Jonathan Lynn was born in Bath in 1943 and educated at Pembroke College, Cambridge. His many credits include co-writing the immensely popular television series, *Yes, Minister* and *Yes, Prime Minister*. He is also the author of the bestselling books of the series. An award-winning stage and film director his credits include *Nuns on the Run* (which he also wrote), *My Cousin Vinny* and *The Distinguished Gentleman*. He has recently directed, as well as acted in the film *Greedy*, which stars Michael J. Fox and Kirk Douglas.

Jonathan Lynn is married with one son and lives in Beverly Hills.

JONATHAN LYNN

———

MAYDAY

PENGUIN BOOKS

PENGUIN BOOKS

Published by the Penguin Group
Penguin Books Ltd, 27 Wrights Lane, London W8 5TZ, England
Penguin Books USA Inc., 375 Hudson Street, New York, New York 10014, USA
Penguin Books Australia Ltd, Ringwood, Victoria, Australia
Penguin Books Canada Ltd, 10 Alcorn Avenue, Toronto, Ontario, Canada M4V 3B2
Penguin Books (NZ) Ltd, 182–190 Wairau Road, Auckland 10, New Zealand

Penguin Books Ltd, Registered Offices: Harmondsworth, Middlesex, England

First published by Viking 1993
Published in Penguin Books 1994
1 3 5 7 9 10 8 6 4 2

Lines from 'Hooray for Hollywood' by Johnny Mercer, copyright 1935,
'That's Entertainment' by Arthur Schwarz and Howard Dietz, copyright © 1953,
and 'Love for Sale' by Cole Porter, copyright 1920, are reproduced by permission of
Warner Chappell Music Ltd/International Music Publications

Extracts from *Fear of Flying* by Erica Jong are reproduced by permission of Martin
Secker & Warburg Ltd

Printed in England by Clays Ltd, St Ives plc

To Rita and Edward

Eve:
I am the first and the last.
I am the honoured one and the scorned one.
I am the whore and the holy one.
I am the wife and the virgin.
I am the bride and the bridegroom,
    and it is my husband who begot me.
I am knowledge and ignorance . . .
I am foolish and I am wise . . .
I am the one whom they call life
    and you have called Death . . .

From *Thunder: Perfect Mind,*
Gnostic poem, 2nd century AD

ONE

'Joanna is in desperate need of $10,000, now or soon. No holds barred.'

From behind his round, fashionable glasses, Ernest Mayday stared myopically at the ad in the Personals of the *LA Weekly*. In spite of his repeated requests, the crowded bookshop down on Sunset Strip had failed to keep a copy of the London *Sunday Times* for him and stubbornly he had refused to buy last Friday's *Daily Mail*. It was stupid of him, he knew that, for he was so out of touch with what was going on in damp and distant London that it really wouldn't have made much difference if he'd bought a newspaper three months out of date, let alone three days. Petulantly he had picked up the copy of *LA Weekly* and taken it home because it was free.

Not that Ernest was hard up, far from it. In fact, he sometimes wondered if the assistants might be a bit more obliging if they knew who he was. On the other hand, the shop was filled to overflowing with the latest Tom Wolfe and Anita Brookner and two generations of Amis and Waugh, and those booksellers' assistants always seemed to Ernest to have a slightly superior air. His books were still in stock, of course, but – depressingly – they were no longer prominently displayed at the front by the cash desk.

Mayday presented a slightly uncharismatic persona to

3

the world. He was a skinny, untidy man of medium height, with a pink face and a curiously well-defined little pot belly. At first glance one might have attributed his flushed complexion to the Californian sun, but closer study revealed a man who obtained most of his daily calories from Johnny Walker, leaving him with little appetite for food. If there was one thing he missed about England – and there was only one thing – it was the pub on the corner. Any pub, any corner. His sweatshirts somehow emphasized his sloping, narrow shoulders and his jeans, suspended below his tummy, hung limply from his hips. His large sneakered feet were continually tripping over invisible obstacles, to the surprise of strangers and the embarrassment of their owner, at least when sober. A shag-pile mat of uncombed greying hair covered a massive head, a head that his slight frame looked only just strong enough to support. The headlamp specs perched on the bridge of his long bumpy nose magnified his anxious blue eyes.

A perceptive bystander could conceivably have guessed that this food-stained individual was a refined intellectual of cultivated tastes, he might even have guessed that his intelligence would make him attractive to some women in spite of all appearances, but certainly no browser glancing casually in his direction would have guessed that this crumpled forty-six-year-old individual with deep brown bags under his listless eyes had enchanted the sun-oiled beach readers of the world with his second-hand Olivetti, and enthralled the airport lounges of five continents with his free-wheeling imagination, spinning yarns of international financial collapse, banking wizards trading in treachery with oil-rich sheikhs while romancing their dazzling lady friends, who were always distinguished by their full yet firm breasts bursting with unquenchable longings, their lithe limbs and moist clefts lusting with fierce desires. 'Sorry, sorry, excuse me, sorry,' he said, getting under the feet of the customers queueing at the cash desk. Who would have thought that this insignificant-looking klutz crawling around on all fours, hamfistedly picking up the loose change that he had dropped all over the bookshop floor, had held travellers and holiday-makers spellbound in nineteen languages with his conspiratorial plots of Byzantine complexity and double-dealing, his apparent familiarity with Wall Street and Threadneedle Street, his knowledge of street-smarts and easy street, of high places and low morals, exotic foreign worlds where hookers are lookers, drug traffickers are hanged, heroes are hung, the best women are bad and sex is always, always good.

Mayday was defiant and defensive about creating the sort of literature that Melvyn Bragg wouldn't choose to discuss on TV, books in which life was what people wanted it to be, fictitious worlds where all ambiguities could be straightened out, books whose purpose was not to pinpoint literary truth but to keep the pages turning. Perhaps that is why he had felt so drawn to Los Angeles. Unfortunately for him, Tinsel Town was immediately drawn to him too, so it took some time after he arrived there before he realized that he was in trouble. For in spite of his fame and wealth and the apparent warmth of his welcome, he was that figure about whom no one ultimately cared less: the novelist in Hollywood. Worse still, a novelist with writer's block. For when Ernest Mayday went west so did his ideas, and his famously fertile imagination dried up like a puddle in New Mexico.

Actually, it was Ernest's divorce and depression that sent him from England, and a cash offer (plus the temporary elation that only drugs or cash offers create) that drew him to El Pueblo de Nuestra Señora la Reina de Los Angeles, the village of Our Lady the Queen of the Angels. But although Hollywood optioned his books, nobody there could work out how to adapt them into films. Nor could he, to start with. The books were never filmed, but Ernest had soon been seduced by LA – the blue skies, the tennis courts, the valet parking, all the comfort and ease of a luxury Caribbean holiday home in a place where he could earn money.

Although he wasn't earning anything but royalties he acquired an agent, Fanny Rush, who in turn helped him acquire a lawyer, Dylan Kanpinchowitz. 'Everyone has to have a lawyer,' she said. 'This is America.' They were a skinny pair. She was a tall, scrawny, blonde woman of a certain age whose taut skin and blue eyes, oddly Asian and slanted in an otherwise Caucasian face, revealed the ravages of much face-lifting, lipo-suctioning, dieting and disappointment. Dylan, somewhat younger, a rising star at his firm, was hawk-faced, bright-eyed and jogged for an hour every morning. They seemed to work well as a team. Together they explained how he had to sell his books to the studios if they were to get off the ground as movies.

'A movie has to be High Concept,' said Fanny.

'That means its content can be so encapsulated for easy marketing that the audience knows everything about it from one line of advertising copy,' said Dylan.

'Or, better still, from the title itself, like *Jaws*, or *Rocky V*,' added Fanny. 'Like – what else did the public need to know about them? Nothing!'

'You see, nobody greenlights a movie if they don't know how to sell it,' explained Dylan. 'I'm sure you can understand that. And it has to be a real simple sell.'

'And you've got a problem there, Ernest,' continued Fanny, 'because there's too much going on in your books. Ideally, a screenplay should have just one central idea.'

'If that,' said Dylan.

'If that,' echoed Fanny.

Dylan, who was no fool, also explained Ernest's new

environment to him: the world in which making the deal is the highest point in the history of a film because if the film hasn't yet been made it hasn't yet failed to live up to expectations; the world of the grandiose title, in which a secretary is an assistant, a middle-manager is a vice-president and even somebody called the President of World-wide Production does not have the power to greenlight a movie. 'Only the chairman can do that,' said Fanny.

'Or the man with the only meaningful title in America,' added Dylan.

'What's that?' asked Fanny.

'Owner,' replied Dylan with a grin.

Mayday had also enjoyed a tantalizing glimpse of American television. Although he had never written a TV script in England, he had been admitted through the golden portals of a major studio with much submissive body language from the Armani-clad executives deeply impressed with his (reported) income, and there to his great surprise he discovered a kingdom in which the writer is such a low form of life that nobody owns up to being one at all if they can help it.

'If you invent the series,' the morose but highly success-ful comedy-writer Sidney Byte explained to him in the commissary over a delicious Chinese-chicken salad, 'and if you are the head writer of it, you're called the executive producer. If you're a regular writer on the series, you know, like, a member of the writing staff, then you're a supervising producer. If you're an occasional contributor you're a consultant – better yet,' he added as an afterthought as he sipped his iced tea, 'better yet, a creative consultant. Creative is a very important word in LA.'

'If your title doesn't state that you're creative, how the hell will anybody know that you are?' inquired Max. Kirsch. Kirsch was an even gloomier and even more successful humorist. Max.'s name was short for Maximil-ian and pedantically he insisted that the abbreviation of his name was followed by the appropriate punctuation. He was known around the back lot as Max Period Kirsch.

'If you're not an important enough writer to be a supervising producer or a consultant,' continued the plaintive Sidney Byte in that drawling, fey, cultivated Californian accent, 'you have to settle for being a mere producer, an associate producer, a story editor or – at the very least – a story executive.'

'And,' concluded Max Period mournfully, 'if all you are is a writer, God forbid, you will be ignored, rewritten, sent to get the coffee and bagels and if you make a suggestion at a story meeting you'll be told to shut the fuck up.'

'That'll teach you,' added Sidney.

The redoubtable Fanny Rush quickly capitalized on Ernest's bestselling status to make sure that he began in television as a consultant with a lot of money. He didn't actually have to write anything but once or twice a week he drove to the studio in his Mercedes 300, the Beverly Hills equivalent of the Chevy and the Ford Cortina. Tentatively he would contribute a few thoughts, an idea or two, even an occasional line of dialogue to the script meeting, although Ernest (being essentially a descriptive writer) always found dialogue difficult. His ideas would be received with respect, perhaps because he was rich and successful, perhaps also because he spoke with a British accent, which to Angelinos has always denoted class, culture and a superior intelligence. There may have been a few supervising producers, story executives and Executive Vice-presidents of Creative Affairs who muttered quietly in corners that he was an asshole and an overpaid British asshole at that, but in the main his suggestions – although never followed – were received with courtesy and described as very clever.

At first Ernest thought this was a compliment. He of all people, an ex-civil servant, should have known better and recognized this as the old Whitehall too-clever-by-half syndrome. It took Sidney Byte to explain it to him: 'Once someone in authority in Hollywood has stigmatized your ideas as clever, it is doubtful that anything you write will ever reach the screen unless and until someone less clever than you has rewritten it.'

And every day, as the sun set over the ocean at the end of Sunset, he would return to his Hollywood Hills hacienda, motoring smoothly through his fearsome, heavy, spiked gate that creaked open automatically as he approached it – unless LA was suffering one of its frequent power cuts, in which case he would find himself locked out. An 'Armed Response' sign was welded across the gate's steel bars to frighten off any crack-brained, thieving, gun-toting addict who might otherwise scale the heights, break into the house and murder him with one of those little Saturday Night Specials that look and sound like cap pistols but which kill you just the same.

In the beginning Ernest worried about the great divide between the rich in their Westside mansions and the homeless sleeping out on the sidewalks downtown and on the coarse tropical grass in the shadows of the giant palms on Ocean Avenue above the Santa Monica seafront. He fretted about the effective apartheid that made Los Angeles, though chock-full of self-styled liberals, as segregated as Johannesburg. He was bothered about the gang killings and burning buildings just beyond the invisible frontier at Pico and Fairfax, only three or four miles away, and the broad-daylight rapes that took place at gunpoint and knifepoint on beautiful sandy Santa Monica beach and even in the UCLA library right there on the campus in the middle of Westwood Village. But gradually, on becoming an Angelino, he learned to focus his anxiety on eating salt and red meat. Furthermore he never ate Chinese food if they added MSG, he avoided caffeine and, wherever possible, diet sodas. After all, chemicals can kill you.

Most of all, however, he worried about his writer's block. In the old days his ideas may not have been all that original but at least they were plentiful. His two huge bestselling books (huge in both senses, hardbacks too heavy to read in bed) had been written with little mental effort. But doubt had now set in. He questioned their value. He wanted to be more than a mere story-teller. Like a rabbit transfixed by a snake, Ernest Mayday had become both hypnotized and paralysed by posterity. While Samuel Beckett seemed to demonstrate that less is more, an increasingly bitter and depressed Ernest Mayday had self-critically reconsidered his monster books and reluctantly concluded that, in his case, more was less.

He had always rather despised minimalists, on the grounds that they're usually so minimal. He had always believed in the splurge, the big fat read. But now, reduced to this terrifying inertia by the fear, indeed the certainty, that he stood head and shoulders below his contemporaries, he was at last face to face with the ultimate nightmare: returning the publisher's advance for his next book. There was only one problem – he'd spent it. It had disappeared into the bottomless pit he called his home, along with all the money he'd made when he'd worked at the studio. The deadline was approaching and not a word was written, not even a title.

Now, sitting at his imposing mahogany reproduction desk, looking through his cinemascope-wide window high in the Hollywood Hills, gazing down through the purple bougainvillaea and sunny lemon trees that fringed his hot brick terrace, he was a far cry from Haslemere where he'd lived with Ellen (the first and – so far – only Mrs Mayday) and from which he had commuted every day to Threadneedle Street. He stared blankly at the distant misty towering outlines of Century City, the futuristic perpendicular business district risen from the old bankrupt back lot of Twentieth Century Fox, the high-gloss finish of the skyscrapers dulled to matt and the sharp edges turned soft focus by the thick white gauze of the morning heat haze. Enervated by the already high temperature and his own profound inertia, he turned the smudged inky pages of *LA Weekly* expecting to find little or nothing of any interest to him.

Half the morning was gone again, and he knew he couldn't write in the afternoons. That morning he'd managed to spend nearly two hours and forty-five minutes learning how to make his word processor paginate, ready to be used in haste when the long-hoped-for torrent of words, ideas and thoughts gushed out as it had when he wrote his celebrated first novel *Lies*, typing as fast as he could for fear of losing his next thought. But on that hot, still April morning, like every morning since he'd signed his new deal with Mark Down at Cockerel Books, no thoughts of any kind at all had occurred to him. Ernest Mayday the novelist (as he liked them to refer to him whenever he had appeared on a talk show) sat apathetic, unthinking, unwashed and unshaven as the encroaching, all-enveloping depression made him turn from his massive safety-glass earthquake-proof picture window to stare hopelessly at the rough white stucco library wall, carefully and roughly textured in the most expensive Mediterranean style, just like the walls of every Frith Street trattoria.

Though picturesque, the wall offered no more inspiration than the window. Morosely he telephoned his writer friends, Max. and Sidney. Answering machines answered. He left no messages. He had nothing to say. His eyes flickered over the notes on his blotter. Nothing. Only the feeblest ideas had occurred to him in nine months, nothing that could form the basis of another bestseller. All he could think of, slowly filling up the spaces inside his head like sodden rice, was the deadening weight of the huge advance that he had accepted and spent.

He sighed and glanced at the *LA Weekly*. Then, right in the middle of the Personals, he saw the ad. 'Joanna is in desperate need of $10,000, now or soon. No holds barred.' The wall of concrete blocking the front of his brain began to crumble. He stared at it, hardly daring to hope. 'Joanna is in desperate need of $10,000, now or soon. No holds barred.' What sort of replies would a girl get from an ad like that? No skills were advertised. But she said she'd do anything. It seemed obvious that the only offers she could possibly get would be to do something illegal, for no one would pay that kind of money otherwise. And wouldn't such potential employers inevitably regard her as expendable? Might she be asked to do something exciting, something dangerous? Certainly. Would she be willing to take the chance? Of course. That was precisely what she was advertising. He realized that within his grasp was a dead-cert set-up for a plot – and one that he didn't even have to think up for himself. Would she be approached by Colombian drug smugglers? By Iraqi terrorists wanting to bomb jumbos? He knew that his literary career depended on persuading her to go along with any offer that came in.

Whatever was going to happen to her, this would be the real McCoy. This would be his window into real-life. He still didn't have an idea. But now, suddenly, he knew how to get one.

TWO

To my agent,
Who believed in me when everyone else did.
                                    Jack Douglas

It was some time before he heard from Joanna. So long that he'd given up hope and forgotten all about her.

He had written a careful letter, thinking long and hard about it. In the end he'd kept it simple:

Dear Joanna,

  I write in reply to your advertisement in the 'LA Weekly'. Please contact me at (213) 555–7476 between the hours of nine a.m. and three p.m. If I do not answer the phone in person, hang up immediately and call back.

  We may be able to help each other.

He considered that last sentence carefully. He felt it had just the right mixture of mystery and allure, and yet it said absolutely nothing. Years of experience at the Treasury had taught him how to say nothing in public, nothing quotable, nothing memorable, nothing incriminating. He had learned the converse skill as well, how to reveal new and important information so boringly that no one would ever notice it. Unfortunately, this aptitude proved of even less use to him in his career as a novelist.

He didn't use headed notepaper but a plain white sheet of copy paper. He didn't want a strange young woman to turn up at the gate unannounced. What if Randi were home?

Randi Toner was what his more arch LA friends called his significant other. Why didn't he tell Randi that he was writing to Joanna? Ernest certainly didn't know. Perhaps she was more other than significant. Or perhaps it was that, as a former civil servant, secrecy (or discretion, as he preferred to call it) was second nature to Ernest. Perhaps he thought that Randi would disapprove. Perhaps he thought it would excite her possessive instincts – and Ernest, having escaped from one barren marriage, did not wish to be possessed by any more women, especially one as sparing with her sexual favours as Randi had turned out to be since she'd found God. Or perhaps it was simply that the secrecy added to the excitement.

At any rate, it was with a shaking hand and a breathless guilty feeling that Ernest Mayday sealed his letter and mailed it off to an unknown female adventurer named Joanna, hoping that he was about to be exposed to a new underworld of illegality and corruption, excitement and adventure, fear and squalor, in short, a world even more disreputable and treacherous than government or the movies. Being a careful man, he had taken one further precaution: he had signed his letter Norm de Plume, which he assumed would both amuse his correspondent and simultaneously advise her that he was using an alias.

Normally he left letters in his mail box outside the gate. In LA, unlike London, the mailman not only delivers but takes your mail. But as Mayday didn't want to run the risk of Randi seeing it, he drove down the winding hill and posted it on Sunset, outside the Frozen Yogurt and Korean Manicure shop.

Randi was returning as he got home. Tall, slim, strong, no make-up, the feminine shape of the nineties, Randi's fitness, muscular frame and determinedly positive and healthy attitude typified California for Ernest. Perhaps that was why he had fallen for her. Or was it those wide-set, sincere brown eyes that looked at him with so much attention, interest and love, and so little comprehension.

'Where've you been?' She was curious. 'I thought you were trying to write.'

'Just to the shops on Sunset Plaza.'

'You hate shops.'

'Not always.' Ernest testily denied the truth. But Randi was concerned about him.

'Ernest, why don't you try coming down to the Church one day? It's so full of love.'

He felt a twinge of acid indigestion as he wondered how he could ever have got involved with a woman who could utter such banalities, and – worse still – mean them. But she had been so relaxing, especially after Ellen, and so full of admiration for his wit, his intelligence, his brilliance. He had been entranced with himself as seen through her eyes. The only other writer she'd ever known was on the staff of *The Young and the Restless*. She made him feel like Tolstoy reincarnated. But he could imagine the patronizing smiles she'd evoke in Berkshire. Of course she hadn't talked in these puerile banalities when they'd first met, and although he knew why she did so now, although he fully understood the spiritual change that had occurred in her, it still embarrassed him profoundly. 'What did you do at Church today?' he inquired with as much interest as he could muster.

'We were planning this year's Sincerity Awards. They're having them at the Beverly Sheraton.'

'Sincerity Awards,' repeated Ernest, slightly glazed. He poured himself a glass of purified filtered water from the special purified filtered-water tap. 'I may vomit,' he added, cheerfully seizing the opportunity to quote Sheridan Whiteside, his favourite American curmudgeon, without attribution.

'What's wrong with sincerity?' she asked, genuinely perplexed. He hadn't the energy to answer the question. It contained far too many buried assumptions. He looked at Randi. She was staring at him, tears welling up. Oh God, he thought, she's hurt again. How would it ever be possible for him to marry this sweet, good-natured, ingenuous masseuse?

His male friends always nudged and winked when he told them what she did for a living. For some inexplicable reason they assumed that as she was a masseuse she must be a profoundly passionate and sensuous creature, and there was no denying that in a way she was. Unfortunately, it was in a sublimated way. Ernest's friends would still cast knowing and envious glances at him. He felt fraudulent but, after all, there had been a time – not so long ago, actually – when he and Randi had been dynamite in bed, before Jesus made her frigid, before her sexuality turned to sanctity, in the days when Ernest did to Randi what the Church was now doing to her.

Ernest had installed Armed Response hoping that it would help to return Randi to her former sensuous self, but it made no difference. Nothing seemed to remove the trauma of that blisteringly hot night when Randi nearly went to meet her Maker, soon after the revolt of the underclass that was known so misleadingly as the LA riots. The additional security offered by Armed Response hadn't reduced her level of anxiety at all, and it merely altered Ernest's. For apart from the irritation of being barricaded out of your house by your own security system whenever there was a power cut, the great danger of Armed Response was that it was all too real. The LA Police Department customarily took at least forty-five minutes to respond to an emergency call, but private security guards were said to be on the scene in less than eight. That, as far as Ernest was concerned, remained to be tested. However, if you accidentally set off the alarm while you were inside your own house, it was generally agreed you were safer off staying indoors because if you stepped outside to greet the armed patrolmen on arrival they might just shoot you.

Randi's voice broke in on his thoughts. 'Ernest – what's wrong with sincerity?'

'Nothing.' He sipped his water. 'When are these awards presented, anyway?'

'Peace and Harmony Day,' she replied. She flinched, but there was no onslaught from him. He simply smiled. 'Is that another manufactured Hallmark Card day? Like Mother's Day? And Father's?'

'No, it's not.' She was indignant. 'It's not commercial. It's the day that the Church and the Institute created three years ago to reach out to people.'

Mayday stared up at his elegant Hollywood cypresses. So far as Mayday could understand it, the Church, the Institute and the Foundation were all different tentacles of the same octopus. The Church's full name was the Church of the Community of Personal Truth. It spawned, for purely charitable purposes (such as the giving of self-serving awards), the Caring and Sharing Foundation (motto: *You Care, I Share*) and tied up somewhere in this Nutrasweet package of goodwill was the Heartwarming Institute, though Mayday didn't know what that was for and didn't much care.

Prior to her sudden experience of being reborn, Randi had known of the Church because of her tireless devotion to self-realization. Realizing one's self was big in Southern California, and perhaps this church would have had the same impact on any traumatized Californian masseuse who had stumbled across it. She'd already tried EST (Erhard Seminars Training, not electric-shock therapy) and Lifespring, and various others, but as far as she was concerned there was nothing to touch the Heartwarming Foundation's SCREAMS. These SCREAMS had already energized and inspired her to work towards her new state of consciousness. On the whole Ernest felt that her new consciousness was slightly less conscious than her old consciousness, but he didn't like to say too much because her new consciousness had made her so happy. The SCREAMS had fulfilled what appeared to be a deep-seated need to go away for the weekend and pay a great deal of money to be locked in a room with four hundred other masochists and be abused by so-called trainers, and not be allowed to leave the room to pee except when they gave her permission. SCREAMS was an acronym invented by the Church's inspirational leader and founder, the Reverend Dr Abel Pile, and it stood for Self-Creating Realization, Energization and Assertivization Mode Seminars. The Reverend Pile had a real talent for mangling language, though the addition of extra syllables wherever possible was, Ernest had noted irritably, a general American trait: teachers were called educators (the additional two syllables apparently adding considerably to their status), transport was known as transportation, and only that morning the weather man on *Good Morning America* had announced a thirty per cent probability of precipitation. He meant that it might rain.

Randi's friend Marge, a make-up artist, had told her all about SCREAMS some months ago. Randi's eyes were bright and sparkling that night. 'I want to share this feeling,' she'd told a gloomy Ernest over a veggie burger at Cravings Restaurant. 'I want to put myself in touch with myself, I want to feel good about myself, I'm going to be myself and *by* myself.'

'And play with yourself?' inquired Ernest.

Her fork stopped halfway to her mouth. 'What's that supposed to mean?'

'All this "be myself" and "discover myself" shit generally ends up with divorce and becoming very poor.'

'We're not even married,' she pointed out.

'Marge is. Her marriage is in enough trouble as it is.'

She ignored that. 'Anyway, most people's marriages and relationships are not perfect.'

'Good God! What a shock!' Ernest exclaimed.

She smiled. 'They just need more love, Brad and Marge.'

'Don't *we*?' he asked.

She was surprised. 'Do we?'

'Well . . .' Ernest decided to offer a compromise. 'Perhaps not more love, exactly. But what about more sex, just to be going on with?'

'The modern woman needs self-realization and assertiveness more than sex,' was Randi's firm reply. Ernest realized he was getting the brush-off again.

'You mean "no"?' he inquired, tight-lipped.

'No.'

'"No" you mean "no", or "no" you *don't* mean "no"?'

'Yes,' she replied.

He stared at her. '"Yes" you mean "no" or yes you *don't* mean "no"?'

She thought for a moment. 'Yes,' she said again.

'Yes, *what*?'

She was becoming confused. 'Yes, please?' she asked cautiously, trying like hell to give the right answer.

He sighed impatiently. 'Yes, please what?'

Now she was baffled. 'What?'

He tried again. 'Did you mean "yes please", more sex?'

'If you like. What's the big deal?'

Ernest somehow felt less than satisfied by this reply. Her enthusiasm seemed limited.

Whether or not Randi's friend Marge achieved full Self-realization Ernest never knew. But she certainly achieved Assertiveness, and perhaps even Aggression – or Aggressivity as they called it at SCREAMS. When she left him, her new-found confidence cost her husband Brad most of what he owned, including fifteen years' advance alimony and a house that he'd lived in for seven years before he'd ever met Marge. And only four months after Marge first went to SCREAMS more than sixty thousand dollars had been spent on legal costs. Mayday decided that EST, Lifespring, SCREAMS and all those other so-called seminars must have been started by lawyers.

Ernest Mayday had been to a session once but had rapidly tired of the camp young man and belligerent bejowled woman in brass-tipped cowboy boots hoarsely screaming 'You're an asshole, you're an asshole' at him and the other 'students' most of the day. 'If you pay all that money to be told you're an asshole for two days,' Ernest remarked to Randi on his early return, 'you probably *are* an asshole.' Randi had asked him to work it through, telling him he'd feel differently by the time he finished the weekend, but he refused. He never went back to SCREAMS and Randi had never understood his hostility to the Church which filled her and all her friends with such love for their fellow humans, and animals, and indeed for the whole planet really except perhaps their spouses.

'If only you'd seen it through to the end.' She held his hand gently and stared into his eyes. 'You never do. You give up too easily. Nothing's valuable if you don't see it through.'

Ernest had thought that was pretty unfair at the time. Anyone who writes two big books is certainly someone who sees things through to the end. Except . . . it was true that he'd given up on book number three, that he'd left the Civil Service, that he'd torpedoed his first marriage and that he wasn't looking too positively at his current relationship. None the less he was in no mood to concede anything. 'Balls,' he replied, without rancour.

She was not deterred. 'Ernest, you need a little more self-knowledge. You just don't ever get involved in anything or anybody, do you realize that?'

'Yes. It's conscious.'

'Well, why not? Why not get more involved?'

'In what?'

Ernest didn't care for the way this conversation was heading. More involved? Was this a veiled proposal of marriage? Though Randi often stayed the night he had never even considered letting her move in, for on the West Coast even living-in ran the risk of rich palimony settlements. Californian lawyers, Ernest knew, ensured that he and Randi and millions of others lived alone, and lonely. He sipped his Scotch and soda and watched a tiny delicate hummingbird suck some nectar from the white roses.

Her voice came through again. 'Why won't you make any commitment?' She was gently insistent, kneeling beside him now on the warm evening terrace.

'I'm a writer,' he replied inadequately. 'I don't commit, I observe.'

She didn't buy it. 'Why don't you get a therapist if you won't let the Heartwarming Institute help you?'

'Because I'm *not* an American,' he said. 'I don't need a therapist, I'm not crazy.' And he strolled calmly through the French windows into his study and shut the door. There, in the magnificent solitude of his white stucco, surrounded by shelves of imported leather-bound books that his decorator had bought by the yard to fill up the vast, embarrassingly empty, built-in bookcases, he would freely acknowledge – to himself, at least – the fear that analysis might somehow crush his fragile talent, or what was left of it. He would rather be productive than happy and, ignoring the fact that he was neither at the moment, he protected his psyche from investigation as if it were a literary Ali Baba's cave, the secret repository for verbal treasures of Dickensian proportions. He simply wanted to write another book and was frightened he'd never do it.

He had wondered about pinching some story and making it his own. You can do wonders, he'd noticed, by taking some fairy-tale, myth or legend like *Cinderella* or *Beauty and the Beast* or *Faust* and setting it in the present or the future – indeed, you can even win points for it from the critics. 'Ernest Mayday has been taking a new look at an archetypal story.' Of course, you risked being accused of writing a stereotypical story instead. 'Stereotype is just the pejorative word for archetype,' he had once written angrily in reply to one of the dozens of publishers who had rejected his first novel on the grounds that it contained too many stereotypical characters. The publisher was sufficiently irritated to write in reply: 'We are still unable to publish your manuscript, but would you like us to shred it for you?' When his books were high on the bestseller list, Ernest gloated, that man must have kicked himself.

But Ernest was unable to think of a suitable myth to jump-start his new book, and finally he had been reduced to wondering if he could get away with some sort of re-hash of his first two volumes – after all, his publisher had made it clear over lunch at Clarkes back in Kensington Church Street that loyal readers are those who buy your new book in the hope and expectation that although it will be superficially different from your last one it will also be fundamentally the same. 'It's called plagiarism if you copy someone else's work,' Mark Down had explained to Ernest as the novelist pushed some decorative *nouvelle cuisine* monkfish and shredded greens around his vast white plate, 'but if you copy your own work they call it your style.'

Ernest Mayday was not, in his own life, a fantasy merchant. While others would describe him as a pessimist, he would describe himself as a realist. Having left Britain in disgust at the constant negativity, he remained British enough to take a thoroughly negative view of anything and everything American, to the confusion of his new Californian friends. Years ago, back in London, Ernest had a slightly more positive attitude, and in those days he had developed a theory about what sells books, a theory that had made his fortune. Why, he had asked himself as he rode bumpily to work in Whitehall on the Circle line, did *Day of the Jackal* appeal to so many readers? It was because it introduced them to a world that previously they didn't know – the world of the professional hit man, the mythical assassin, Carlos the Terrorist, about whom everyone read in the tabloids. Ernest didn't know if Frederick Forsyth really knew how terrorists worked, but it was enough for the reader that he seemed to know and that everyone believed that he knew. The book had been written in the sort of compelling detail that impressed him: the way that the gunman had obtained his forged passport, for instance, had stuck for ever in the mind of Ernest Mayday and millions of others – including John Stonehouse, the renegade Labour cabinet minister who copied the trick so that he could vanish without trace. It was this plethora of information that seemed to make the fantasy real. John le Carré used the same literary device, Ernest Mayday noticed as he rumbled home again under London, working his assiduous way through the Smiley canon. Was Le Carré ever a spy? Who knew? Was that his real name? Who cared? It was all part of the magic, for Le Carré had introduced the reader to a world of moles and the Circus and safe houses, and it didn't matter whether it was revealed truth or inspired invention. It was the detail that carried the day. Many other authors, whose books Mayday had laboriously trudged through, enjoyed success built solely upon their information, their endless facts, their liberal use of designer brand names, their leaden-footed research of – for instance – airports for *Airport*, hotels for *Hotel* and (presumably, though he had never read it) wheels for *Wheels*.

For fifteen years Ernest Mayday had been a Treasury civil servant. In so far as anyone understood economics,

Ernest did. On becoming an author he had found that weaving his fantasies of Wall Street crashes and junk bonds, of Sloanes in wellies, of pink nipples and pork bellies came easily to him. Of course it was the pork bellies rather than the pink nipples that were researched in the sober corridors of the Treasury but, overall, Ernest's theory had been put to the test and he prospered: it turned out that his readers did indeed yearn to be introduced to a new world, a world of power and excitement about which they knew absolutely nothing. But now Ernest Mayday had a problem. In his first two books he had told his readers everything he knew about the City. From now on he would have to invent. And until that fateful morning when, irritably, he had picked up the *LA Weekly* containing Joanna's advertisement he had absolutely no idea where to begin.

For a few days after Ernest Mayday posted his letter he had waited by the phone. He didn't even attempt to go on inventing a story for the novel, confident that after he met Joanna it would no longer be necessary. But days, then weeks, went by and she didn't call.

So he played golf with his thin, tense accountant Aaron Bookman, a man in search of a loophole, and assured him cheerfully that his looming financial problems would soon loom no more. He and Randi dined with friends at the local Japanese place and discussed how LA restaurants were changing fast – 'Oh tempura, oh sushi,' he'd remarked lugubriously, to smiles of appreciation from Max. Kirsch and Sidney Byte but a puzzled glance from Randi.

'I thought you liked sushi,' she said, surprised.

'I've gone off it,' growled Ernest. 'When I first got here everyone took me to sushi restaurants. I ate so much raw fish I felt like a sea-lion.'

He passed pleasant sun-filled weekends with Randi at the beach, watching her athletic older brother Pete Toner (the Vice-president of Parking at one of the major studios) as he surfed, then dining with Randi's mom and pop at Art's Deli in the Valley. Randi's pop, Milton Toner, ran the Universal mail room.

'Is that a real place or a metaphor?' Ernest had asked. As always, he was unable to resist showing off.

'It's where I work,' a puzzled Milton had replied. 'Why?'

'It seems to me,' smirked Ernest, 'that so many things get lost there that it's probably both.'

What with the Toner family's social life and a new regular early-morning tennis game with his athletic, competitive lawyer Dylan Kanpinchowitz and the bi-weekly poker game with Sidney, Max. and the other melancholy misanthropic comedy-writers he'd met at the studios around the punch-up table, he couldn't find time to consider his book anyway and springtime vanished in a sweet, carefree, jasmine-scented haze. Clearing his desk seemed to occupy all his working hours – replying to phone calls and letters from fans he didn't want to meet, visitors from London he didn't want to accommodate, agents whose client he did not wish to become, gold and platinum credit card offers he didn't solicit, remortgaging finance he didn't need, publishers to whom he didn't want to give pre-publication quotes, and requests for lectures he couldn't be bothered to give. Though his desk stayed clear his mind did not, and Ernest simply hoped that things would work out somehow.

And they did. Joanna was forgotten but the financial crisis diminished. The television pilot season was on the horizon again and he was still on the payroll as a consult-ant. His first book was about to be re-optioned by a film company for the fifth successive year, and meetings that appeared to be serious in intent were being arranged with the new optioning producer-director, Oliver Sudden. So when his new, electronic and cordless phone yelped and a voice said, 'Hello, it's Joanna here,' Ernest didn't immediately realize who it was.

'Joanna who?'

The voice was cool, friendly but businesslike. 'You replied to my ad in the *LA Weekly*.'

Ernest suddenly remembered. 'Oh. Joanna.'

'Yes.'

'Yes. Er . . . no holds barred, right?'

'That's what I said.'

'You need ten thousand dollars?'

'Yes.'

Ernest handled the situation with his customary aplomb. 'Um . . . well, ah, um, should we, ah, you know . . . ah . . .'

'What?' said the voice.

'Um, I mean, meet. A meeting.' Ernest fell back on the Hollywood solution to everything. 'Let's take a meeting.'

'Where?'

Ernest's mind was now completely blank. He'd had weeks to think about what he'd say if and when she called, but somehow he hadn't ever thought about where they'd go.

'Hello? Are you still there?' she said after a while.

'Yes. I'm . . . ah, trying to think of a place to, you know . . .'

She waited. 'Well, where do you live?'

He didn't want to tell her. 'Hollywood Hills.' There was no harm in saying that much.

'Look,' she said, after another pause, 'perhaps you've changed your mind.'

'No, no!' He was upset with himself. He knew he sounded anxious and he'd wanted to sound cool. 'No, it's just that, I may have a, you know, proposition that might, ah, interest you.' He stared desperately out of his window, at Sunset Strip far below. 'How about the cocktail bar of the Bel Monde Hotel?' It was the only neutral ground he could think of on the spur of the moment. 'It'll be quiet, we can talk there.'

'Sure. When?'

'Um . . .' He was free today, but didn't want to seem too eager. He tried to sound casual. 'I think I've got some free time tomorrow.'

'What time?'

He thought frantically for a time that he could guarantee that Randi would be elsewhere, so that he wouldn't have to explain himself.

'Six o'clock?'

'OK. See you then.'

She hung up.

THREE

*Trash novels are the popular girls of modern fiction.
They're a good time, but you wouldn't take one home
to meet your parents.*

Carolyn See

Ernest Mayday arrived at the hotel early. He'd wasted the
day, reading Thomas Mann without absorbing anything,
listening to Mozart without hearing anything, unable to
concentrate. He was excited.

Unusually for him, he spent time considering what
he would wear for the encounter. He opted for the
bookish look that would reinforce his proposal – horn-
rims (or to be precise, in the age of the Greens, plastic
imitation horn-rims), an unstructured silk jacket and tie
from Fred Segal's, white linen button-down shirt, baggy
paisley trousers and moccasins, not sneakers. He wanted
her to know, if she were the kind of woman who could
tell, that he had money and that his plan was not
frivolous.

He drove slowly down the windy hill, windows
down, sun-roof open, breathing in the hot smell of
eucalyptus that he loved and always associated with Hollywood. He edged along Sunset, bumper to bumper in the
rush-hour traffic, past the chic restaurant Pogo – only in
LA could the movie business's trendiest A-list restaurant
be a shed on legs flanked by two massive billboards on
rusting steel lattice-work stilts fifty feet high, overlooking
a crumbling concrete yard full of used cars and the big
translucent fluorescent orange and black plastic sign for

Budget Rent-A-Car. Was this really the Knightsbridge of LA?

He turned down San Vicente and hard left into the forecourt of the Bel Monde Hotel, a nine-storey adobe-coloured cube, its drive cluttered with doormen and bellmen in adobe-coloured uniforms, and Mexican valet-parking men in strangely inappropriate little blue oriental-style tunics and black trousers. Taking the car receipt from one of them, he strolled into the long hotel lobby, the heels of his leather moccasins clicking like dice on the marble floor as he negotiated the jungle of potted palms in the porch.

He had forgotten that the cocktail bar was a piano bar. A blond pianist was hard at work, wearing a little too much eye-liner, crooning Cole Porter's 'Love For Sale' into a sound system apparently designed for a concert at Wembley Stadium. Mayday, accustoming his eyes to the darkened room, stared curiously at this person whose hair was beautifully coiffed but whose five o'clock shadow was beginning to show through at ten minutes to six. He wondered if this entertainer could be persuaded to lower the volume. He spoke to the barman as quietly as he could, not wanting the scattered drinkers to hear.

'Excuse me, I'm expecting a lady to meet me here. I don't know what she looks like. She may ask for me.'

'Whatsa you name?' The barkeeper was from south of the border.

He almost said Mayday. 'Er. It's, Mister, er, de Plume.'

'Mister Erdeplum. Certainly, sir.'

'Er no, no, it's just de Plume. At least . . .' Ernest decided to simplify things. 'Plume will do, I think.'

'Bloom?'

Ernest realized that he was not projecting adequately above 'Who will want to pay the price, For a trip to Paradise?' He tried again. 'Plume. Plume. With a "P", and an "e" on the end.'

29

'Huli?' said the barman, inexplicably.

Mayday stared at him. 'OK, OK. Forget it. Bloom's fine.'

The barman beamed. 'Ah, Bloomstein. OK, sir, you got it.'

'Look,' snapped Mayday, 'can't we turn that sodding music down?'

'What?' said the barman.

'Can't you turn down the music?' He mimed and pointed.

'Why?'

'Because it's too loud.'

'I can hear you, Mr Bloomstein.'

'The name's Bloom.'

'What?'

Ernest felt rage rising in him. He controlled himself. 'Mineral water!' he shouted, and departed from the leather-topped bar. He seated himself at a corner table furthest from the piano, only to find himself right beside a loudspeaker. Angrily, he picked up a handful of assorted salted nuts from the glass-topped table and stuffed them into his mouth.

The bar was nearly empty. Just a holiday-making elderly married couple in one corner, and a couple of businessmen between him and the pianist (now performing 'Girl From Ipanema' in a deafening whisper) who seemed to be going over their quarterly sales figures. Ernest sipped his San Pellegrino and surveyed the salted nuts, which were of every kind and *big* – walnut and hazel and almond and pecan and macadamia. Even the peanuts were Hollywood huge.

He waited, and wondered. At the far end a girl walked in. She looked around, hesitated in front of the opaque glass doors expensively engraved with art deco lilies, glanced at Ernest Mayday, then sat at the bar. He watched her. She said something to the barman, who listened and shook his head.

She was slim, medium height, short brown hair with a forelock overhanging her forehead, minimal make-up, not unattractive but the sort of girl you wouldn't really notice unless you were trying to guess whether or not she'd come to meet you. She ordered a Margarita, sipped it, then looked again at Ernest. He felt a flutter in his chest. Was this Joanna? She slid down from the bar stool, straightened her tight black mini-skirt which had ridden up close to her crotch, and walked towards him. 'Are you Mr de Plume?'

Ernest jumped up, knee-capping himself on the chromium edge of the cocktail table. 'Ouch,' he said painfully, by way of greeting. She watched him curiously as he hopped up and down for a little while, holding his knee and nodding.

'May I sit down?'

'Oh yes, please, sorry, I just banged my knee.'

'I saw.' It was the same as when she had phoned. She didn't seem to have much use for unnecessary words.

She settled comfortably in the maroon velvet armchair opposite him, and stared at him with candid grey eyes. Her legs were long, slim and straight. She crossed them. She was attractive but no stand-out. She was wearing a black business suit with a well-tailored double-breasted jacket over a cream silk blouse. Her skirt was mini but not micro. A designer suit, thought Mayday, not quite what he'd expected. He hadn't known what to expect, but he hadn't expected this.

'The barman said your name was Bloomstein,' she remarked, without either making a comment or asking a question.

'Yes, he got the wrong end of the stick, I'm afraid.'

'So your real name is de Plume.'

Again it was more a statement than a question. He looked at her sharply, to check for irony. But no, apparently there was none. So. What should he say? How should he start? He hesitated. 'Um . . . you want a drink?'

She looked at him puzzled, and indicated her full glass. 'I just got one.'

He felt foolish. 'Yes. I just wanted to get you something.'

She smiled. 'I'll give you the tab for this one. OK?'

'OK.'

'You English?'

He nodded. 'And you?'

'I'm from the south.' She said it with a cheerful smile. Her teeth were straight and white. Her smile was movie-star perfect. 'Atlanta.'

'Like Scarlett O'Hara?' Ernest remarked foolishly.

'That's right.'

'It had to be you,' sang the piano player softly and deafeningly. Ernest excused himself, went to the piano, waved a twenty-dollar bill in front of the pianist's nose and placed it on the music stand in front of him, turned the amplifier volume control right down and returned to his corner banquette. As he passed them the elderly couple applauded him, and one of the businessmen grinned and gave him an approving nod.

'A man of action, I see,' said Joanna, flirting.

'Who, me?' Ernest smiled modestly, and felt stupidly pleased with her admiration. She smiled back. He wondered if she had been joking. He glanced at her again. He couldn't tell. He decided to broach the subject of the meeting.

'Thank you for coming.' Graciously she inclined her pretty head. 'Perhaps we ought to talk about ... er ... you know, what we ought to talk about.' She was looking at him askance. What's the matter with me, he wondered, why am I so diffident? It's a very simple plan. Joanna made him nervous and he didn't know why. 'The thing is,' he began, 'I'm a writer.'

'Oh yes? What kind of writer?'

'A novelist, actually.'

She waited. He sipped his drink.

'Ever had anything published?'

'Of course, it's my profession, I do it for a living.'

'I don't think I've ever read anything by you.'

'How would you know?'

'I read a lot. Norm de Plume? I don't recall that name.'
She was looking at him with what he felt might be suspicion.

He thought quickly. 'I . . . er . . . I write under a . . .' He
stopped himself saying it in the nick of time. 'Under a pen
name.'

'Oh, I see.' French, apparently, was not her best subject.
'Like Bloomstein?'

'Sort of. Anyway, I've written some bestsellers and I'm
quite able to pay you your ten grand. But I want
something in return.'

She shrugged, and smiled. 'No such thing as a free
lunch, huh?'

Ernest paused for a moment as he reflected upon how
Milton Friedman's dictum had become a cocktail-bar
cliché. She seemed to think he was at a loss. 'Haven't you
ever heard that expression?'

'Oh, yes. Certainly I have.'

'So, what is it you want?' She smiled encouragingly at
him. 'Suggest whatever you want. Don't be shy. I meant
it, no holds barred. I'm broadminded.'

Ernest stared at her, impressed. 'You mean, you'll try
anything?'

She was pretty confident. 'Sure. There's not much I
haven't tried, between you and me.'

He felt slightly in awe of her. She could see it. She
threw back her head and laughed, a surprisingly deep
throaty laugh. She was enjoying his uncertainty. He
noticed her neck was long and slim, somehow erotic.

He swallowed. 'Anything?' he repeated.

'If it's for money, sure. That's the promise.' She was
casual, if not cavalier. 'I told you, I'm broadminded.'

'You'd smuggle drugs? You'd put a bomb on a plane? You'd be a gun-runner? You'd work for BOSS or Mossad?'

'Boss who?'

'You don't know BOSS?'

'Boss who?' she repeated carefully.

'The South African Secret Police? Bureau Of State Security.'

Her smile faded a little, her eyes flickered momentarily around the shadowy bar. 'You a cop?'

'I told you, I'm a novelist.'

She had become noticeably cooler and more reserved. 'What, exactly, do you want me to do?'

'Well, how broadminded *are* you?'

'Very, I told you.'

'Then give me an answer.'

'Sure.' She hesitated. 'What's the question?' Ernest Mayday sighed. 'You mean, would I smuggle drugs and things? No. I don't quite know what you're driving at.'

Ernest Mayday took the plunge. 'I need a plot for my next book. I saw your ad. You say you'll do anything, no holds barred. You want a lot of money for this. You advertise no skills. You need the cash at once. It follows that you're willing to do something illegal. Am I right so far?'

She lit up a cigarette, an act that marked her out as a pariah in Los Angeles. She nodded.

'So,' he continued, 'I imagine that you'll get some replies. I will not give you ten thousand bucks *cash down*. But if you show me every letter you get in reply, and tell me *exactly* what happens as a result, keeping nothing back from me, I promise that I'll match – dollar for dollar – every penny you earn from the ad.'

She looked at him for a long time. He thought she was considering it. Then she spoke. 'I still don't get it.'

Ernest Mayday didn't get why she didn't get it. Was she cautious, evasive, or was she simply stupid? He couldn't tell, so he had another try. 'Look. Have you had any replies to your ad, other than mine?'

'One or two, yes, but they didn't grab me.'

'Why not?'

'They were grubby and obscene.'

'Oh.' Ernest was disappointed. This was not working out as planned. She tried to encourage him. 'But the ad goes in again this week. It usually gets results.'

Ernest was surprised. 'You mean, you've placed this ad before?'

'Oh, yes.'

'In Atlanta?'

'Yes, and in Savannah, but it's not so easy there. It's kind of a small town, though they hate it if you say so. But after a while everybody gets to know you.'

'Why were you desperate then? And what were you offered?'

She wouldn't reply. She gazed at him from under her thick black eyebrows, then flicked some cigarette ash into the whopping glass ashtray. 'Look, I just want to understand what *you're* offering.'

'I'm offering', said Mayday enthusiastically, 'a sliding scale. It may be less than ten thousand. It may, on the other hand, be twenty thousand. I'll match whatever you earn, because I need a good story. So if, for instance, a Colombian cocaine cartel asks you to courier crack to LA, all you have to do is tell me everything that happens. Everything: how they contact you, what they're like, the way they speak, how they phrase their offer, how much they pay you, who you meet, how the crime is committed, every detail. It's the detail that counts.'

She shook her head. 'I'm afraid you've got the wrong end of the stick,' she murmured. 'I don't do that kind of thing.'

He was baffled. 'You said you did. You said you did anything.'

She was silent. Perhaps she thinks I *am* a cop, he thought. 'You can trust me,' he said earnestly. 'I'm not a cop, I promise.'

She laughed aloud, that warm, dark, experienced, smoker's laugh. 'No, you're completely missing the point, Norm.'

Mayday, though he wasn't sure why, was insulted. 'What point? How am I missing the point? If I'm not a cop, what's your problem? I won't tell anyone what you tell me. And I'll fictionalize it all, obviously, because I want people to think I made it all up. No one will ever be able to link it to you when they read it.'

'Is that how it's done?' She was intrigued.

'Of course!' He was emphatic. 'It's for my safety too – if you're dealing with dangerous men and they knew that I knew what *you* knew, I'd be putting myself at risk. So, although anything you knew you'd make sure that *I* knew, I'd know and you'd know that they mustn't *know* that I know.'

Joanna stared at him for a moment. 'Truthfully, you're not that good at communicating, are you, considering you're a writer?' She picked up her Margarita and knocked it straight back. 'Can I get another of these? I can see that's all I'm going to get out of this evening.'

Ernest was nonplussed. He tried again. 'You won't even consider my offer?' Quickly he snapped his fingers at the barman. 'Another drink for the lady.' The barman cupped his hand around his ear. Mayday mimed the order.

She was looking at him with an air of amused affection. 'You have a wonderful line in fantasy,' she informed him.

'I do?'

'Fuckin' A. You know what? I can believe you're an author.'

'Of course I am. Why would I lie?'

'Men lie to me all the time.'

'I'm not lying. This is a bona fide offer, please consider it carefully.'

Slowly she shook her head. 'I can't.' Carefully she selected a huge macadamia nut, then looked up at him. 'Because that's not the kind of offer I'll be getting. No one has asked me to do anything with drugs or guns, nothing that exciting, nothing that dangerous.'

Ernest couldn't understand. Everything she said to him seemed to be a contradiction, yet he was convinced that she was telling the truth. 'So . . . what kind of offers *do* you expect?'

'I'm afraid it wouldn't interest you.'

'What wouldn't?'

She leaned across from her plush upright armchair and kissed him gently on the cheek. 'I told you, I'm broad-minded,' she whispered. Then she put her tongue in his ear. And he understood that broadminded was the code word.

'You're a hooker?' he whispered. He couldn't believe it. Hookers were tarty painted creatures on Hollywood Boulevard or Wardour Street, not this attractive, clean, pretty young woman. She smiled wryly. 'I don't like that word much. I'm a working girl. And an actress. Well, an actress model really.'

He swallowed nervously. 'So what did you mean by broadminded?'

'You name it.' She smiled a mischievous smile, grey eyes twinkling. She patted her handbag. 'I've brought my toothbrush.'

He was suddenly flushed and embarrassed. This was not what he'd expected, certainly not what he had hoped for.

'So that's why you thought I'd contacted you?'

'Sure. And why else would you meet me in a hotel?'

His curiosity was now getting the better of him. 'What else did you bring?'

'You mean, toothbrush aside?' He nodded. 'Well, a clean pair of panties, obviously. And some condoms, of course. Why?'

'I like to know details. Details interest me.'

Her drink arrived. He signed for it on his platinum credit card. He noticed that she noticed. 'Well, I don't want to keep you,' he said.

'No problem. I'm enjoying my drink.'

He looked at her. She was like his friends' teenage daughters, fresh, untouched by any tawdry experience. A college senior, perhaps. There was nothing painted, nothing cheap about her. 'Have you always been a . . . working girl?' She looked him in the eye. 'I'm sorry, do you mind my asking?'

'Nope.' She stubbed out one cigarette, then lit another. 'No. I'm a nurse, actually, by profession.'

'A nurse?'

'That's right. That's what I was in Charleston.'

'Charleston?' Confused, Ernest had visions of wild dancing in the roaring twenties.

'Charleston, South Carolina.'

'Not Atlanta? I thought you came from Atlanta.'

'Both. And I was in Savannah for a bit, I told you. But . . .' she sighed deeply, 'I needed much more money, all of a sudden.'

'Why was that?'

'I'd had a lover. My first, actually.' She leaned over to Ernest, and nuzzled his face with her little nose. He felt an immediate erection. She leaned back again in her chair. 'Do you use Ralph Lauren Polo aftershave?'

Ernest was taken aback. 'Er . . . yes.'

'I recognized it. So did he.'

'Who?'

'My first lover.'

'How did he recognize it, he's not here?'

'No, I meant he used Ralph Lauren Polo aftershave.'

'So, what happened with him?'

'When we split I owed him money. He threatened me.'

'I see.' Tentatively he continued asking questions. 'So

then what happened?' He hoped he had a suitably diagnostic 'what seems to be the trouble' manner, investigative and objective rather than prurient. In any case, she didn't seem to mind answering his questions.

'When I was in New York I did a day job as a doctor's receptionist. If I needed money I got work from an escort agency.'

'Does that mean ... I mean, is escort a euphemism for ...?'

'Obviously.' She giggled. 'Where have you been? Ooh, you've gone all pink.'

'Have I?'

'You're sweet.' She patted his hand. Her hand was cool and firm. His erection returned immediately. He hoped it would go away before she noticed.

'So, you get well paid for this?' he asked.

'Sure.'

'And you did well in New York?'

'Sure. It's an American tradition, since the Civil War – the North has always fucked the South.' She laughed again, softly. Ernest decided to use that line. He was glad that she was from the Deep South, and he suddenly knew that there must be a southern element somewhere in the new book. It made him feel safe, for the South is to American literature what India is to English, with its nostalgic air of lost empire, illusory power, faded gentility, dumb NCOs, rednecks and deferential natives, the elaborately courteous and the casually cruel, bounders and cads, life and death in the hands of transported suburbanites pretending to be cool and upper class despite the sweaty humidity at these last outposts of the civilization, and real ladies and gentlemen whose superficial reserve and manners hid the torrid secrets and violent sexual passions which flourished in the sweltering wet heat. She interrupted his train of thought: 'You still here?'

'How much did you hope to get from me tonight?'

'Three hundred, four hundred? Why, you want to try?'

He wanted to, yet he didn't want to. He looked at her. She smiled encouragingly. 'I've brought my . . .'

'Toothbrush, I know. And you're broadminded.' They smiled.

'Sure am,' she said cheerfully.

But this was not what he wanted to get into. Was he too sensible or too scared? He didn't know.

She shrugged. 'Thought not.' She downed her drink. 'So. This is goodbye?'

Mayday didn't want her to leave yet, and furthermore her story didn't quite make sense to him. 'No, wait a minute, I don't get it. Your ad says you desperately need ten thousand dollars. You tell me that you thought you might earn three or four hundred from me tonight. Where did you expect to find the other nine thousand six hundred?'

'I wasn't really looking for just one trick tonight. I was hoping that you'd be in the market for something more permanent.'

'Marriage, you mean?'

'God, no!' she laughed. 'Marriage? Please! Spare me. I don't want to spend my whole life as a working girl, that's what marriage is. No, see, if I could have been your mistress – not yours,' she added hastily, 'I know that, but, say, someone like you – for a few weeks, or even a few months, that would do it. In that time I'd perform unlimited services as often as you want, whatever you want. That's worth ten grand easy, don't you think?'

'Services?' He leaned back casually, the way he thought a man of the world would.

'Sexual services.' She looked him straight in the eye. 'Of every kind you can imagine. And some that you can't.'

'Can't I?'

She ignored his question. It wasn't worth answering.

'Unlimited. Not two or three hundred bucks for one short time, but as much as you want for a month or six weeks. Anything, any time, day or night.' She ran her tongue around her lips slowly, sensually. It was a slight gesture yet it was somehow full of lust, a stunning aphrodisiac when viewed with her fresh, soft, creamy peach complexion and bright eyes. She seemed, to Ernest, to be – above all – healthy in her attitude to sex. 'It's like a buffet,' she explained, 'or Sunday brunch at this hotel. You'd get as much as you can eat, for a month.'

'As much as I can eat?'

She giggled. 'Or as much as I can. It's a fixed price. It's a great deal, believe me, an experience you'd never forget.'

'A great deal for a rich man.'

'You're a rich man, Norm.'

'I haven't got three hundred dollars on me.'

'I'll take a cheque. Or a credit card.'

He swallowed. His cheque book and credit cards had his real name on them. He couldn't possibly use them, he didn't dare. Randi might see the bill. His business managers and accountants might see. He was ashamed of his lust.

'Yes,' he replied, 'but this is not the deal I'm looking for.'

'I know that. I'm not trying to talk you into it. You asked, so I'm telling you.'

'Yes. Sorry. Yes.'

She picked her handbag up off the floor. 'So. Is that it now, can I go?'

He didn't want her to leave. 'Um ... well ... wait a moment. Can I ask you a couple more things?'

She thought for a moment. 'Why not? I'm not going anywhere.'

'I don't mean to pry,' he said, prying, 'but what do you need the money for?'

'My mother has cancer. And she doesn't have any health insurance.'

He felt a pang. 'Is she very sick?'

She nodded. Suddenly she looked like a little girl. He felt that she needed help, support, sympathy, but he said nothing. He didn't know how to and, being English, he preferred to say nothing than say something inappropriate. She blinked back a tear. 'Anything else?' she asked.

'Yes.' He was tenacious. 'I'm sorry to ask you what I'm sure you think is a naïve question. I mean, it's a sort of what's-a-nice-girl-like-you-doing-in-a-place-like-this question. But . . . how do you *feel* about your – ' he swallowed, 'your work?'

She sighed. Too late, Mayday realized that she'd been asked this many times before. 'Look, I earn the sort of money that I can't possibly earn nursing. And, frankly, there's very little difference between nursing and what I do.' She glanced around, then lowered her voice a little. 'I've been trained to touch people's bodies, in all their private places. I wash them, powder them, make them feel better, more comfortable, less tense. So, if I'm their escort – or their mistress – what's the difference? I let them inside me, that's all. It's no big deal.'

Ernest was fascinated by her matter-of-factness. 'No qualms?'

'Why should there be?' She tossed her head, flicking her soft brown glossy forelock back out of her eyes. 'Lots of men want sex without any emotional complications. I don't blame them. I happen to like that too.'

'Isn't that rather . . . unusual, for a woman?'

She smiled wearily. 'No, it's pretty common, actually, Norm. But men don't like to think so. They want women to need them, they like to think women are emotionally involved with them – it's good for the male ego, I suppose.'

'I guess some women want emotion with sex?' he ventured cautiously.

'I guess.' She didn't seem particularly interested in such

42

women. 'So do I, sometimes. But men have such romantic notions about women. Believe me, most of us have a much more clinical attitude to our bodies than most men realize. It's not such a momentous event to get fucked. Well, not usually. Personally, I enjoy it a lot. I like sex. And I like it with different guys. I like the variety. I *really* like feeling a man inside me, filling me up. I do no harm, I give people pleasure, and I enjoy myself. I'm not ashamed of what I do, OK?'

He was startled by her outburst of defiance. 'I didn't say you should be ashamed.'

She looked at him gravely, then nodded to acknowledge that he was right. 'No, you didn't.'

'But if you're not ashamed of what you do – does your mother know?'

She flared up again. ''Course not. You think I'd tell my mom that I sell my body?'

'So you *are* ashamed.' The cross-examination was concluded.

She stood up. Her pretty mouth was set in a hard tight line. As she stood over him he was uncomfortably aware that her breasts were close to his face, breasts he would be allowed to touch, to feel, hold, suck ... if he just gave her three hundred bucks and took a room upstairs. That's all it would take. That is, if she wasn't too angry with him, if he hadn't just blown the relationship.

'I'm not ashamed.' She was repeating it, emphatically. 'But there are double standards, Norm, as you well know. That's why I had to leave Savannah. You can't lead a double life in a small town like Savannah.'

Ernest stood up, uneasily close to her. He smelled her perfume. It made him giddy. 'I'm sorry,' he said. 'I didn't mean to upset you or insult you.'

She nodded cursorily. 'Will you ask the bellman to get me a taxi?'

Ernest was surprised. This was LA, where everybody

had a car, where you couldn't get around without one. 'You haven't got a car?'

'It's not working. And I can't afford to have it fixed. I'm stone broke. I told you, I need money desperately.' She looked into his eyes. Was she asking for money, for help, for charity? Or was she saying she'd earn it and be independent? Ernest simply couldn't tell. So he didn't offer her money, although he had taken up so much of a working girl's time. But he didn't offer anything, and she didn't ask. This was something that he would later come to regret.

Instead he said: 'I can give you a lift home, if you like.'

She brightened up. 'Can you? You sure?' She seemed pathetically grateful. 'Thank you.' He liked that. It made him feel good, somehow strong and masculine, even while he was aware that this was a ridiculous response.

They waited outside the hotel for some minutes while the valet sorted out Ernest's Mercedes from all the others, and, like an old-fashioned sugar daddy taking his squeeze home from a date, he held the door open for her as she got into the car. It also gave him one more chance to look at her legs – trim ankles, slim calves, perfectly turned thighs and that tight little bottom, available for cash, cheque or credit card – as she slid herself into the front seat of the Mercedes. He'd expected her to be impressed by it but he saw at once that she'd ridden in them many times before. As they swung back out on to Sunset and motored silently up into the Hollywood Hills she deftly adjusted the air-conditioning to just the way she liked it, then slid her seat back to give her long legs more room. She knew where the handle was, without even having to feel for it.

She lived, it transpired, in a condo in the Valley, in the the neighbourhood known as Toluca Lake. It was a deceptive name, conjuring up – like Shepherd's Bush, Swiss Cottage or Wood Green – a pastoral fantasy that bore no relation to the reality. If there had ever been a lake at Toluca, thought Ernest, it would now probably be nothing more than a patchwork of cracked dry mud. They drove in silence up and across the Santa Monica Mountains, zigzagging up through scrubby, arid Laurel Canyon Pass and down the San Fernando Valley side of the Hollywood Hills to the flatlands of ugly, built-up, suburban Ventura Boulevard, left past Universal Studios, then right, towards the Warner Bros lot at Burbank. Some days it was possible to see, on the far side of the Valley, the snow-topped San Gabriel Mountains, rising steeply behind Burbank airport. But that day the air was so polluted that hazard warnings had been posted, and on the TV and radio news the elderly and asthmatic were being advised not to go out jogging. The San Fernando Valley, once a vast quiet plain at the foot of the High Sierras, fragrant and filled with orange blossom, was now somewhat less fragrant and filled with orange smog.

At Toluca Lake, on Riverside, beside the empty concrete river bed, he parked where she directed. 'Sorry I can't ask you in or anything,' she said politely as she opened the passenger door.

'That's OK. I have to get home anyway,' he lied.

'You see, I share an apartment with a girlfriend and it's all a bit of a mess.'

'That's OK,' he repeated. 'I'm sorry I wasted your time.'

'You didn't at all,' she said with considerable charm. 'I enjoyed meeting a bestselling author. My first. I'm just, well, disappointed that I got no work tonight. Not your fault. I like you, you're sweet.'

'And I like you,' he said. Feeling slightly shy, he extended his hand for a handshake. Grinning, she took it. Was she also thinking, he wondered, that this was – for her – an unusual and incongruously distant form of contact with a man who had answered her ad? Holding on to her hand he said urgently: 'The offer's still open. If anyone calls you with the kind of proposal that I had hoped for – you know the sort of thing I mean – please phone me at once. You still have my number?' She nodded. 'I'll match any offer that's made to you, remember that, dollar for dollar.'

She smiled. 'I assure you, no one will call with that kind of offer. At least, no one ever has so far.'

'They might.' He still hadn't let go of her hand.

'I don't think so, Norm. Everyone but you who answers that ad will know what I'm advertising.' She kissed him lightly on the cheek. His heart fluttered. 'You're a real innocent, you know that?' He was hot and embarrassed. 'You're blushing again,' she whispered. 'You're really cute. Sorry. I'm really sorry I can't help you.'

Gently she removed her hand from his grasp and slid out of the car. She turned and leaned down towards him. He tried not to look at her cleavage, now partially and temptingly revealed. He had a brief glimpse of a delicate, lacy, see-through white bra. Aware of his glance, she quickly put her hand across the top of her blouse, holding it to her chest-bone. Was she embarrassed? Surely not? Was it because Mayday hadn't paid to see her breasts? Of course not. Ernest Mayday saw instead that this was an instinctively modest gesture. He was intrigued by the paradox of this modest and intelligent whore. There was no doubt at all in his mind that, when she wasn't working, this working girl was a lady.

FOUR

*If my books had been any worse, I should not have
been invited to Hollywood, and if they had been any
better, I should not have come.*

Raymond Chandler

Sex with Randi suddenly improved again over the next
few weeks. Ernest didn't know why, but he was greatly
encouraged by her renewed enthusiasm. He speculated
about it quite a lot. Maybe it was as a result of their
conversation about self-realization. Maybe she just felt
more loving towards him. Maybe her libido had returned.
Perhaps, he thought, I've become more patient and understanding. His love-making certainly acquired a freshness,
for while Randi was in his bed Joanna was in his mind.
He shut his eyes and saw those long legs, those frank grey
eyes, that warm smile with such promise, that sensuous
tongue moistening full lips, and he wondered how such a
girl could sell her body without any apparent regrets,
indeed with pleasure. It ran counter to everything that he
thought he knew about women. It was her candour, the
open pleasure that had been implicit in her attitude to sex,
that had really turned him on, more even than the perfec-
tion of her body or her skin, about which he fantasized
whenever he was inside Randi.

Meanwhile, Randi began to respond to him as she had
done when first they met. Better still, although Ernest's
book was still stalled, he found that his inability to write it
no longer made him feel impotent. Inexplicably, rather, he
felt free. This was fortunate as his first meeting with

Oliver Sudden was being set up by his agent Fanny Rush.

She took him to dinner at Pogo, to explain to him how she had 'positioned the deal', one of her favourite phrases. 'Where's Randi?' she asked when they met in the chic crush at the Hostess's desk beside the restaurant's front door.

'Your table will be ready in two minutes, Miss Rush,' the slim, elegant young lady in charge of the table plan assured her, turning to explain to six other parties (mere members of the public) that there would be no tables available for at least two hours.

'Randi's at a meeting.' Ernest didn't want to get involved in explanations about the Church of the Community of Personal Truth, even though he'd discovered that nothing weird phased the average Californian agent. Instead, as the hostess seated them at a moderately good table, not at the front by the big windows but far enough from the kitchen and the toilets that it could not be construed by Fanny Rush as a slight, Mayday marvelled at how people in show business allowed their status to be determined by the maître d' of a hot restaurant. Money didn't do it. Restaurateurs were incorruptible in that one regard. The maître d's skill was to determine who was hot and who was not and that was that.

'Did you read your contract?' Fanny asked him, as they were being seated.

'Sure.'

'It's a longer option than usual. It sunsets in five years, not one.' Ernest Mayday was not sure that he was prepared to recognize the word sunset as a verb, although generally he felt he was mildly approving of Californian creativity with the English language. 'Because of that,' she continued, 'it's worth quite a lot more, but they want to pay it in stages.'

'Am I guaranteed the money?'

'If they renew, yes.'

'Oh.' He was surprised. 'I thought it didn't sunset for five years.'

'It's a one-year option, renewable. But we can't force them to renew.' She had ordered some of the famous chef's equally famous pizza to start with, and she nibbled at it while she waited for her salad and her fish, broiled with no butter. On the whole Mayday would have preferred to have a hungry agent.

'What about my credit?'

'Billing, you mean? The usual. Based upon the novel by Ernest Mayday. If they use your screenplay you'll get a separate credit for that: Screenplay by Ernest Mayday.'

'Yes, but what about my producing it with Oliver Sudden?'

'But you're not a real producer.'

'I *know* that, Fanny. But how many producers are?'

'Oliver Sudden is. He's a major *major* hyphenate.'

'Hyphenate?'

'Producer-director,' she explained. 'Or writer-director. Or writer-producer. In his case, all three.'

Mayday noted that the word major had become so devalued that if you were major you now had to be described as major *major*.

'Look, Fanny, I can guess how it's all to be billed. "Oliver Sudden Productions presents a film by Oliver Sudden. Produced and Directed by Oliver Sudden." Right?' She picked at her salad of mixed baby lettuce hearts in raspberry vinaigrette. 'Well, it's my book and it'll be my script. It's as much my film as his and I want it to say so.'

'But he's not only the producer, he'll be the director too,' she explained. 'It's his vision.'

'Bullshit. It's my fucking vision, he's just the director.'

Fanny shook her head sadly. Would these writers ever understand? 'Ernest, film is a director's medium. By definition it's his vision.'

'He can't direct his film', replied Ernest stubbornly, 'without my story. It would be like if he directed Shakespeare and called it his.'

Fanny smiled. 'When I lived in London I remember people talking about Richard Eyre's *Hamlet* and Jonathan Miller's *Merchant*. Don't you?'

'But everyone knows who wrote them, for Christ's sake.'

'So?'

'So it isn't right to call my film a film by Oliver Sudden.'

'Ernest, Hollywood has zero interest in right and wrong. You were a civil servant, you of all people should understand how irrelevant right and wrong are to almost anything. Since when did right and wrong have anything to do with power and money? Hollywood is about the bottom line.'

'And ownership,' Ernest insisted. 'It's about ownership. And I own this project.'

'Above all, Hollywood is about perceptions,' countered Fanny. 'And if this isn't perceived as an Oliver Sudden film, he won't do it. Is that what you want? Is this a deal-breaker?' She knew that it wasn't. He needed the deal.

Ernest Mayday dug into his seared swordfish steak with a scowl. 'It's bullshit,' he growled again. 'I went to the Hollywood Bowl last Sunday and heard the LA Symphony – I suppose it should have been advertised as an André Previn Concert, scored by Ludwig van Beethoven.'

Fanny was rapidly tiring of the conversation. It was one she had almost daily with all her non-hyphenate writer clients. 'Let me tell you about Oliver,' she said, moving right along. 'He's very smart. But he's easily bored, he has a lot going on, he moves fast, he's wired. He's known as the Electric Italian.' She giggled.

'You know him well?'

For the first time in their entire acquaintance she didn't have an immediate answer. She smiled awkwardly, then confessed: 'Actually, I've never met him myself but of course I know all about him from my colleagues at the agency.'

'Of course,' he muttered, embarrassed for her. But he needn't have been. It took much more than that to cause her genuine embarrassment.

The next day Ernest Mayday drove to the stark white concrete and glass California-modern court of the Electric Italian, high on a peak in Pacific Palisades, overlooking Santa Monica Bay. Persil white and Omo bright, the house sparkled and dazzled in the sunshine. Max Period and Sidney had explained to Ernest that the movie business, like fifteenth-century Florence, was divided up into a number of princely courts not unlike those of the Borgias and the Medicis. These courts were the seven major studios plus the two or three top talent agencies and a handful of major major producers, and the powerful princes at the head of each court were surrounded by their courtiers, their mercantile advisers, their pirates and their mercenaries, and they held undisputed power until they were – inevitably – treacherously usurped. As they strove through Machiavellian manipulation, persistent feuding and the occasional use of terror to increase their already extensive plunder they – almost as a by-product – hired the local artists (and even imported a few from foreign parts), and commissioned works of art. Some of the commissions were very specific, some left the better artists alone to do the work their own way. Thus history has treated these princes more kindly than they deserve and they are most often remembered today as discriminating patrons of the arts.

Oliver Sudden was reputed to be one such Hollywood nobleman and Ernest was hoping to get an inside glimpse of a real movie-mogul's mansion. Instead, on arrival he was escorted straight into an office near the front door. 'Hi, I'm Debbie, Oliver's assistant,' said the pretty blonde girl in skin-tight hotpants who let him in, then disappeared saying, 'I'll just check into his status,' meaning, presumably, that she'd see if he were free. Mayday peered out of the open office door at the hall. It was all that he could see of the house. It had lots of cool, pale yellow marble all over everything. Every possible surface – floor, stairs, walls, pillars – wherever you could stick a piece of marble, they'd stuck it. This was indubitably the residence of a major major hyphenate.

Oliver Sudden bounced enthusiastically out of a door across the hall. He was wearing knee-length shorts and a T-shirt inscribed with the words: *It's not what you are, it's what you wear. Who cares what you really are?* He greeted Mayday with intense enthusiasm, shook his hand vigorously and joyfully and headed for the jug of hot brewed coffee on the marble shelf behind his desk. He spoke in one continuous sentence, without ever pausing for breath. 'So *you're* Ernest Mayday, hi, want some decaf, I didn't think you'd look like that, how'd you like Hollywood, seen the London papers recently, do you live here or there, sugar and cream?'

As Oliver turned around to face him, Ernest held his hand up abruptly for silence, like Charlie Chaplin in *The Great Dictator*. Thrown by the abruptness of the gesture, Oliver stopped talking for a moment and the Englishman seized the opportunity. 'Yes I'm Ernest Mayday, yes I'd like a decaf, what did you think I'd look like, I like Hollywood, I don't read the London papers, I live here and no cream or sugar thank you very much.'

Oliver Sudden's face was suffused with delight. 'Hey, that's neat,' he exclaimed, with admiration and interest. He handed Mayday the coffee mug. 'Sit down.' He stared with open curiosity at this Englishman who appeared, at any rate at first glance, to have a brain as quick as his own. Ernest sat dutifully in the chair indicated. Haslemere and Hollywood gazed at each other for a moment, sizing each other up. Oliver Sudden saw a suspicious, paranoid, weedy, watery-eyed, bespectacled, bulging-browed intellectual – a writer, in short. Ernest Mayday was looking at a tousled, fit, muscular, boyish tycoon in his late thirties, with curly black hair, trim black beard and a disarming grin. Oliver Sudden was not surprised by what he saw, but Ernest Mayday had not expected this youthful casual charm. The producer put his sneakers up on the vast open spaces of his desk top and sipped the hot decaf. 'Jet-lagged?'

'No,' said Ernest.

'Been here long?'

'A couple of years.'

'That explains it,' said Oliver and he grinned again. 'So, where shall we begin, you want to talk about how we should adapt *Lies* for the screen?'

'May I be impertinent?' asked Mayday.

'Sure,' Oliver grinned some more, 'but I may throw you out on your ass.'

'Is Oliver Sudden your real name?'

He didn't mind the question. 'Yes it is, weird isn't it, I'm Italian and it's a real waspy type name but the thing is it's an Ellis Island name, my dad's real name was Giuseppe Giovanni Improviso, he was a master baker from Milan, you should have tasted his *biscotti*, they were great, he's dead now, anyway the immigration guy couldn't write his name down, imagine! Giuseppe Giovanni Improviso, I mean, that's like "Huh?" Know what I mean, Ernest? So some good Samaritan there translated Giuseppe as Joe and the Ellis Island moron asked somebody what *improviso* meant and he was told sudden so suddenly my dad became Joe Sudden. When I was christened I don't think it occurred to him that Oliver Sudden would sound funny to people, I mean like he pronounced it Olly-*vair*, but you wanna know something cute, I think he named me after Olly Hardy, he loved Laurel and Hardy, do you, I think they're the best, know what I mean, the *best*, and Poppa always liked Oliver more than Stan, I guess it was because he was the fat one, I mean like my poppa was a baker, a pastry cook, whaddya expect, he'd like *thin* people? Ridiculous!' Ernest wasn't sure how to reply. But fortunately Oliver didn't seem to expect him to. 'Ever heard of Rip Torn or Elvis Presley, that's their real names too, weird, huh? So having that name is a cross to bear but I guess it was good for me it gave me something to react against, to fight, a little ambition that's what my therapist says, so I don't regret it I don't have regrets I believe in being positive, no negativity, making the most of what you got, of what God gave you, I think I've done that, whaddaya think?' The flow of words had come to a sudden halt.

'I think,' replied Ernest, 'that you can breathe in through your nose while you're talking through your mouth.'

Oliver stared at him for a moment, then grinned, flattered. 'Let's cut to the chase. You want to script the movie?'

Ernest was taken aback. 'It's agreed, isn't it?'

Oliver Sudden ignored that. 'Do you know how? Tell me the difference between writing a novel and a screenplay.'

Ernest answered easily. 'In a novel you can write what you like, as long as you can hold the readers' attention and keep them turning the pages. You don't have to write the leading characters in a way that flatters the ego of some star you're trying to cast. There's no budget, except the cost of the paper, so you can whisk the reader from Bombay to Brighton to Bel Air in one easy paragraph at no extra cost. I can write a story with a multitude of themes instead of one simple story with a little sub-plotting. I can tell my readers what they need to know, instead of depending on actors, for God's sake, to help them infer it from the way they speak the dialogue. I can . . .'

'Hold it, hold it,' interrupted the producer. 'This is great. Absolutely fucking great. So, why do you want to write a screenplay? Why not write another novel and hand your book over to a screenwriter?'

Mayday didn't want to admit his fear that he'd lost his ability to write another novel. 'Because I want the film to be the film of my book,' he lied.

'Why do you care?' Oliver wasn't trying to persuade him, he was genuinely puzzled.

'I don't want to disappoint my readers.'

Oliver shrugged. 'You can't help it. A movie's always a disappointment to someone who liked the book it's based on. Readers have their own private screening rooms in their heads, they already see the movie as they're reading it. But it's their movie, not yours. And it's not your version of the book that they're reading, either, it's theirs. You know what'll disappoint them less? If you stay right out of it. Then they'll blame me, not you.'

This sounded like a trap to Ernest Mayday. He said nothing. He was deadpan. He knew how to play poker. 'Anyway,' Oliver continued, 'you missed out the biggest difference between writing books and movies.' Mayday raised his eyebrows in the unspoken question. 'Books are about words, but movies are pictures, action, the fewer words the better. Books can be an intellectual experience, you can transmit ideas, profound thoughts, but not in the movies, baby.'

'Not in American movies, maybe,' said Ernest, getting a xenophobic word in edgeways.

'Not in any movies, period. Trust me, movies are an emotional experience, they're scary, they're funny, you laugh, you cry, you may be rootin' for the little guy in a movie about Wall Street but if you want to understand supply-side economics you'd better read a fuckin' book.'

He leaped to his feet, energized, enthused. 'Same with theatre, kiddo – words, words, words, no action! Just a bunch of people talking to each other, like, how much action is there in *Hamlet*, it lasts four hours and there's maybe five minutes of action *total*, a couple of guys get stabbed, what's his name, the old fellow . . .?'

'Polonius?'

'So he gets iced along the way, a few more at the end get wasted, you know, poisoned and stabbed, what's the song –

> The ghost and the Prince meet
> And everyone ends in mincemeat,
> La la, lalalalah,
> That's en-ter-tain-ment'

– Oliver was up on the desk now, singing and dancing – 'but that's it, man, one fuckin' fight at the end, other than that, talk! Nothing but talk. *Great* talk, I grant you, great fuckin' talk, but talk. No action.' Ernest Mayday was reeling. First Fanny had talked of *Hamlet*, now Oliver Sudden – was there no end to all this scholarship? Who said there was no culture in Hollywood? Oliver Sudden jumped off his desk, and was now nose-to-nose with him. 'The question is, Ernest my friend, brilliant writer though you are, can you turn your book into pictures or are you going to be British about it and cling to all those words?'

Mayday mentally reviewed the subtext of this conversation so far. 'You don't want me to write it, is that it?'

Oliver Sudden backed off. 'Hold it, hold it, hold everything, stop the presses, I didn't say that, OK? Look, I got no ulterior motive, believe me. I *want* you to write it' – he became emotional – '*if* you *can* write it.' He picked up the mug of decaf and sipped. 'But not if you can't,' he added. 'So. Can you?'

Ernest Mayday didn't know if he could or he couldn't, so he changed the subject and, for the second time, avoided a difficult question by asking one. 'Do you plan to change the title of my book?'

Oliver Sudden also knew how to answer a question with a question. 'You think *Lies* is a good title?'

Ernest hesitated. 'I think so.'

Oliver Sudden grinned. 'Nailing your colours to the fence, huh?'

Mayday was indignant. 'Just trying to give a thoughtful, honest answer.'

'Let me tell you about titles.' Oliver was now lying on the floor, his knees clutched to his chest, rolling forwards and backwards on his pelvis and spine. 'I gotta bad back,' he explained. '*Cocktail* was a terrible title. *Cocktail starring Tom Cruise* was a great fucking title.'

'You mean it depends on who stars in *Lies*?'

'Maybe. Hold my feet down. On the floor, there you go.' Now Ernest was on his hands and knees, holding Oliver's Patrick Ewing sneakers down as the producer did some sudden energetic sit-ups. 'Stars are not the only thing, but the movie must have top-spin. All I'm saying is, if it sells, it's a good title. How many copies of *Lies* did you sell?'

'Around the world? Hardback or paperback? Book club?'

Oliver Sudden sat up and threw his arms wide in an expansive gesture. 'Total!' he demanded.

'Seven or eight million.'

'Then you know what?' Oliver Sudden shouted and leaped athletically to his feet. '*Lies* is a great fucking title!'

The meeting was over. Oliver promised they'd meet again – soon. He'd talk to Fanny. He gave Ernest a big affectionate hug, as if they'd known each other for twenty years. 'You're terrific,' he said. 'I love you.'

Ernest drove home, hoping he'd get to write the screenplay. It would keep his mind off his book, and off Joanna. He felt at a loose end. At the Sunset Bookshop he picked up another free tabloid, this time called the *Learning Annex*. TAKE ONE, IT'S $FREE! screamed the headline, so he took one. It advertised all kinds of self-improvement courses. 'How to Write a Movie in 21 Days' attracted his attention. He didn't actually *need* that one – he hadn't confessed this to Oliver Sudden but he'd already written a screenplay for *Lies*. He wanted Oliver to commission it, pay for it and then wait for it, so that Oliver would feel he had contributed, feel that he'd achieved some 'input'. 'What To Do When Your Bills Exceed Your Paycheck' was another course that seemed relevant but which, Ernest felt, would offer no particular solution other than the obvious. His mind went back to an icy winter's morning when, as a lonely eight-year-old sent home by his Indian army parents from the warm and comforting British diplomatic compound in Bombay to his preparatory boarding-school on the South Downs just outside Brighton, he'd bagged a classroom desk by one of the big clanking iron radiators and hugged it as old 'Spotty' Spottiswoode had read to them from Dickens. 'My other advice, Copperfield,' said Mr Micawber, 'you know. Annual income twenty pounds, annual expenditure nineteen nineteen and six, result happiness. Annual income twenty pounds, annual expenditure twenty pounds ought and six, result misery.' Now, having made the move from Bombay to Brighton to Bel Air – or, at least, the Hollywood Hills – Ernest felt he was unlikely to go bankrupt ever again, even though he might be forced to move into a smaller house with a smaller pool if he didn't deliver the book within the year. The luxury had lulled him into a true sense of security. He was no longer driven to write.

But it had also, paradoxically, made him feel that the way he lived now had to be preserved. Downgrading his home would be a tremendous loss of face. He sat in the Mercedes and continued leafing through the free broadsheet. Anything to avoid going home to work. 'Earn up to $100,000 a Year as a Balloon Artist', it said. If mastering hot air was the trick, Ernest felt that he had already earned much more than a hundred thousand with it. 'How to Strip for Your Lover (For Women Only)', warned an enticing ad for a course that he'd have liked to attend, but for which he clearly wasn't eligible. 'How to Begin and Continue a Conversation' ... He shook his head in wonderment, stunned that there was a market for this one. He kept the paper in case he decided to attend the movie-writing seminar – under an assumed name, of course.

Randi was waiting for him at home, anxious to know how his meeting with Oliver Sudden had gone. Although she'd never moved in with him he'd given her a set of keys soon after their affair began, and now he wasn't sure how to ask for them back. He hid the *Learning Annex* from her – on the front cover was a course called 'How to Make Love All the Time', with a banner quote from some MD in a fat typeface: IF YOU AREN'T IN THE MOOD FOR SEX, SAY NO TO SEX, BUT SAY YES TO LOVING. Ernest felt it was too great a risk to show a quote like SAY NO TO SEX to someone as impressionable as Randi, especially when the quote was credited to a doctor and especially when she was showing signs of coming to life in bed once more.

Three times in the next two days he phoned Fanny Rush, to try to establish whether he and Oliver had a done deal to write *Lies* for the screen. She was, her assistant informed Ernest each time he called, in a meeting. 'Well, who are you?' he demanded.

'I'm her assistant, Sherry.'

'You mean, her secretary?'

'Her assistant, yes.'

'Well, can't you interrupt her meeting?'

'It's a closed-door meeting.'

'What does that mean?'

'It's behind closed doors.'

'Don't they have hinges?'

She hesitated. 'I don't get the question.'

'If they're closed, Sherry, open them.'

'I can't do that. But I'm sure she'll call you back momentarily.'

'American momentarily or British momentarily?'

'Huh?'

'In a moment or for a moment?'

'Huh?'

There was a pause. Then a sigh. 'OK, Mr Mayday, I'll try and establish her status as of now.'

'Her status,' replied Ernest dyspeptically, 'as of now, as of this moment, at this point in time, as you circumlocutory people like to say, is that she's my agent. Her status may change to ex-agent momentarily, in the American sense only, in other words *in* a moment but certainly not *for* a moment, unless she returns my calls. Which she should return momentarily, also in the American sense, i.e. very soon.'

There was another pause. 'May I tell her what you're calling about?' Sherry sounded distinctly cooler.

'Do you know what I'm calling about?' he inquired.

'No, sir, I don't.'

'Then how can you tell her?' He hung up in triumph, but his pleasure evaporated in seconds as he realized that a victory over Fanny's secretary was somewhat Pyrrhic. So he called his lawyer, Dylan Kanpinchowitz, whose assistant explained that he was in a closed-door meeting. 'Another fucking closed-door meeting?' said Ernest. 'Tell him it's about his paternity suit.' There was a brief pause, then the assistant came back on the line. 'I'm putting you right through,' she said.

Dylan came on the line. 'Ernest?'

'I hope I didn't embarrass you,' Ernest lied.

'Not at all,' said Dylan. 'Which paternity suit?' They both laughed immoderately. Ernest explained that although Fanny had made a deal there was in fact no contract yet with Oliver Sudden. There was only a deal memo. 'So in what sense is there a deal?'

'There's a letter of intent,' replied Dylan, 'outlining major points – your financial compensation, your profit participation, that kind of stuff.'

'So what about a contract?'

'There won't be a contract', the lawyer explained, 'until I've negotiated all the small print with the studio's business affairs department.'

'But Oliver Sudden wants the screenplay within a few weeks.'

'Do you want to write it?'

'Yes.'

'You sure?'

'Yes. Don't *you* start.'

'I thought you had a deadline on your novel.'

'So?'

'OK, OK, don't be so *English*.'

'What's that supposed to mean?'

'Well, you're being a little persnickety.'

'I don't think I am,' snapped Ernest, wondering how pernickety became persnickety as it crossed the Atlantic.

Kanpinchowitz sighed. 'Jesus, I envy you, I wish I were writing a novel. I'd like to do that more than anything in the world.'

'Why?' Ernest was puzzled. 'You've already *got* a job.'

'What's the matter with you today?' Dylan was getting irritated now. 'Why are you being so snot-nosed?'

'Fanny told me before the meeting with Oliver that it was agreed I'd do the screenplay.'

'Did Oliver say you couldn't?'

'Not exactly. But it's clearly an open issue.'

'Why do you want to do it? Do you need the money?'

Ernest didn't want to admit it. 'It's not the money,' he replied, 'it's the principle.' Dylan, at his desk atop one of the shiny black skyscrapers in Century City, smiled. He knew from long experience that whenever anyone said 'It's not the money, it's the principle', they meant that it was the money. He put this theory to the test.

'Then make it a deal-breaker,' he suggested. As Ernest didn't care for this suggestion, a brief silence ensued. Dylan was relentless. 'If it's a matter of principle, surely you must?'

Ernest said: 'We've already *made* the deal, Dylan, and I want everyone to stick to it. That's what a deal's for, isn't it?'

'Not in Hollywood,' explained Dylan cheerfully. 'Here, everything's negotiable and re-negotiable and re-re-negotiable.'

'Then why make a deal at all?'

'Because then you have a deal that's the deal that you have until you make a better deal. You want my opinion? Oliver may want to write the movie with you. Joint credit. I'd go for that because in protecting his own position he'll have to protect yours too.'

Ernest saw the sense of this. But he wanted Dylan and Fanny to discuss it, just in case. So when Fanny finally phoned him back at the end of the day, he told her assistant that she should talk to Dylan instead because he was behind closed doors. The next day, a huge basket of fruit and assorted European cheeses and crackers arrived, with a handwritten note of apology on a card with the printed heading FROM THE DESK OF FANNY RUSH. 'Dear Desk,' Ernest wrote back, 'thank you for the apology and for the provisions, which will certainly help to keep me going next time I have to wait in for several days for you to call me back.'

Dylan Kanpinchowitz had guessed correctly. Oliver Sudden was delighted to write *Lies* with Ernest. Ernest insisted that in the film's credits the words 'An Oliver Sudden Film' would be followed by Ernest's own proprietary credit, so that the whole thing would read:

An Oliver Sudden Film
of Ernest Mayday's
LIES

Honour, the euphemism for ego, was thus satisfied on all sides.

FIVE

*The law was the tree . . . for when the law said, 'Eat
this, do not eat that,' it was the beginning of death.*

Gospel of Philip

Ernest Mayday was obsessed by Joanna. He thought
about her for most of the day, he dreamed about her at
night. In his dreams she would confess that she loved him.
In his dreams he seemed to be endowed with a penis that
grew like Jack's beanstalk and which she caressed lovingly,
yet although it was attached to him he could not feel it.
All day, as he sat alone at his desk, he was tormented by
the questions that he should have asked her but didn't.
Was she, for instance, married or single? What was her
surname? Would she often need large sums of money, or
was it just this once as a desperate measure for some
particular treatment for her mother? Where exactly did
she live? He knew on which corner he'd dropped her, but
there were thousands of houses and apartments within
easy walking distance. And why hadn't he asked for her
phone number?

The problem was, he couldn't find her. And she had no
reason to call him. Perhaps if she'd known who he really
was . . . but why, even then, would she call him again? She
had apparently believed he was a bestselling author. He
was glad that he had not revealed his real name. He didn't
want her to know just how rich he really was. Not that he
was *rich* rich, not by Hollywood standards, but compared
to most of the world – compared to most Americans,
indeed – he was very well-heeled and his royalties alone

could keep him going (albeit with a reduced standard of living) more or less for life even if he never wrote another lousy word. He could have afforded to give her the ten thousand dollars on the spot, and he felt a little guilty about it. There was absolutely no reason for him to feel responsible for her, a total stranger, nor for her mother. Yet he couldn't help it.

Sometimes he felt an overwhelming sense of relief that he had not got involved with her and that his palpitating encounter with the *demi-monde* had been so brief and so safe. Prostitution, he knew, was illegal in Los Angeles. The client, too, commits a violation, though – since it's with a prostitute – only in the legal sense of the word. But that meant criminal proceedings, a prosecution, press coverage, humiliation, disgrace. Though never recognized in the street, Ernest Mayday's name was known to anyone who had ever read a book and the publicity if he were to be involved in vice charges would be too awful to bear. Furthermore, the temptation to prosecute someone rich and famous would be, for almost any DA (especially one with a forthcoming re-election campaign) well-nigh irresistible. None the less, while confident he'd done the safe thing, he still found that he couldn't stop thinking about her.

Ernest had promised Oliver that he'd finish a story breakdown of *Lies* within three weeks. Since he'd already written the whole thing, this précis took him only two days. So he returned to the problem of the unwritten novel, which he now hoped could be about a working girl from the Deep South. The next morning he sat down in front of the word processor and tried:

FLAGRANTE DELICTO
A new novel by
Ernest Mayday

Chapter One

He paused. That was the easy bit. Now what? Five hundred blank sheets of paper sat in the printer, awaiting him. Each blank sheet contained no boundaries, no limitations. It was limitless, infinite space. Because he could begin anywhere, he couldn't begin at all. Instead, he brewed some coffee. He sipped it. Then he made himself a peanut butter sandwich on toasted wholewheat, which he enjoyed guiltily. He wandered around the terrace for a while. Then, suddenly, he saw how he could hit the ground running, and he hurried back to the study.

At the far end of the darkened hotel bar, a girl walked in. She looked around, hesitated in front of the opaque glass doors expensively engraved with art deco lilies, glanced at me, then sat at the bar. I watched her. She said something to the barman, who listened and shook his head.

She was slim, medium height, short brown hair, with a forelock overhanging her forehead, minimal make-up, not unattractive but the sort of girl you wouldn't really notice unless you were trying to guess whether or not she'd come to meet you.

She ordered a Margarita, sipped it, then looked again at me. I felt a flutter in my chest. Was this Joanna? She slid down from the bar stool, straightened her tight black mini-skirt which had ridden up close to her crotch, and walked towards me. 'Are you Mr de Plume?'

He stopped typing. What now? Of course he could describe the rest of their meeting. But then what? He still had no story to tell. With a mixture of exhaustion and despair he switched off his word processor and stared for a while at the dead, flat screen. With little else to do, he began to check out his own status.

Why was he so anxious and depressed? Was it really because he wasn't able to work? He could always heed Mr Micawber and live on nineteen pounds nineteen and six. So was it perhaps guilt? Guilt about not having to do a proper job, guilt about earning so much for – finally – so little. Or was it fear, not a fear of the cash running out exactly but a fear of failure, or (to be precise) a fear of being perceived as a failure in this town of unreal perceptions, a Hollywood fear of not being able to look your accountant in the eye, or the Vice-president of the bank's Entertainment Division, your attorney or your business manager. Ernest realized that he feared status failure. Like an aging jumbo jet lumbering clumsily along the runway, grounded by metal fatigue, Ernest felt that status fatigue was imminent. He feared that he might break up under its stress.

He went downstairs to get himself another cup of coffee. Consuela his maid, little, pudgy, smiling, Mexican and illegal, was bustling around the kitchen. Consuela had been Randi's cleaning lady when she'd had her own apartment in the days before she'd been born again and joined the commune down at the Theological Institute and Seminary. Consuela had looked after both their places in those days. Although Randi still had the keys to his house, often stayed the night with Ernest and kept some clothes at his place, she absolutely never cooked anything or cleaned up. Consuela alone cleaned Ernest's house, and Randi went to the Seminary all day where she struggled to find inner cleanliness. Sex had become a more complex issue than ever owing to the Church's latest drive for Inner Purity (and Randi's subsequent confusion on this important policy issue), but Ernest still loved her innocence and her sweet nature. Most of all, he loved that she loved him.

As Ernest sipped the strange vanilla-flavoured coffee that he had bought inadvertently at Gelsen's, he decided to hire a caterer to come and cook for a dinner party. He would get Consuela to come in and clean up. But he did not discuss this with her. He would wait till the gardener came on Thursday, to tidy the garden and translate.

Consuela was one of the very few human beings with whom Ernest spent the day and with whom he interacted in a way that was wholly satisfactory to him. For Consuela spoke no English, and as he spoke no Spanish the relationship was simplified to a level at which he felt entirely comfortable. Not only did she clean the house efficiently and silently, she was a hawk about sell-by dates – if any food passed the sell-by or eat-by date she would seize it with triumph, bustle to find Ernest wherever he was in the house or garden, interrupt him with impunity even if he was writing and point dramatically to the date with a look which spoke volumes and somehow managed to be both reproachful and gleeful. Then she would hurl it dramatically into the garbage bin or the waste-disposal machine and grind it up. Ernest would nod his intense approval and return to his study, happy that this relationship had once again been re-established, and in such a wholly manageable form. He enjoyed the performance and the ritual so much that, in order to safeguard its future and thereby the future of the relationship, he asked Randi that she never throw away any food or drink if it was either old or off for he did not want to deprive Consuela of the immense and apparently cathartic pleasure of her search and destroy missions, and he wanted to watch her doing it. Indeed, whenever he went to the supermarket he made a point of finding two or three items that were close to the end of their shelf-life so that she would not be disappointed on her next visit to the house.

Ernest wished that Randi could cook. He longed to eat at home sometimes. But she always found fun places to go and that evening she drove him to dinner in one of the hottest new Westside restaurants, a large echoing cement cube of a room with extra large pinky-yellow ceramic tiles on the floor, smooth bare walls, extra large tables and no drapes of any kind, so that when the restaurant was full there was a kind of comprehensive echo and acoustic chaos which when loud contemporary music was added to the mix guaranteed that it was impossible for anyone in the restaurant to hear anything that anybody else said, including the waiter and all of the people on the other side of your table. Ernest was fed up with eating out but the pasta was said to be excellent, though there was an element of pot-luck unless your waiter's lip-reading was of a high order.

'Hello, I'm Bobby.' The camp young waiter with moussed blond hair slicked back from his thin face introduced himself very loudly. 'I'll be your waiter tonight.'

'Just give us the menu,' replied Ernest, *mezzo forte*. He was in no mood for small talk with the waiter, with whom he had no desire to be on first-name terms.

'Do either of you folks want a drink tonight? Who's the designated driver?'

'I'm the designated drunk,' yelled Ernest above the background noise, and he proceeded to prove it by drinking several glasses of Chianti Classico while Randi admired the huge three-dimensional painting of three leather-clad bikers which was generally agreed to be 'interesting'. The place was packed with chic Westside diners eating very little at great expense while shouting themselves hoarse. It seemed to Ernest that it was the very impossibility of conducting a coherent conversation that made the place so popular.

Fortunately, since Randi and Ernest were alone together, they could sit at adjacent sides of their table and they were thus able to get close enough to each other's ears to discuss someone she described as her new-found support in life.

'The Reverend Abel Pile?' he asked.

'I was referring to God,' she explained.

'Well, if you're going to get support,' said Ernest cheerfully, 'why not get it from the best?'

'You're not taking me seriously.' She was reproachful.

'I am, darling.' He soothed her. 'But I'm not taking God seriously.'

'Why not?'

'Let me correct that. I do take Him seriously, in the same way that I take Macbeth or Raskolnikov seriously. He's one of the most remarkable and enduring characters in fiction. If not *the* most.'

'God's not a character. He's the author.'

Ernest grinned. He didn't always expect wit from Randi. But then she spoiled it by asking him one of those preprogrammed questions from EST or SCREAMS. 'Seriously, Ernest, what are you running away from?'

He simply couldn't bring himself to reply. He sighed and he wondered why he'd chosen pasta with an artichoke and ginger sauce. Or perhaps he hadn't. 'Don't you believe in some higher elemental force of nature, that's greater than us?' she persisted.

'You mean, other than Warner Brothers?'

'Ernest, why are you laughing at me?'

'Why do you think?'

'I'm trying to be serious.'

'That's why I'm laughing.'

'Won't you come to the Church with me, and see for yourself?'

'You know I won't do that.' He abandoned the disgusting pasta and started eating the bread instead.

'Do you realize what you're turning down?'

'God, you mean? I think so, yes.'

At a distant table three or four gay waiters carried in a birthday cake, placed it with triumphant smiles in front of a pretty girl diner, and sang 'Happy Birthday' to her. Ernest watched, fascinated.

'Darling, I'm talking to you. Are you willing to take a risk?'

Reluctantly he looked back at her. 'Depends.'

'Meet Abel Pile. Listen to what he has to say.'

'No thanks.'

'Admit you're afraid.'

Ernest pushed his plate away in irritation. 'Randi, you're extremely gullible and you're ruining my dinner.'

She was implacable. 'Ernest, you've got to work from the other part of yourself. Have you the courage to make this choice?'

He was beginning to lose all patience. 'Darling, who teaches you to ask these dumb questions?'

She was guileless, as always, and answered his question without hesitation. 'The seminar trainers. But they're not dumb questions, they're good questions. I wish I'd known how to ask them before.'

'OK,' responded Ernest, 'try this question, it's the one everybody asks and nobody answers: why should we believe in a God who allows the Holocaust, the God who ignores all the suffering in the world?'

'I don't think He ignores it.' She was resolute.

'Torture, murder, children dying of cancer?' said Ernest. 'If He doesn't hear their prayers, He's not God. If He hears them, but doesn't answer them, He *shouldn't* be God.'

'We must have faith that He knows what He's doing.'

'Why?'

'Why do you keep saying "why"?'

'Why not? What are *you* running from?' said Ernest. 'You say He answers all prayers. You say He has His reasons for all the pain and misery that He causes or allows. But it's a theory that you can't test. Logically speaking, there's no difference between a world in which God isn't listening and a world in which God doesn't exist.'

'It's not the point, that bad things happen to people. That doesn't prove anything. Have you read the story of Job?'

'Certainly have. A very skilful attempt to justify belief in a God who makes us suffer for no reason other than to please Him.'

'He makes us suffer *so that* we'll believe in Him. You know that's what happened to me.'

Of course she was referring to the night she was shot. Ernest Mayday knew that, but he wouldn't accept her argument. In fact, her gullibility was starting to anger him. 'That's not the whole story. I'm afraid the Reverend bloody Abel Pile is what happened to you, he exploited your fear and your suffering, and he's using you. I understand why you need to believe in a God, but don't you see . . . the same incident that makes you need God is the very one that makes it impossible for me to believe in Him. And all I see is that bloody Pile exploiting and manipulating you and lots of others who are as frightened as you are.'

She was angry now. 'You don't know Abel. He's a saint.' And she stood up abruptly and left the restaurant, leaving him to phone LA Checker Cabs and make his own way home. Bobby the waiter was worried: 'She didn't like the pasta?' he shouted.

'It's not your fault,' yelled Ernest into Bobby's ear as he paid the bill. 'It's God's.'

'Hey, man, what isn't?' Bobby shouted back agreeably.

'The thing is,' Ernest hollered in explanation, 'she was shot recently.'

'No shit!' screamed the waiter, with sympathy.

When he got home from the restaurant she was waiting in the hall. He was surprised. He thought she would have gone straight to the Church Commune, down on Hollywood and Western. She wanted to make peace with him, but after waiting forty minutes for a cab he was in no mood for that. 'You're obsessed with yourself,' he said. 'A true Californian. A true narcissist.' He took off his linen jacket, preparing to go to bed, and switched on Ted Koppel's *Nightline*.

'What's that mean?'

'Feeding yourself is your only concern.'

'I don't eat much.' Puzzled, she followed him into the master bedroom, muted the giant television set at the foot of the bed and stared at him.

'Emotional feeding. That's why you're perpetually involved in all this crap – EST, *Insight*, SCREAMS, all this self-psychology garbage.' He sat back in his revolving, swinging, tipping, lolling, leatherette armchair and watched her.

'I don't get it.' She was wide-eyed, smiling with incredulity. 'That's bullshit. What's your problem? What's *wrong* with joining a Human Potential Program?'

He laughed aloud at the name. 'And you accuse *me* of talking bullshit?'

'You smug prick. You're jealous because I'm part of a group. Don't you *get* it? I'm *less* self-seeking, I'm relating to others, members of the Church, society, I'm giving something back – what are you doing for anybody else?'

'I'm an observer.' It was his usual reply.

'That's not narcissistic?'

'Not necessarily.' Ernest was becoming defensive now.

'It's supposed to be some kind of contribution, is it, observing?'

'Writing is, yes. If literature is a criticism of life . . . '

She interrupted angrily. 'We!l, I put up with enough criticism from you.' She picked up her car keys. 'I waited for you. I was going to go to bed with you. Now I've gone off the whole idea.' She slammed the door and was gone.

Nothing had been the same between them since the shooting. They'd been driving home from a dinner party at the Marina, just south of Venice. Venice is a 1930s development in which some lunatic tried to recreate in LA what is known locally as Venice Italy. In a neighbourhood close to Los Angeles International Airport he built a network of canals, and a few offices, apartments and shops with cheap imitation Byzantine frontages. There's a beautiful beach there, populated at the weekend by deeply tanned musclebound weight-lifters who look like four-hundred-pound gorillas (and are every bit as harmless), acrobats, rollerskate dancers, country and blues singers and various other forms of street theatre. By night, however, and only a few blocks inland from this ocean paradise, the dank streets near the canals are populated by large rats with sleek, smooth black hair and shiny, round, expressionless button eyes, casually insolent, especially the human variety who tend to be on crack cocaine and trigger-happy. Unlike the shy wildlife, the human rodents come out in the daytime too, will attack when not threatened, and are rabidly dangerous.

Taking a short cut down a narrow side street, a service alley between the backyards of bungalows that ran the length of a long block, Ernest and Randi saw (from the density and florid profusion of the blue and red graffiti that virtually obliterated the concrete fences and clapboard garages) that they had stepped into gangland. They reached the end of the alley without incident, stopping for the red light at the intersection with wide Washington Boulevard. Under a nearby lamp-post, well lit and clearly visible, they noticed three Latino boys, no more than seventeen years old. Although Randi subsequently con-cluded that God had saved her, Ernest felt that – at best – God had helped those who helped themselves. As luck would have it neither of them had been drinking, they weren't deep in a heavy conversation, they had observed the boys under the street light and were well aware of their presence. Randi's front passenger window was up.

As she watched for the light to change to green she

took her eyes off the three boys for a split second. In that moment the one with his back to her spun on his heel. Out of the corner of her eye she saw his arms swinging down, two-fisted, the gun pointing straight at her head, only four or five feet away, no time to scream. She ducked as he fired. Simultaneously Ernest, seeing everything, floored the accelerator and powered out across Washington Boulevard through the red light, narrowly missing an oncoming truck which screeched and skidded across the street. Sparkling glass slivers from Randi's shattered window shimmered in front of his eyes. 'This is it!' thought Randi. She had lots of time to think. She had a sense of absolute realism, – not 'This can't be happening to me' but 'It's me, so this is what it's like, I'm the one you always hear about.' She experienced that sense of elongated time, seeing the events in slow motion because her brain was racing, her perceptions coming at twice the usual sluggish speed. She had plenty of time to photograph in her mind an unforgettable picture of the smiling Latino kid at the moment that he pulled the trigger. And then the bullet entered her head and with the glass fragments cascading all around her face she felt with her fingers the warm wetness of her blood seeping through her hair.

Screaming loudly, hysterically, uncontrollably, convinced that she was dying, assuming that the bullet had lodged in her brain, she lay half on and half off her seat, nearly strangled by her safety belt, clutching at her head, trying to stem the flow of blood as Ernest sped up on to the freeway, roared recklessly forward for three exits and careered back down a slip road, ignoring and negotiating one busy red-light intersection after another. Within ten minutes they were at the hospital, where she was examined by an intern who gave her the miraculous news: the bullet had penetrated her scalp but not her skull, an exit, wound was visible, and there was no serious injury. The bullet had been fired by a .32, a fairly small calibre of gun, and it seemed that the impact on the passenger window had deflected it. That, and Randi ducking simultaneously, had saved her life.

By wheelchair, ambulance and wheelchair again she travelled to the upscale Cedar Sinai Hospital in West Hollywood, where the stars of the silver screen routinely die or are saved. There she waited in the Emergency Room for five hours, not because of any stars but so that cat-scan priority could be given to those people who had been shot that night in and around town and who had bullets actually *in* their brains. At dawn, her wound now infected from several hours of waiting untreated in the bacterial hospital air, Randi's scalp was finally cleaned out and, stitched up. Then, together with Ernest, she staggered home to his ungated, unalarmed mansion.

For some weeks afterwards they were in a state of shock. It was during that period that he installed the Armed Response security system. They drove only on well-lit thoroughfares. At traffic-lights they were watchful and suspicious. They began to collect similar horror stories about other people who had been shot – and usually killed – in their cars, sometimes in broad daylight. They discovered that this was not an uncommon phenomenon. Randi, a native-born Angelino, was even more shocked than Ernest to discover that random violence was beginning to travel great distances, crossing the frontiers from the black and Hispanic neighbourhoods south and east of Dodger Stadium into the wealthy white havens of West Hollywood, Beverly Hills, Brentwood and Pacific Palisades. The War on Drugs was not working. It had seemed a good idea at the time, for there were no more bad guys overseas to fight – the Russians were our friends, Iraq, Panama and Grenada had been defeated, and war could not be declared overtly on the Japanese as they owned so much of America. So all the enemies were within: thus there had been declared a war on drugs, a war on crime, a war on racism, a war on homelessness. Americans need a war. But, as in Vietnam, America's other lost war, the enemies in the War on Drugs seemed curiously elusive and hard to identify. Perhaps it was because they were right here at home: the customers.

Both Ernest and Randi had read *Bonfire of the Vanities*, of course, or at least the first third of it – very few Hollywood people manage to get all the way through long books – and found that since the insurrection in South Central LA folks were beginning to feel as unsafe out here as they did in New York. This was new, because LA was so thoroughly and efficiently segregated, and in the most convenient manner: financially. The city's segregation had come about through the free market rather than legislation, which meant that no one had any moral or ethical qualms about it.

All forms of discrimination in Los Angeles were illegal, and to a greater extent than Ernest had ever encountered, even in Britain. Playing golf as a guest of one of his WASP friends, a surgeon, at the Los Angeles Country Club, he learned that no one could legally be barred from membership on the grounds of race, colour, religion, marital status, national origin, ancestry, sex or sexual orientation, physical or mental handicap, medical condition or age. However, as it cost a minimum of sixty thousand dollars to join any decent LA golf club plus thousands in annual dues, it turned out that the *only* grounds on which anyone could legally be refused membership was poverty. It was illegal to discriminate against anyone except the poor. Ernest considered this a truly American concept. So did Dylan Kanpinchowitz, his lawyer, with whom he'd discussed the matter on the third fairway. 'To be poor is somehow slightly un-American,' Dylan remarked in his usual drily humorous way as he addressed the ball. 'It shows a certain disrespect for American values, don't you think? We country club members certainly don't want to accept the poor, because poverty is not something we wish to encourage.' The splendid and legal result was that segregation could be maintained in both social and recreational circumstances for reasons that appeared to be economic (in other words, right and proper) rather than racial (and therefore beyond the ethical pale).

If money was really the only justification for exclusion, both the LA and Bel Air country clubs would have had a few more Blacks and multitudinous Jews among their membership, and the Hillcrest Country Club might have had more than a few token *goyim*. None the less, for decades both Jews and white Christians alike had been happy about the geographical apartheid whose benefits they shared in the safe, green, well-watered Westside.

The day after Randi was shot the two of them had to venture back into a slightly less safe neighbourhood when they visited the police station at Mar Vista to give evidence. Deputy Sheriff Joe D'Angelo had been assigned to the case, a task he had accepted with some reluctance. He was pudgy and tired and not much interested in some shooting incident which only had a minor injury to show for it. Attempted murder being a commonplace event in his daily life, it took an actual death (or preferably two) to excite his interest.

Randi's thirst for knowledge, however, was unquenchable and she was not deterred by D'Angelo's apathetic attitude. 'Why would he have shot me?' she asked.

He hazarded a guess. 'Pleasure?' He slipped a piece of gum into the side of his mouth.

'Pleasure,' she repeated, at a loss.

'Yup.' He chewed methodically, enjoying the minty taste that would last so little time. He could see that she didn't understand so he elucidated further. 'The sheer pleasure of killing somebody.' His little eyes gleamed.

Ernest suggested that it might have been a mugging.

The Deputy Sheriff was unimpressed. 'Did it look like a mugging?' he inquired laconically, sitting forward uncomfortably in his chair and scratching his arse. 'Or like a shooting?'

Ernest nodded. 'A shooting,' he acknowledged.

Randi found this hard to accept. 'Is there no other explanation?'

Joe D'Angelo nodded. 'There is one,' he obliged. 'Could've been an initiation rite. In some gangs, before you can join, you have to kill somebody you don't know.'

SIX

And wretches hang that jurymen may dine.
Alexander Pope

'You don't know what that Latino kid has suffered,' said
Frankie, the wife of Professor Leonard Lesser of the
university's Social Science department.

Ernest Mayday and Randi Toner were at a dinner in
Westwood, at the home of Professor and Mrs Craig
Rosenbaum, a young and extremely ambitious member of
the English faculty at UC Santa Monica. They were both
a little on edge, Randi because she always had difficulty
following the conversation at dinners with members of the
English faculty and Ernest because he had arrived late
following an unscheduled and unsettling meeting with
Joanna.

'May I speak to Mr Norm de Plume?' the husky voice
had whispered when he answered the phone which rang
while he was in the shower. He was standing dripping and
naked in his bedroom, his feet making dark wet circles on
the carpet.

'Who is this?' he asked.

'VIP Escorts,' said the voice. It didn't sound like
Joanna. 'Is that Mr de Plume?'

'Er ... ' Ernest decided to own up. 'Well ... yes?'
Fortunately Randi was at the Church.

'Please hold, I have a call for you.' Click. He was put
on hold. Then Joanna's unmistakable Southern voice came
on the line. 'Hey. Norm.'

'Hello,' he replied stiffly.

'Can we meet again?'

'When?'

'How about tonight?'

'I'm not free. I have to go to a dinner party.'

'Where?'

'Westwood.'

'That's where I am now. What time do you have to be there?'

'Forty-five minutes.'

'Meet me first for a drink at the Beverly Westwood. Please.' She hung up.

It was another dark hotel bar. Ernest got there as soon as he could. She was sitting on a bar stool, sipping a Margarita again. She was wearing an elegant masculine pinstripe suit, with a double-breasted jacket, a cream silk blouse open at the neck and a tie knotted down towards her cleavage. 'Thank you for coming,' she said with a warm smile, and kissed him on the cheek. Her perfume was as intoxicating as before. 'You need a shave.' Gently she rubbed his face with the back of her long slim fingers. 'All sandpapery. Very *macho*.' He was dizzy from her scent, her proximity, her touch, her warmth, above all from her obvious availability.

'I was going to shave,' he apologized unnecessarily. 'But you called. There wasn't time.'

'Thank you for coming right away,' she said.

'Of course,' he shrugged, and meant it. There had really been no choice for him. 'But I haven't got long,' he added.

'So,' she began. 'What about it?'

Ernest was blank. 'What about what?'

'Our deal. The one I offered you.'

He hesitated. 'I don't ... I don't understand. Is that why you asked me to come over here? I already said no.'

She nodded and smiled. 'But you were tempted, weren't you? I can tell.'

Ernest swallowed. 'Tempted?'

'Tempted,' she repeated softly, and took his hand in

hers, entwining her slim, cool fingers around his. 'And I thought you were such an innocent when I met you. I bet you knew all along what my ad really meant.'

'I didn't,' said Ernest, feeling hot. 'And of course I'm tempted. Who wouldn't be? But I don't want a mistress, I told you, I want a story.'

'I think you want a story and a mistress too,' she insisted gently. 'All married men want a mistress.'

'No they don't,' Ernest replied. 'And I'm not married, by the way.'

She looked at him with surprise. 'No?'

He shook his head.

'You seem married.'

'Perhaps that's because I have a mistress,' he grinned.

She was cool. 'Do you mean a girlfriend?' she inquired.

He shrugged. 'A girlfriend, I guess.'

'And there are problems, right?'

'Aren't there always?'

'She doesn't put out. Or at least, not enough? She gets a headache, right?'

'So do all women.'

'I don't, Norm,' she murmured softly. 'Not if we've come to an arrangement. Headaches wouldn't be part of the deal. I'd be yours any time. You'd just have to say the word.'

She was looking him straight in the eye. 'Sounds good,' said Ernest nervously. 'But it's not why I answered your ad.'

'It *is* good, Norm. A fantasy relationship. Without problems.' Ernest glanced at his watch. He was already late. She noticed. 'Is your girlfriend going to this dinner party?'

'Yes. She'll be there now.'

'Then let's go back to your place and have a nice time.'

One part of Ernest wanted to, but he knew that he

couldn't. He prevaricated. 'Don't you ever go back to your place with the customers?'

She smiled ruefully. 'Not unless I know them really well. I mean, would you?'

'I suppose not.' He pulled himself together. 'Joanna, I can't do this. Not now, anyway.'

She stared at him for a moment. 'Would you like to see a photo of my room-mate? She's gorgeous.' She delved in her handbag and pulled out a snapshot of a wholesome blonde girl aged about eighteen, wearing shorts and a T-shirt, with a friendly freckled face and a snub nose. 'Pamela,' said Joanna. 'Pretty, isn't she?' She lowered her voice to a whisper. Her lips brushed against his ear. 'We could do a threesome, if you like?'

Ernest cleared his throat. 'Are you and Pamela lovers?'

She seemed to hesitate. 'Well . . . I like men too,' she answered carefully. It seemed to Ernest that she didn't want to put him off.

But Ernest felt that he was getting in too deep. 'I've got to go,' he said firmly, and stood up. She held on to his sleeve. Her voice sounded pleading. 'I need money, Norm. My mom's not getting any better.'

'I'm very sorry to hear that,' he said. 'But surely you can see that you can't expect me, a total stranger, to take on responsibility for . . .'

'Do you know that thirty-seven million people in this country have no health insurance? Isn't that terrible?'

'Terrible,' he agreed.

'Either they can't afford it, or the insurance companies won't insure them, or they lose it when they lose their jobs. There's a recession on.'

'I know that,' said Ernest helplessly. 'But it's not my fault, I didn't cause the fucking recession.'

'That boyfriend I told you about, remember . . .?' Ernest tried to remember. 'My first lover? The one who uses the same aftershave as you? Well, he's still threatening me.'

'You never paid him back what you owed him?'

'Not completely.'

This was beginning to sound like a whole lot of problems with which Ernest had no desire at all to be involved. 'Look, Joanna, I'm really sorry you've got all these problems. But I've got my problems too. I've told you the deal I was willing to make. And I still am.'

'Well, that's what I'm leading up to,' she said. 'I've got another proposition for you. Why don't you do a book about a working girl? It could be very sexy. And quite exciting. For instance, that boyfriend of mine turned out to be a pimp and a pretty scary guy. You'd sell loads of copies. I'll tell you all my adventures.' She looked at him hopefully.

Ernest hesitated. 'But ... I mean, what's the plot? Where's the story?' he wanted to know. He stared at her. She stared back at him. 'Look, Joanna, let me explain, that's not an idea, exactly. A novel about a working girl – that's just what we call an arena. That's just a subject, just one character. An idea for a novel, even a pulp novel, has to be more than just some anecdotal experiences. I mean, you could find that sort of stuff in any soft-porn magazine.' She nodded, biting her upper lip in disappointment. 'D'you see? I'm looking for something more than that. So, I've got to rush now, but call me if you get the kind of reply to your ad that'll interest me. OK?' He excused himself hurriedly and left.

'But I won't,' she called forlornly after him. 'Bastard didn't even pay for my drinks,' she remarked to the barman, leaning down for her handbag.

So it was that Ernest arrived hot, late and unsettled at Craig Rosenbaum's English-faculty dinner party. Randi was already there. The Rosenbaums lived in a small and unremarkable suburban house fronted by spindly neo-colonial columns holding up an entirely irrelevant portico. When Ernest arrived everyone at dinner was trying to find explanations for Randi's missed appointment with the Grim Reaper.

'One per cent of US citizens own forty per cent of the nation's wealth,' Professor Lesser was saying. He was a corpulent yet smooth presence, intelligent, with twinkly amused eyes and a fat rubbery face with chins all around his neck. He was an interloper from Social Sciences, and he didn't teach at UC Santa Monica but at the expensive, private USC, which variously stood for the University of Southern California or the University for Spoiled Children. Frankie hastened to agree with her husband. 'These people have no education, no family life, no hope!' she twittered. She was a tiny bird-like creature with a road map of fine but deeply etched lines converging on her pinched mouth from all directions. 'You just can't blame them. You don't know what they've suffered.'

Ernest had drunk nearly an entire bottle of Californian Cabernet plonk at lunchtime, he had had an irritating headache all afternoon which seemed to be worse since his meeting with Joanna, and suffering fools gladly was in any case not his forte. He had an almost irresistible desire to tell Frankie she was a moron but he managed to opt for moderation. 'Frankie, I'm up to here with all this politically correct shit. I feel within my rights to blame someone for trying to kill us, OK?'

'You don't know what he's suffered,' reiterated Frankie. 'You can't know, you're British.'

Ernest didn't much care for repetition, except in Mozart. Repetition of the 'you don't know what he's suffered' variety was specially designed to get right up his nose. 'Frankie, I don't care what he's suffered,' he remarked. She looked up at him sharply, a scrap of scrawny quail wing dangling from the fork halfway to her taut mouth.

Why, Ernest wondered in passing, do Angelinos always serve quail to the English? Does it say something about them, or us, or their view of us, that we always find these little trussed-up birds on our plates? 'I just wish you'd spare us all this bleeding-heart liberal crap.' Moderation, apparently, was more or less exhausted for the evening.

Cora Malloy, an associate professor in her early thirties with black circles under her eyes and lank yellow hair down to her earlobes, intervened from the far end of the reproduction Sheraton dining-table. 'We at the University of California observe the law.' She went though the litany, like a good Catholic saying the catechism, restating the faith. 'Employment at the university cannot be denied to any person on account of race, colour, religion, sexual orientation . . .'

'Which means gays,' explained Craig.

' . . . age or any other handicap.'

'Physical or mental, right?' added Leonard.

'Physical or mental,' confirmed Cora self-righteously.

Leonard turned subversively to Ernest. 'Does that surprise you? That mental handicap is not a suffi-cient reason to deny people employment at our great university?'

Ernest glanced around the table at his dinner companions. 'I wouldn't doubt it,' he replied jovially. Leonard snorted into his wine glass.

Among the other dinner guests that night was a fellow Brit for Ernest to meet, Dr Julian Genau, a tall, enthusiastic psychiatrist with a prominent nose and wryly humorous expression who appeared to be an expert on absolutely everything. 'The problem is, if I might just explain,' he explained before anyone could stop him, 'the problem *is* that the bloom is off the orange groves.' This didn't seem like much of an explanation to the roomful of people, all of whom felt that they too were excellent at giving explanations of almost everything, and all of whom would rather explain than be explained to. Nevertheless, Dr Genau continued with enthusiasm. 'There are some tremendously complicated dynamics here, between the various racial and ethnic tribes, as one might perhaps delineate them if one were an anthropologist – which', he added modestly, 'one *is*, actually, in a small way – but be that as it may, I must say that I've noticed since I've been here that the Asians – one mustn't call them Orientals, I've discovered, apparently that's like calling Blacks niggers or native Americans *Red* Indians, absolutely *infra dig* – be *that* as it may, the Asians, who are among the highest achievers of what-one-might-call-the-*new* immigrant groups, in other words, those who came to America the Beautiful since the first influx of Jews and Swedes and the Irish – who may still be coming here, of course, but who are none the less part of one of the oldest immigrant communities . . . um . . . uh . . .' And here he lost track of his own digressions. 'Where was I?'

'Be that as it may?' suggested Ernest unhelpfully.

'Yes, be that as it may, the er – um . . .'

'The Asians?' obliged Leonard Lesser.

'Yes, yes, the *ASIANS* . . .' he was back on course, 'the Asians look down on the Blacks and the Latinos, and the next generation of Asian children are winning all the places at college and the whites and the Jews – the high achievers of the last generation – are being squeezed out, many of them actually leaving California to cool out up north in Oregon and Washington State.'

Leonard Lesser yawned. He knew all this. 'So?' he asked. He glanced around the table. Everyone was wondering the same thing: why was Dr Genau telling them what they already knew? But Dr Genau was the kind of person who wasn't sure that he knew something until he was able to explain it to somebody else. This was a man in the grip of an irresistible desire to impart knowledge. Like an airliner on automatic pilot, like the psychopath who can't stop himself from strangling his victim, Dr Julian Genau did not feel that he was alive unless he was telling extremely interesting facts to other people. 'So the exodus of the white middle class,' he continued, his enthusiasm unabated by the politely incredulous looks upon the faces around the table, 'the *next* emigration from California, is changing the economic balance of this city. Out of the fifteen poorest suburbs in America, five are in LA. Did you know that?'

'Yes,' said Ernest, Leonard, Craig, Frankie and Randi. Even Craig Rosenbaum's wife Judy, who hadn't said anything all evening, piped up in agreement.

Genau was pleased that they knew. 'Good. Good. That's *most* interesting. Did you know that the majority of the population of greater Los Angeles will be Spanish-speaking by the year 2000?'

'Yes,' chorused everyone once more. 'And did you know,' asked Ernest, delighted to join in the game, 'that if the number of lawyers in this country continues to increase at the current rate, by the year 2025 everyone in America will be a lawyer?'

They all laughed.

Julian was still more pleased to have fallen in with such an intelligent crowd. He leaned back in his dining-chair, rocking on the spindly rear legs. Judy eyed him with concern, as the conversation continued along favoured middle-class lines, balancing the horrors of black crime and 'wilding' in New York City against the horrors of police violence and racism. Everybody around the table was completely united against racism, of course, even though all of them had few actual black friends who'd ever come, Sidney Poitier-like, to dinner. The conversation moved on to the abortion debate between Pro-lifers and Pro-choicers (this being America, no one was *against* anything) which was, as always, a deeply gratifying

conversation and one to which they were all happy to
return whenever they met since everyone present was
adamantly pro choice; and thence the discussion proceeded
to the ritual condemnation of the gun lobby and the
National Rifle Association, scoffing at the NRA's insist-
ence on both the right to bear arms and the belief that
when the Founding Fathers wrote this right into the
Constitution it had been intended to apply to all weapons
including semi-automatic pistols that could fire thirty
rounds in one burst.

'And perhaps you haven't noticed,', Dr Julian Genau
asked rhetorically of his now glazed audience, 'that the
people who are pro life are the same people who support
capital punishment.' Everyone nodded woodenly, wondering how much longer Dr Genau would drone on and
whether all Brits were such bores, while Frankie politely
expressed her amazement at this intriguing cocktail of
reactionary attitudes.

Ernest Mayday felt obliged to dispel that impression.
National honour was at stake. 'It all makes sense to me,'
said Ernest. 'It's like grouse shooting and salmon fishing.
The grouse must be protected so that there'll be enough of
them for us to enjoy killing on August the 12. And you can't
fish for salmon till they're fully grown, either. There's no
contradiction between being pro life and pro capital punishment. The Right-to-Lifers are simply stocking the lake.'

No one around the table knew what to make of Ernest's
intervention. He was just about to suggest that one or two
of the liberals present might perhaps secretly own guns
and be in favour of the electric chair when the *other* chair
– Dr Genau's – broke up under the stress of his rocking.
As he picked himself up off the floor, embarrassed but
using the opportunity to explain the history of chair –
making since the early Middle Ages, several of the other
guests suddenly remembered that they had to be up early
in the morning and the dinner party, too, broke up.

Craig asked Ernest (and therefore Randi) to stay behind for a cognac and talk with a couple of members of the English department who had been down at the other end of the long thin dining-table. Owing to the verbose Dr Genau, a completely different conversation had been going on at the far end of the seating-plan. 'We think you are the perfect person to teach creative writing here in our faculty,' began Rosenbaum with a warm smile.

'That's nice,' said Ernest. 'Why? And may I have a large cognac?'

'Because', Rosenbaum replied, pouring what he considered a very large brandy and Ernest considered no more than a dirty glass, 'your own use of signifiers in your work, sequentially so formless and uninteresting in themselves, creates excellent openings for new reading and linguistic strategies and for a healthy emancipated subjectivity among the students. And, of course, this is coupled with your experience of film, where semiotic analysis is so productive.'

Ernest tried to process the above information and failed. 'What was that again?'

'Perhaps I can explain,' chimed in Alfred Hare. He was tall, young and confident, with a JFK square head and resentful blue eyes. 'What didn't you understand?'

'Just ... well, everything he said,' confessed Ernest. Craig and Alfred exchanged puzzled looks. 'Um ... look, I'm delighted you think I'm the perfect person to teach creative writing – but why?'

'Well,' replied Hare, 'how would you propose to teach writing?'

Ernest chugged back his brandy, what little there was of it. 'Haven't the foggiest. Actually, I don't suppose writing can be taught, so I suppose I'd let them write whatever shit they want to, then I'd force the other members of the class to read it – why should I be the only one to suffer?' He chuckled. They nodded seriously. 'So then we'd discuss

it and I'd make such suggestions as came to mind. If any.'
He held out his glass for a refill, but Craig Rosenbaum
took it from him and placed it on the coffee table. The
idea of giving Ernest another large cognac didn't seem to
occur to him spontaneously.

'Excellent, excellent.' Cora Malloy had returned from
the bathroom and was standing awkwardly in a dark
corner, listening to him with enthusiasm. The dark brown
bags under her eyes suggested that she needed to catch up
on several months' sleep. She was five foot one at the
most, and her sniffly nose was slightly pink around the
nostrils. She stepped forward in jubilation. 'Excellent,' she
enthused again. 'The creation of texts is exactly the direction we should be going in, especially trashy post-modern
texts. We're on the cutting edge here. It's actually better to
create our own texts so that we can decode their semiotic
significance ourselves. God, is it the smog or the pollen
count that's so awful today?' She sniffed and wiped her
nose on the back of her hand.

'By "the creation of texts",' Ernest asked, slightly
confused, 'do you mean the creation of literature?'

A sudden silence fell. Craig Rosenbaum, Alfred Hare
and Cora Malloy looked at each other. They couldn't
quite comprehend this question. Alfred Hare tried to
explain. 'Literature is there, *to be written*,' he said. 'It is
not constructed. It is called upon.'

'Oh yes?' said Ernest with a smirk. 'Where is it then?
I've been blocked recently, I'd like to call upon it. What's
the phone number?'

Puzzled professors gazed at bemused philistine. Randi
suddenly spoke, breaking the deadlock. 'Is this something
to do with Jung's Collective Unconscious, maybe?' she
asked tentatively.

The academics looked at her with interest. 'In a sense,
perhaps, yes,' murmured Craig, meaning in a sense
perhaps no, but grasping the lifeline and trying at the

same time not to appear too confrontational. 'What we're saying is, the ideas are there already, they're out there, they only need to be written down.'

'Only?' snapped Ernest with open derision. '*Only?* So that's what English professors think. Well, let me explain something to you academics, with your tenure and your exceptionally heavy workload of about six hours' teaching a week: writing it down is the difficult bit. Lots of people have ideas. Even good ideas. Ideas are two a penny, as a matter of fact. Tens of thousands of people out there believe they have a novel in them – if they could "only" write it down. *Only?* All I can say is, if literature is out there, waiting to write itself, I'd like to know where the fuck it's hanging out so that I can take a piece home and type it up.'

When Ernest and Randi had called to see Deputy Sheriff Joe D'Angelo again a few days after the shooting, they had leafed through mugshots of suspects with previous records of drive-by shootings, freeway shootings, gang-related shootings and just plain ordinary shootings. The Deputy, a firm believer in the electric chair, would have liked their assailant to be identified, tried and fried, but he listened equably as Mayday rehearsed the usual arguments against capital punishment. 'There's no proof that it acts as a deterrent. In states which have no capital punishment, the murder rate rises no faster than states which have it. So the only point of the death penalty is revenge.'

D'Angelo saw no problem with that. 'So? Don't you want to see the little fuckers fry?'

Mayday shook his head. 'If killing people is wrong, killing people is wrong. A rose is a rose is a rose.'

D'Angelo's brow puckered up. 'I can't see how roses come into it.' Ernest Mayday noted that the Sheriff's Deputy was not familiar with the works of Gertrude Stein. Apparently unconcerned by this deprivation,

D'Angelo unwrapped a stick of gum and slid it slowly and carefully into the side of his mouth. 'Gum disease,' he explained. 'I haven't been flossing.' Randi was quietly leafing through the grimy transparent plastic pages of mugshots, taking no notice of either the Deputy's dental problems or the capital punishment debate that Ernest was still pursuing with single-minded determination in the face of the Deputy's apathy.

'It's him!' said Randi suddenly, pointing to a picture and saving Ernest the embarrassment of a reply. 'Isn't it?' She looked at Ernest for confirmation.

Ernest chewed his lip. It certainly looked like the same guy. 'I think it is.' He hated to commit himself.

Joe D'Angelo watched him closely. 'You think so, or you know so?'

'I know.' Randi was positive. She was not the kind of person who was assailed by doubt. She stood up. As far as she was concerned, the search was over.

'Come,' beckoned fat Joe D'Angelo. They followed him under the fluorescent lights through a maze of little cubicles until he reached his own. He eased himself slowly into his chair. 'Now, listen up. I want you to think carefully about this before you answer: are you prepared to prosecute that guy?'

'Of course,' said Ernest.

'Damn! What did I just say?'

'You said, are we prepared to prosecute.'

'And before that I asked you to think carefully. You didn't think at all! You just went ahead and answered right away.'

Randi was confused. 'What do you want us to think about?'

'What I want you to think about is, once you've identified him, once he knows you're prosecuting, he may come after you. Or if we can hide you until the case comes to court, his friends may come after you when the judge sends him to jail.'

Ernest Mayday glanced nervously at Randi. 'Come after us?'

'Yup.'

'Why?' But Ernest knew the answer even as he asked the question.

'Git even.'

'You mean, they might, er, shoot us?'

'Shoot, maybe. Or knife you, or cut your throat, slash your face, buddy, I can't guess which. And I'm not sayin' it'll happen for sure, it may not happen. It depends who this kid's friends are. It depends if they want to bother. All I'm doin', since you're British and since you don't seem to know nothin', is I'm tellin' you there's a risk. OK?'

Ernest licked his lips, which had suddenly gone dry. 'Can't you offer us police protection?'

'Nope.'

Ernest naturally reverted to British pomposity. 'I should have thought you would have a duty to do so.'

Joe D'Angelo waved two stubby grubby fingers at them. 'Two reasons why not, pal. In the first place, if we had to provide officers to protect witnesses in every case of violent crime, we wouldn't have one officer left out there doing the job. In the second place, there's nothin' we can do to protect you until they commit a crime. Until they assault you – we can't stop them doing it.'

'What if they kill us?'

'They'll go to the penitentiary.'

'You serious?' Ernest was aghast.

'Yup. Recently, two released convicts from LA County Jail staked out the house of the guy that put 'em inside. He called us. They were right outside his front door, waitin' and watchin', in a Buick. We couldn't do nothin'.'

'Why?'

'Because they hadn't done nothin'. You're allowed to sit in a car, on the highway, if the parking's legal.'

'In England you could arrest them for Threatening Behaviour or something. Anything.'

'Not here, *amigo*. In this county we're very high on civil rights.'

'For criminals?'

'For everyone.'

'What about the victim?'

'You ain't a victim till you're a victim.'

'But then it's too late.'

'You got it.'

Ernest Mayday fell silent. He looked at Randi. She looked at D'Angelo. 'What happened, in that case? Those people staking out the house.' He hardly dared ask, for he could guess the answer.

The Deputy took his time, masticating the gum for some moments before replying. 'They shot him. He's dead. We picked them up. They're in San Quentin now, for life.'

'But they shot the man,' Ernest said. The Deputy Sheriff just nodded and chewed. 'Is there no way we can protect ourselves?'

'Git a gun.'

'I don't want to do that,' said Ernest. 'I don't like guns. I don't approve of private citizens being armed. I think there should be gun-control laws.'

'Suit yourself,' said Joe. 'But if you do get one, remember this: technically, you can only shoot an intruder once they're inside your home.'

'What if they're in the backyard?' asked Randi. 'Or coming through the window.'

'I'm not tellin' you what to do. I'm just telling you the law,' said the Deputy. 'So if you shoot one of these scumbags in your yard, drag the body into the house before the cops arrive, OK?'

'Wouldn't they be able to tell?' asked Ernest. Joe stared at him, puzzled. 'I mean,' Ernest continued, 'forensic scientists.'

'If they wanted, maybe. But there ain't nobody gonna look.'

'I see,' said Ernest thoughtfully. He turned to Randi again. 'We have to think about this, don't we? I mean, whether we want to prosecute or not.' She nodded.

The wall of hot air from the street hit them as Joe D'Angelo showed them out of the police station's air-conditioned lobby. 'I want to ask you one question again,' he said. 'Are you *sure* that was the guy who tried to kill you?'

Randi answered without hesitation. 'I'm sure. I'll never forget his face, as long as I live.'

Ernest nodded. 'I'm sure it was him too. But we need time to consider what you've said. Don't proceed with this unless you hear from us.'

Deputy Sheriff Joe D'Angelo never heard again from Ernest Mayday or Randi Toner, and rightly concluded that they didn't want to prosecute. He was pleased. It made life so much simpler. Mar Vista was his beat. It was only a matter of time before he came across Emilio Fernandez, the boy who'd tried to kill Randi. He identified him. He checked the ID carefully. He tried to question him, but Emilio wouldn't talk to a cop, he'd have been shot by his gang. D'Angelo taunted Emilio. There was an altercation. Emilio pulled a gun. The Deputy Sheriff was ready and shot him dead. It was so much easier than arresting him, taking him to court, hoping that Ernest and Randi's eye-witness identification wouldn't wilt under cross-examination, all ending up with appeal after appeal and a nominal prison sentence because he was a juvenile. The Deputy's way, the problem was solved once and for all.

The headline in the *Los Angeles Times* said AUTOPSY SHOWS YOUTH DIED FROM SHOT AT CLOSE RANGE. The *Times* report confirmed that the bullet was fired during a confrontation between drug-dealing gang members and sheriff's deputies, and was fired at point-blank range. Sheriff's Lieutenant Bill Harvey, the spokesman, said that the conclusion supported the contention of sheriff's investigators that Emilio Fernandez, seventeen, was shot to death as he struggled for control of a deputy's handgun. Coroner's spokesman Mort Dyer did not comment on whether the report supported or refuted anyone's version of the incident, but he said there were no plans to continue the county's investigation into Fernandez's death.

Both Ernest and Randi read the report in the *Times*. Neither mentioned it to the other. But it was not long after Emilio's death at the hands of law-enforcement's amiable gum-chewing Joe D'Angelo that Randi Toner, who had already attended meetings at the Church of the Community of Personal Truth, first met the Reverend Doctor Abel Pile, an encounter that would change all their lives in a way that none of them could foresee – as did the next phone call that Ernest received from Joanna.

SEVEN

In the shimmering countries that exude the summer,
the day is blanched in white light. The day
is a harsh slit across the window shutter,
dazzle along the coast, and on the plain, fever.

Jorge Luis Borges

'Yes?' He always answered the phone abruptly, giving nothing away.

'Is that Norm?'

'Who?'

'Norm de Plume?'

Acute anxiety hit him in the pit of the stomach. Mayday glanced furtively around at Randi, who was clattering around in the kitchen, trying to find utensils and heating up pizza again. 'Yes,' he muttered into the receiver.

'This is Joanna.'

'Yes?' he repeated cautiously. At Randi's suggestion, and in the early days when he'd thought of marrying her, before the shooting, before Randi found purity and before sex was doled out like food stamps or social security payments, Ernest had had his kitchen done up – or remodelled, as they call it in America. Somehow the sculptural terminology added a touch of elegance and art to what was the essentially appalling business of having the builders in. Since it had been remodelled it had never been used except to make coffee, pour orange juice or heat up the pizzas and other convenience food delivered at the drop of a hat from Greenblatt's deli, LA Pizza, Thai Garden or Genghis Cohen (the local Chinese).

'I've had an offer,' said Joanna's excited voice on the phone.

'Yes?' he said again.

'Do you want to know about it?'

'Yes.'

'I think it's the kind of offer that you were hoping for.'

'Yes?'

There was a slight pause. Quizzically: 'Norm, are you ever going to say anything but yes?'

'Yes.' He hesitated. 'I mean, yes I do, say other things I mean, but I can't talk now.'

'Got company?'

'Yes.'

'The girlfriend?'

'Yes.'

'Do you want to meet me and hear about it?'

'Yes.'

Another pause. 'OK, I can see that's all you're going to say.'

'Yes,' he said, and laughed. So did she; that delicious, husky, sexy chuckle, so mature in a woman so young.

'Meet me at the Hamburger Hamlet, on Beverly, tonight at seven.'

'Fine,' said Mayday. 'Bye.' And he hung up fast.

'Who was on the phone?' said Randi.

'Jerry,' said Ernest, lying easily as usual. 'Poker game with the guys next Wednesday.' He made a mental note to reinstate the old Wednesday evening game. It would cover his story, and he'd been missing his night out with the boys.

Randi served up the pizza. Even the green salad had been driven up from the pizza parlour on the Strip rather than prepared at home, and the dressing had that processed, metallic taste. Ernest picked at the lettuce, ate a slice of pizza and drank a beer.

'You're coming to the Church tonight, remember?'

He'd forgotten. 'Oh. I can't.' He tried to be casual about it. 'I've got more work to do on that synopsis for Oliver.'

'Can't it wait? You promised.'

'Sorry.'

'We're drawing up guest lists for the Sincerity Awards.' He sniggered. 'All right, all right, I know you think it's funny.'

'I certainly do. And you don't need me for that. What else is there?'

'Abel is preaching tonight. It's a special meeting, for the initiates.'

'Are you an initiate?' She nodded, eyes shining. 'That settles it then,' he said with finality. 'I'm not, so I'm staying home.'

'If you would only open up, you could become all that you were meant to be,' she pleaded. 'Why won't you try to contact the inner you?'

'I've got enough trouble with the outer me. Every time I look in a mirror, there it is.'

'It's not funny, Ernest. Please come.'

He understood full well the cause of her new fervour but he didn't want an extended discussion, not if he was meeting Joanna in less than an hour. 'Look, forget it, OK?'

'God won't forget it. You're part of His perfect plan.'

'I'll take that as a compliment.' He smiled across the table at her and sipped his ice-cold Budweiser.

'Don't you *ever* wonder about God?'

He nodded. 'I do. God is either the biggest lie or the greatest truth,' he said, 'and I wonder which. Do you want to know what else I wonder?'

She nodded.

'Well, I wonder: when God created the Universe did He simply have a generalized notion of the stars, the black holes and planet earth? Or did He actually envisage, for instance, that forty-foot high Marlboro cigarette billboard on Sunset outside the Château Marmont Hotel? And, if so, what the fuck was He playing at?'

She'd heard him talk this way before. She ate her pizza with pepperoni, without comment, staring at him.

'Was it also', he continued amiably, 'a part of His master plan – sorry, perfect plan – that this city would be built around dozens of freeways in the fifties that would be completely jammed for six hours a day in the nineties? What made Him think of that little jape, I wonder? Did He foresee, in His glory, in that void before Genesis – if indeed you can be glorious in a void, even if you're God – that the salami in our fridge would smell funny today, that Consuela will enjoy consigning it to the outer darkness tomorrow, and that meantime there'd be nothing else to eat in this fucking house which is why we always have to send out for Domino's Pizza?'

She smiled. 'You're a very funny man.' She stood up and kissed the top of his head. 'I love you. This planet is blessed that you are on it.' And with that she left for the Heartwarming Institute.

He was trying to be tolerant, though tolerance did not come easily to Ernest. He knew that she had to have faith, she had to believe in God's plan, because otherwise she couldn't handle the senseless attempt on her life and the subsequent death of her would-be assassin. Randi felt deeply remorseful that Deputy Sheriff D'Angelo had executed Emilio Fernandez and she also felt, dimly, that in some way it was her fault. In one way she was right: if she and Ernest had had the courage of their convictions, the nerve to prosecute him, the moral strength to give evidence against him in open court, he might now be alive. They, on the other hand, might be dead.

There was something else too. The more she considered the threat to their safety, the more she went over it in her mind, the less convinced of it she became. It occurred to her that the Deputy Sheriff might have been trying to persuade them not to prosecute so that he could quietly take the law into his own hands. She lay awake for hours at night, tormented by this fear. Had she been duped? Was the reported altercation just a fake, a put-up job? Or was it real, but provoked? Either way, she felt inexplicably guilty that she had survived and that Emilio Fernandez – this unknown assailant whose fate was irrevocably tied to hers but whom she had glimpsed for a mere split second and knew only from his mugshot and a brief news item that she saw by chance – was dead. She was haunted by the responsibility. She realized that she had pronounced his death sentence.

These questions and anxieties crowded in on her during the sleepless early hours of the morning, every morning. She needed solace. She tried discussing them with Ernest but in reply he occasionally grunted and generally snored. Even in daylight he evinced little interest in these preoccupations. As far as he was concerned, it had all had a splendid outcome. Ernest believed fervently in the rule of law, he believed that all alleged criminals should be tried by their peers, presumed innocent unless proven guilty and *certainly* should not be executed on the streets by the police. On the other hand, he also believed fervently that Emilio Fernandez might have murdered them both and he was consequently delighted that he was dead. He shed no tears over Fernandez and suffered no sleepless nights.

In vain Ernest tried to explain to Randi why she should not feel guilty. 'Religions need guilt. They can't exist without it. Without guilt we don't need to be saved, and if we don't need to be saved we don't need God.'

'You think I *want* to feel guilty?' asked Randi over breakfast, her face tear-stained, her eyes red, dark bags under them.

'Unconsciously, yes. Unpleasant though guilt is, for

most people it is preferable to feeling helpless or insignificant. It makes us feel powerful because whatever we did or didn't do, it was something that affected others. So guilt gives us a feeling of importance, it flatters us. That's why we cling to it.' Randi didn't follow the argument, but it was for these reasons that the Church had suddenly become central to her life. Ernest, meanwhile, still in his own impotent God-like void before Genesis, sat at the word processor and continued to worry about his inability to create his own universe.

But not this evening, for as soon as Randi had driven away he set off for the Hamburger Hamlet. Joanna was already seated when he got there. He was asking the Host for a table for two, non-smoking, when he saw a pretty girl waving from across the room in the smokers' section. He didn't recognize her in the dim light till he reached her table.

'I've already ordered,' she said as he slid into the maroon leather booth beside her. 'Hi,' she continued belatedly, squeezed his hand affectionately and hugged him close for a brief but glorious moment. Her body moulded itself to his as she pressed herself against him. He could feel the softness of her breasts through her blouse and his T-shirt. As she let go of him he looked at her. It was Joanna, but she looked so different from last time. Her hair was blonde now, and long. Her make-up was trendier, dark-brown eye shadow, she was wearing tight jeans with a fashionable tear across the right knee, a little cotton blouse – and he noticed at once – no bra.

'I didn't recognize you,' he said.

She smiled. 'I forgot to warn you. This is the real me.'

'You dyed your hair.'

Her smile widened to a grin. 'You're such an innocent. You can't grow this much hair in a few weeks.' She twisted a cascading strand of her shoulder-length blonde tresses round a finger in a childlike gesture. 'That was a wig I was wearing before.'

'Why?'

'I felt like it. Also, you have to keep changing your look if you go back to the same hotels. They get to know you. They sling you out on your ear.'

'I've been to that hotel regularly. They don't sling me out.'

'They're different with single women. In bars. They think we're all trying to pick up men.'

'But you are.'

She was indignant. 'Yes, but I might not be. How dare they assume that? And why shouldn't I anyway? Men try to pick up girls whenever they can and no one objects to that.'

'True. But what you're telling me is, you've been to those hotels before, soliciting. So you're not just doing this because you need the money desperately, you do this all the time.'

'I've done it before, yes.' She was defiant, chin up. 'I was trying to get a gig for ten grand. I told you. And I *do* need the money desperately, my mom's really starting to go downhill. But I know that's not your problem.'

'Large Stoly on the rocks,' said the waitress, placing a tumblerful of neat vodka and ice in front of her. 'Can I get you a drink, sir?'

Mayday ordered a Diet Coke. At a distant table a birthday cake was carried in by a convoy of six or seven waiters, who gathered around a table with a magnificent flourish and sang 'Happy Birthday to You'. It seemed to Ernest that it was the desire of every citizen of Los Angeles to spend their birthdays in restaurants being sung to by a bunch of strange waiters and waitresses whom they would never invite to their homes. He turned back to Joanna. 'So? What's happened now?'

'I had a letter. I don't know who it was from. He called himself John Schmidt. Not many people have the balls to give me their real name, Norm, like you did.'

He felt guilty about deceiving her. 'Do you give people your real name?'

'You mean Joanna? Sure. Why not? Cheers.' She raised her glass in a little toast.

'You look terrific tonight.'

'Thank you.' She accepted the compliment with accustomed grace. 'I'm only sorry you can't see my best feature.'

What did she mean? 'Why not?'

'I'm sitting on it.' She gave him a sly wink, then came that delicious throaty laugh. Ernest was sipping his Diet Coke, and it went straight up his nose. While he spluttered, choked and recovered, embarrassed and mopping his shirt front, she ordered the biggest burger on the menu. 'I love meat,' she explained to Ernest. 'I can't seem to get enough meat. I'm insatiable when it comes to meat.' Ernest wondered if she intended the *double entendre*. He had already eaten pizza and wasn't hungry, so he ordered a slice of cheesecake and picked at it while she coated the inside of her massive burger bun with a thick lining of mustard, ketchup and relish. She eyed his cheesecake with surprise. 'You're not worried about cholesterol?'

'No.'

'Most men of your age are.'

'What's the good of worrying?' asked Ernest. 'I had a friend who died of a heart attack caused by the stress of worrying about whether his cholesterol was so high that he might die of a heart attack.'

'That's cool,' she said. She took a huge mouthful of burger and chewed it with gusto while looking at him, wide-eyed with admiration.

He was pleased with himself. 'Let's get back to John Schmidt, can we?'

'OK, John Schmidt. He wrote to me. I'll show you the letter. He wanted to meet me, just like you, in a hotel. So

I met him in a bar at the Bonaventure, downtown. I was dressed the way I was when I met you, conservatively.'

'Did he know you were a working girl?'

'Of *course*.' She giggled.

'Even though there was no mention of anything to do with sex in your ad?'

'Norm, it doesn't make any difference how you sell sex. You don't need to mention it. Men expect to find sex everywhere and they just assume that's what you're offering. Often enough, they're right.'

'I didn't assume that.'

'No, Norm, but you're one in a million. You're special. You're nice.' Ernest wasn't so sure about that. He felt quite a hypocrite as she squeezed his hand affectionately again. 'Anyway, he took me up to his hotel room, because he said he wanted to talk privately.'

'What did he look like?'

She thought carefully for a moment, before describing him. 'He's about five six or seven. He's dark, could be Spanish, or Jewish maybe, I couldn't tell. Small but very dishy.'

'Uh-huh.' Ernest took out his pencil, and started making notes on the inside back cover of his cheque book. 'Dishy in what way?'

'Attractive crinkly laugh lines around his eyes. Blue eyes, actually, which is funny since his hair's so dark, that makes him interesting. Slim, almost skinny really, nice buns. His nose is a bit odd, sort of flattened – probably had a nose job, or maybe it was broken in a fight or an accident.'

'How old?'

'So hard to tell – twenty-six, twenty-eight?'

Ernest was surprised. 'I see. Young.'

Joanna glanced at him with a slight smile. Instantly she sensed an older man's jealousy. 'Oh yes, young,' she continued, enjoying herself. 'Just a kid, almost, probably not long out of college.'

'You think he went to college?'

'Sure. I think he's quite educated.'

'How was he dressed?'

'Expensive Italian suit. Three-piece, like a lawyer. The label's from one of those fancy shops on Rodeo Drive. You know, where you have to make an appointment just to get into the shop.'

Ernest didn't know. 'How much?'

'For the suit?' She considered. 'Three, four thousand dollars, more maybe. 'Course, that's only if he got it retail. But he seemed to have a buck or two. An old Cartier watch, for instance, definitely not a copy, designer shirt, designer boxer shorts.'

Ernest's eyebrows shot up. 'You saw his boxer shorts?'

'I see most men's shorts, in the end.'

'Was this because you fancied him?'

'I was attracted to him, yes. But that's not the point at the moment. He took me up to his room, which he wasn't staying in. He'd just rented it to meet me.'

'How do you know that?'

'I always look around carefully whenever I go into a man's hotel room. I try to wander around as casually as possible, but obviously I have to check him out. It's for my own safety. So I idly open the closet doors, pop into the bathroom, see what books or mags he's reading, that sort of thing – you know, find out who I'm dealing with. Is he a perv, or a cop, or what? Well, guess what I saw?'

'What?'

'Nothing.'

'Nothing?'

'Nothing. No clothes in the closet, no luggage, no toiletries bag, no aftershave, no nothing.'

Ernest smiled. 'He hadn't brought his toothbrush.'

'That's right, angel, he wasn't staying the night. So I assumed he'd just rented the room for sex. But he wanted to talk.'

'Like me?'

'In a way. He sat me down very seriously, in an armchair – so he wasn't trying to cozy up to me – and he said: I've got a proposition to make to you. I said: I'm used to being propositioned, and he said no, not that sort of proposition. He said: "We think there is a forthcoming criminal trial downtown here, and there are indications that a friend of ours is to be indicted. If so, it is imperative that this friend, this accused person, is acquitted."'

'Who's "we"?' asked Ernest.

'What?'

'Who was he speaking for? Who did he represent?'

'I don't know. I didn't ask.'

'Pity.'

'Norm, I don't think he wanted me to know just yet. If he wanted me to know I think he'd have told me, don't you?'

'Go on,' Ernest ordered. 'What else did he say?'

'Then he said: "I must tell you that there is absolutely no doubt about our friend's innocence. But, just to be on the safe side, we will want you to get a selected juror into a compromising sexual situation. He will then feel obliged to vote for acquittal, and justice will have been done!"'

Ernest's eyes were dancing. 'This is perfect.' He was excited. 'This is exactly the kind of thing I was hoping for.'

'I *knew* it,' she said with delight. 'Well, they said they'll pay me the ten thousand dollars I asked for. So, are you on?'

He nodded. 'How are they going to pay you?'

'In instalments. He gave me five hundred so far.'

'Five?' Ernest agreed immediately. 'I'll do the same. How can I get the cash to you?'

'A cheque will do.' Ernest hesitated. He had been writing notes in the back of his cheque book. He suddenly realized that earlier she could have noticed the name E. F. MAYDAY printed on the face of the cheques. His address was printed there too. She'd just been telling him how observant she was, what a good detective. He had a sudden twinge of panic. His cheque book was lying face down on the table, maybe she hadn't read the name. He glanced at her. He had to think of a reason to say no to giving her a cheque, and fast. But he just couldn't think of one.

'No,' he said blindly, without offering any reason at all.

'Why not?' She picked up the cheque book. He grabbed her wrist and twisted it, so that she had no chance to read it. She gasped. His grip was unexpectedly strong.

'Ouch! Let go, you're hurting!'

'Sorry,' he said, but he pried the cheque book out of her grasp. 'I said I don't want to write a cheque, OK?'

'Why not? Christ, you're fucking rough!' She rubbed her twisted wrist as he slid the cheque book into the side pocket of his jacket, the side that she couldn't reach. Her eyes were surprised and hurt. 'What was all that about?'

'I said I'll give you cash. I don't want any record of this transaction.'

'Why not? I wasn't going to declare it.'

Thank God, he thought, a plausible reason at last. 'That's why,' he said slyly, grateful that he had come up with an excuse for his curious behaviour in the nick of time. 'I'm protecting you. And me. I don't want any repercussions with the taxman, I like to do things legally, OK?'

'Well, don't protect me so painfully.' She was still angry.

Ernest apologized again. She relented. 'OK, Norm, I'm sorry too.' Relieved that she was still calling him Norm, he asked how John Schmidt had paid her.

'In cash.'

'This is great. So, shall I meet you tomorrow, with the money?' He stood up.

'Don't you want to know the rest?'

Ernest hesitated. He hadn't realized there was more. 'The rest?' He sat down.

'He said he had to interview me, to ensure that I was the right girl for the job.'

Ernest was intrigued. 'How could he do that?'

She giggled. 'You're so funny, Norm. How do you *think* he interviewed me? That's when I saw his designer shorts.'

EIGHT

*Christianity is always turning itself into something that
may be believed.*

T. S. Eliot

'"I am the way, the truth and the light," said Jesus, and
that is why our Church, the Church of the Community of
Personal Truth, a church of our own very unique personal
integrity, takes our initiates on the Shining Bright Journey,
the Journey of Light and Truth to Inner Purity.'

The Reverend Abel Pile was charismatic. Randi Toner
had no doubt that he was the very incarnation of goodness. She sat listening to him at the Church and Theological Seminary. It wasn't the sort of church that Haslemere
Man might recognize as such. No Gothic spire, no
Norman belltower, no perpendicular stained glass – and
not a flying buttress to be seen. It was instead a crumbling
1930s deco heap, originally designed to resemble the
superstructure of a trans-Atlantic liner, and it must have
seemed very chic at the time it was built. It now stood
marooned in a declining area of Hollywood, itself a declining area, on a grubby, run-down corner of Hollywood
Boulevard near the intersection with Western Avenue,
about a third of the way if you're driving (which of
course you always are in LA) from green Beverly Hills
towards the glistening, towering, financial district
downtown, a typically American vista now largely owned
by those nefarious Japanese who had become so
thoroughly unpopular for trying to subvert the United
States by offering Americans good cars and TV sets at

prices they could afford. Next to the church, in its wide shadow, stood an adult bookstore, and bright in the evening sunlight stood the other neighbour, an ex-shoe store now converted to Equity-waiver theatre, proudly billing its long-running hit *Legendary Ladies of the Silver Screen – a one-man show starring Frank Cook*.

Inside the Church, Randi sat at the back of the meeting room, listening intently. There were no pews, no Hymnbooks Ancient and Modern, just shabby sofas, lumpy armchairs and a couple of glass-topped coffee tables; in short, a sort of Junior Common Room. Abel Pile, tall, handsome and cherubic, goodness shining out of him like a butter commercial, cheeks pink with good health, his thick blond hair flying as he paced back and forth, was preaching and teaching with his customary energy and enthusiasm. Randi wrote copious notes on the yellow legal pad on her knee as he spoke, but she still found an opportunity to ask him how she could make a start on her own personal Journey of Light and Truth.

He smiled at her. She felt safe and loved. He was pleased with the query, and pleased with her.

'Good question. A very good question.' Such praise from Dr Pile made her profoundly happy. If only Ernest would come to listen to him, she thought, he would surely see how spiritual and truly truly special the man was.

'You have *already* started on your Journey' – Abel Pile was answering the question – 'or you would not be here. I have selected all of you here today to be our Initiates. You are to be the priests and priestesses, the rabbis and teachers. When you are ready to open your hearts to God's goodness, through me, there will be an ordination ceremony and you will all be ordinated.' He hesitated, then corrected himself. 'Ordinationized. Many more Americans, week by week, day by day, hour by hour, are – like the late, great St Paul – finding their road to Damascus. Yet, my friends, there is a traffic jam on the road to Damascus – you are to be God's traffic cops, and your job will be to get the traffic running smoothly again.'

'What's causing the traffic jam?' asked a deeply lined, slim blonde lady with a few miles on her, and a diamond-studded Rolex on her too.

'The pseudo-scientific world of the social scientist,' replied the spiritual leader without hesitation. The class was quite taken aback by this reply and they looked completely blank. 'My children,' he continued, 'you look puzzled.' Obligingly they rewarded him at once with more puzzled looks and nods. 'When I was a kid, if you wanted to blame somebody else for your sins, the best candidate was undoubtedly the Devil. Or maybe the Demon Drink. But everyone knew that your sins were your own and that you were personally responsible for them. But now what do we hear? We hear the word "illness", we hear the word "compulsion", we hear the word "addict". Is sin, is criminal behaviour, is all wickedness simply beyond our control? I'm asking you, is sin *really* a form of illness, merely a form of compulsive behaviour?

'The psychiatrists are lining up to explain our sins as obsessive-compulsive disorders. If we drink, if we fornicate, if we kill – yes, if we *kill* – it's not because we are wicked. Oh no! We simply have abnormal DNA sequences in our genes.

'Let me tell you some of the other new medical conditions that have been discovered around these parts. Shopaholism, have you heard of that? That's what we used to call avarice or greed. Workaholism? Sexaholism?' His audience was laughing now. He was working the room well. 'And if you do nothing to help your spouse, that's not your fault either – you're simply in a co-dependency situational disorder. I've even heard of Bank Robbing Syndrome!' The initiates were laughing aloud.

'But don't forget this.' Suddenly he was serious again. 'If vice is merely disease, then virtue has no virtue. But virtue is not just good health. This is not what *we* believe, my friends. We believe that there *is* sin and that there *is* salvation.'

Challenging them to disagree, he looked around the room. When no one did, he moved on to the key question. 'So how do you find salvation?' No one in the room noticed, except perhaps subliminally, that Abel Pile did not feel that he needed to find salvation, only his congregation, his disciples. 'You, my friends, have now started out on the Journey of Light and Truth, you are already on the road to Inner Purity. You are the Pilgrims. I offer you Pilgrims the hope of escape from the wheel of death and rebirth by ascending in triumph over the planet earth's negative force fields into a completely positive state of being, close to God, which is known to our Church as the Pilgrim's Omniscience. The only reality is God. Negative notions like poverty, sickness and fear are unreal, and if you work hard on yourselves and attend our seminars assiduously these negative feelings will no longer exist. Death is unreal, for life is eternal. But because the word death has negative connotations we shall never refer to it again – for death is real only in that it is a transcendent experience, a transition to another plane. It is this very Pilgrim's Omniscience which will, in turn, grant to those of you who have eliminated all negativity the ultimate state of goodness and spiritual consciousness.' Here he lowered his voice with hushed reverence. 'This is the state we call Yahweh Perception. This is the work that I have come down here to do. You initiates are those who I am taking home with me to God. Amen.'

And he left the room.

There was a long silence. The initiates felt not only deeply privileged, they felt almost sacred. Abel the good, the embodiment of a Christ-like power, had 'come down here' to take them home to God.

Later on, much later, his enemies (and other people he

accused of being godless) made much of this statement when it was reported by one or two disaffected followers, charging him with both blasphemy and fraud. But the good Dr Pile always insisted that when he said he had 'come down here' he was referring to his descent from his hilltop home on Mulholland Drive to Hollywood Boulevard, rather than from heaven to earth. 'How could anybody have thought that I would commit such blasphemy as to equate myself with Christ? Who would believe it?'

The initiates believed it. For the Church of the Community of Personal Truth was the Cadillac of cults and the initiates were, within months, to attend their ordination. Having been ordinationized, they would then be the Ministers of Truth in the Pilgrim Priesthood.

While Randi was undergoing these first days of her priestly initiation, Ernest was struggling with more mundane problems. He drove to the 7-11 shop just off La Cienega Boulevard and tried to get the cash for Joanna from the instant teller machine. Instant fury rather than instant cash was what normally came out of an encounter between Ernest and the instant teller and today was no exception. He punched in the number 1464, which had been allocated to him by the bank. The liquid crystal letters told him it was not a valid number. He knew for a fact that it was, so he tried twice more, and the third time the machine ate his cash card and refused to regurgitate it. Angry and frustrated, he drove home and, still thinking about 1464, he punched that figure into his gate decoder, then realized it was wrong, then punched in a different number, and the decoder immediately jammed and refused to either open the gate or accept another code. Swearing and sweating he scrambled up and over the spikes, tore a gaping hole in his shirt, landed heavily in the concrete carport twisting his left ankle, hobbled up the drive to the front door where – to his consternation – the seven-digit code number of his burglar alarm completely deserted him. He ran through all the possibilities, but the only number that occurred to him was 1644 which, he belatedly realized, was the correct number for his sodding cash card. As always, his head was awash with numbers, not just for the cash card and the gate and the burglar alarm but also for his two telephone lines, his AT&T calling-card, his fax, his car phone, Randi's car phone and the CLEAR codes on both car phones without which he couldn't unlock either of them – and they had to be lockable so that the car valets at valet parking couldn't phone home to Mexico, the Philippines or South Korea while he was lunching at Le Dôme.

Ernest Mayday stared hopelessly at his burglar alarm's touch-tone key-pad, wondering how to get into his home without automatically summoning Westside Security and knowing that, if he did, he had forgotten the numerical code which he would need to tell them when they phoned to check that he wasn't an intruder, in which case if he couldn't remember it they would dispatch all those private police to his house, armed to the teeth, bristling with guns and low IQs. While deep in this indecision and misery the front door opened and Consuela the maid smiled at him. Overcome with relief, he hobbled into his office, intending to open the wall safe so that he could check the various codes that he'd forgotten – when he remembered that he'd forgotten the number that would open the combination lock of the safe. Kicking the wall in impotent rage, he injured his other ankle, and in search of solace he limped painfully into the kitchen looking for the excellent bottle of 1976 Château Haut-Brion that was still half full after last night's dinner. It was nowhere to be seen. He asked Consuela, using extensive mime. It took a while. With great happiness she showed him the now empty bottle at the bottom of the trash bin. Baffled, he asked her if she'd drunk it, miming and going glug glug glug. She understood clearly, shook her head and pointed to the vintage date on the bottle. With a heart-rending shock Ernest realized that she'd poured it away, thinking that 1976 was the 'drink-by' date.

Completely overwhelmed by the tragic loss of half a bottle of irreplaceable wine, Ernest sat silently at his kitchen table, unable to speak, unable to think, able only to sweat. When he calmed down he remembered where he'd written the code to the safe. He found his list of numbers within it, and phoned the bank requesting them to messenger five hundred dollars to the house in cash, plus an application form for a new cash card since the other one was gone for good.

Armed with the money, he headed for Cravings, on Sunset, where he was to meet Joanna and conclude the deal. When he got there she was looking in the window of a lingerie shop close to the restaurant. He noticed with relief that her hair was the same length and colour as the night before. She was wearing a different blouse but the same jeans, and because she was facing away from him he saw that they were carefully torn not only across the knee but also horizontally across the top of her left leg, immediately below the buttock, a tear that was tantalizingly and expertly placed.

'Buying yourself some lingerie?' he asked as he sidled up behind her.

'Oh, hello.' The usual peck on the cheek. Ernest Mayday wondered for a moment if her lips lingered just that much longer today. 'No, women don't buy lingerie, they buy underwear. Lingerie is what men give you. Underwear is what you have to go out and buy for yourself.'

He stood behind her, pretending to look in the shop window too. But he was much taller than she was and looking over her shoulder he could see down the front of her blouse. She was not wearing a brassiere and she didn't seem to need one, for her breasts were as firm as any he'd ever seen. 'I see you're not wearing much of either today,' he remarked.

'Either?' She turned to look at him.

'Underwear or lingerie.'

She regarded him with new interest. 'How can you tell? Ooh, Norm, were you peeping down my front?'

'No,' he lied, and then wondered why he couldn't admit to such an ordinary, natural, male impulse. It was hardly so wicked or so shocking, especially not to a girl who sold her body. 'No bra straps,' he explained lamely.

'I don't usually wear a bra when I'm not working.'

He was surprised. 'I should have thought it would be the other way round.'

She was intrigued. 'Why?'

He looked around, embarrassed again. This was not a conversation that he would have chosen to have on a busy shopping street. 'Well, I mean, don't your clients like you to be naked?'

'That's what *you'd* like, is it?' She smiled mischievously.

Mayday suddenly found that he had a frog in his throat. He cleared it noisily. 'Um, well, if I were paying for sex with you I think I'd want to see your body, yes.'

'At the start?'

'How do you mean?'

'They mostly want to see me, eventually, yes. Not all, but most. Most people like to fuck naked, *eventually*. But to start with they usually like lingerie. Most men like taking my bra off. And my panties. Or watching me take them off. Undressing raises the whole level of excitement and anticipation, don't you think? That's why I wore that blouse with lots of buttons when I first came to meet you. It's such fun to unbutton, don't you agree?'

'Well, nothing succeeds like undress,' he quipped, hoping to hide his English inhibition at discussing sex with a woman without the cover of euphemisms. She could see that he was covered in confusion but she was enjoying herself too much to let it go. 'Seriously, Norm, don't you enjoy unbuttoning ... and unzipping ... and unclasping?' She was staring at him innocently.

'Let's just say', he replied, 'that you look terrific fully clothed and I'm sure you look great in, or out, of anything. This is for you.' And he produced the envelope with the five new crisp one-hundred-dollar bills that had been biked over from the bank. The bank always messengered over their best banknotes.

'Thanks,' she said, and stuffed the envelope into the pocket of her jeans. He realized that she didn't carry a handbag when she wasn't working. Presumably her handbag contained all her working equipment: the toothbrush, the panties, the condoms and other stuff that he'd have to ask her about in due course if his novel were to contain enough voyeuristic detail to become a bestseller. But something surprised him. 'Aren't you going to count the money?'

'What?'

'The money? Aren't you going to count it?'

She looked at him with those candid grey eyes. 'Why? Can't I trust you?'

'Sure you can.' He felt silly now.

'Look, I'm not some grubby streetwalker. I'm not going to count your money. I trust you, don't you trust me?'

She made him feel ashamed. 'I know that. I'm sorry, I didn't mean to insult you.'

She was rubbing it in. 'Norm, this is a straightforward business deal, isn't it? If we can't trust each other, it has no future.'

'I know that,' he said helplessly.

'If you had been stupid enough not to put five hundred in here, then I wouldn't tell you any more about John Schmidt, would I? I need the money, you need the story, right?'

'Right.'

'So can I assume that there's five hundred in here?' She took the envelope out of her pocket and held it in front of his face.

'*Yes.*'

'Fine.' She put it away. 'I'll be in touch.'

After she was gone, Ernest Mayday realized that he still didn't have her phone number.

NINE

It is a truth universally acknowledged, that a single man in possession of a good fortune, must be in want of a wife.

Jane Austen

Summer. Hot is what everybody wants to be in Hollywood, but not literally. The temperatures were rising every day and pollutants filled the air. If you drove to the top of Sunset Plaza Drive and stood on top of the mountain behind Ernest Mayday's house you could see the thick blanket-yellow cloud of smog that lay over the whole of the Los Angeles basin, obliterating the distant hills south of the city and even the Pacific Ocean. You wondered why you couldn't see all the filth in the air when you were right down there in the middle of it, breathing it in, living on it, and you wondered about how beautiful the land must have been in the days before fumes filled the city, when the San Gabriel Mountains, that dramatic rocky snow-peaked backdrop to the original village of Hollywoodland, were visible every day, not just in the winter and spring on occasional clear bright days after the rains had blotted up the smog and the sea breeze had then whisked it away.

In this heat people developed prickly eyes, and coughs, and felt out of sorts. 'I've got a virus,' they'd say to each other, and retreat to bed with inexplicable headaches and upset tummies. People forgot how far south they were living. Ernest Mayday's appetite, never good even in the most clement weather, vanished altogether. He could not stand the intense heat as he sat at his office desk in the afternoon and the desert sun beat in on him, his plate glass picture window acting like a giant rectangular magnifying glass. Ernest had always been told that if you lived on the city side of the Hollywood Hills with a breeze blowing through from the ocean, you didn't need air-conditioning. 'That may be true for the Americans,' he said to himself, sweating and gasping, 'but not for the Brits.' Clutching his heart, overwhelmed by the claustrophobic heat, and by the illusion that he could hardly breathe, he beat a retreat from his desk, staggering across the antique Tabriz shipped from Haslemere to lie prone on the enormous chocolate-brown leather sofa in the furthest, darkest corner of the sauna that he called his office. Some days, some nights, the bath-tub or the swimming-pool were the only places where he could bear to lie down.

Mayday's Mexican gardener Ricardo retimed the automatic sprinklers to water for fifteen minutes each day instead of every other day. They were set to go off at five a.m., before the sun rose east of the city beyond the downtown skyline, revealing in the cool grey dawn over East and South-central LA the previous night's bodycount from the gangland wars and drive-by shootings. As the cops hosed blood off the ghetto streets the sprinklers refreshed Ernest's garden, well before the sun could dry up his carefully tended, newly nourished lawns and flower-beds.

Randi didn't mind the heat and her business was thriving. The work kept her fit and healthy, and with the support of God and Abel Pile she began to get her old confidence back. She had given up her apartment and enjoyed living in the commune at the Theological Seminary down in Hollywood, though she still spent many a night with Mayday. As an initiate into the Pilgrim's Priesthood she was given her own bedroom and bathroom at the Seminary. Life there was communal, but not too communal. When she first went to the SCREAMS she gave ten per cent of her income to the Church. Mayday gave ten per cent of his to his agent. He wasn't sure which of them was the less rational. But now that she lived at the Church, nominally at least, she gave them fifty per cent. Mayday neither approved nor disapproved. She was pleased that he wasn't judgemental. Actually, he just didn't care one way or the other.

Overwhelmed by the relentless heat, which continued day after day, week after week, Mayday more or less abandoned what little work he was trying to do. A few royalties trickled in from Cockerel Books, Bedford Square, WC1 (or from some place out in the sticks where they kept their accountants), plus the measly maximum remittance of five thousand pounds from the Public Lending Right, his annual gratuity from Britain's free lending libraries. This sum represented thousands upon thousands of presumably satisfied readers who had borrowed the books over which he had laboured and on which he depended for his declining income. Rather than write his new book he wrote indignant letters to *The Times*, the *Guardian*, the *Independent*, even the *Telegraph*, railing against the injustice of the system, but none of them were ever published. The people of Great Britain (he'd been told) bought one-ninth of the number of books bought by the people of West Germany, which Ernest chose to think was not a reflection upon British literacy but upon the fact that they could read any book without paying for it if they just took a bus to the public library. In rural areas they didn't even have to do that, as the library itself was on a bus. The British did buy paperbacks, admittedly, but they persisted in regarding hardbacks as too expensive. This was completely baffling to Mayday. Why, he asked, would an Englishman happily pay a tenner for a round of drinks at his local, and twice that for a ticket to a play or a curry for two at any old Indian restaurant, and yet resent buying a book? It was obvious to Ernest that a copy of one of his books (or even a copy of somebody else's book) was much better value than either a seat in the stalls or a chicken biryani, even with a couple of poppadams and a Bombay duck thrown in. For if you have the book on the shelf you can keep coming back to it and, unlike the curry, it doesn't keep coming back to you. Mayday had no objection in principle to free public libraries but for the life of him he simply couldn't see why they should be subsidized, as he put it, by authors. The state paid all other workers when it provided subsidized services, and in the case of libraries the librarians were paid for their work – why, he wondered bitterly as he sat in the shade of his palm trees beside his black-bottomed pool, should there be a ceiling on what bestselling authors were paid? Especially as they might never write another sodding book anyhow.

Sipping his rum and Diet Coke from one of the plastic unbreakable tumblers that were compulsory around his pool (he didn't want to be sued for one million dollars by some litigious guest who might step on a piece of broken glass), he waited daily in the shade hoping to hear from Joanna, confident that sooner or later she'd call. It was still too soon to call Oliver Sudden and give him the storyline of *Lies – the Movie*.

Meanwhile, Randi began to feel less threatened. When they were in bed together she began to talk of marriage, and consequently Ernest began to feel threatened instead. He had tried marriage before of course, back in Haslemere, and it hadn't turned out at all well. Ellen had been a strikingly good-looking woman and everyone agreed that they were a perfect match. Like Ernest, she had taken a First at Oxford – Ernest in law and Ellen in philosophy, politics and economics – and everyone perceived them as the couple most likely to succeed. Even their differences seemed to make them suitable for each other, Ernest with his quiet English reserve and dry humour and Ellen's red hair, startling green eyes (made so much more startling by the bright-green contact lenses that he never knew about till after they were married) and her superior Anglo-Irish intelligence. But in retrospect it seemed to Ernest that as soon as a relationship was formalized by marriage vows or even by the assumption that a man and a woman would henceforth live together always, the sex stopped working. Ellen began complaining to him that she didn't 'get off' when they made love. For a long time Ernest had felt guilty about it. Not guilty enough, however, for in due course he started a loveless lunch-hour affair with his secretary Sharon at the office which, although it made him feel even guiltier, also made him feel better about himself for Sharon seemed to 'get off' without any difficulty.

When eventually he discovered that Ellen was getting laid by a tubby clown called Barry who had the face of a shifty gerbil and was Chairman of the International Division at the merchant bank where she worked, he felt sure that his guilty feelings would diminish. But no, he seemed to feel even worse about it, for she continued to remind Ernest that she hadn't been 'getting off' with him, and that was the reason she'd had the affair with Barry. Later, when she was promoted to the board of directors of the International Division, Ernest became less convinced that it had all been his fault, though she insisted that her promotion had been properly earned in the office and not on her back in the bedrooms of the Strand Palace Hotel, where she and Barry had apparently got each other off satisfactorily. Ernest now felt that she was projecting her guilt on to him, and he intended to hand it right back to its rightful owner.

When they had discovered each other's infidelities (he voluntarily admitted his relationship with Sharon when he learned about Barry), they sat down in the idyllic thatched cottage outside Haslemere, which was the envy of all their friends, and discussed the matter sensibly, like adults. 'It's equality,' she had explained to him patiently. 'If you fuck around, why shouldn't I?'

'But you were doing it first,' he pointed out.

'What difference does that make? You didn't know that.' Female logic, he thought. He was about to explain that she could hardly use his affair as a justification if she didn't even know about it when she continued: 'If men can do it, so can women. This is the eighties.'

'It's nothing to do with the eighties.' Ernest stayed cool, trying to keep the conversation on some logical track. 'Women have always been unfaithful.'

She flared up at that. 'Oh? And men haven't, I suppose.'

He took a deep breath and tried again. 'That's not what I was saying. Of course men have too. I merely said that it's nothing to do with the eighties.'

'Well, what is it to do with? What do you *feel* about my affair with Barry? What do you *feel* about the fact that I don't usually have an orgasm with you? You must feel something.'

The only feeling Ernest had ever had any talent for expressing was rage, but to his surprise he didn't even feel that. In fact, he didn't feel much of anything though he knew he ought to. He sighed, and tried to feel something. 'Actually, you know what I feel? I feel that perhaps there's no point in being married at all. I mean, why should I stay committed to having sex with one woman – you – and support you and share everything equally with you?'

This made her angry. 'You don't support me, I earn nearly as much as you do. And if I'm willing to commit myself to that, why shouldn't you be?' He didn't reply. He stared out of the leaded casement window at the drizzle falling through the limp red and gold leaves. 'Why don't we try again?' she asked.

'You're willing to give up Barry?'

'That's over long ago. The sex was good but nothing else was. I really like you, Ernest. Let's try again?'

It was truly tempting. In the firelight that wet autumnal Sunday evening she was even more beautiful to look at than the night he fell in love with her at the Balliol Commem Ball. She was wearing her pink satin dressing-gown loosely wrapped around her naked body, drying her hair after her shower before they went out to dinner with friends who lived near by. Yet tempting though she was that night, something had changed in him. 'Yes – but why?' he asked. He leaned against the warm Aga. His head almost touched the black oak beams that supported what the estate agent had claimed was the original seventeenth-century ceiling. 'Look,' he said again, 'we neither of us believe in religion. I'm an atheist, you're an agnostic, for us marriage is not a sacrament. So what else is it?'

'I don't know.' She inhaled a long deep drag from her cigarette and stubbed it out in the overflowing ashtray. 'What is this, "Twenty Questions"?'

'I'll tell you what it is. It's a contract. That's all. It's a deal.' At last the lawyer in him had found a way of dealing with this painful situation. 'You're a banker, you understand deals. A marriage has got to offer something to both parties if it's going to last.'

'I don't know what this is all about. What don't I offer you? I let you fuck me whenever you want. Even though I don't get off, usually.'

He kept his temper. 'Apart from the fact that you make it sound like you're doing me some big favour, I'm not saying that marriage is a sex contract, Ellen. It's a contract for life. I sort of expected – I realize now how foolish I was – I expected not only sex, but children.'

She was surprised. 'You don't even like children.'

'Other people's, perhaps,' he agreed. 'But I might like mine. Anyway, I'd have liked the name of Mayday to continue.'

'Talented though I am, darling, I can hardly guarantee you a son.'

'Well, even a daughter would have been some sort of continuity.'

'Well, I'd be willing to have a child for you. I just don't want to be at home all day with the little brat, that's all.' She was beginning to feel very defensive.

'Ellen, you can't ignore biological facts. Children need mothers.'

'They need parents. Mothers bear children, fathers can look after them.'

'But I have important work, at the Treasury.'

'And I have important work, at the bank.'

'That's right,' he agreed. 'I'm not saying you're wrong, I'm just pointing out that the contract between us doesn't work. Look, what can I offer you? Economic security. In return, I hoped for children, housekeeping, sex and so forth. The usual bourgeois deal.'

'You make it all sound so romantic.' She was sounding increasingly bitter.

He was puzzled. 'But you're the one who doesn't want romance. You want equality.'

'I want both. They're not mutually exclusive. Let's start again, and be faithful to each other this time.'

'Fine. I offer you economic security. But what can you offer me in return? Economic security. I don't need that deal, I've got that already. Our marriage isn't working because we're offering each other an exchange of similar goods.'

She was getting upset but was determined not to show it. She stood, filled the kettle and considered her response, refusing to look him in the eye. He watched her with regret, suddenly knowing for certain that this was the end, sad that this tall handsome woman and he were soon to go their separate ways. 'I see that you'll never understand,' she said. 'I'm a liberated, educated woman. I know that you like that in theory, but you don't in practice. You don't realize this, but you are an unreconstructed, paternalist, sexist, male chauvinist caveman.'

He shrugged. 'Maybe. I don't know what's in it for you, but I'm just saying that our deal turns out to have nothing in it for me.'

'Nothing? *Nothing?* Do you realize how insulting that is to me? You're saying you don't want me because I won't cook and clean for you, and give up my career for you.' She poured the hot water from the kettle to the teapot and stirred the Earl Grey vigorously. 'I think this all boils down to sexual jealousy. It's all because I fucked Barry and Ahmed, isn't it?'

Ernest blinked. 'Ahmed? I never *heard* of Ahmed! Who's *Ahmed?*'

'Oh!' She grimaced. 'Whoops! Um . . . he's one of the Saudis I do business with,' she explained as casually as she could. 'You met him at the Christmas party last year. You liked him.'

'Oh, that's OK then,' said Ernest. '*Ahmed?*'

'He's very nice. I hope you're not going to get racist about this.'

'I'm not concerned with Ahmed's race,' said Ernest. '*Ahmed?* You say it's over with Barry. And with Ahmed too, I presume?' She nodded. 'That's fine. But can you see that, from my point of view, there's no point in my committing to have sex with only one woman, committing to support her – especially when she can perfectly well support herself – especially when *Ahmed* could perfectly well support her – support *everybody*, I should think! – why should I commit to share everything equally with you, when I have to get a housekeeper to run our home, I have a choice of restaurants to dine in, a dry cleaner who sews on my shirt buttons, and no kids? What do I get from you – you particularly? Sex. Well, the truth is I can get that anywhere, with more variety and fewer complaints.'

'So can I,' she snapped.

'As you've demonstrated so clearly.'

'But . . . what about kids?' She knelt beside him at the table, and put her hand on his knee. 'Do you *really* want them? Because if you do, let's do it. It might make all the difference.'

'I used to want them,' he said. 'But you know what? My heart's no longer in it. The way I feel now, they're expensive, they're an intrusion. All I want now is to live my life the way it is, selfishly, without guilt or regrets.'

She stared at him. Then she stood up, poured the tea and placed a steaming mug of it in front of him on the old pine refectory table that they had polyurethaned together in the first flush of their romance on a similar wet Sunday afternoon years before. 'You're even more self-centred than I thought. It's like the way you make love. As soon as you're satisfied, you stop, roll over, go to sleep. What about me? You drove me to those men.'

Suddenly Ernest was exasperated. And he no longer felt it was his problem. 'Ellen, it's not my responsibility if you don't "get off", as you call it. Whose orgasm is it we're talking about? I mean, whose cunt is it, actually, yours or mine?'

'Sex is supposed to be a mutual pleasure,' she said. 'I do it for you, you should do it for me.'

'But that's the point, Ellen, don't you see? That's not what I married you for. *I don't have to be married*, I don't have to be in love with the woman, I just have to be sexually stimulated and there are lots of women around of every shape and size who do that just fine. Better than you, actually.'

She tipped her mug of tea into his groin. He gasped, then jumped up, as he felt the hot tea scalding him through his trousers and underpants. 'Ellen, what the fuck?' He pulled his trousers down and with his pants round his ankles bunny-hopped ridiculously over to the sink. She was laughing so hard that she was almost fighting for breath. He grabbed a dishcloth, soaked it in cold water and gently soothed his reddening skin. She was still laughing, now mopping her eyes, blowing her nose, watching him as he stood there ludicrously naked from the waist down. 'What was the point of that?' he shouted. 'Stupid bitch.' She walked upstairs and started packing.

Years later, over a game of poker at Jerry's, he'd told the story of his marriage to Max Period and Sidney. 'I was willing for it to be a fifty-fifty arrangement. She seemed to think eighty-twenty was fair.'

Sidney nodded sympathetically. He was on his fourth wife. 'Anybody who thinks that marriage is a fifty-fifty deal', he said, 'doesn't know anything about women.'

'Or fractions,' added Max. 'So how long were you married?'

'Eight years.'

'Not bad,' Max. commented. 'Arlene and I have been happily married ten years.'

Ernest was astonished. 'Only ten years?'

'Ten out of thirty ain't bad.' They all laughed uproariously.

Lying in bed with Randi now, Ernest thought back on his marriage. Ellen had truly believed that everything in a modern marriage should be shared. And that was certainly the prevailing Californian view. It had led to some similar fights with Randi, over restaurant bills for instance. 'You want it both ways,' he'd tried to explain to her once at Genghis Cohen's Chinese restaurant. 'If I don't pick up the check I'm a cheap son-of-a-bitch. But if I do, I'm an aggressive male chauvinist pig. I can't deal with this and I don't want to.' On that occasion *he* had stalked out of the restaurant. But he had never been able to get Ellen's last words to him out of his mind. After she'd packed an overnight bag she'd come downstairs and gone straight to the front door. 'Is this *goodbye*?' he'd asked, melodramatically, trying to lighten the moment. He failed. He saw that she was crying now, and not with laughter. The hysteria had not lasted long. Big tears were rolling down her face. But she looked him in the eye.

'You know what I think, Ernest? You want to know why it didn't work? I think you're not capable of a real relationship with anyone.'

It was a sweltering night when Randi snuggled up to him in bed and suggested, as she chewed gently on his ear, that they might marry. He dodged the suggestion with a muttered 'maybe' and then they made love. Afterwards she fell asleep, apparently contented. Even after all these years he wished that Ellen could witness Randi's satisfaction. Ernest lay stretched out across his king-size Californian bed and watched her sleeping, curled up on the hot rumpled sheets, graceful as always, the breeze from the humming fan gently ruffling her hair. He thought how loving, how kind she was. Again he saw Ellen saying 'I think you're not capable of a real relationship with anyone', as he had seen her say it so often over the past seven years, rerunning and rerunning the scene in what Oliver had called the screening room of his mind. He wondered if it really had been his fault. He wondered if she were right.

He knew that he couldn't marry Randi. He didn't think he could ever get that involved with any woman again. He remembered that Ellen had told him more than once that she thought he was disturbed. Now Randi often suggested that he should get therapy. He didn't know why. He wondered if they were both right. He heard the screech of the barn owl in the tree outside the bedroom window and the screams of the police sirens down on Sunset. Hot weather always meant trouble in LA. Through the fronds of the palm tree he saw a new moon and, below, the twinkling jewel-box of multicoloured lights of the city, so deceptively beautiful at night.

That night Randi had told him her good news: that she was being considered for priesthood, with full powers. He had pretended to be pleased for her, but not only did he despise her Church and her work, on some level he also feared it. And yet, he didn't know why.

TEN

*Nowhere is woman treated according to the merit of
her work but rather as a sex. It is therefore almost
inevitable that she pay for her right to exist . . . with
sex favors. Thus it is merely a question of degree
whether she sells herself to one man, in or out of
marriage, or to many men.*

Emma Goldman, *The Traffic In Women*

'God is very well adjusted,' the Reverend Abel Pile
explained to Randi, 'and he wants us to be well adjusted
too.'

'I understand that.' She wondered what this was leading
up to. She had been called to Dr Pile's private summer
cottage at the end of an unobtrusive dirt track out in
Malibu. It was nearly an hour's drive from the Heartwarming Institute and Theological Seminary, all the way
along Sunset past the Will Rogers State Park to the
Pacific. She turned right at Gladstone's, the huge fish
restaurant on the beach which she had never been back to
since she ordered catfish one night and they brought her
the whole creature on a plate, standing up on its belly in
swimming position, complete with whiskers, belligerent
though fried, rather like Ernest at a party. She drove
north along the Pacific Coast Highway, past the impressive
gates that mark the entrance to the Getty Museum,
a secluded reproduction of a Roman villa standing
high above the highway on one of Malibu's crumbling
cliffs, containing rare and valuable artefacts from all
centuries including a smallish rectangle of canvas called
Irises, covered with thick diagonal strokes of blue and

yellow and purple oil paint, not the best example of the demented vision of Vincent van Gogh but 'worth' forty-seven million dollars, obviously not as art but as currency.

How can you put a price on art? Ernest had wondered when he stood in front of this crazed colourful work, wondering also whether the fart that he was about to let loose would be noticed by any of the other people in the gallery. He thought not. It was a large room and a weekday, and all the other members of the public were too far away to notice any smell. If they did, he reasoned, they would have no reason to identify it with him. But he hadn't considered the noise, and when he let go it was like a bull elephant's call to the herd, a huge trumpeting blast, a tremendous raspberry. Amazed, all the respectful tourists in this hushed temple of art turned and looked in his direction. The mighty fart could only have come from him or from Randi who was standing next to him, and as she too was staring at him in open-mouthed astonishment there seemed to be no way at all for Ernest to deny authorship. Attack being the only available form of defence, Ernest defiantly stared back at the array of incredulous faces and said loudly: 'What are you all staring at?' None of them spoke. 'It was me. I farted, OK? Haven't you ever farted?' He looked from one to another. Apparently they hadn't, or if they had they certainly weren't prepared to admit it. The culture-seekers turned away, appalled, disgusted, pretending he hadn't spoken, pretending this wasn't happening, especially not in the Getty, especially not in front of a masterpiece by Van Gogh. All except Randi, who suddenly guffawed. Encouraged, Ernest continued addressing the general public. 'If you want to know, that's what I think of paying forty-seven million dollars for this painting. Not just this painting,' he went on, getting into his stride, 'but any painting. What is art anyway, what's so fucking sacred about it, paintings are a form of interior decor, that's all. Painters paint them in the hope that someone will like them enough to buy them and hang them on their walls. You're all acting as though I'd farted in church ... not that there's anything wrong with farting in church either, farting's a perfectly natural function. The way I look at it is: if God hadn't intended us to fart he wouldn't have given us arseholes. Or beans,' he added as an afterthought. People were hurrying out through every available door. 'What's the matter?' he called to the departing backs of three middle-aged Canadian ladies in tartan headscarves, fighting to get out of an emergency exit at the far end of the room. 'You think Van Gogh never farted?'

The gallery was deserted except for Ernest and Randi, who was lying on the polished oak floor crying with laughter, and the solitary figure of an approaching security guard who asked them both to leave the museum immediately.

That was a year or two ago, when they first started dating, when they could hardly keep their hands off each other. Randi grinned as she remembered. It was only later that she realized Ernest was half serious. They had discussed the studies of Velázquez they'd seen there earlier that day, which Ernest had greatly admired, and the Rembrandts too. 'These are profound statements,' she'd said reverently as they drove home that evening.

'Statements?' he had asked. 'Statements about what? What are they stating, do you suppose?'

For a while she was stumped by the question. 'They're statements about character,' she said finally.

'You know, I'm not sure that painting can be profound,' Ernest had replied. She couldn't decide whether or not he was putting her on, or testing her. 'Painters paint what they see, don't they?' he asked.

'Yes,' she said, 'and so do writers.'

'No,' he argued, 'paintings are just exercises in light and

shade. Look at the Impressionists. Full of theory but no thought. Light and shade. That's about as much in the way of thought that any painting can contain.' She knew she didn't agree but she could never find the right words to argue with him. He was still in love with her in those days so he helped her out. 'Do you mean that a portrait by Rembrandt is as profoundly descriptive of character as, say, a novel by Dostoyevsky?' That was exactly what she'd meant, she said. He nodded, but made no comment.

That whole day came back to her as she turned right off the Pacific Coast Highway and drove some distance up dusty Malibu Canyon. When she reached her destination she found that Abel's pile was a Californian ranch house, or what in Britain would be called a bungalow. But a very large bungalow. Discreetly unimpressive when viewed from the road, it contained every creature comfort both within and without – a huge pool (known to Westside realtors as a 'swimmer's pool'), a jacuzzi (known as a spa), a bar (known as a 'wet' bar – heaven knows what a dry bar would be, other than a contradiction in terms), a north/south tennis court (a required luxury in Californian real estate, so that the low morning or evening sun didn't get in anyone's eyes), a library, a den, a 'gourmet' kitchen (that's any modern kitchen), plus a couple of living rooms and bedrooms and no less than twelve toilets known as bathrooms – even though several contained no bath – rest rooms, powder rooms and other assorted euphemisms. Like most wealthy American households, the plumbing facilities were apparently planned with a diarrhoea epidemic in mind. It did not occur to Randi to speculate about the source of this opulence, so concerned was she to learn the reason that she had been summoned to Abel's private residence.

It turned out to be a private talk, a sort of annual appraisal interview like they have in secular corporations.

Also present in the den was a charming young man with crinkly blue eyes and incongruously black hair called John Schmidt. 'Have you ever met John?' Abel Pile courteously introduced them. 'He's one of the guys.'

'One of the guys?' she repeated. He was real cute, she thought.

John Schmidt seemed to think the same about her. 'So pleased to meet you.' He took her hand in both of his. 'I mean it most sincerely, this is a *real* pleasure.' Gently he shook her hand, up and down, several times. He didn't seem to want to let go. He was looking deep into her eyes, almost – she felt – into her soul. She felt naked, transparent. She was happy. She felt appreciated, admired, understood.

'I call them the guys,' explained Abel Pile, pouring her a Diet Coke. 'John is one of our seven High Priests of Yahweh Perception.'

She looked at John Schmidt with awe. 'So what do I call you?'

'Call me John,' he said with a smile. 'We don't care too much for formality, except on strictly religious occasions.'

'Like the Sincerity Awards Dinner at the Beverly Sheraton,' added Dr Pile.

'Or Easter?' she offered.

The Reverend Doctor and his High Priest exchanged a look of warm approval. 'That's right,' said Pile. She was pleased.

'Smart girl,' said Schmidt. 'I can see why he chose you to be a Pilgrim.'

'You could be one of the guys too,' said Pile.

'You mean, a High Priest?' she whispered, blushing.

'Yes indeed. But only if you can find it in your heart to be sufficiently committed,' added Abel.

Randi was astonished. She couldn't think what he meant. 'Sufficiently committed? You *know* how committed I am.'

'I certainly do,' he replied. She waited. He said nothing more. She looked from one man to the other. They seemed to be waiting for her to speak. 'Are you saying I'm not sufficiently committed?'

Abel Pile shook his blond curls sadly. 'You know we wouldn't say that,' said John Schmidt. 'We don't believe in that kind of negativity.'

'*Any* kind of negativity.' Pile corrected him firmly.

'That's right, we don't believe in any kind of negativity,' agreed John Schmidt. 'Negativity reveals a lack of spiritual depth. It also reveals a lack of loyalty to Abel.'

'Negativity begets negativity,' concluded Abel in a magisterial summing up. 'Nothing comes from nothing.'

Randi was shocked. 'But . . . are you saying that I'm being negative?' Abel Pile raised his eyebrows. 'No, no, of course you're not, that would be saying that *you* were negative, that would be negative too, right?' He smiled. She understood. 'I guess, you're saying that I'm not positive – sorry, I didn't mean that, what I mean is that I could be *more* positive and *more* committed, is that it?'

Abel Pile inclined his head forward almost imperceptibly to indicate both agreement and approval. She was suffused with gratitude and relief. He rewarded her with his warm, wonderful, yet very human smile. She felt safe again. But only for a moment.

'So, the question is, *how* can you be more committed?' Dr Pile asked her.

She thought hard. She couldn't think of anything more she could do. 'I don't know. I mean, I live at the Church now, I'm always around to help anyone who needs love or support. I devote all my free time to the Institute. I do household chores there, more than at home, I'm helping with the Sincerity Awards . . .'

'Home?' John was puzzled. He crossed his legs and leaned forward. She noticed how hairy and masculine his thighs were, dressed as he was in large-checked Bermuda shorts and a running singlet that left one in no doubt that he worked out rigorously every day. 'I thought you said you lived in the Seminary and Commune?'

'Well, yes, I do but . . . I used to have my own apartment and now I often stay with my boyfriend. Is that wrong?'

Abel shook his head slowly from side to side. She was frightened that he was going to say that it was. 'Of course not.' Again she was relieved. 'But we never seem to see him at the Church, do we?'

At once she realized the problem. 'I've tried,' she began, 'but he's an atheist.'

'But you're not going to accept that, are you.' This, from Abel, was a statement not a question.

'Well, no, but . . . '

'Perhaps you mean an agnostic,' suggested John gently, helping her out. 'Someone who doesn't yet know God.'

'I'm sorry to disagree with you, but no, he just says he knows God doesn't exist. I can't change that. Sorry to be negative,' she added hastily, 'if I am being negative, but that's just the way he is.'

John Schmidt was intrigued. 'He's a very confident person, then, to assert that there is no God. How can he prove that?'

'He says you can't prove a negative. It's not up to him to prove it, it's up to me. He says there's no evidence.'

Abel Pile and John Schmidt smiled at each other, the sad smiles of the wise. 'He's a novelist, isn't he?' asked the good doctor.

She nodded.

'He writes bestsellers, doesn't he?'

'Yes,' Randi admitted, 'but you mustn't hold that against him.' She could see that they were both puzzled. 'He says he's trying to reform. Also, he says he wants to be remembered.'

'*I have immortal longings in me,*' murmured Abel.

'You too?' Randi was surprised. 'But surely, all our

souls are immortal? Why do you long for something that's already yours?'

'I was speaking for your boyfriend,' he explained. 'Since an atheist doesn't know that he's immortal, he may long for immortality.'

'You see,' said John, 'we would like your friend Ernest to be involved with the Church of the Community of Personal Truth.'

'So would I.' Randi was in emphatic agreement there.

Pile raised his eyebrows. 'For personal reasons, no doubt?' She nodded. 'Good. But as Jesus said – and, in my opinion, quite rightly – it is more blessed to give than to receive. As you know, at the end of each of our Self-Creating Realization, Energization and Assertivization Mode Seminars we ask all the participants to donate money so that others may be able to participate at a subsidized rate. We want to reach out to people all over the globe, that they may share the experience. Remember the motto of the Heartwarming Institute: *You Care, I Share.*'

Randi's eyes were opened. 'So that's what it means.'

'Indeed. Even some ordinary participants in our SCREAMS, not members of the Church, contribute cheques for as much as ten thousand dollars after completing the seminars.' Pile watched for her response.

'I give you fifty per cent of my income. It's not enough, I know, but it's all I can do.'

'No, my dear Randi, please don't misunderstand me, you are generous beyond compare.'

John Schmidt intervened. 'Abel's talking about Ernest.'

She couldn't see what they wanted of her. 'I know you think I'm being negative, but he doesn't believe. I can't do anything about that. I can't get him to donate to something he doesn't believe in, not even for me. It's his money, after all.'

Abel Pile was extremely understanding. 'Of course it is.

By the way, to change the subject completely, how are things between you?'

'Fine.' She was a shade defensive.

Pile was probing. 'You are just good friends – or are you, as they say, in a relationship?'

'I'm seeing him, yes,' admitted Randi, using the current Los Angeles euphemism for fucking.

'Mmm.' Even Abel Pile's thoughtful grunts sounded warm and supportive to Randi. 'And how are things – forgive me for prying – in the bedroom?'

'Fine,' she repeated. Actually, she didn't find it all that easy to forgive his prying, but she did her best and she was determined not to be negative.

'Sexuality is good,' said Dr Pile. 'You must use it. It is a gift from God. God made you a sexual creature with healthy sexual drives and desires.'

'Not just you, all of us,' John Schmidt hastened to explain.

'Even me,' added Abel encouragingly. 'It is nothing to be ashamed of. It is something to enjoy, to relish, to luxuriate in. Every living creature, every part of the Good Lord's creation, knows and enjoys sex.'

Randi was blushing. Though far from inexperienced in matters sexual and sensual, she had never been good at discussing them with men, and especially not with men who seemed so far above such squalid matters, men who operated on the sublime and spiritual plane to which she so deeply aspired. 'You look shocked, Randi,' he added.

'No.' She was actually less shocked than confused. She picked up a Bible that lay conveniently to hand on the coffee table, thumbed quickly through Genesis and read aloud. 'Listen, this is God, speaking to Woman: "I will greatly multiply your pain in childbearing; in pain you shall bring forth children, yet your desire shall be for your husband, and he shall rule over you." And to Adam He said, "Because you have listened to the voice of your wife, and have eaten of the tree of which I commanded you, 'You shall not eat of it,' cursed is the ground because of you; in toil you shall eat of it all the days of your life; thorns and thistles it shall bring forth to you; ... In the sweat of your face you shall eat bread til you return to the ground, for out of it you were taken; you are dust, and to dust you shall return."'

She lowered the Bible and looked at them. Abel Pile said patiently: 'I know that passage. Did you take special note of the words "Your desire shall be for your husband"?'

'Yes?'

'Randi, many Christians believe what St Augustine taught us on the strength of the story of Adam and Eve, namely that sexual desire is sinful, that all babies are born with original sin, and that Adam's sinful disobedience, prompted by Eve, corrupted the whole of mankind. But, I ask you, how can that be? Isn't sexual desire a part of God's creation? Isn't suffering and death? How can they be unnatural? How can they be bad, or wrong? If God created them, then they are good. So they cannot be a result of Eve's sin, for God created Eve and therefore she was good.'

Randi shrugged hopelessly. She felt she was getting a little out of her depth. She was completely unable to answer this barrage of rhetorical, theological and impossible questions. She waited for Pile to explain further. He was happy to oblige. 'I believe in the essential goodness of God's creation. And I believe in the freedom of the human will. I also believe that even if we were stained by sin, baptism cleanses the believer. Isn't that what everyone knows, that Jesus came to save us? As Didymus the Blind said of baptism: "Now we are found once more such as we were when we were first made: sinless and masters of ourselves."'

Randi was overwhelmed by his learning, and by the honour of this personal (Abel would have called it personalized) seminar. She wanted to make sure that she'd got this straight. 'So you're saying that death is not the result of Eve seducing Adam into eating the Apple?' She was dimly aware that her near-miss with death and her subsequent devotions were all connected in her mind to a sense of sexual guilt for which she was trying to repent. Had she been barking up the wrong tree? Is that where all this was leading?

Abel Pile held his arms out wide, palms up. 'How can that be? How can our deaths be Adam and Eve's fault? God is just. Why should God punish anyone but Adam for Adam's sin? Would he condemn the whole human race? Of course not! No, death – physical death, death of the body – awaits us all. And it always did. As Julian of Eclanum said: "God made bodies, distinguished the sexes, made genitalia, bestowed affection through which bodies would be joined, gave power to the semen, and operates in the secret nature of the semen – and God made nothing evil."'

Randi was more confused than ever. 'But I thought Genesis taught us that death is punishment for sin. God said to Adam: "You shall surely die."'

'That's right. Adam died, morally and *spiritually*, from the day that he chose to sin. And each of us faces the same choice, sanctity or sin, morality or immorality, immorality or death.'

'So . . .' Randi having started a question, hesitated before she continued. 'How does this affect me, exactly?'

'Sexuality is not only sweet, it is positively God's will. How else can we follow God's command "Be fruitful and multiply, and fill the earth"? Genesis one, verse twenty-eight.'

Randi couldn't think of any other way. 'I don't know.'

'So marriage is a sacrament. Marriage is God's *Good*

Housekeeping Seal of Approval. Marriage is monogomous and indissoluble. "What therefore God has joined together let no man put asunder" – Matthew, chapter nineteen, verse six.'

Randi decided to get to the point. 'You want me to marry Ernest? Because, you know, like, it's not just up to me.'

'Want?' Pile looked amazed. 'I want nothing. But if you're asking me, do I think you *should*, then yes, of course I do. That is the Christian position: sex within marriage.'

Randi was still trying to get it all straight in her mind. 'Is the Christian position the same as the missionary position?'

Abel Pile was losing it. 'Randi, baby, this is not a discussion of the Kama Sutra or *The Joy Of Sex*. Do it any way that gives you pleasure. But we believe that, if you want this sexual relationship to continue, it should be blessed by God within the holy sacrament of marriage.'

She thought carefully. 'And if I don't want it to continue?'

An unexpected googly. Momentarily (in the English sense) Messrs Pile and Schmidt found themselves batting on an awkwardly sticky wicket. But Pile made a worthy recovery. 'Our Church', he blocked firmly, 'has no place for nuns. We do not think that women should be the brides of Christ. We do not think that women should deny themselves the good things that God gave us, and sex is one of the best things. Women, too, are part of God's perfect plan. We are not a sexist Church. We believe in equal opportunities. After all, you, a woman, are in line to be one of the guys.' He spoke in ringing tones.

But she hesitated. Something was still wrong, he could see that. 'The only thing is,' she began tentatively, 'sex isn't always one of the best things. Not with Ernest. You see . . . ' Randi started to explain and then she saw the look in their eyes. 'Am I being negative again?'

They nodded yes, in unison.

'Well, what if he's reluctant to marry me? He has been married before, you know.'

They nodded again. 'We know,' said Schmidt. Again she realized that she was expressing negativity. Feeling despair, she wondered how on earth she'd ever learn to change.

'By the way, does he pay alimony to his first wife?' Pile inquired casually.

'I don't think so. There weren't any kids. He's never mentioned anything like that.'

Pile smiled. 'That's fortunate. For you, I mean,' he added hastily.

'Yes,' she agreed enthusiastically, seizing a chance to be positive for a moment. 'But . . . as I said, you know, marriage depends on sex, at least until you *get* married anyway, and at the moment . . . well . . .'

John Schmidt leaned forward and took her hand in his. 'Would you like help with it?'

Randi was startled. 'With what?'

'With the sexual side of your relationship?'

'No . . . I mean, how?' She smiled nervously. 'You mean, advice?'

'Yes,' he replied smoothly. 'Or . . . practical help.' His voice was low, his gaze hypnotic. They were staring deep into each other's eyes. Then she realized that Abel Pile was watching closely and, remembering that she was to marry Ernest, slid her hand gently away from John Schmidt's grasp.

'Just remember that every problem is also an opportunity.' Abel Pile was winding up the meeting fast. 'Randi, God has given you a beautiful face and body. God has given you feminine wiles and a nice ass. Go read a sex manual, watch a porn movie, buy some open-crotch panties at Trashy Lingerie, I don't care how you do it. But by marrying Ernest Mayday you will save your soul and his too, by bringing him into the body of our Church.'

They watched her drive away in her station wagon, bouncing over the pot-holes in the dirt track, back down the long dry hill towards the ocean below the peach pink cloudless evening sky. In the distance the seagulls called, swooping and climbing on their invisible roller-coaster. Abel Pile and John Schmidt deeply breathed in the good, clean, smog-free sea breeze. Malibu was a fine place to live. Abel Pile turned to his High Priest. 'What do you think?'

'I think she'd be a great fuck. If she could only get off that guilt trip.'

'I *mean*', grinned Abel, 'what do you think she'll do?'

'I think she'll do her damnedest.'

'How much do you think Ernest Mayday is worth?'

'Who knows? Millions. He's sold a whole lot of books.'

Abel Pile smiled. 'Thank God the courts take proper care of wives in this state.'

John Schmidt chuckled. 'Yup, thank God for community property.' They strolled back into the house.

ELEVEN

*The author in his book must be like God in his universe,
everywhere present and nowhere visible.*
                                        Gustave Flaubert

Ernest Mayday returned to see Oliver Sudden, the Electric
Italian. In earlier days Oliver had been known as the
Electric Wop, a nickname which had a better rhythm and
undoubtedly created a funnier mental picture. But the word
Wop was now considered offensive and racist, and was
never used in polite society, even though it was merely an
Ellis Island acronym for With-Out Papers. Wop, like
Kike, Yid, Jewboy, Nigger, Negro, *schwarze*, Red Indian,
Wog and Chink, was a forbidden noun in Los Angeles
society. Even the word Jap, Ernest noted, though merely
the short form of Japanese, was wholly *verboten* because it
had been used pejoratively in World War Two. Lenny
Bruce seemed to have lived in vain. The curious thing was
that the words asshole and motherfucker were in daily use
in all strata of LA life and were not apparently considered
vulgar or offensive by anyone.

Mayday had been summoned for a 'strategizing' meeting. This was in itself good news, for it seemed to signify
that the Electric W. liked the synopsis he had sent him.
He was right. In the event, Oliver's enthusiasm was
unrestrained, for he went so far as to open his own front
door as Ernest drove up, and he waved the synopsis at the
Englishman. 'This story outline is a real kick in the ass,'
he yelled exultantly, indicating that Ernest should step
inside.

Ernest was suddenly nervous. 'You mean, it's bad?'

'No. It's good.'

The first fifteen minutes of the strategizing meeting, devoted to Oliver's brief comments on the shape of the story, took place in his office. Then they jumped into his Jeep and zigzagged down Paseo Miramar to a café in the chic shopping mall in Palisades village, where they strategized over tall tumblers of iced tea. Twelve minutes later Oliver, with Ernest breathlessly in tow, was leaping back into the Jeep and strategizing as they headed for the house again – not the office, this time, but the garden. 'Can't you get iced tea at home?' Mayday had complained at the café as he tried to gulp the last third of his drink before being hurried away from the table. 'Can't you get iced tea at home?' he repeated querulously as he sat in the garden and surveyed the tea stains on his shirt.

'Sure, I got a housekeeper and a cook – and a wife and a daughter, come to that – I just get bored sitting in one place for all that time.'

'Less than half an hour?'

'Too long.'

'How long is too long?'

'Half an hour.' Sudden grinned at him. 'I get bored easy.'

Ernest Mayday managed to resist the almost overwhelming temptation to murmur 'easily'. Oliver intrigued him. He had never previously encountered an educated man with such a cavalier attitude to adverbs, nor had he ever before encountered anyone with such a low boredom threshold. As an ex-civil servant, his own tolerance for boredom was considerable. 'So how do you manage to stick it out all day at your office?'

'Easy. I never have a meeting longer than twenty-five minutes. Tops. Now, you gotta write the screenplay *fast*, OK? Virginia Spearmen is gonna be the new President of Production at the studio where I have my deal, nobody knows yet, OK, *nobody knows*.'

'So how do you know?'

'I know, I just know, OK, I know, take it from me, I know. You wanna know how I know, my nose is so far up her butt I'm nearly coming out of her mouth, OK? I want her to see this screenplay before her deal is nailed down three to four weeks from now. If we're late, that's a real kick in the ass.'

'You mean, that's good?'

'No. That's bad. The moment her deal leaks out she'll be swamped with every piece of shit in town, every dead script will be exhumed from every bottom drawer, dusted off and offered to her as if it's brand new, we gotta get a jump on them, can you do it in time, that's the question, can you do it in time?'

Ernest, who already had the completed script on his desk, pretended to think long and hard. 'Well, if I work flat out, day and night, if I start at five every morning . . .' He stuck his chin forward like Jack Hawkins in *The Cruel Sea* and murmured in his best heroic gritty voice, 'I think . . . maybe I can, yes.'

Oliver hugged him. 'You're great, you know what, you're *great*, this could be the start of something big, you pull this off, it'll be an incredible kick in the ass.'

It was clear that this time he meant that it would be good. Ernest found Oliver's all-purpose idioms refreshing. Who said that words should have to mean anything specific? Oliver was ushering him out into the vast old brick courtyard where his and Oliver's Mercedes were parked. 'Now if you got any problems with the script I want you to share them with me, OK? You're my partner. Partners, right?' Oliver extended his right hand for Ernest to shake.

'Partners, yes,' said Ernest, who had no intention of sharing his writing problems. He took the view that, when it came to writing with producers, a problem shared was a problem doubled. Nevertheless, he nodded agreeably and shook Oliver's hand. Oliver clapped him on the shoulder. 'You know how to find me, if I'm not at the office I'll be working out of my house.'

'You mean *in* your house?' asked Ernest, who was determined to get the hang of the local lingo.

'That's what I said, out of my house,' repeated Oliver. 'OK, write well, I'm gonna go hit the phones.'

Perhaps literally, thought Ernest, as he drove home in the sunshine, smiling and contented. This new rush to have the script written before Virginia Spearmen's deal was carved in stone meant that Oliver Sudden's 'input' would be severely curtailed, especially as Ernest planned to delay the delivery of any portion of the script until only a day or two before Ms Spearmen's appointment was announced in the trade papers. That night he took Randi out to a celebration dinner at the Olé Kosher Nostra.

'Have you a reservation?' asked the friendly maître d'.

'No.'

'Well, we should have a table soon.'

'How soon?'

'You're looking at five to seven minutes.'

While Ernest wondered how you look at minutes, Randi ordered mineral water. Then, to Ernest's disgust, Randi's robber bandit loony girlfriend Marge turned up. Randi hadn't mentioned to Ernest that they were to be a party of three. Ernest, though he had only met her a couple of times while she was divorcing Brad and making off with his house and his money, remembered her well, especially her attachment to EST, Lifespring, SCREAMS and all the other psychobabble seminars.

'Where've you been, haven't seen you for months?' he asked without the slightest trace of interest.

'Iraq.'

That got him. 'Iraq?' Mayday was mystified. 'Why did you go there?'

'Curiosity.'

'Was it gross?' Randi wanted to know.

'No, it was neat.'

'Neat?' Ernest didn't know what she meant. He had visions of a very tidy bazaar in Baghdad with everything nicely stacked and folded. 'Real neat,' she added by way of explanation and amplification.

'That's it? *Neat?*'

'There was only one disappointment. I didn't see an amputation.'

Mayday gaped. 'You *wanted* an amputation?'

'No, I didn't exactly want one, but . . . if one was going to happen I'd like to have been passing by, so I could've seen it. They often have them at four o'clock on Friday afternoons. I just didn't get lucky.' Ernest acquired a new perspective on Marge and Brad's expensive divorce. It was clear that Brad had got off lightly.

Later, driving home in the Mercedes 300E (what did E actually stand for? Exclusive? Not in West LA. Extortionate, presumably), he remarked that Brad was fortunate that he wasn't still married to her. Randi sighed. 'I know. But I think marriage must be neat with the right person,' she said, and snuggled up to him. Ernest didn't say anything. He no longer thought that there was such a thing as the right person. He thought Ellen had been the right person. He thought he had been the right person for Ellen. Randi watched him and knew what he was thinking.

Although Randi had rediscovered the joy of sex, and with a vengeance – the night that she returned from her Malibu rendezvous with Abel and John Schmidt she had astonished Ernest by appearing from the bathroom wearing red-and-black nylon open-crotch panties – Ernest was feeling less and less like making any kind of commitment to her. He enjoyed their love-making, now that she too approached it with an enthusiasm bordering on the greedy, but somehow – when he closed his eyes – he still saw only Joanna's calm grey eyes, her playful grin, her provocative walk, her cool casual attitude (both to men and to her own body) which had completely bewitched him. Randi, whether kissing or pumping iron, praying or making love, was never cool. On the contrary, she had become infused with a hot, fervent, committed, almost manic energy that went into both Scripture and sex and which Mayday was beginning to find slightly alarming.

Randi was now seriously interested in marrying Ernest. She had been persuaded by Abel Pile and John Schmidt that a marriage which would bring Ernest, his celebrity and his money into the Church and the Commune was God's work. This was to be no cynical move, at least not on Randi's part, for she was a true believer. She was now convinced that sex within marriage was a sacrament and that marriage to Ernest, if it was the only way to bring him into the fold, was God's work. If God's work involved fellatio or sitting on his face, so be it.

Freed from guilt, she was thoroughly enjoying her reawakened sensuality, and the moist, torrid, sweaty scenes that now took place regularly in Ernest's vast mirrored master bedroom were something to which, purposefully rejecting negativity, she found that she positively looked forward.

The more sexually energetic and enthusiastic she became, however, the more Ernest began to feel a primitive fear of engulfment that perhaps accounts for the ambivalence that many men feel when faced with a libidinous woman, which makes them both lust after them and yet mock them, using them with passion only to despise or discard them later with contemptuous sneers and locker-room jokes about man-eaters and nymphomaniacs. In her desire to fulfil God's wishes as revealed to her through the prophet Abel Pile her response to him had become so voracious and demanding that all of Ernest's old traumas with Ellen were reawakened. The more insatiable she became the more worried he was about his performance.

And so, as Ernest's relationship with Randi apparently heated up, his thoughts turned more and more to Joanna. This was partly because he had not yet tasted her, nor even touched her. She was hardly ever out of his mind. She was in his dreams and his day-dreams. Part of the attraction was the belief that she wanted nothing from him. She had never spoken of marriage, except as a loss of her freedom, and clearly she wanted no commitments from men other than short-term business arrangements. Whenever Randi and Ernest were making love his vision of Joanna, her sweet innocent smile that was in such contrast to her dirty laugh and lewd hints, his half-imagined fancies of her rapacious and lustful exploits with other men, seemed to give him the renewed virility and staying power that he needed.

But he knew he was scared of Joanna, which was why he kept his distance. For sex with Joanna did not have to remain a fantasy. He could easily have afforded her price, and she would not have made the pursuit long, difficult or tantalizing. Quite the reverse – all Ernest had to do was put his hand in his pocket. Even credit cards, indeed *all* major credit cards, would be accepted by Joanna. But he sensed that, like the Black Widow, her sexual power was potentially so threatening, her capacity for destruction of the male so overwhelming that although he wanted her he preferred to dream in safety. Tempting though she was, he chose not to buy Joanna for an hour for three hundred dollars, nor for a couple of months for ten thousand. He told himself that it was a matter of pride. If he couldn't have Joanna except at her hourly rate, it meant that he couldn't truly have her at all. In that sense she was hard to get, so much harder to get than Randi, and thus so much more attractive.

The more that he thought about Joanna, the more confident he was that his new book, *Flagrante Delicto*, could be about her. He began again with his meeting with Joanna in the bar of the Bel Monde Hotel. He still had his first three paragraphs stored in the computer's memory:

At the far end of the darkened hotel bar, a girl walked in. She looked around, hesitated in front of the opaque glass doors expensively engraved with art deco lilies, glanced at me, then sat at the bar. I watched her. She said something to the barman, who listened and shook his head.

She was slim, medium height, short brown hair with a forelock overhanging her forehead, minimal make-up, not unattractive but the sort of girl you wouldn't really notice unless you were trying to guess whether or not she'd come to meet you.

She ordered a Margarita, sipped it, then looked again at me. I felt a flutter in my chest. Was that Joanna? She slid down from the bar stool, straightened her tight black mini-skirt which had ridden up close to her crotch, and walked towards me. 'Are you Mr de Plume?'

He was about to continue, but he hesitated. Without thinking, he had written the first three paragraphs in the first person.

He couldn't go on. He had plenty to write about now, even though he didn't know where the tale might end: there was his first meeting with her at the Bel Monde when he learned what her ad really meant, there was the third meeting at Hamburger Hamlet when she looked so different with her own long blonde hair and she told him of the letter from John Schmidt, there was her encounter with John Schmidt and his hiring her to nobble a juror. It was a good start to his kind of book and, while he awaited the next developments, Ernest knew that he could certainly write a spicy scene in which Schmidt examined her credentials, and other euphemisms.

But why, he asked himself, had he automatically started writing in the first person? He would have to change that. He certainly didn't want people to think that the book was autobiographical. He would not want people to think that he ever suffered from writers' block, nor that he had bought his plot from some hooker. He was proud of his popular reputation as a spinner of yarns and a teller of tales. In numerous interviews with the press he had played the master storyteller, making much of his meticulous research, explaining that he studied what he called his arena until he was so familiar with it that he could simply go to his desk, sit down and make up the whole story.

Ernest was perversely proud that he had never written about anything that had happened to him nor anything that touched him personally. Admittedly, he had set his two previous books in places that were familiar to him, the City and Whitehall. But Gstaad, Monte Carlo and Aspen also loomed large in his books, and he had never been to any of them until long after they were both written and he had become a bestselling author. He had never set foot on a private yacht (though he had described several in detail), he had never bought a designer suit (though Ellen had once given him a designer tie for Christmas), when he started writing he didn't know a Smith and Wesson from a Magnum .357, and he was profoundly uninterested in brand names of every kind. All the hot brand names in his books were taken from a list compiled by Becky, his patient and long-suffering copy editor at Cockerel Books, and he then inserted them at regular intervals into the finished text, just like the sex scenes.

More than one journalist had hinted that the lack of personal content was the reason why his books were considered third-rate by the literary press. When questioned about his lukewarm reviews he always managed to sink to the occasion: 'You must never believe what you read in the papers,' he admonished one interviewer-cum-critic, 'especially if you wrote it.' When asked on another occasion why he revealed so little of himself, he quoted Nietzsche: 'I am one thing, my writings are another.' But even his publisher Mark Down, whose lease on a crumbling early Georgian heap just off Bedford Square would shortly expire and who desperately wanted him to continue writing the same sort of saleable stuff (only better, of course), had casually mentioned that he should perhaps consider writing something just a *little* less mechanical and more personal. Ernest exploded. 'I've made you a fuck of a lot of money,' he snarled, 'so fuck off, OK?' Mark had back-pedalled immediately but Ernest was left fuming for weeks because the criticism just wouldn't go away.

Now, here he was about to embark on a tale of a Hollywood expatriate British writer and a hooker. The potential for embarrassment was considerable. Everyone would assume that he was writing about himself, and the fact that they would be right didn't make it any better.

Or would they be right? Ernest wondered. For where does fiction end and autobiography begin? If her real-life story proved more interesting than his fantasies (which, God knows, was more than likely) he'd go with real life. None the less, he would still have to fictionalize the story superficially, both for reasons of legal safety and because art needs to have a better shape than life. Ernest decided that if people thought he was the novelist in the book, so be it. But one thing was certain: he did not intend to reveal any more of himself than in his previous books, nor would he delve uncomfortably into his own feelings. What Joanna discovered, and what happened to her as a result, he told himself, was nothing but research. What happened (if anything) between Joanna and him was nobody else's business.

TWELVE

Every morning, to earn my bread
I go to the market where lies are bought.
Hopefully
I take up my place among the sellers.
                                        Bertolt Brecht

Nearly a month after they met to strategize, Oliver Sudden let Ernest Mayday know that Virginia Spearmen's new job would remain confidential for only one more week. In other words, half the film community already knew about it and someone would leak it to the trades any day now. Accordingly Mayday delivered his screenplay to the Sudden mansion, secure in the knowledge that it would be read overnight. It was. Oliver phoned, pronounced it great (Ernest expected nothing less, great being the minimum Hollywood praise) and summoned him to his clifftop home for more strategy.

They sat under a massive eucalyptus beside the huge blue pool, which was an irregular shape surrounded at one end by weeping willows, landscaped so that it looked more like a pond than a pool. Mexican gardeners toiled in the distance, out in the midday sun. The Englishman sat in the shade and drank more iced tea. Oliver didn't have time to drink anything, he was talking so fast. 'OK, so we deliver this script to Ginnie Spearmen, we deliver it today, OK, we tell her that three other majors are interested in it . . .'

'Are they?' interrupted Ernest, surprised.

'They will be,' said Oliver. 'So, let's tell her that four other majors are interested . . .'

Ernest interrupted again. 'You said three.'

'Let's make it four.' Oliver was decisive. 'OK, we tell her that four other majors are interested, let me finish, we give her till lunchtime tomorrow to respond.'

'What if she doesn't?'

'She will.'

He was right. Three days later, Virginia Spearmen's appointment was announced and the following morning Ernest trooped into her spacious new office with Oliver and two of his Creative Development Executive Vice-presidents, Chuck (who didn't look old enough to have left high school though it turned out that he'd majored in film criticism at UC Santa Barbara and his father was a major major agent), and Tiffani (who had shoulder-length golden hair and a great ass, though Oliver insisted that she also had a great story sense and that was why he'd given her the job straight out of college). Both had perfect large white Californian teeth. Before the big meeting they all assembled in Oliver's office for a serious and urgent discussion of how to handle Virginia Spearmen.

'Chuck and Tiffani have read our script,' explained Oliver. Ernest realized that Oliver meant his script.

'It's great,' said Chuck.

'Really great, really *really* great,' emphasized Tiffani, the sincerity turned up to full.

'It's so intelligent,' said Chuck.

'It's *beyond* intelligent,' enthused Tiffani.

'Thank you,' said Ernest, 'I'm quite pleased with it myself.' He wondered what beyond intelligent meant. He couldn't let it pass. 'What does beyond intelligent mean?'

'Really neat,' she said.

Chuck was perturbed. 'You're only *quite* pleased with it?'

Oliver reassured them. 'He's British, he's a tight-ass, he means he loves it, he just can't say it.' Oliver kicked off his shoes. 'Now, Chuck, what's the game plan?'

'We tell her why she should make this deal.'

'Good. Why should she?'

'OK, we tell her it's based on a book which is a major bestseller, that it's been optioned no less than nine times by various producers and studios but it has always been held in a major holding pattern till now because no one could ever see how to make it. It's easy to adapt long novels into mini-series but no one could see how to compress a book this big into a two-hour theatrical feature film till you and Ernest had a brilliant insight and saw how to do it. We tell her that Ernest wrote the script in less than three weeks so that she could get a first look as soon as she took the job, we tell her that if she greenlights it it should be easy to cast.' He paused. 'That kind of stuff, right?'

Chuck sat back in his Eames chair, waiting for approval. None was forthcoming. 'Wrong, wrong, wrong!' denounced Oliver emphatically, leaping to his socked feet. 'Completely fucking wrong.' Then he waited. But Chuck and Tiffani were in a silent panic, frantically trying to work out why. Ernest had no such inhibitions, he didn't have a job to lose. 'Why is it wrong? Everything he said about the project was true, wasn't it?'

'True? Maybe.' Oliver shrugged. 'So what? We're pitching a movie, not trying a court case. Is Virginia Spearmen gonna grab us as we walk into the office, thrust a Bible into our hands and make us swear to tell the truth, the whole truth and nothing but the fucking truth?'

'No, but ...' Ernest was intrigued. 'Well ... what should we say, then?'

'First I'll tell you what you don't say, OK? You don't say it's been optioned nine times ...'

'Doesn't that show how many people have thought it

would make a good movie?' interrupted a slightly defensive Chuck.

'It also shows that *nine times* people have put up money for the book and nine times they've run into problems. We don't say anything negative, Nothing negative, OK? Nothing negative, get that, only positive, we only say things that are positive, nothing negative, only things that'll make Ginnie want to buy, nothing that'll put any doubts in her mind, OK?' Ernest was struck not only by the ferocious speed of Oliver's speech, not only by the fact that he said everything at least twice to make sure that it had been taken on board, but also by his absolute refusal to countenance the expression of any negative thoughts. So like that other Californian super salesman, he thought, so like Abel Pile.

Oliver was off and running, pacing around the room, punching the air, the wall and the desk for emphasis. 'So, we don't tell her it's been optioned nine times. We don't tell her no one could see how to adapt it – why suggest there was a problem? We don't tell her it's not easy to adapt a long book into a two-hour movie, we list five big books that have become hundred-million-dollar movies, for instance *The Hunt for Red October*, *The Color Purple*, *Dr Zhivago*, *Lawrence of Arabia* . . .'

Ernest interrupted him again. 'That wasn't based on a novel.'

Oliver stared at him blankly. 'There was a book, wasn't there?'

'If you mean Lawrence's autobiography *The Seven Pillars Of Wisdom*, yes,' replied Ernest carefully in his best Oxford Senior Common Room voice. 'And there was a biography of Lawrence by Anthony Nutting, I believe. But . . .'

'So whaddya telling me? I don't get it. There was a book, two books even. We tell her about some *big* hit movies that were based on books, that's what I said, right? What we *don't* do is utter the words 'mini-series', we don't even let it cross her mind that our movie might really be television. Big mistake. Big. BIG. Next, we don't tell her it was written in three weeks flat, not even specially for her, she'll think it's a botched job, rushed, hurried, not thought out properly, she'll tell us it needs work, come back when we've fixed all the problems. No, what we do is write "Third Draft" on the title page, that way she'll think we've been into all the problems, spent money on three drafts from you (and I'll tell her you don't come cheap), taken two more passes at the script and ironed out all the glitches, and we're ready to cut a deal and go make the fuckin' movie.'

Ernest was deeply impressed. 'I see.'

'Wait, I'm not through yet, let me finish. You know what else we don't tell her? We don't tell her we can cast it if she greenlights it, she knows that, she's not stupid, she's a bright cookie, what she wants to hear is that everyone is all jazzed up about our movie already, she's gotta feel that she's got one chance, just one chance, to jump on a bandwagon that's already moving, to get on the train as it's pulling out of the station. This ship is sailing – the only question is, is she gonna be on board?' He looked around the room and waited.

'How do we make her feel she's gotten this one chance, Oliver?' asked Tiffani sincerely, dead on cue.

'We name the cast and the director.'

Ernest sat up. 'You're the director, right?'

'Maybe.'

'What do you mean, maybe? Everyone told me you're going to direct it.'

'Everyone? Who's everyone?'

'My lawyer, my agent . . .'

'Who's your agent?'

'Fanny Rush.'

'I don't know her, who's your lawyer?'

'Dylan Kanpinchowitz.'

Oliver beamed. 'I know Dylan, you ever play golf with him?'

Ernest knew he was being skilfully deflected. 'What's this about your not directing it?'

'I didn't say that, I said maybe. So, we'll tell her I may direct it, we'll name the cast . . . '

'But I didn't know we had a cast.'

'We don't, we don't, but we *will*, right? She'll ask us who we have in mind. We'll round up the usual suspects, Mel Gibson, Robin Williams, Arnold Schwarzenegger, Eddie Murphy, whoever's hot.'

'Arnold Schwarzenegger?' Ernest was astounded. 'Which part could he play?'

'Where does an eight-hundred-pound gorilla sit?' asked Oliver. Tiffani and Chuck answered in unison: '*Wherever he likes!*' They all laughed happily. Ernest stared at them. Oliver explained. 'Arnold's an eight-hundred-pound gorilla, meaning he's the biggest movie star in the world, he can play any part he wants to play.'

'But there isn't a part that's right for him.'

'So we'll rewrite it for him.'

'How?'

'OK, OK!' Oliver backed away from a needless confrontation. 'I'm not saying he has to be in the movie, I'm just talking about how we pitch it, OK? We mention a lot of hot actors who could be in it, then directors'll come up, she'll want to know about directors, she'll want me to commit but I don't know yet if I can so we'll say maybe me but if I can't I'll be executive producer *and* Spielberg has read it and he's interested too.'

'I know we're not on oath,' asked Chuck, 'but is that true?'

'It could be true,' replied Oliver with a smile.

'What if she checks up?' Ernest was by now profoundly impressed with Oliver's manipulative skill.

'He's filming in Africa, Virginia's gotta make up her

mind long before she can get ahold of him, we're giving her a deadline, remember? If she buys it I'll get him on the phone somehow and by the time I've finished talking to him he *will* be interested, that's a promise. Now, next, we have to strategize the meeting itself.'

'I thought we just did that.' Ernest was having trouble keeping up with all the deception.

'No, all I did so far was tell you guys what *not* to say. So now, what *do* we say?' His three students looked at each other. None of them wanted to speak. They knew they were sitting at the feet of the master. They wanted to listen and learn. He grinned. 'OK. This is the play. We go in. I introduce Ernest, I give you a big build-up, then you talk.'

Ernest was aghast. 'Me? I can't pitch a movie. What do I know about Spielberg and Arnold Schwarzenegger?'

'Nothing. I know that.' Oliver was impatient. 'So, you tell her a joke.'

'Tell her a joke?' Ernest repeated, thinking he'd misheard.

'You remember that joke you told me about the Irishman and the porch, tell her that.'

'Why?'

'It's funny. It'll make her laugh.'

'But it's nothing to do with the movie.'

'That's the idea. But she'll like you, she'll think you're a funny guy instead of some up-tight, tight-ass English novelist, we don't want her to be nervous of you, we want her to see you as a regular guy and not some sort of over-educated intellectual like Noël Coward. OK, so, now you've made her laugh, we're on first base, now I'll tell her some gossip, what's going on around town, anything rather than talk about the movie. OK, so we're at least ten minutes into a half-hour meeting, now we pitch her the idea of the movie in two or three sentences.'

'How do we do that?'

'We tell her the title, tell her it's a romantic comedy –
romantic comedies are hot – tell her it's very funny yet
very warm . . . '

'Hot *and* warm,' murmured Ernest to himself.

'Won't she have read it?' asked Chuck.

'Sure. Well, maybe. We'll only messenger it to her the
night before, so she doesn't have too long to consider it.
But even if she's read it all she'll only have read the *words*,
they're just a blueprint, we're pitching the movie, the
concept, the marketing, the wanna-see ingredient, the
reason why people'll put up seven-fifty to go see it on the
opening weekend. We're telling her why she should buy it.
So then she'll ask us about the numbers.'

'What numbers?' asked Ernest, truly amazed. 'You
mean, musical numbers?'

'No. The numbers. The budget.'

'Oh,' Ernest relaxed. 'I see, the figures.'

'So,' Oliver turned to Chuck. 'What's this budgeted at,
ballpark?'

'It's only a guestimate,' replied Chuck. 'Eight million,
below the line. But with the kind of above-the-line names
you've been mentioning it's a whole different ballgame,
could be forty or fifty mill.'

'OK. We'll tell her seventeen, all in.'

'But Oliver . . . ' Chuck began. Oliver brushed him
aside.

'Listen, Chuck, it's simple: eighteen is the average
budget for a picture today. We pitch it at one million less,
it sounds like she's getting a great deal.'

'We can't tell her she'll get Spielberg and Arnold all in,
for seventeen mill,' remonstrated Chuck. 'What if she
takes us up on it?'

Oliver sighed and rolled his eyes heavenwards. Why
were they all such dunces? 'She wouldn't, she knows, she's
running a studio, she knows it'll cost more if we get those
guys, and you know what – she wouldn't care! OK, enough

about the numbers, I'll handle that part of it. You guys be sure to agree with anything I say, be impressed at Ernest's track record, laugh at his joke. Ernest, I'll hand it back to you to tell her all that good stuff about how many copies you sold, hardback and paperback, how many languages you been translated into and therefore what a humungous audience there is for this film, especially foreign, worldwide, not just Europe. Then you tell her what it was like when you went to the Palace and met the Queen . . . '

'I didn't. I haven't.'

'She doesn't know that, you're English, you're famous, she'll believe it – and believe me, she's a sucker for royalty. Trust me. So you keep talking till I decide it's time for us to go, and that way we don't have to say any more about the numbers or the cast.'

'How will I know?'

'Know? Know what?'

'When it's time to go.'

'I'll give you a signal.'

'What signal?'

Oliver thought for a moment, then he had an inspiration. 'I'll take off my shoe,' he said. They were ready for the meeting.

Virginia Spearmen's office was very beige and spacious and had two secretaries sitting in the ante-room. She only kept them waiting two or three minutes. He hadn't known what to expect, but he met a strikingly attractive tall blonde woman, slim (of course), large mouth, wearing a white linen double-breasted jacket, a silk tie, co-respondent's brogues – in fact, she was dressed pretty much the way he had always imagined Bugsy Segal would dress. Maureen O'Connor, a slim young woman with a pale face and auburn hair, introduced herself to them as a VP and offered them decafs, sodas, Pellegrino or popcorn.

Oliver introduced Ernest to Virginia. 'This is Ernest Mayday, from England. He's been a novelist for years, but now he's a writer.'

To start with, the meeting went exactly as planned. Oliver gave Ernest a big build-up, then spontaneously appeared to remember that Ernest had told him a very funny Irish joke. They all urged Ernest to tell it, especially Tiffani and Chuck. Virginia's several assistants or vice-presidents were also all agog.

'Well,' began Ernest, 'an Irish odd-job man comes to the front door, rings the bell, and a yuppie answers it. "Hello," says the Irishman, tugging his forelock. "Oi wonder, have you got any odd jobs that oi can do for you sir?"' Ernest was speaking in a thick Irish brogue. '"If t'ere's anyt'ing oi can do for ya, any odd jobs, t'at sort of t'ing, know what oi mean, sirr?" So the yuppie says: "Well, yes, actually, my man, there *is* something I need doing. Go round to the side of the house, you'll find a large pot of white paint there. I want you to paint the porch." "T'ank you, sirr, t'ank you," says the Irishman. "God bless you, sirr," and off he goes round the side of the house to find the paint and the porch. Well, half an hour later the front doorbell rings again, the yuppie opens the door, and there's the Irishman. "Sirr, oi've finished, oi've painted the porch, 'tis all done." "Thanks very much," said the yuppie, rather surprised. "How did you do it so quickly? Have you painted the whole porch?" "Oh yes, sirr," replied the Irishman emphatically, "the whole porch is completely painted white, every bit, every little bit of it. There is one t'ing oi t'ink oi ought to mention, though – it's not a Porch, it's a BMW."'

Everyone rocked with laughter. 'Cute joke, isn't it?' said Oliver.

Maureen O'Connor wasn't laughing. 'Don't you think that kind of ethnic joke is a little out of date?' she asked, very cool.

'Politically incorrect, is it?' smiled Ernest. 'I'm sorry, Maureen, it's just a joke, I'm certainly not anti-Irish, my ex-wife Ellen was Irish, as a matter of fact.'

'I just wanted to point out', replied Ms O'Connor, undeterred, 'that those kind of jokes seem slightly out of place in an equal opportunities corporation.'

'Ellen was all for equal opportunities too,' said Ernest. 'She was an equal opportunities wife. She believed in getting laid by everyone, regardless of race, creed, religion . . .'

Everyone broke up. Even Maureen smiled. 'Funny guy, see?' said Oliver but immediately changed the subject and started to discuss studio politics over at Warners. After ten minutes or so Virginia suggested they discuss *Lies*. All went well till Chuck mentioned Arnold Schwarzenegger. 'There's no part in this he could play, is there?' she asked. 'Henry's a wimp.'

They all glanced at each other. So she had read it. 'In the *book*, Henry's a wimp, yes,' agreed Oliver cautiously, sitting up.

Ernest jumped in, eager to agree with her. 'Virginia, I think you're right. Schwarzenegger's great, but I think that the part should be played a lot older, I mean, the man is reaching retirement.'

Now Ms Spearmen sat up. Slowly she lifted her feet off the glass-topped coffee table. 'Retirement?' She was alarmed. 'But we want this picture to be young and hip, don't we?'

Oliver Sudden knew how to take a cue. 'Young and hip, yes, that's it exactly, that's exactly what this picture is gonna be, young and hip, boom boom boom, young and hip.' He looked at Chuck and Tiffani. 'Young and hip,' they chorused. 'Boom boom boom!' Virginia seemed to relax a little.

After a cursory discussion of the numbers she asked about the start date. 'Right away,' said Oliver, 'just as soon as we have the deals in place, the cast lined up, we can start prepping to shoot late fall.' Immediately he turned to Ernest and told him to tell Ginnie about what happened when he met the Queen. Ernest extemporized for two or three minutes, trying to remember what anyone who met the Queen had ever told him about her. All he could remember was that she was very short, so he talked about that for a while, about how surprised he'd been that she was such a titch and about how Princess Margaret was even titchier and Lord Snowden was a real shortarse too as a matter of fact, in fact *all* the royals were really, even the corgis had very short legs. It rapidly became clear that Virginia was not as much of a sucker for royalty as Oliver had thought, for her eyes started wandering and she glanced at her watch.

'Why am I telling you all this?' he said. 'I can see you couldn't care less about Her Majesty, I'll shut up about her.'

'Thanks,' she said, flashing a gorgeous smile at him. 'Oliver told you to tell me all that shit, to distract me from discussing the project, right?'

Ernest didn't know how to answer diplomatically. Oliver came to the rescue. 'Yup, my fault,' he admitted with his disarming grin.

'You're such a bullshitter, Oliver,' she told him. She seemed amused rather than upset.

'Well, that was my strategy. Actually, I did think you'd be interested in the Queen, but . . . hey! You wanna know the rest of my strategy for this meeting?'

'You bet.' Virginia sat up. She was really interested now.

'I told him to talk about the Queen till I gave him the signal that it was time to leave.'

She laughed. 'Maybe you'd better give him the signal now,' she suggested.

'OK,' agreed Oliver cheerfully. He looked at Ernest. 'What was the signal, I can't remember?'

Everyone in the room was laughing now. 'You were going to take off your shoe,' Ernest reminded him. More laughter.

'Oh yeah,' shouted Oliver, took off his shoe and waved it in the air. Now they were all screaming with laughter.

'OK, here's a signal from me, the meeting's over,' yelled Virginia, pulling off her shoe and waving it above her head. Amid gales of laughter everyone in the room yanked off their shoes and, waving them around their heads, hobbled out of the room, wheezing, gasping, wiping tears away from their eyes.

After the meeting Oliver, Ernest, Chuck and Tiffani stood and deliberated in the parking-lot. 'Great meeting,' they all agreed.

'Do you think she'll greenlight it?' asked Ernest.

'Not yet, we don't have a cast,' said Oliver. 'But she'll put it on their fast track for progress to production – if we give it to her.'

Ernest was baffled. 'Well ... why wouldn't we? I thought that's what we wanted.'

'She's gotta make us the right offers. OK, leave me alone, now I gotta jump on the phone and tell the other studios that Virginia's made us an offer.' Oliver waved them away, and began talking on his car phone.

'It's been a real pleasure to meet you, a real *real* pleasure,' said Tiffani, sincerely.

Chuck was equally sincere. 'A real pleasure, sir,' he agreed.

Originality wasn't Chuck's strongest suit, thought Ernest, but at least he was respectful. Ernest liked that.

THIRTEEN

Everything and nothing in my work is autobiographical.
Federico Fellini

While awaiting the outcome of the meeting with Virginia Spearmen, Ernest Mayday continued work on his book. He had only met Joanna four times, however, and it wasn't long before he ran out of material and found himself killing time, waiting for her next call. He was agitated, anxious, unable to occupy himself, for these days Ernest Mayday was finding reading almost as difficult as writing. He seemed to have lost the knack of reading large novels and was suffering from readers' block no less than writers' block. Perhaps they were intertwined, for reading also requires that you first gain access to your own mind. Mentally scattered, unable to focus on anything except the most transient and trivial, he spent many tense hours on his sun-drenched terrace under the lemon trees reading the newspapers from cover to cover, even the baseball and basketball coverage. He read both the *LA Times* and *The New York Times*, although they were awfully similar. Eventually he became engrossed in the controversy about capital punishment which was raging – not whether or not it was right to execute people, but whether or not the executions should be televised.

Ernest had always regarded public execution as a sign of barbarism and assumed that the British had taken a giant stride along the long and difficult road to civilization on the day that public hangings were abolished and the gruesome and painful deaths of convicts were no longer presented as a public spectacle. The idea that the death of a fellow human being could be an excuse for a day out at Tyburn, a family picnic with grandma and the kids followed by the entertainment spectacular of watching someone choke to death seemed to belong to the dark ages, to Nero's degenerate Roman circuses, to the tumbrils of 1789 and the lynch mobs of crazed fundamentalists in the streets of Tehran in the aftermath of the Ayatollah's succession. Yet serious Americans were now proposing – nay, insisting – that executions in the gas chamber, in the electric chair, on the gallows, should be televised.

As he sipped his decaf and Consuela's freshly squeezed orange juice one morning he read in a *New York Times* leader that 'the state has sequestered an important, controversial government process without any compelling reason. That seems an abridgement of the First Amendment.' The First Amendment, Ernest knew, was the one that guaranteed freedom of speech. Ernest couldn't see how freedom of speech had much to do with it. He did realize, however belatedly, that Marge, who had wanted to see a public amputation in Iraq, was expressing a perfectly respectable view: that any act by the state should be completely available for public scrutiny, and it is not for the government (or anybody) to limit what the media may show to the public. In the cause of free speech liberal intellectuals – who might otherwise have scorned (at least in public) the pornography of killing on television – could be found defending this ultimate act of voyeurism. It made him feel better about the idea of relating Joanna's real life experiences as she seduced a juror, for if the morality of the 'snuff' movie could be justified by the First Amendment, the voyeurism of his book somehow paled into insignificance.

Ernest felt comfortable in America. A society in which

the morality of the peeping Tom was protected by the Constitution was clearly an excellent environment not only for journalists but for other writers too. Yet Ernest remained puzzled by what was protected and what was not. Hard-core pornographic films were showing at the Pussycat Theater down on Santa Monica Boulevard, and at the All Nude Theater not a mile from his home he understood that naked girl dancers would show absolutely everything to frustrated men for a couple of dollars' tip. Though such entertainment was unquestionably sexist when offered to men, it would presumably be politically correct if any lesbians could be found to watch such an exhibition and, as such, qualified as freedom of expression. Yet a performance of sexual intercourse, though readily available to the public if rented from the 'adult' section of every video store, was apparently not protected as freedom of expression if it were performed live in front of an audience. He discussed this pressing matter at Jerry's poker game that Wednesday evening.

'What I can't figure out,' said Ernest, 'is what constitutes free speech that's protected by the First Amendment, and what constitutes pornography that's punishable by law.'

'It's very simple,' replied Max Period Kirsch, as gloomily as ever. 'It's the old question of pornography versus art. Pornography is whatever turns the district attorney on.' They all chuckled, and Max.'s deeply tanned leathery face creased with pleasure. It had a number of purply-pink patches, from which small cancerous growths had recently been removed. He came from that older generation of Californians who hadn't known about the ozone layer and who had never worn sunblock creams as they drove their chromium-fronted convertibles around town. He didn't seem concerned, however, because he'd been told the problem was nothing to worry about and Southern California was comfortingly full of elderly men and women, the golden girls and boys of previous generations, who now went around with slightly piebald faces.

Ernest always looked forward to the poker game at Jerry's. As all four men were professional writers they had absolutely no interest in discussing literature, unless it was to trash the latest work of some mutual friend. 'I don't resent anybody else's success, unless they happen to be friends of mine,' explained Sidney Byte courteously when Ernest chided him once for lack of charity. 'Overly successful friends are always a little hard to take, don't you think?'

Ernest, Sidney, Max. and Jerry would, like all writers, confine their professional conversations to complaints about their agents, their publishers, their studio bosses, and the non (or late) payment of royalties and residuals, these being the issues that preoccupy writers in their daily lives somewhat more than the love of literature or the meaning of life. The three Americans loved to discuss politics and in these discussions they, with the natural paranoia of all employed writers, invariably took the side of the underdog although all of them were unmistakably overdogs. Capitalist, conservative and *laissez-faire* in their business dealings, their rhetoric was left over from their youth and was that of Roosevelt Democrats.

Furthermore, being elderly, they still suffered some residual depression from the Depression. And like most rich Hollywood liberals with no experience of government or politics other than the payment of campaign contributions, they were utterly confident that they knew the answers to all the nation's ills. Ernest, on the other hand, fresh from the Treasury, was coming to the conclusion that although economics was called a social science it was not a science at all, probably not even an art, more like a series of deeply held religious beliefs. Unlike his zealous New Deal friends, Ernest was an ecomomics agnostic, and he preferred to discuss show business.

'Let me tell you about my pitch meeting with Oliver Sudden,' said Ernest as they sat down to play, eager to share his latest lunatic experience.

'I hear he's really an asshole,' remarked Max., dealing the cards.

'Yes and no,' said Ernest.

'You're so *English*,' drawled Sidney, with feigned contempt as he studied the cards in his hand. "Yes and no", what kind of answer is that? Can't you be a little more definite, man, which is it, yes or no, is he an asshole or isn't he?'

'Your problem', countered Ernest good-humouredly, 'is that you Americans are not comfortable with ambivalence. Which, by the way, is why you don't understand irony in this country. You like everything to be definite and clear-cut, good guys v. bad guys, black hats and white hats, that's why you all voted for Ronald Reagan. You don't understand Europeans because we *like* ambivalence, we're comfortable with not having to make up our minds about anything, we like having things both ways.'

'Well, in my view we were right to vote for Reagan and Bush,' said Jerry. Jerry was younger than Sidney and Max. with a thoroughly un-Hollywood beer-belly bulging over his belt. He had the sort of figure that you saw in other parts of California, a state which contained both the most emaciated and the most obese men and women on earth.

'Who cares about Reagan and Bush any more?' sneered Sidney.

Jerry enjoyed provoking Sidney by paying compliments to the Gipper. 'Ronald Reagan's the man who brought the Soviet industrial military complex to its knees and George Bush ended the Cold War. We Americans showed great wisdom in electing them.'

'I hope that's ironic enough for you,' Sidney growled, and flicked his long greying hair out of his eyes as he ate a huge messy mouthful of pastrami on rye. 'Apparently Reagan was a great statesman after all,' he added, wiping most of the mustard off his beard and moustache with a paper napkin. 'Apparently we were all completely wrong in thinking he was just a senile old actor.'

'That's right,' agreed Max., his rheumy brown eyes twinkling. Ascetic and skinny, he was picking at a pickled cucumber. 'He was a statesman.'

'A statesman is just a retired politician,' said Ernest.

'That's almost an epigram,' complained Sidney, as bits of red meat, mustard and crusts exploded out of his mouth and cascaded over the small pile of accumulated coins in the middle of Jerry's kitchen table. 'Do we have to take this Oscar Wilde shit from you?'

Ernest smiled. 'Are you suggesting', he inquired as he discarded a two of clubs and looked at Jerry, 'that Reagan and Bush knew what they were doing?'

'Are *you* suggesting', replied Jerry, 'that *any* politicians know what they're doing?'

Sidney was getting irritable. 'Look, Reagan may have inadvertently ended the Cold War with his schoolboy threats of Star Wars, but what about the recession here?' Sidney's question was rhetorical. 'What about all the homeless out there in the cold, on Ocean Avenue?'

'This is California,' said Max. 'Many are cold but few are frozen.' The others chuckled. Pleased, Max. twisted open a beer bottle and took a swig. He seemed completely satisfied with his answer, somehow feeling that his joke had made some useful contribution to the problem of the homeless.

'My difficulty with Reagan was that he believed in Nancy's astrologers,' said Sidney. 'Remember all that? Imagine! The finger on the nuclear button, dependent on that sort of superstition.'

'Didn't bother me,' said Ernest, studying his cards. 'I don't see any objective difference between a belief in astrology and a belief in God. Except that there's slightly more empirical evidence to support a belief in astrology.'

Max. smiled. 'You know, I never thought of that, but it's perfectly true,' he agreed.

Jerry leaned back in his chair, sweating as always. His pallid face was wider than it was long. This was a man who seldom saw the sun. He was enjoying Ernest, and he egged him on. 'Why d'you keep going on about God?'

'Yeah, give God a break, *puh-lease*,' exhorted Sidney. 'Why don't you?'

'You wouldn't if you lived with Randi.' Ernest defended himself. 'She's obsessed.'

'So who should we trust if we can't trust God?' asked Jerry, ambling over to the fridge to pick up a cream soda. 'Scientists?'

'God forbid!' said Ernest.

'More irony,' explained Sidney to the others, in a sardonic stage whisper. He cut the deck.

Ernest ignored him. 'We can't trust scientific discoveries, they keep getting out-dated. Look at Galileo, Copernicus, Newton, Einstein. Science is merely about the reproduceablity of experience, whereas religion is much more interesting: it's about killing your enemy while claiming that you love him.'

'But Ernest . . . I thought scientists had replaced God in your atheistic universe,' said Max.

'Certainly not,' said Ernest. 'Scientists are the people who brought us the hydrogen bomb and can't cure the common cold. At least God can't do us any harm.'

Max. put his cards down and stared at Ernest with genuine interest and astonishment. 'Can't do us any harm?' he said. 'At Bergen-Belsen millions of Jews who did not believe in Christ were murdered by a few thousand men and women who did.'

Ernest slugged back his Jack Daniel's on the rocks. 'Yes, but Max! God didn't create religion. It's the other way round. God is a fictional character, we invented Him.'

'I had nothing to do with it,' said Sidney defensively. 'Don't blame me, OK?'

'God is just a peculiarly capricious character in the world's oldest and most potent book,' Ernest continued, ignoring him still. 'If you say that God's responsible for the state of the world, you might as well say that Hamlet is. Or Oedipus.'

'Oedipus *was* responsible for the state of his world,' remarked Max. irrelevantly.

'You see, what I can't agree with', intervened a languid Sidney, leaning back in his chair, 'is the notion that fiction is less damaging than religion. Quite frankly, I think you underestimate the effects of bad fiction.' The others laughed.

'And as for *good* fiction,' added Max., 'if God is an example of it, then the pen *is* mightier than the sword.'

'Look, I'm tired of God, OK?' intervened Jerry. 'OK? This is a poker game, not a fucking theology class. I thought you were going to tell us about pitching *Lies* with Oliver Sudden.'

'Do we have to hear this?' whined Sidney, now deep into the tub of coleslaw. 'I'm not sure that I can bear to hear about any more of your fucking successes.'

'I thought you wanted to know about Oliver Sudden?' Ernest said

'No,' said Sidney. 'He's a movie mogul. What's he got to do with me? I'm never going to have any dealings with him, he's stratospheric. I'm a TV writer, I'm not open to acquiring any knowledge I can't use.'

The others grinned. Sidney was on fine *kvetching* form that night. 'Listen, Sidney,' said Jerry good-humouredly. 'Max. and I want to hear all about it, so shut up.'

Ernest told them the whole story. When he got to Oliver's shoe signal, even this hard-bitten bunch was incredulous. 'I've only just heard of this person', remarked Max. with reluctant respect, 'and already I'm having to revise my opinion of him.'

The consensus of opinion around Jerry's kitchen table was that so long as Oliver Sudden was pushing it, Ernest's screenplay would be bought, if not by Virginia Spearmen then by somebody, and that Ernest was about to become even richer. They all behaved as if they were absolutely disgusted by this, and amid the ribbing and hilarity that this elaborate performance of disgust and envy produced they were able to hide their true feelings of disgust and envy.

After the game, at which Ernest won more than three hundred dollars, they sat out on Jerry's pink-tiled terrace, overlooking the city. Unusually for midsummer it was a clear night, there having been a brisk wind from the ocean the day before. Some small intense twinkling lights slowly moved across the distant deep blue cyclorama of the sky like half a dozen Stars of Bethlehem, westward leading, still proceeding, before landing at Los Angeles International Airport just south of Venice Beach. 'Tell us about your new book,' said Max.

'I told you before, it's about an English writer in Hollywood.'

'Not another fucking Hollywood novel?' exclaimed Sidney in his most aggrieved tone.

Ernest considered that comment for a moment. 'Well . . . it's set in Hollywood. But it's not about Hollywood, really.'

'So why not set it in England?'

'Because I'm here. And because this is the place where the difference between fact and fiction, between fantasy and reality, is the most blurred.'

'Tell me,' said Max., 'I wouldn't really know, because I don't write prose, I write dialogue, and I seldom write a soliloquy or, as we call it in the movies, a voice-over. But you, as a novelist, have a sort of omnipotence, don't you? I mean, you can tell us what your characters think, and how they feel. You describe their souls, their essence. Doesn't that make writing a novel a dangerously personal thing to do?'

Ernest Mayday felt he was confronted both with his own inadequacy and his own intimacy. Rather than reply, he smiled enigmatically.

'You say it's about an English writer here,' repeated Jerry. 'So may I ask the obvious question?'

'Yes,' said Max. 'This is the question I was kind of edging towards.'

'The answer's no, it's not me.' The three writers eyed him doubtfully. Was he protesting too much? Then he remembered his new plan, which was neither to confirm nor deny the autobiographical content. He smiled. 'But of course, in one sense, you always write about yourself. How can one do anything else?'

'You can't. That may have been the obvious question, in that the answer was obvious,' said Sidney. 'But quite frankly, I don't care if it's about you or not. I'm not interested in whether or not you're in it. The *important* question is – and I hope you don't think that I'm being too narcissistic here – the important question is: Am *I* in it?' The others fell around, laughing uproariously. 'Because if I am you'd better be careful. If I'm not portrayed as a very warm and wonderful human being I'll fucking sue you.'

Max and Jerry wanted to know the story of the book. Truthfully, Ernest said that he didn't yet know, that he was launching out on a sort of voyage of discovery. He told them the basic idea of the story. 'What I don't understand', complained Sidney, 'is, if this bestselling novelist is so rich, why don't you just give her the money?'

'Why don't *I* just give her the money?' queried Ernest. 'It's not me.'

'No, 'course not, sorry,' apologized Sidney. 'What I

mean is, why doesn't he just give her the money if he's got so much of it?'

The others stared at him. 'Whoever heard of just giving ten grand away?' asked Max., quite perplexed. 'You mean, a kind of *nouveau riche oblige*?'

'No,' said Sidney. 'I mean, make a deal. Why doesn't he give her the dough and fuck her for a couple of months?'

'He wants a book, not a fuck,' said Jerry.

'So he can write a book about fucking her,' suggested Sidney.

'That wouldn't be nearly as interesting,' said Ernest.

'It would interest me,' said Sidney.

'Your trouble, Sidney,' said Max., 'is that you're just not an artist.'

'Thank *God*,' said Sidney. 'More irony, dear,' he muttered to Ernest.

Jerry spoke up. 'But she's a hooker. If he fucks her, and she does it just for the money, and there's no feeling between them, it makes them both too unsympathetic.'

'I think it makes it honest.' Sidney's face was deadpan. 'Prostitution is the only honest relationship, wouldn't you say Max?'

Max. nodded gravely. 'As writers with studio contracts, I think we have to take that view.'

When Ernest was driving home that night he smiled to himself as he thought again about the evening. He loved Max. and Sidney, their anger and their cynicism. He turned on the radio. First there was news of a plane crash somewhere in North Dakota which had, according to the news-reader, 'evinced a one hundred per cent mortality response.' He realized that he flinched more at the mangled language than at the news of a hundred mangled people. Then came the bombshell: 'Dr Abel Pile, the spiritual leader of the Church of the Community of Personal Truth in Los Angeles, was tonight arrested and charged with fifty-one counts of fraud.' The news-reader went on to report that Pile was the host of the upcoming Sincerity Awards, that he was a friend and confidante of many celebrities in the world of films, television and popular music. It seemed that Dr Pile had been taken to jail in handcuffs, like everyone who is arrested in Los Angeles no matter how non-violent, no matter how certain their release on bail. It is simply one of those rituals of law enforcement in the wild west. From outside the jail Ernest heard a brief interview with Pile's spokesman, who was called John Schmidt, saying that Dr Pile had a complete answer to all the charges against him and was confident that no jury would ever convict him.

When he got home there was a message on his answering machine from Joanna. His heart, as they say, skipped a beat.

FOURTEEN

We intend to be good stewards of God's money.
                                          Jim Bakker

Randi was distraught. There were pictures on all the TV
news programmes of Abel Pile being frogmarched out of
his Malibu house in handcuffs. There were shots of his
arrival at the jail, and more shots of his release from jail
the following morning. She was determined to express her
faith in her spiritual leader by going straight to him, to
show him that her love and support for him was as strong
as ever. If the Federal Court was to be his Calvary, she
would neither be his Judas nor his Doubting Thomas.
Ernest Mayday, on the other hand, was eager to return
Joanna's phone call so that he too could become a
Thomas, peeping not doubting. However, he could find
no privacy that morning. Randi insisted that he express
his loyalty and support for her by accompanying her to
the Church on Hollywood Boulevard, there to demonstrate
that Abel Pile did not stand alone.

The Church of the Community of Personal Truth had
been founded in the mid sixties up in San Francisco,
under a different name. It was originally a draft-dodging
device, to help educated young men who very sensibly
didn't want to fight and die in Vietnam for John Foster
Dulles's outdated domino theory. The First Amendment
not only guarantees freedom of speech but also freedom
of religion. Ministers of a pacifist church could be exempt
from military service as conscientious objectors (so long
as nobody thought of challenging the good faith of the

church in the courts) and Abel Pile was one of those who paid one dollar and was immediately ordained as a pastor. Like most of the other young men, the Reverend Abel Pile (as he could now style himself) did not take his religious duties very seriously, though he was amused to learn that he was entitled, by law, to marry couples, to bury corpses, to baptize babies and to perform all the other duties and avail himself of all the other privileges with which men of God are empowered by that helpful First Amendment. At first, apart from conducting three or four hippy beach weddings, at which he married three or four couples who were friends of his, just for the hell of it, he took little notice of his new God-given powers, and as the war wound down he continued with his previous profession of selling used cars. Or, as he preferred to call them, 'pre-owned' or 'experienced' cars.

It was some time in the early seventies that, in a blinding flash of enlightenment that was to change his life for ever, he realized that churches made more money than car dealers. And unlike car dealers, who had to make cash deals to avoid paying tax, church profits were automatically exempt from taxation because churches were deemed non-profit-making. This meant that whoever owned the church got all the tax-free profits. The question was: who had the power to recognize and acknowledge that a church was a church, and could thus operate tax free? Abel Pile was gleeful when he discovered the answer: nobody had that power, not the State government in Sacramento, not the Federal government, nobody – the separation of Church and State is enshrined in the Constitution, and any attempt by government to say what is or is not a church is in itself an infringement of the First Amendment. Only if a church is prosecuted for a violation of a secular law will the question be raised, and then the matter can only be decided by a jury.

Encouraged by this revelation, he returned to San

Francisco. By now the Church was nearly defunct. He spoke to the original founder, who had lost interest in it as Nixon was bringing the war to a close and Watergate was now the hot issue. Impeaching the President did not require being a member of any church. The Reverend Abel Pile paid another dollar into the Church's coffers and awarded himself a Ph.D – he was now Dr Abel Pile, Doctor of Divinity. No legal problems resulted. So he took the list of all the other draft–dodgers and sent them letters offering doctorates to all the Reverend young men for a fee of fifty dollars. Most of them ignored the letter, but some thirty-five responded. Maybe some of them were doing it just for the laugh. The upshot, however, was a tax-free profit of seventeen hundred and fifty dollars for the investment cost of a couple of dollars in postage stamps. This was the best mail-order business yet.

For a small portion of the doctoral profits, Pile paid off the founder and owner and assumed control himself. He installed a board of trustees, containing one or two trusted friends and a few easily manipulated believers, the kind of westerners Stalin once memorably described as useful idiots. Like the yuppies on Wall Street who were to achieve such notoriety in the eighties, like the junk-bond salesmen and leveraged buy-out manipulators, Abel Pile realized that asset-stripping was the answer. It would have been no mean task to start a new church, for it might have drawn the attention of the Internal Revenue Service to the transition in his occupation from used car dealer to bishop, but it was remarkably easy to assume control of a bona fide church which for years had gone unnoticed on account of its being no more weird than anything else in California. The Church's assets, as far as Pile was concerned, were neither physical nor financial, merely historical. It was there, established, unchallenged, respectable.

The Reverend Dr Abel Pile also realized that, like the medieval Church, he now had many offices to sell and many tithes that he could collect. A self-educated man with considerable flexibility of mind, he studied church history. He even visited Rome, and could hardly fail to be impressed by the Vatican's wealth. He was well aware that the Church no longer sold its offices and titles, and that its great wealth had been collected from the faithful over many centuries and often in small amounts. But, he said to himself, we all have to start somewhere, and in any case he did not feel the need to overtake the oldest and richest of all his competitors. He simply felt that there was room in the market place for them all, and Church history gave him much food for thought.

He resolved that he could sell something just as implausible. Implausibility, he realized, was the key to founding a great new profitable religious enterprise – after all, nothing could be less plausible than the son of God being born to a virgin and rising from the dead after three days in order to save the world. Abel Pile concluded that these ideas were simply expressions of natural human fears (in this respect, he had much in common with Ernest Mayday) and that anything that could be done to make people feel better about their mortality would fulfil a real spiritual and emotional need.

America loves a good con man, and if the snake oil salesman or the Music Man brings happiness in one form or another he is easily forgiven or excused. Abel Pile understood the American dream and – adopting a thoroughly ecumenical approach, broadly tolerant of every spiritual enterprise, arguing that everyone from the Romans to the Lutherans, from the Baptists to the Scientologists, from the Muslims to the Jews, were all in search of the same Nirvana, all had equally valid ways of climbing the mountain or killing the cat – he renamed his own enterprise the Church of the Community of Personal

Truth and was at pains to insist in his sacred teachings that membership of his church did not preclude membership of any other religious group.

Common to all these religions, and to all the even more primitive religions that he began to read up on, was some element of sacrifice, of a gift to God or the gods. Vows of celibacy and poverty had been Rome's major sacrificial lambs. Abel Pile knew that celibacy would be a hard sell in California. Cash, he decided, was the most profoundly meaningful sacrifice to twentieth-century Americans, a sacrifice that would make his followers feel a lot better and which, coincidentally, would make him feel a lot better too.

The Prophet Joseph Smith of the Mormons had written a sacred book. So had L. Ron Hubbard of the Scientologists. So had the Disciples of Jesus, Jesus himself not having had the time, not being in it for the money and not intending to found a new religion anyway. So Abel Pile wrote his book too, which he called *The Journey of Light and Truth*. It was about a shining bright journey to inner purity, through Perception, Sensibility and Recognition of a Higher Consciousness, taking the committed student out of negativity into a Total Positivity, and thence through Pilgrim's Omniscience into the sublime state of being called Yahweh Perception. It was in this sacred book that Abel Pile laid out The Route for the members of his church, the initiates, and for those who were to be ordinationized, and for those fortunate followers who, God willing, would eventually be appointed Pilgrims if they worked hard enough and sacrificed enough.

Was this a real church? Some conservative followers of the older, more established churches might say no. But in America a church is a church is a church. It's a church unless and until a jury says that it isn't. Only by the judicial examination of its tenets and practices may a church be said to be real or phoney. In a recent Californian case, which Abel Pile had followed with intense interest, an attractive woman had founded a new church in which the essential religious rites and observances consisted of men coming to visit her and paying her to have sex with them. The payments were called donations. She was prosecuted, and the jury, which had absolutely no sense of humour, convicted her of prostitution. The story had a happy ending, of course, because this was America and on her release from prison she became a television celebrity and bestselling author. But when a case is put to a jury it is not always so cut and dried. It is not always so easy to decide what is or is not a real church. Is it simply a body of people who gather together to worship something that cannot be empirically proved or disproved? Apparently so, and that is why all religions stress the sanctity of faith, for if the existence of God could be proved, if indeed the tenets of any religion actually made sense, then there would be no need for faith and hence no religions at all. It might be argued that the Church of the Community of Personal Truth was flawed because Abel Pile did not himself believe in its precepts. Yet how could that be proved? And even if it could be, this would not be unique – many churches, notably the Church of England, are led by men who are assailed with doubts and who may or may not fully believe their own theology. Still others have argued that some of these lesser cult churches are fatally flawed because they threaten those who criticize their doctrines, or ridicule them, or try to leave. But few churches tolerate such behaviour willingly. It was not Abel Pile who invented the laws of blasphemy. History suggests that a thorough-going campaign of intimidation, terror, even war, is the sign of a real church – whatever a real church may be. Remember the Inquisition? Remember the crusades? Remember Galileo?

But one important question remained for the enterprising

Dr Pile: how to discourage members of his own Church from leaving. Many, obviously, would not want to leave because he would be providing them with a sufficient sense of sacrifice and spiritual fulfilment. But something had to be done to prevent the weaker brethren from falling by the wayside. He did not have the resources of the State behind him, so an Inquisition was not a practical possibility. Unlike King Henry VIII he was not strong enough to sack the monasteries, nunneries and churches of his competitors, wiping out the competition to establish a monopoly. The traditional threat of hellfire and eternal damnation worked well with believers and waverers, but not so well with those who had ceased to believe. For them, something more of this earth had to be contrived.

Pile had always felt that the notion of Satan, the fallen angel, had distinct possibilities. In the Church of the Community of Personal Truth whispers began to circulate about a being called the Angel of Darkness. The name had been a slight problem to begin with: at first it was known as the Black Angel, but that seemed to have racist overtones; then the Red Angel, but that seemed to have an old-fashioned, cold war feel about it; the Avenging Angel was corny; the Dark Angel had been used as the title of some movie or novel; the Angel of Darkness seemed to be the best option.

There was only one problem. This Angel could not be spoken of easily because, unavoidably, as the Disciplinary Force of the Universe, it had elements of negativity about it. Indeed, if threat of the Angel of Darkness was to have any *gravitas*, negativity was not only inevitable but desirable. Yet even the slightest acknowledgement of negativity was discouraged by the Church and perceived by the members as a sign of spiritual failure, necessitating further study, further seminars, and the payment of further fixed donations. In one of his inspirations Abel Pile realized that this could be turned to advantage: the answer was indeed to shroud the Angel of Darkness in mystery. The Angel of Darkness could be spoken of, yet could not be spoken of. It could be mentioned only obliquely, and therefore only fearfully. Thus nobody, not the followers, not the disciples, not the initiates, not even (it was rumoured) the Pilgrims, knew exactly who or what the Angel of Darkness was, nor whether he was metaphysical, spiritual or a human enforcer. Was he a supernatural form of Satan, or was he the Terminator? No one knew except Abel Pile, and no one wanted to reveal their negativity and risk disapproval by asking.

Ernest Mayday knew nothing of Abel Pile's chequered past. that morning, though he was slightly suspicious of the man. But Randi's distress was so great, and her determination to be wholly positive on Pile's behalf so strong, that he felt he must accompany her down to the Commune and Heartwarming Institute on Hollywood Boulevard for the first time. As they drove there the radio reported that Abel Pile faced one hundred and twenty years in a federal correctional facility if convicted on all counts which, considering that Pile was already in his forties, sounded to Ernest like overkill. Randi wept, not because she believed him guilty but out of frustration, anger and a sense of the tragedy that was about to envelop them all.

Abel Pile, on the other hand, was quietly confident. He had gone straight to the Church on his release from jail and was calmly reassuring his many followers who were gathering there in an apparently spontaneous demonstration of support. All those years of teaching them not to be negative was certainly paying off now. Most of the celebrities in the congregation were, it must be admitted, conspicuous by their absence, having had hasty early-morning conferences with their agents, press agents and business managers, for much as they loved and admired Abel, business considerations would dictate that they start to distance themselves from criminal proceedings. Yet their support for the Church was on the record, they had participated in (and sometimes received) the Sincerity Awards in past years, and the press would be hounding them all for responses to the good doctor's arrest. Most of them would be unavailable for comment.

It was the morning rush hour and the traffic on Sunset Boulevard was moving slower than a family Christmas. As Ernest turned off Sunset, up Vine, into Hollywood and crawled slowly towards the Church, Randi pleaded with him to come in. He refused. 'Abel can help you,' she said.

'Help me?' Mayday was amazed. 'I thought he was the one who needed help. I thought you were coming here to show solidarity.'

'Today he needs help, yes. That doesn't mean he can't help you.'

'I don't need help, I haven't been indicted on fifty-one counts of fraud.'

'Has it occurred to you that your writing may have dried up because of your spiritual crisis?'

'I haven't *got* a spiritual crisis, Randi. You have.'

'Then why are you so blocked?'

He chose not to reply. He was about to deny that he was still blocked, but he realized that he might be. After all, describing Joanna and writing down everything she told him about herself and her exploits was barely creative. He remembered watching a television interview of Donald Ogden Stewart, a smiley, white-haired, charming old chap who had written the screenplay of *The Philadelphia Story* and had been a friend of that other Ernest, Hemingway. Stewart had not been much impressed with his friend's writing. 'He just wrote about things that happened. In *The Sun Also Rises*, you remember when he goes up into the mountains with an American friend? That was me, I was that guy. Ernest just described what we did, what happened to us. What's so great about that? 'Course, he described it OK, I guess.'

As they drove along Hollywood Boulevard, where the stars are on the sidewalk and the fumes obscure the sky, Mayday was struck, as he always was, by the irony of it all. The glamorous images on the Walk of Fame, each paving-stone along the wide sidewalks on either side of the street embossed with a star and a brass plate memorializing some famous movie name, some current, some dead, some forgotten, a shrine to gods and goddesses of celluloid, a celebration of fantasy and dreams, contrasted oddly with the panhandlers, bums and the homeless who everywhere, fifty years after the Depression, were begging bystanders to be a buddy and spare a dime.

They lapsed into silence until they pulled up in front of the Church, which was being doorstepped by a small crowd of TV and radio people, with camcorders and transmitter vans, all trying to force their way inside, all trying to get comments from anyone who went in or out. As Randi jumped out of Ernest's Mercedes and walked up the steps to the massive oak doors below a huge geometric art deco sunset in grey pre-cast concrete she was accosted by several of them. Questions were fired from all sides. She ignored them, and strode purposefully forward and into the building. One of the reporters was transmitting live. 'No one going in or out this morning will answer any questions about the Church, about Dr Pile or about the future of the Sincerity Awards.' Ernest, immediately hemmed into a deep canyon between a grimy yellow school bus and a tall eighteen-wheeler truck and trailer, both exuding clouds of noxious gases while loud and even more noxious pop music throbbed in the battered rusty Mustang convertible directly in front, was trying to listen to her on his car radio. 'Outside the Church of the Community of Personal Truth, I'm Melissa Gambini,' said the reporter, signing off. Ernest felt the bile rising again. 'Who are you when you're somewhere else?' he shouted at the radio. 'Stupid bitch,' he muttered to himself, and dialled home to see if his answering machine had picked up any more messages from Joanna.

He was in luck. She had called again. 'It's Joanna. Call me.' As terse as ever. To Ernest's surprise she'd left a phone number with a 213 area code. Toluca Lake, where she lived, was in the Valley, which meant it should be an 818 number. He called back from the car.

'Hello,' said a woman's voice.

'Can I speak to Joanna please?'

'You want to see Joanna?'

'I want to speak to her.'

'Who is this, please?'

Ernest was getting hot and irritable. 'Look, just let me speak to her, OK?'

'I'm afraid that's not possible.'

'Why not? She told me to call her at this number.'

There was a pause at the other end of the line. 'You know her?'

'Yes.'

'What's your name?'

'Er . . . Norm.'

'OK, Norm, give me your number and Joanna'll call you.'

'Just let me talk to her.'

'I can't do that. We have to call you back.'

Ernest sighed. 'OK, she's got my number. Tell her I'll be home in twenty minutes.' He hung up.

As he came into the house the phone was ringing. He grabbed it. 'Joanna?'

'No,' said Randi, 'it's Randi. Who's Joanna?'

'Oh, ah, she's . . . ah, she's Fanny Rush's assistant. Well, one of her assistants, anyway.'

Randi didn't seem interested in his explanation. 'I'm

194

going to be here all day, Abel's here, so are the guys, we're all going to pray for him.'

'Fine,' said Ernest, relieved that she had lost interest in finding out about Joanna, 'I'm sure that'll be a big help. Got to go.' Ernest only had one phone, but it had AT&T's Call Waiting facility – he could hear that little blooping noise, indicating that someone else was trying to get through to him while he was already on the line.

Randi was curious. 'What's the big hurry?'

'The other line's ringing. There's someone on callus interruptus.' He hung up on Randi and took the other call. It was Joanna.

They met in the frozen-yogurt and ice-cream parlour at the bottom of his hill. Little round formica-topped tables on spindly black pedestal legs surrounded them, and they sat on curvy chrome chairs with flowery plastic seats. Other people came in, only to buy cones or family-size quarts and then leave. Ernest and Joanna were the only customers sitting down and eating.

She was already there, waiting for him, when he arrived. She was still blonde. She was wearing another little suit, sort of chocolate brown in colour, with a tiny tight skirt and a blue silk shirt or T-shirt underneath the jacket. The blue in the shirt seemed to bring out the blue in her eyes. He hadn't noticed before how very blue they were. He started to shake hands with her but she held on to his hand, stood up and kissed him on the cheek. It was a chaste kiss, but Ernest was momentarily intoxicated by her perfume and the softness of her breasts pressing against his chest again. Flustered, he hurried straight into questioning her, even while they stood at the counter and ordered. 'Where were you when I called? Why wouldn't that woman let me speak to you?'

She waited till the sullen Korean behind the counter was out of earshot, getting some nuts as a topping for Ernest. 'It's the escort agency. They always call the clients back. Something to do with security, I don't know whether it's for safety or whether it's to check that you're not a cop.' He paid, and as they returned to their table she ran her tongue smoothly all the way round the top of her frozen yogurt cone, loading her tongue with vanilla yogurt in one long skilful lick. He watched. Slowly she drew it into her mouth, and smiled at him. 'Good, huh? I've got the best tongue in the business.'

He didn't know how to reply. 'You have?'

'You should try it sometime.'

Ernest went pink. He concentrated on finding out more facts for his fiction. 'Does an escort service ever mean just that – an agency for escorts? Or is it always a front for . . . working girls?'

'All the ones I've ever come across are. But sometimes a client just wants a *real* escort. No sex, just company. That's half price. I like those gigs, sometimes I meet really interesting guys. But then I dress like a professional woman, you know, like an executive or something.'

'How do professional women dress?'

'You know,' she grinned, 'they wear pantyhose.'

He looked at her glorious long legs, now demurely locked together at the knees as she sat and licked the top of the cone. They were encased in a smooth nylon sheen. 'Isn't that what you're wearing now?'

'Oh, no,' she said. 'I'm wearing stockings with a garter belt. Look.' She stood up, handed the yogurt to Ernest, glanced around to check that no one else was looking, then, tilting her neat little bottom slightly towards him, she pulled one side of her skirt up a few inches to reveal a stocking top, suspenders, and that teasing, tantalizing patch of white skin between the black stocking top and her black lacy panties. 'That's quite different from pantyhose, that's sexy, don't you think? Especially under a tiny little skirt like this?' He swallowed, and nodded. She sat down again, satisfied she had proved her point, took back her yogurt and licked it suggestively never taking her eyes off Ernest.

He watched her for a while. 'Do you ever do any nursing any more, to help pay the bills?' he asked.

She shook her head. 'No money in it. Too much like hard work.'

'So what do you do if you can't find a man to support you?'

She gave him a cool hard look. 'I don't need a man to support me. I had that once. Now I have my freedom.'

Mayday was slightly bemused. 'But I thought that's what you were advertising for. I thought you wanted ten grand to be some guy's mistress.'

'That's a purely short-term thing. I told you, my mom's *dying*.' She looked away. She seemed to be blinking back tears. Ernest felt guilty that he never asked about her.

'How is she?'

'She's hanging in there,' said Joanna. 'Can I have a coffee, please?'

He walked over to the counter and ordered one for her. As he sat down beside her again she wiped her eyes with the back of her hand in a curiously childlike gesture.

'Here's your coffee,' he said, sitting down. 'So what do you live on?'

She swung round towards him with defiance in her voice and said: 'OK, if you want to know, sometimes I'm a strippergram, sometimes I do table dancing, sometimes I work in adult movies . . . I told you, I'm broadminded.'

'Table dancing? What's table dancing?'

'Yeah, you know, nude, on tables.'

'I've never heard of that,' he lied. 'Is this an American thing?'

She shrugged. 'Must be. There's good money in it. First you strip, then the men stuff dollars into my garter when I show . . . myself. And there's no sex, which is great.'

'You mean, no contact?'

'Yeah that's right, no contact. No sex. Just looking. No touching. Touching's against the law.'

'So's prostitution. The law never stopped you doing that.'

She sighed, staring at him, brows knotted with impatience. 'Norm, I do wish you wouldn't use words like prostitution and hooker.'

Ernest probed gently. 'Don't you, didn't you ever, feel . . . shy? Embarrassed?'

'About what?'

'Dancing nude in front of a crowd of people?'

'No! Fuck you.' She was indignant. 'Look, it's just an erotic dance, it's kind of artistic, I like doing it, I have a great body, I like the way I look, OK?'

He was surprised by her vehemence, which made him hesitate for a moment. 'I'm not saying you should be ashamed or anything, I was just asking, that's all.'

'I bet you'd like to watch.'

'I expect I would,' he admitted.

'I've never met a man who wouldn't.' She seemed to have recovered her composure. 'It's not so different from what you do, anyway.'

This surprised Ernest. 'It isn't?'

'You're a writer. You expose yourself for money.'

He smiled a complacent smile. 'Some writers do. I don't.' She was staring at him. 'My stories don't reveal me.'

Her expression didn't change. She continued to stare at him without a flicker, considering what he'd just said. 'I don't see how that's possible,' she commented eventually.

'Well . . .' Mayday, surprised again by her intelligence, modified his argument. 'In one sense they may. But I keep my soul to myself.'

'Me too,' said Joanna. 'My dancing doesn't reveal me, either. Not the *real* me. Just my skin. But it's great to watch, it really turns the guys on.'

'There's something I'm confused about,' he said. 'When

we first met you told me you like the sex, and that anyway it's no big deal to you one way or the other. Now you say you like the dancing because there's no sex involved.'

She smiled. 'Well, honestly, Norm, it's like anything else, it depends who the sex is with or what the job is. It's like when I was nursing, there were some jobs that were less attractive than others. I liked to do things for my patients but, I mean, for instance, giving an enema wasn't that great. It's the same with this, there are some jobs I'd rather not do, but it's all part of the service. You can have too much of a good thing, you know.' Slowly, suggestively, she pushed the remainder of the yogurt cone straight into her mouth. He watched her swallow it, then run her tongue slowly and sensuously along her lips. 'But I never hate work.' Her eyes sparkled in amused anticipation. 'And I'm always game to try new things with fun guys.'

She was gazing at him provocatively. Ernest found that he couldn't out-stare her and, unnerved, he looked away. She waited and watched him. He pulled himself together and looked back at her. 'You say you only work ... as a working girl ... in private. But an adult movie isn't private. There must be quite a few people on the set, and thousands will watch you eventually.'

She was outraged. 'That's different. Movies are acting. When I act in a movie I'm an actress. That's not me up there on the screen, that's the character I'm playing.'

'Well ... not exactly,' sneered Ernest. 'Not in that kind of movie.'

'No? So why is it different from what any other romantic actress does? I just go a teeny bit further, that's all.'

'There must be some difference.'

'Why? All those legit actresses strip. They show us their tits and their asses, they kiss guys, they're in bed with guys, they simulate blowjobs, they *look* like they're fucking even if they're not.'

Ernest was sure there was a difference between acting in porn movies and other movies, but he couldn't exactly explain it. He ducked the question. 'Aren't you worried about AIDS? They don't use condoms in adult movies, do they?'

'I only ever acted in movies with my boyfriend as my partner.' She smiled as she realized the implications of his question. 'So, you watch adult movies, huh?'

'No, I don't.' Ernest went pinker again.

She stared at him. 'Don't deny it, Norm, let's be honest with each other, OK? I'm being honest with you.'

He swallowed. 'Well, I've *seen* them, yes. I mean, in passing.' Shamed into telling her the truth, he made it sound as though he saw them by accident. 'Most people have.'

'There seems to be some kind of double standard here – I mean, what are you saying, that it's wrong to act in an adult movie but it's OK to watch it?' She stared at him, appraising him. 'Because I don't think it's wrong.'

Ernest cleared his throat. 'All the women I know say that pornography degrades women, because it just treats them as sex objects, and it encourages violence against women and rape.'

'I guess some women believe that', she said, 'but plenty more don't. Why should pictures of women having sex be degrading? Is it because women are supposed to be uninterested in sex? Well, I'm interested in it, and most of us are. It's, like, we're still supposed to be innocent and pure? I personally think that this female purity shit is what women have been struggling to overcome. We're allowed to have sexual fantasies too. That's not degrading. Sex isn't degrading. Nearly as many women rent adult videos as men. And rape's been going on for thousands of years – it didn't start with adult videos.'

'OK, OK, act in them if you like, I don't care!'

She softened. 'I think this is how you get your kicks. Talking about it. If that's what turns you on, I can talk dirty for you if you like, if you want to get your rocks off.'

Ernest's colour went from pink to puce. 'It's not that at all,' he replied with ridiculous self-righteous indignation. 'It's just that if I'm going to write a book about you – or someone like you – I have to ask questions, that's all. It's research.'

'Oh, that's what it is.' She smiled a faint, private smile, and played with the white plastic teaspoon in the saucer of her coffee cup.

Ernest waited a moment and then continued prying. 'So, are you working as an escort now, or what?'

She turned back towards him, her eyes wide with surprise. He noticed that her lashes were long and dark and thick. He wondered if they were mascaraed or if they were naturally so beautiful. They looked natural to him. 'You mean *now*?' she asked. 'Don't worry, Norm, the meter's not running today. This is your research, right?' He nodded. 'We made a deal. I'm not charging you extra for my time today, we agreed ten grand inclusive, a deal is a deal.' She chuckled playfully. 'Unless you want me to dance for you, or have sex. That's extra.'

Ernest took the plunge. 'Maybe I do,' he said.

'Maybe you do . . . what?'

'Want to have sex with you.' He swallowed. For some reason that he couldn't have explained, he felt profoundly embarrassed. He looked down at the table, feeling strangely humiliated. Then looked her straight in the eye.

Her smile faded. A look of real sadness clouded her face. 'You know what, Norm? I don't think that's such a good idea.'

He was dumbfounded. 'Why not?'

'Because . . .' she searched for the right words, 'because I don't think it's smart to mix business with pleasure.'

'We'll make it business,' he offered immediately. 'I'll pay you.'

She seemed sad, almost disappointed. 'No, I don't think so – you know, once a man and a woman have had sex, everything's different. You'd be jealous of other men, I may become jealous of your lady, I don't think we could be friends once sex has entered into it.'

He couldn't understand it. 'Surely we can, since it's you . . .' She raised her eyebrows. 'I mean, it doesn't mean anything to you, does it? It's just a sort of quick in and out thing, isn't it?'

She took his hand and held it between both of hers. 'No, not with someone I know. Not with a friend. I'm human. I'm a woman, not just an orifice.'

'I know that.'

'I have emotions too. And I wouldn't dream of charging you money – I wouldn't want you to be just another john. And anyway, how could I take more money from you when you're paying me such a lot anyway?'

'So why did you suggest it?'

'I'm sorry,' she said. 'I didn't mean it, I was just playing, I never thought you'd . . .'

'I see,' said Ernest sadly. But he didn't really. 'Is there no way?'

'Not unless . . .' She hesitated. 'You know, only if it were a long-term arrangement, like I told you I was looking for originally.'

'You mean – ten thousand dollars for a few weeks?' She nodded. 'But I'm already giving you ten thousand dollars.'

'I know, Norm, you're really very generous. But that's for my work for you, on your book, on this trial. If you want *me*, I'd want you to take care of my apartment – financially I mean – my clothes, my expenses, car, you know, all that shit . . . and a cash allowance for me.' She blinked back a tear. 'Well, not for me, of course, for my mom, not even for her, for the doctors.'

Ernest was moved. And he really wanted her. But Ernest was also careful with money, and this was quite a price when it was all added up. He wasn't poor, but he wasn't *rich* rich and even though he'd have more cash when the film deal was finalized this sounded like buying a yacht. If you have to ask yourself if you can afford it, you can't afford it. He just couldn't see why she couldn't be more flexible. 'But you *are* still working as an escort?' he persisted.

'Well, you see, that's the thing, I'm not, not any more. I don't need to, thanks to you and John Schmidt.' And she folded her arms around him gently and kissed him on the cheek again.

Ernest disentangled himself. Bells were suddenly ringing in his head. 'John Schmidt?' She nodded. 'Was that the name of the man who hired you to nobble the jury?' She nodded again. 'I heard that name on the radio last night, I think . . .'

She was smiling. 'Me too. And I saw him on *Eyewitness News*. He's the lawyer for that fundamentalist preacher who's just been arrested.'

Mayday shook his head for a moment in silent wonderment. 'So. That's what you called to tell me. You're going to help get Abel Pile off fifty-one counts of fraud,' he said softly, more to himself than to her. He shook his head again.

'Something wrong?' she asked.

'No. Well, yes and no.'

'What gives?'

'Nothing. '

She knew something was on his mind. 'Is there some reason I shouldn't do this?'

He wondered how to answer her. Of course she shouldn't do it. Jury tampering was a serious criminal offence. Blackmailing a juror was perhaps even more serious. Abel Pile was manifestly criminal and ought to be stopped bilking gullible believers out of their life savings. And in helping, supporting, encouraging her he would be an accessory, at the very least. And yet . . . what a *great* story! 'No,' he replied. 'There's no reason not to. I definitely think you should do it.'

FIFTEEN

In the aristocracy of success there are no strangers.
                                    S. J. Perelman

In Hollywood, Ernest told himself, you must strike while
the insincerity is hot. The meeting with Virginia Spearmen
was universally agreed to have been a great meeting.
They'd all agreed it at the time, as they'd staggered hilari-
ously out of her office. Oliver, Tiffani and Chuck had
assured Ernest afterwards, in the parking-lot, that it had
been a *really* great meeting. That night Virginia had called
Fanny Rush to tell her what a great meeting they'd had,
and even Fanny found time to call Mayday to let him
know that the studio was excited because it was such a
great meeting. Later the same day Virginia's assistant
called Tiffani, then Chuck and Tiffani made a conference
call from their compact Japanese cars to Oliver's
Lamborghini as they drove home, and they congratulated
themselves and each other upon how great the meeting
had been. Hollywood is a small company town, a gossiping
village in which everyone knows everyone else's business,
and in a matter of days everyone who was anyone seemed
to have heard about the great meeting. The word of
mouth on the meeting was so great, in fact, that the
greatness of the film itself seemed virtually assured, and so
no one was at all surprised when Virginia Spearmen
greenlighted the movie, subject to everyone being able to
make their deals. Shortly afterwards, deal memos having
been agreed on all sides, the news was published in
the trades and the *Hollywood Reporter* mentioned that
everyone concerned was thrilled about the great meeting

that had taken place. It also mentioned that Ernest Mayday's deal, including his screenplay and the rights for his novel, was thought to amount to well over a million dollars.

All of a sudden Ernest found that he was in considerable demand. Like *Vogue*, Hollywood is in the fashion business. Producers and their assistants (the ones known as Development Executives, because they couldn't be called assistants because secretaries were called assistants) buzzed around Ernest, then homed in on him like flies on to shit. ABC TV called him to see if he were available: 'We have a limited window for a hooker movie,' enthused a hopeful young Senior Vice-president. Mayday explained that he didn't want to do it because he was already writing a hooker novel, and this got them very excited and they asked if they could read it. When he said no they got even more excited and asked him to lunch.

No sooner had he hung up than Casey Boddichek, a twenty-five-year-old Creative Executive from International Studios, called and explained that he'd always been one of Ernest's biggest fans. He asked if he could send over – by special messenger – a story that he believed would make a wonderful wonderful major major movie. Ernest was delighted. He still had plenty of time on his hands, for his screenplay was largely written and, though he had made copious notes for *Flagrante Delicto* after the recent meeting with Joanna, there was little further progress because nothing much had happened to her yet. A studio with a ready-made story to send to him made him very excited. He was looking forward to being given some parameters, some guidelines, just like he used to get in Whitehall, where the politicians told Ernest and his colleagues what to do and, using that as a basis, they then did what they liked. So his feeling of disappointment could hardly have been greater when, upon tearing open the envelope, the story of *Cinderella* fell out. Believing that there must be some mistake, he rang Casey Boddichek, the Creative Executive, to check if he had been sent the wrong package in error.

'No,' replied the young man, slightly puzzled. 'Why?'

'Well,' said Ernest, 'by some strange coincidence I know this story.'

Boddichek was not good at irony. 'I knew that there was that possibility,' he said, 'but we have a great new way to treat it, and I thought you might want to reread it before taking a meeting.'

'Reread it?' said Mayday. 'We are talking about Cinderella, and the wicked stepmother and the Ugly Sisters and Buttons the page and the Fairy Godmother, "Cinders, you *shall* go to the ball but be sure you're home by midnight or you'll turn into a pumpkin"?'

'Hey, you know it pretty well,' said young Casey with admiration in his voice. 'But I've found a new directionality for this story.'

'Do you mean direction?' asked Mayday.

'I guess I do.'

'Then', snapped Mayday, 'why don't you fucking say so?' He hung up and turned on his answering machine to screen all further calls.

For a while he sat there and fumed. As he calmed down he began to wonder why he was seized so often with these uncontrollable bursts of anger. What did it matter when he had so much of everything? Not that he exactly had it yet. A million-dollar deal was what he had at this point, not a million dollars. But a million-dollar deal was sufficient to be perceived as a success and Hollywood is a place where the perception is more real than the reality. In the film industry you are only as good as your last movie, but Ernest didn't have a last movie. His only track record was two bestselling novels and a million-dollar deal, and that record of success, never put to the test, placed him right at the top of the greasy pole.

*

He was looking forward to Oliver Sudden's annual summer barbecue and ball at the Pacific Palisades mansion that weekend, for he expected to be the centre of attention. But when he got there he realized that virtually all the other guests were industry insiders who knew each other, and he hardly knew anyone at all. Oliver was not on hand to introduce him.

Wandering disconsolately around the edges of the vast chattering crowd that thronged the green lawns and old brick terraces of Oliver's magnificently lush gardens, staring out at the picture postcard ocean views, he bumped into (of all people) Dr Julian Genau, the English analyst. Ernest hadn't liked him much when they had met at Professor Craig Rosenbaum's dinner party, but in this huge crush Julian was one of a very few familiar faces and Ernest greeted him warmly. Close by, a string quartet of tired-looking elderly Jews in dinner-jackets sat on a small rostrum at one end of the lake-sized pool and played the songs of Irving Berlin for the networking, wheeling and dealing guests, all drinking mineral water and working the party. Ernest and Julian sat in a cool corner of the perfectly manicured lawn under a huge avocado tree and talked about the terror of the blank page.

'I've written several rather good books myself, actually,' sympathized Julian, 'psychotherapeutic, of course, rather than fiction, but one knows the feeling ... the proverbial blank sheet of paper is not what one might call a safe, maternal holding environment. We all need boundaries, and it's jolly hard to set them for oneself.'

'Especially here,' agreed Ernest, 'in this land of plenty.'

'So, do you prefer living here or in England?' Dr Genau was curious.

'You know, it's strange,' said Ernest, 'I don't feel I really belong in either place. I'm half in and half out of both English and American life. I'm at home in both places, but now I'm a foreigner in both places too.'

'I know what you mean,' enthused Genau, always

pleased to play with a new thought, however slight. 'You're English to the Americans and yet, living abroad, especially in a fantasy world like this, you're somehow Americanized to the English.'

'That's it exactly!' Ernest was delighted to have found someone who was willing to talk to him about himself at such length and with such apparent interest. He was really beginning to like Julian Genau.

'I suppose', continued Genau, 'that explains why you're such a thoroughly mean-spirited observer of life in both places.'

Ernest was taken aback by the sudden change in the tone of the conversation. 'What's your problem with that?' he asked belligerently.

'Nothing.' Julian Genau grinned suddenly. 'It's about the only thing one can say in your favour.'

Ernest wasn't sure how to take this remark. It seemed rather a backhanded compliment, but at least the conversation was still about him. 'People seem to think that I'm aloof,' he said, 'but it's just that I don't vomit my innermost feelings all over everyone the way the Californians do. But I'm sure people can distinguish my good intentions and genuine feelings of warmth from my misanthropic exterior, don't you think?'

Julian Genau pondered this for a moment. 'I would say not,' he answered with a tactful but judicial air.

'Oh,' said Ernest. He was beginning to sink into one of his depressions. He looked around for a waitress with a tray of booze. There were none in view. Julian looked around too. He seemed to be losing interest in Ernest as a conversational topic, but Ernest was disinclined to let it go. 'So why do *you* think things like pomposity and stupidity make me so angry?'

'Well,' said Julian Genau, inclining his head at a professionally sympathetic, therapeutic angle and starting a nod, 'it sounds like projection to me.'

'Projection?' Mayday didn't understand.

'You project your feelings on to others because you don't want to acknowledge them in yourself.' His nodding was in full swing now, that familiar psychotherapeutic understanding nod, like a toy dog on the back shelf of a moving car.

'Huh?' inquired Ernest, slightly blurred. The seven Scotches were taking effect. Alone among a thousand guests, he'd had much too much to drink. 'I don't get what you mean.'

Dr Julian Genau refused to be drawn further. 'You seem to be an intelligent man,' he explained. 'I'm sure you do.'

'Wait a minute. You're telling me I'm pompous and stupid, and that's why I get angry when I see it in others?'

'I'm not telling you anything.'

'*You*,' said Ernest, the Scotch articulating slowly and carefully for him, 'are telling *me* I'm pompous and stupid. And then you have the nerve to say that *I'm* the one who's projecting?' Julian Genau smiled enigmatically. Ernest was pissed off. 'Psychobabble,' he added dismissively. 'Why should I be angry with myself?'

'Why do you care, if it's psychobabble?'

'No, go on.'

Genau smiled. 'Well, as I said, it's not for me to say. You're not my patient.'

Ernest Mayday hesitated, then took the plunge. 'Could I be?' he asked.

Julian Genau was taken aback. 'Oh,' he said. 'Why would you want to be?'

'I've been blocked for a while. I wonder if . . . I mean, could it be anything to do with this anger?'

Julian Genau shrugged. 'I suppose it could be. Or it might just be that you have nothing to say. Or you may be so comfortable that you have no incentive. But I can't take you on.' Ernest sank deeper into his mire. He hadn't thought it possible that he could be rejected by Joanna or Julian Genau, let alone both of them. 'We know each other socially,' explained Genau, turning to greet Oliver Sudden's wife Lori. She had heard about Genau from her best friend's therapist who had heard him speak at a UCLA seminar and pronounced his lecture awesome, which in LA was a major major compliment. Lori had attended one of his subsequent lectures, been quite overwhelmed with his mellifluous British accent and his torrential articulacy.

'You're becoming a hot psychoanalyst,' she said, kissing him on both cheeks.

'Hot?' he queried the word. 'I'm not in show business.'

'But you're invited to A-list parties,' she pointed out. 'How would you like your own talk radio show?'

'There's a thought,' he mused.

'You must,' said Lori. 'Every therapist who's anyone is on talk radio.'

Ernest decided he needed another drink. Near the bar he finally bumped into skinny Fanny Rush, who introduced him to a tall young man with long shiny black hair, slicked back with gel and tied in a ponytail. 'Hi, I'm one of your greatest fans, I work at the same agency as Fanny.'

'How strange we've never met,' remarked Ernest.

'That's because I only handle talent,' said the young man.

Ernest, ever in search of an insult, thought for a moment that he'd hit the jackpot. He stared at Ponytail with unfocused alcoholic incredulity. 'Are you saying I'm not talented?' he asked.

Ponytail laughed uproariously. 'God no, I told you, I'm one of your biggest fans. Hey, I see what you mean. No, you're a writer. Talent means actors and actresses, like, you know, performers?'

'I see. It's from the Latin, I take it,' remarked Ernest superciliously.

'Huh?' said Ponytail.

'Apparently,' commented Ernest, 'you have not had the benefit of a classical education.'

'Huh?' Ponytail repeated.

'Talent, meaning a unit of currency.'

Ponytail laughed loudly again though his heart didn't seem to be in it, for he told Ernest immediately that it had been a pleasure to meet him, a real pleasure, as he moved swiftly away into the crowd. Ernest turned away from the bar with a replenished tumbler of neat whisky and bumped into his host, Oliver Sudden.

'Hey!' Oliver greeted him. 'Have you talked to Virginia?'

'Virginia?' Ernest couldn't think what Oliver meant. 'Why, was I supposed to?'

'Sure, she's here.'

'What am I supposed to talk to her about?'

Oliver Sudden took him aside. 'You gotta talk to Ginnie, she's on point for this movie, she greenlighted it, it's very important that you cozy up to her, invite her out for lunch or dinner, lunch or dinner, dinner would be better than lunch because you can spend a little more time together, get to know each other, there's not so much pressure to get back to the office if it's dinner, it's an open-ended time frame you know what I mean so make it dinner but if she can't find the time for dinner take her to lunch, OK? OK, so, you take her to lunch or dinner, dinner would be better but lunch would be fine, and when you get there there's three things you gotta remember, three things, OK? One, don't get drunk, two, don't fuck her, three, don't talk about the movie.'

Mayday was fascinated. 'Does she fuck?'

Now Oliver was fascinated. 'Everybody fucks. What are you, a Trappist monk?'

'No.' Ernest felt impelled to defend his manhood. 'I live with a masseuse called Randi.'

'A what?'

Ernest translated. 'A massoose.'

'Hey!' said Oliver, and turned to greet another guest with a big hug.

Ernest wandered around the party till he found Virginia. She was sitting on the edge of the pool, dangling her feet in the cool water, seemingly deep in conversation with some star actor whom he dimly recognized but couldn't put a name to. He hung around awkwardly for a minute or two, then she looked up and saw him. She smiled her gorgeous smile. 'Hey!' she said by way of a greeting. 'Ernie baby, howya doin'?'

Ernie baby was flustered by this sudden familiarity. 'Fine,' he muttered monosyllabically. The star kissed Virginia and moved on to hug and embrace some other guest.'Quite a hunk, isn't he?' she said, standing up.

Ernie baby stepped forward. 'I . . . ah . . . I was wondering if we could have lunch or dinner sometime. Dinner would be better,' he added hastily.

'Sure,' she said. 'Call my office on Monday and set up something with my assistant.' And she turned to speak to a determined bespectacled young woman with long straight brown hair who brushed past Ernest to interrupt their conversation without ceremony. 'Ginnie, I've got to talk to you,' she began in a New York accent, and stood between Ernest and Ginnie.

At the other end of the pool Ernest saw Julian Genau sitting on the edge of the huge jacuzzi in his swimming trunks, holding a glass of champagne and peach juice, talking volubly to Oliver who was holding a glass of San Pellegrino. Relieved to see a conversation in progress between two people both of whom he knew, he wandered over to listen. As he arrived he heard Oliver saying that he was leaving his analyst and switching to a new psychologist.

'I'm not a psychologist,' said Julian. 'I'm a psychiatrist and a psychoanalyst.'

'What exactly is the difference?' Oliver wanted to know.

'A psychiatrist is an MD, qualified to prescribe. An analyst has undergone his own experiential training analysis, so that he's qualified to deal with issues of transference and counter-transference. A psychologist is someone who has a degree in psychology. It's merely an academic and research qualification.'

'In America we call therapists psychologists,' said Oliver.

'We don't in Britain, unless they're clinical psychologists,' said Julian. 'As far as I'm concerned, a psychologist is a man who pulls habits out of rats.'

Oliver laughed. 'Who said that?' he asked.

'I did,' said Julian. 'Didn't you see my lips move?'

'I want to ask your advice,' said Virginia to Julian, sliding into the hot tub beside Oliver. 'Your professional advice.' She looked good enough to be one of her movie stars in her one-piece swimsuit.

'Shall we make an appointment?' suggested Julian.

'What's wrong with right now?' said Virginia, who loved being the centre of attention. Julian glanced around the jacuzzi, which now contained Ernest, Tiffani, Oliver and the Hunk who Virginia Spearmen had been embracing earlier, all sipping Bellinis or San Pellegrinos. Then he shrugged a why not.

'My therapist has been behaving disgracefully', began Virginia, 'and I want to know what I should do about it.'

'What's he done?'

Everyone in the jacuzzi turned to Virginia, all agog. 'He asked me if he could borrow ten grand from me.' Everyone in the jacuzzi gasped. 'What do you think of that?' she demanded.

Julian Genau hesitated. 'Well, it doesn't sound like the usual therapeutic stance,' he agreed. 'Um . . . why did he ask you, do you think?'

'He said he needed the money.'

The little audience in the jacuzzi looked at Julian. 'And you didn't believe him?' asked Julian. Ernest looked around the audience. It was clear that they all thought this question was a bit naïve. If he wasn't careful Julian would be a good deal less hot by the end of the afternoon.

Oliver was incredulous. 'So you think that's OK, for your therapist to ask you for ten thousand dollars?'

'I'm reluctant to comment, old chap,' said Julian cautiously, 'since I don't really know anything about her, or him.'

Virginia's Hunk joined in. 'I know you doctors like to stick together – is that what's going on here?'

'Doctors are like the Pope,' interjected Ernest. 'They never admit a sexual indiscretion or a professional mistake.' This won an appreciative chuckle from the folks in the jacuzzi, and Ernest was happy that he'd managed to deflect a little of the limelight away from Julian. But Virginia Spearmen wouldn't let go of her question. 'Let me ask you this, Doc – would *you* ever ask an analytic patient for money?'

'I never have done,' said Julian, 'but . . . how long have you been in therapy with him?'

'A couple of years.'

'Getting anywhere?'

'Don't think so.'

'Well . . . maybe he did it for you, not for him.'

Virginia stared at him. 'I don't get it. What do you mean, for me?'

'Well, perhaps he can't get through to you any other way. I mean, I would say, from our brief acquaintanceship, that money might be the most important thing in the world to you, more important than anything else. So perhaps by asking you for money he touches something fundamental, something primitive in you, something that makes you angry, something that creates a genuine emotional response. Perhaps that's the only way to get through to you.' He stopped. Virginia was nodding, genuinely impressed. The little crowd in the jacuzzi had now grown to nine or ten people, all of who were gazing at Julian Genau in open-mouthed admiration of both his insight and his nerve in talking to the rough and tough Virginia Spearmen like that. A star was born before their very eyes. His stock in the company town had just climbed about three hundred per cent.

'And then again,' added Julian, in a carefully casual throw-away, 'perhaps he just needs the money.' His timing was perfect. They all laughed and applauded, especially Virginia. Lori had been essentially correct. In Hollywood, everyone's in show business.

SIXTEEN

American society encourages dreaming, both as a key to success and as an antidote to failure.

John Lahr

The best that Gilbert Hoolahan, the federal prosecutor in charge of the LA District department of religious crime, had been hoping for was a judgeship. But when the Abel Pile case fell into his lap he saw that, if he played his cards right, he might have a career in politics after all. A successful prosecution, if high profile enough, can be that lucky break that separates you from the crowd, and he hoped that this could be his chance to run for Mayor of Los Angeles or State Attorney General, thence onwards and upwards to Senator, Governor and – who knows? – even the White House.

Gilbert Hoolahan wanted to succeed in politics and undoubtedly he stood as good a chance as anyone else because he had the one essential gift needed by all gubernatorial and presidential hopefuls: a thick head of hair. He wanted to make his mark, in case his asset started to wear thin, and he could see an opportunity at City Hall. The incumbent Mayor was floundering in the opinion polls and the competition was either weak or relatively unknown. Hoolahan, of course, was not very well-known either and the Abel Pile case was just the opening he had been looking for. When Jim Bakker, the TV evangelist, had been prosecuted for fraud it had been one of the hottest trials for years, a media jamboree, a heaven-sent opportunity for the prosecutor. Of course, the

Bakker case had enjoyed the inestimable advantage of a defendant who was a national television personality, plus the voluble Jessica Hahn, a mystery woman who (according to whichever story you believed) was either an innocent virgin seduced by Bakker or an experienced call girl with an eye on the big bucks – her two subsequent appearances in *Playboy* magazine did not do too much to bolster up her claim to be the former. When Bakker confessed to a 'forty-minute affair' with the girl he brought notoriety upon them both, and – this was the key as far as Hoolahan was concerned – fame and glory to those who put him behind bars. Any case that could occupy front-page space in both the *National Enquirer* and The *New York Times* was a godsend to a federal prosecutor with political ambitions. Jimmy Swaggart had also been brought down by revelations of contact with not one but two prostitutes: these evangelists fucked like rabbits, noted Hoolahan. So far, he had not succeeded in finding a Jessica Hahn in the Abel Pile case but he wasn't going to give up easily, for a fraudulent born-again Christian would be still hotter news if he could tie in some hot sex, which meant that there would be a much better chance of a conviction.

Ernest had followed Jim Bakker's trial closely in the newspapers and had been astounded by his sentence. Subsequent high-profile trials included that of Ivan Boesky, whose frauds amounted to hundreds of millions. He got three years. A Korean shopkeeper who murdered a black fifteen-year-old teenage girl in her corner grocery store by shooting her in the back of the head after she stole a soft drink worth a dollar sixty-nine was sentenced in LA to probation and community service. But the embezzling evangelist who lived in a mansion got forty-five years – presumably three years for fraud and forty-two years to assuage the envy of everyone in the courtroom who didn't see why he should live in a big house and fuck Jessica Hahn if they couldn't.

Gilbert Hoolahan was sure that he would be able to mobilize that envy in the Abel Pile case too, and he couldn't wait to get started. Hoolahan's official title was Assistant United States Attorney. He was a man in a hurry. He had become a deputy prosecutor right out of law school. His boss, the US Attorney, had divided the office into a number of departments, and when Hoolahan had been given religious crime he felt he had been thrown overboard. But fate had now tossed him a life-jacket and, seizing his opportunity, Hoolahan handled the indictment of Abel Pile with great skill: he found that essentially the same two crimes of obtaining money under false pretences and cheating on his tax return could be turned into a whole range of different charges of fraud; tax fraud, mail fraud and even racketeering. Thus he was able to win national headlines by charging the good Dr Pile with no less than fifty-one different counts, and with these headlines came the certainty that he, Gil Hoolahan, would be interviewed on network television. The contempt laws in the nation's courts had themselves fallen into such contempt that he was able to use the media to assure LA County, and indeed the whole country, of Abel Pile's guilt and the certainty of his conviction. For did not that wonderfully handy little First Amendment guarantee freedom of expression to prosecutors, both inside and outside the courtroom?

Randi Toner was watching this whole process unfold with a profound feeling of despair. Happiness is defined by unhappiness, just as life is defined by death. Now, suffering vicariously the public excoriation and humiliation of her beloved spiritual leader who, in the best traditions of Los Angeles justice, was being tried and convicted in the media long before his case came to court, she realized that although she had been obsessed by her search for the meaning of her life and by her need for some sort of self-realization, she had known considerable happiness in the past and, sadly, had failed to recognize it. Determined to stand by Abel Pile, consumed with bitterness by what she perceived as the unfairness of his prosecution, rightly convinced that it had nothing to do with his guilt and everything to do with Hoolahan's political ambitions, she asked Ernest what else she could do to show her support and solidarity in Abel's hour of need.

Ernest, aware that John Schmidt was organizing a conspiracy to set up a juror in a sexually compromising situation with Joanna, suddenly realized that a social relationship with Pile and Schmidt could open up a whole new angle of research for his novel. He seized the opportunity, and to Randi's surprise he was very encouraging when she suggested calling them. 'Ask them over to dinner,' he offered with unexpected geniality. 'I'd like to meet them.' She hurried to the phone.

Later that week, as they drank their morning decaf and orange juice in the kitchen and Consuela bustled around them, going through the fruit bowl and hurling anything that was less than perfect into the waste disposal, Ernest and Randi watched the increasingly familiar burly figure of Gilbert Hoolahan live on one of the morning talk shows, his open, honest, freckled face topped with that thick ginger mop, telling the viewers what a strong case the State had against Abel Pile. Every few days since the arrest he had skilfully leaked a new piece of evidence from the prosecution's case, keeping himself permanently in the headlines and ensuring that the general public was completely convinced of Pile's guilt.

After the taped interview with Gilbert Hoolahan, Abel Pile himself was interviewed live in the studio. He was good. He was impressive. He did not come across as a man who diddled Uncle Sam. 'What about these allegations of your opulent lifestyle?' asked intrepid little blonde anchorwoman Barbra Riggs, egged on by the applauding studio audience.

'Have you noticed', asked Abel, his clear blue eyes shining with sincerity, 'the pejorative use of the word lifestyle? Poor people have lives, but if they think you're rich they say you have a *lifestyle.*'

'I wasn't trying to load the question,' interjected Barbra, 'but . . .'

'I accept that, Barbra,' said Pile graciously, his warm deep voice comforting his listeners as it always did. 'I'm sure you would want to be fair to me at this time?' She nodded several times, for emphasis. After all, no TV interviewer wants to admit to unfairness. 'So, let me answer your question,' continued Abel, 'openly, honestly, with complete candour and without fear. My lifestyle, as you called it – no, don't apologize again, there's no need – is, well, it's a matter of personal taste. But let me say this: my books, my accounts, are open to everyone.'

'So why', asked Barbra, 'have you been charged with fraud?'

Pile raised his eyebrows and extended his arms out in front of him, palms upwards. 'I have no idea,' he said. 'But I look forward to my day in court, when I know that the jury will declare my innocence.'

Ernest, who was watching closely, smiled. He's good, he said to himself.

'I don't see how they can find him guilty, do you?' asked Randi with passion.

'I think he stands an excellent chance of getting off,' said Ernest carefully, who knew at least one reason for Abel Pile's quiet confidence. Abel was still talking.

'I appeal to you', he was saying to the studio audience, 'and to all of you viewers at home, for help. I need money to fight this case, to defend my honour. I need a defence fund. Please write in, please pledge your support, send your cash and your cheques to the Church of the Community of Personal Truth, marked Defence Fund.' Ernest gaped. This was a *real* con man. To bilk the public out of even more dough when on trial for fifty-one counts of fraud took the kind of *chutzpah* that Ernest could not help but admire. For the first time he almost liked the man.

Pile was being asked about the dangers of television evangelism. 'I am not a television evangelist, as you know,' he explained in his soothing dark brown caramel voice. 'There is an inherent risk in television evangelism, a risk of idolatry, a risk that ordinary folks out there will worship the face on the screen instead of worshipping God. So when I'm on television I pray directly to God. I say to the people who will see me on the screen, I say: you and I will pray together. I reach out to them with all my inspirationality to make it a participatory process.'

Barbra Riggs's face gave no indication of which side she was on. 'Let's take our first phone call from a viewer,' she said. 'We have Sandy, on the line from Tarzana. Sandy, do you want to ask Dr Pile something?'

Sandy's voice came over the telephone line. She sounded emotional. 'I sure do. I gave Abel Pile my support for twelve years. I gave a lot of money to his Church. I was there every Sunday. Then when I ran out of money he told me he would do nothing more for me unless I gave him a blowjob . . .'

'We'll move right along to the next caller,' said Barbra rapidly. The studio audience giggled nervously. Randi's mouth fell open. Ernest was simultaneously amused and extremely disappointed. He wondered what Pile would have replied.

At his home in the Valley Gilbert Hoolahan, also watching the programme, pricked up his ears too. Was this the element of sexual scandal that he'd been hoping to find?

Pile insisted on answering Sandy from Tarzana. 'I want to answer that woman. I don't want to repeat that obscene accusation on the air, but I must tell you one thing: she is lying. She is a stranger to me, I don't know her. We are not acquainted. Now why would she say that? I don't know, I only know that some people do the strangest things to get attention. She must be a troubled woman and we must pray that God will help her.'

Ernest had to concede that he was very good. He turned to Randi. 'Do you believe him?'

'Yes,' she said firmly, 'I do.' Ernest looked at her closely. He wasn't sure that he believed her, she didn't seem to speak with quite her usual certainty. And Ernest was right. She had felt a slight pang of jealousy and shock. But as always she was determined not to think any negative thoughts.

'She'd better be careful,' said Randi quietly.

'Why?' asked Ernest. Then she told him about the Angel of Darkness. Not that she could tell him much, merely that there was an ill-defined fearsome being that loomed, always present, waiting in the shadows, ready to be invoked by Abel to punish any apostate who expressed negativity or who tried to leave. But whether it was spiritual, Satanic or a human enforcer of discipline was unknown because nobody had ever dared to ask. 'I shouldn't even be telling you about it,' she added. 'You must keep the secret. Promise?'

Ernest had some difficulty in believing in the Angel of Darkness. He scoffed at first, but when he saw that this made Randi deeply uneasy he soon abandoned all discussion of it. It was apparent to Ernest that the Angel of Darkness – if there really were such a thing – would not be some vague metaphysical presence but would either be John Schmidt himself or some hit man whom Schmidt would hire. Schmidt obviously ran the criminal side of the operation for Pile. He was organizing the jury tampering. It all made Pile's protestations that he was innocent of fraud sound rather hollow. Ernest was as convinced as Hoolahan that Pile was a crook, for he did not believe that Schmidt would have hired Joanna to nobble the jury without Pile's knowledge. It was also clear to Ernest that a great deal of money must be at stake in the Church of the Community of Personal Truth. He was glad that Randi knew nothing about John Schmidt's arrangement with Joanna. There was nothing more dangerous than a born-again Christian on the make, he decided, and these preachers would stop at nothing. Whether or not the Angel of Darkness existed, Ernest was now sure that Randi would not be safe if they knew that she knew about a conspiracy to pervert the course of justice. Nor would Joanna. Nor, for that matter, would he. He had one small problem in keeping it a secret: he was writing a book about it.

For her part, Randi instantly regretted telling Ernest about the Angel of Darkness, but she was sure that he would keep his promise not to tell. She was grateful for that, and grateful also for the friendly gesture, the dinner invitation. More than grateful, in fact – she was thrilled that at last Ernest and Abel were to meet. Abel had been wanting to meet Ernest for such a long time and Abel and John had always made her feel guilty she had never been able to get them together. But now, to her surprise, Ernest was being unaccountably considerate and obliging and she loved him for it all the more.

It was running into August and the heat was on. First thing in the mornings, the view from Ernest's house in the hills was like an old-fashioned London pea-souper. The Los Angeles basin disappeared into a dark grey haze. All the mountains had been obliterated weeks ago; the San Gabriels, the San Bernardinos, the Santa Susanas. Now you couldn't see the ocean, you couldn't see downtown, you couldn't even see the skyscrapers of Century City from only a couple of miles away. All you could see, and only if you drove to the top of the hills, was the thick, yellow, stagnant smog, enveloping everything. People's throats burned, their eyes itched and watered, their heads ached, and, those without air-conditioning sweated indoors or soaked themselves in the cool of the swimming-pool. Those fortunates who lived in the hills sat out on their patios and terraces in the evenings, hoping that the occasional gentle breezes would not die. Those who lived in the Valley stayed indoors with their air-conditioners for company, their backyards too hot to step into. In South Central LA it became dangerous to sit out on the front porch because the intense heat raised the emotional temperature too – drive-by shootings multiplied and revenge killings followed hard upon their heels, schoolboys and schoolgirls shooting and knifing each other in a deadly toll that seemed to go up and up with the barometer each weekend. On successive Monday mornings movie people anxiously scanned the numbers, the box-office numbers, to see which movies had been hot over the weekend. Everyone else turned to the Metro section of the *Los Angeles Times* and looked up the other numbers, the total of the dead and maimed, the raped and brutalized. Twenty people, give or take a few, were murdered most weekends. One weekend Ernest looked, the death toll was twenty-eight, but the story still only made page twenty-seven of the *Times*. And every Monday morning the kids went back to their high schools, where they passed through the metal detectors and gave up their guns, knives and clubs till it was time to go home at three o'clock.

The drought prevented ordinary people from watering their gardens. Lawns were dried out and cracked, except in the most exclusive neighbourhoods where the law didn't seem to apply. Even the rats with which Beverly Hills is infested, living under the ivy and the brush, were made sluggish by the merciless sun. In the twilight of the day as Ernest emerged from his study he found, to his horror, a large rodent swimming in the pool. When it saw him it scrambled up the steps and scurried away into a dark hole beside the pool filter. The next day he saw it bathing again, and this time it made its getaway in a more leisurely fashion. Sitting at his desk the following morning he saw another slow fat rat amble down the trunk of one of the cypress trees outside his study window and pick an orange off a nearby bush.

Ernest reached for the phone. The ratman came within a couple of hours. Private enterprise ensures a quick response to emergency calls on the affluent Westside. He introduced himself. 'My name is Stefan,' he said in a thick Hungarian accent. He was a smiling, tubby man. Ernest explained what he had seen.

'So, how *many* rats you seen, exactly?'

'Three,' said Ernest.

Stefan was not a bit surprised. 'You probably have a family of rats living in the house. Or several families.'

Ernest was horrified. 'You're kidding.'

'Well, you've seen three in three days.'

'No, wait a minute, I said three but I don't know that I have, I may not have seen three rats once, I may have seen one rat three times, or one rat in the pool twice and a second rat in the tree once, or two different rats in the pool on two separate occasions plus one of those same two rats in the tree, once ... I mean, how do I know, I can't tell one rat from another, they all look the same to me.'

'But if they're strolling around your garden in the late afternoon it means that they've been here for a while and have become confident.'

'Maybe, but how could there be whole families? I've never seen them before.'

'They're out there in the hills all day. At night, when it gets cold, they like to come in. They can be in your roof, your basement, the crawl space under the house.'

'The roof?' Ernest was aghast. 'How do they get into the roof?'

'They climb up the trees. They get in through the teeniest holes, ventilator grilles, open windows.' Stefan liked putting the wind up people.

'Several families? What does that mean? How many could there be altogether?'

'Who knows? Fifteen, twenty-five . . .'

Ernest was panicking. 'Where do they all come from?'

'This whole area – Hollywood, Beverly Hills – is infested with rats. And snakes.'

'I'll say,' agreed Ernest readily.

'Not just rats, pests of every kind. Termites, squirrels, ground squirrels, racoons . . . how do you think I make such a good living?'

'How would I know what you make? We've never met before.'

'I don't have to do this, you know,' said Stefan. 'I went to the Juilliard School of Music.'

'Really?' Ernest was initially sceptical. 'What instrument do you play?'

'Piano. But I'm mainly a singer. A lyric tenor. Let me ask you something, you in show business?'

'In a way,' replied Ernest, suddenly uncertain. Was a novelist in show business? A screenwriter was, he supposed, but what about an unproduced screenwriter? In fact, was an unproduced screenwriter a screenwriter at all?

'So, what you do?' demanded Stefan, interrupting his train of – for want of a better word – thought. 'You a producer?'

'No, what makes you think that?'

'You have time to sit around the house all day.' He laughed uproariously, in a beautifully articulated melodious high tenor's laugh, clear as a bell. 'Ha-ha-ha-ha-ha.' Ernest smiled weakly at the feeble joke.

'No, I'm a writer.'

'A writer.' Stefan whistled respectfully. 'That's great. I have the greatest respect for writers.' That's good, thought Ernest, at last I've found someone in Hollywood who has the greatest respect for writers: the ratman.

'Here,' Stefan went on, producing a little cassette from his pocket. 'Listen to this. I recorded it myself. It's got arias from all the great operas. Plus a few popular favourites, you know, "My Yiddishe Momma", "Quando Quando Quando", "My Way".' Great, thought Ernest, just what I need, the ratman singing 'My Way'. 'Here's my card. If you ever need a Hungarian tenor in a movie or a TV show,' Stefan went on, 'you know where to find me.'

'At Pest Exterminators Inc., I presume?' said Ernest. He pocketed the card and looked at the tape. There was a photo of Stefan on the front, wearing a blue tuxedo, a phenomenally frilly shirt and a huge, purple, floppy bow-tie. Above the photo were printed the words STEFAN KODALY SINGS.

'Does it mean sings?' Ernest checked. 'Or is this music for the deaf?'

Stefan took the cassette back and looked at it. 'Oops,' he said, and bit his lower lip.

He set traps all over the basement and attic. Then he stuck poisoned chunks of something to the tree trunks where Ernest had spied the rats. 'They eat this, they die,' he explained cheerily.

'What if they don't eat it?'

'They will.' Stefan spoke with total certainty. If there was one thing Stefan knew about, it was rats.

'But what if they *do* eat it?' asked Ernest, as a horrifying picture took shape in his mind's eye. 'Won't we have dead rats falling out of the trees all over my terrace?' He had an image of his beautiful patio deluged with rats, cascades of rodents raining down upon chic movie industry guests from Beverly Hills.

'That's not how it happens,' Stefan reassured him. 'They get sick slowly, they crawl away into the hills and die. But if they're in the house we catch them in the traps I set in the attic and the basement. I'll come back once a week to check. If you want to check yourself, before then, and you find any rats, or if there's a bad smell, call me and I'll take 'em away.'

He set the traps in the house, and left, singing 'Celeste Aida'.

That Saturday night Randi, Ernest and Bobby (the caterer Randi hired to cook dinner) busily prepared to receive Abel Pile and John Schmidt. Promptly at seven the gate intercom buzzed.

'It's them,' said Randi with excitement as she hung up, and hurried out into the garden to greet them. As she set foot on the terrace a rat fell out of the tree outside Ernest's study, bounced off her head and lay there on the bricks, twitching. She screamed. He rushed out. She was still screaming. He looked around, bewildered.

'What's wrong? What's happened?'

Hysterical and incoherent, she pointed at the rat. 'It hit me on the head!' she shrieked. Ernest turned, looked, and jumped back, clutching Randi. She screamed again. 'What happened?'

'Nothing,' said Ernest. The rat lay there, apparently dead. 'Shit,' said Ernest, 'what are we going to do?'

Bobby the caterer was now on the terrace. He was a man of action. 'Have you a broom and a dustpan?'

'Good idea,' said Ernest, and ran inside to the broom cupboard.

'Abel and John are coming up the drive,' whimpered Randi to Bobby. After a fight with the tangled brooms in the broom cupboard, Ernest emerged, threw the dustpan at Randi and the broom to Bobby. 'I'll go and delay the guests,' he said.

'No you don't!' screeched Randi, now only semihysterical as her terror was turning to rage. 'It's your house and your terrace and your broom – and it's your fucking rat, as a matter of fact! And they're my guests.' And she slammed the dustpan against Ernest's chest and hurried down the drive just as Abel and John were strolling into view. Ernest turned to Bobby.

'Come on, we can do it,' said the intrepid caterer. 'Put the dustpan down.' Ernest held it beside the rat at arm's length while Bobby swept the corpse on to it. Then they moved cautiously into the kitchen, Ernest still holding the pan at arm's length in case the rat suddenly revived and leaped for cover. 'Get a garbage bag,' shrieked Ernest.

'Where from?'

'I don't know, wherever the maid keeps them.'

Randi saw that the terrace was all clear as she approached with her guests, but she could hear the commotion in the kitchen as Bobby threw open and slammed shut all the kitchen cabinets two by two while Ernest stood helplessly in the middle of the room, arms extended, eyes on the rat. 'Someone sounds awfully busy in there,' remarked Abel Pile. 'Can we help?'

'No, that's just Ernest and the caterer, putting the finishing touches to dinner.' Slam, slam, came from the kitchen. 'Let's stay out here, isn't the view wonderful?'

Abel and John stared at the thick evening smog. 'Well, I can see that on a clear day it must be,' said Abel. 'I'll bet you can see all the way to the ocean.'

Ernest appeared. 'Hello there, pleased to meet you at long last,' he said. 'Come in.'

'Randi suggested staying out here.'

Ernest glanced nervously up at the trees. 'No, let's go in,' he said.

In the circumstances it was inevitable that Ernest would not let dinner pass without some disagreement. 'I hear you want to convert me,' he remarked jovially as he poured the Chardonnay for his guests.

229

'I would certainly like you to join us in Christ,' acknowledged Abel Pile.

'What does that mean, exactly?' asked Ernest, raising his glass. 'Your good health.'

They all clinked glasses. 'Like, born again,' explained Randi as she served the delicious crisp Caesar salad that Bobby had made as a starter. 'Like me. Like him. You know that.' She smiled apologetically at Abel and John. 'I'm afraid Ernest's not a very spiritual person.'

'Yes, it's jolly good of you to offer, Abel old chap,' said Ernest patronizingly, 'but actually I've never been born at all, spiritually that is. And I'm bound to say that most of the people I've met who were born again were somewhat nicer the first time around.' He plonked the bottle of wine down beside him at the head of the table. 'Present company excepted,' he added, with his widest and most insincere smile.

'Jesus's resurrection is our resurrection,' said Abel. '"We shall be changed," said St Paul.'

'Well, that raises *another* interesting question,' remarked Ernest. 'I mean, *was* Jesus resurrected? Was the tomb really empty? Did He die on the cross? Was it all a trick? Let's face it,' he went on, getting into his most truly offensive stride, 'it's a bloody weird religion that turns on whether or not a particular corpse was or was not in a tomb two thousand years ago. A bizarre basis for one of the so-called great religions of the world, wouldn't you say?' They were looking at him in silence. 'Unless you look at it anthropologically, as one of those myths of rebirth that one finds in all societies.'

'It's The Greatest Story Ever Told,' said Abel Pile, fittingly choosing to describe Jesus's life with a movie title.

'The greatest?' Ernest was off and running. 'Well, now, that's quite a claim, my friend.' His enmity was quite transparent. 'Greater than *War and Peace*? OK, for the sake of argument, let's suppose you're right. Supposing it really is the greatest story ever told, that doesn't mean that it has to be true. Wouldn't it be even more exciting if Jesus had never existed – a superlative literary invention, a story of a man who died to save the whole of mankind? Wouldn't mankind be even more wonderful if it had invented such a myth?'

'But He did exist. He was the son of God.'

'Who says?' Ernest topped up his own wine glass.

'For those who believe,' said Abel smoothly, 'no explanation is necessary. For those who don't believe, no explanation is possible.'

'Good answer,' said Ernest with approval. 'Bloody good answer. You know why? Because it completely begs the question.'

'How so?'

'Look. It's simple logic.' Ernest was beginning to hector his guests now and Randi was watching in despair. This was not how he had promised to behave. 'It's so fucking obvious. There are some things – many things – that we don't understand. We can then say either "God is the reason", or we can say "we don't understand". What I'm asking you is: *why* should we believe that God is the reason?'

'Without God,' said Abel, 'isn't it, for instance, just a matter of opinion about whether or not it's right to kill people?'

'*With* God,' countered Ernest, 'it still seems to be a matter of opinion. Isn't that why Salman Rushdie's life's in danger?'

'I can't speak for the Islamic God,' replied Abel Pile dismissively. 'He seems different from my God. My God tells me the difference between right and wrong.'

'Wait a minute, wait a minute,' said Ernest, affecting a perplexed expression, 'I thought there was supposed to be only one God.'

'Yes . . . but there are many ways to perceive him, most of them erroneous.'

'I see,' said Ernest. He was still giving his I'm-just-a-plain-man-trying-to-understand-these-very-complicated-ideas performance. 'So God tells you the difference between right and wrong.' He nodded for a while, as if deep in thought. 'Haven't you thought of the alternative explanation? That we invented God to create standards? I mean, I put it to you that morality exists in spite of the cruelty and intolerance that religion has brought, not because of it.'

'But look around you,' Abel answered. He seemed to be enjoying the debate. 'Look at our wonderful world. Look at the night sky, the stars, the scope of the universe, the trees and the flowers, look at the magnificence of the Creation. God is the obvious inference.'

'No, it's just one possible inference,' said Ernest. 'But why would anyone want to martyr themselves for an inference?'

'Nobody's asking you to, darling,' intervened Randi. All three men ignored her, even though she had recently been initiated into the Pilgrim's Priesthood by two of them.

'So you don't see God as the source of our morality?' asked John Schmidt. Ernest was privately delighted by the knowledge that the man sitting opposite him, talking of 'our morality', had to his certain knowledge hired a prostitute to blackmail a juror to secure a wrongful acquittal of the con man sitting next to him.

'Not my morality,' stated Ernest with certainty. 'You want my opinion? I think that morality exists in every society and for very practical reasons: every society creates a moral code because the members of that society need to co-exist with each other, and for their own mutual defence. All the ancient religious taboos are purely practical: against adultery, against incest, against eating shellfish and pork, against theft . . .' he paused and looked meaningfully at Abel Pile. 'They are just simple rules to ensure society's survival, and the survival of the species.'

'But who gave us these rules?'

'I know, I know, you believe that God did,' said Ernest. 'Believe me, I get it. But I believe that you believe that simply because you need to believe.'

'You don't believe that we need God?'

'Oh yes. No question, I believe that you need God, I believe that the whole human race needs God. I mean, even me, even I need God,' he added generously. 'I admit it. I'd love to believe in God. I'm sure I'd be happier if I were a believer. So yes, the need is real. But that proves fuck all, pardon my French. The question is out there, but perhaps we invented the answer.'

'I guess we shall have to agree to differ on this,' said Abel. He could see that Randi had been right. It was clear that, for the moment, Ernest could not be prevailed upon to join the Church of the Community of Personal Truth but, quite honestly, so long as the trial was pending Pile did not expect many more recruits. The important thing was for Randi to marry Ernest, in California, and thus gain access to the Mayday millions. He saw, as did John Schmidt, that they would have to continue to work on Randi privately.

SEVENTEEN

The prostitute appeals by her fresh and natural
coarseness, her frank familiarity with the crudest facts
of life; and so lifts her customer for a moment out of
the withering atmosphere of artificial thought and
unreal sentiment in which so many civilized persons
are compelled to spend the greater part of their lives.

Havelock Ellis

The evening before the trial of Abel Pile, Joanna met Ernest Mayday at the Bel Monde Hotel, the scene of their first encounter. At the end of their last meeting in the frozen-yogurt shop he had remembered to take her phone number and in the intervening period he had wanted to call her. But for what? He knew that she would call him when she had anything new to report, for she certainly needed the money. He knew that until the trial started there would be nothing for her to do. She had politely but firmly refused to grant him her sexual favours. And yet, or perhaps because of this, his thoughts turned constantly to her. He wondered if he should phone her to make a date, just to see her again, even if only to have a meal together. He fantasized more than before about becoming her friend, her lover, the one man in her life to whom she would make love for *love*, or for fun at least. But eventually common sense would prevail as he reminded himself how they had met. She didn't want marriage; she would allow herself to be kept for a price, but above all she wanted her freedom. Ernest Mayday thought that one day she might agree to be bought but he knew also that she would never be his.

So he waited patiently to hear from her and, sure enough, the night before the trial she phoned. Randi had gone over to Malibu. Abel Pile had asked her to come and pray for him, with 'the guys', the High Priests of the Pilgrim's Priesthood. Randi hurried over there, honoured by the invitation. She remained buoyed up by an absolute belief in Abel's innocence, she refused to think negative thoughts and she was devoting herself more and more to church affairs. Ernest knew that the *paparazzi* were camped outside Pile's house and saw clearly that a prayer meeting the night before the trial began was in the interest of good public relations. 'Are you going to pray for me, Ernest, my friend?' Abel had asked him on the phone.

'You know I don't believe in prayer, but I promise you that you'll be constantly in my thoughts throughout the trial,' Ernest had told him with complete honesty. 'And for a long time afterwards as well,' he added

He thought of asking Joanna to the house, knowing that Randi would be out for the evening, but he realized that if he did so his cover would be blown and she would learn who he really was. All around the house were letters, cheque books, diaries, framed degrees hanging on the wall above the toilet, all bearing his name. She had already told him how carefully she checked out every new room she went into, looking for exactly that kind of information. He was sure that, no matter how hard he tried to hide things, she would leave his house knowing his name and everything else about him. Though she knew his phone number, it gave him a sense of security to know that she didn't have his address.

So he took a bedroom in the Bel Monde. In the public rooms there was always a possibility of their being overheard, and it was a criminal offence that they were discussing. He got there early, helped himself to a very large whisky from the mini-bar and waited. He stood on the tiny terrace outside his ninth-floor French windows and stared at the streaked pink and purple sunset. The sky was the colour of a giant black eye. There was a knock at the door. He opened it. Joanna was there, in a pretty flowered Laura Ashley sort of dress, calf-length, dainty ballet pumps on her little feet, a straw hat on her head, a picture of demure simplicity. She pecked him on the cheek, strolled in, threw her handbag on to the bed and glanced back at him. 'I see,' she smiled, eyes twinkling. 'A hotel room at last. And I didn't bring my toothbrush this time.'

'But I thought that . . . I mean, I asked you and you said no,' said Ernest, covered in confusion.

'I *know*, Norm, I was kidding, darling,' she said, taking off her hat and throwing herself on to one of the sofas. 'God, I'm tired, it's been quite a day.'

He offered her a drink. She took a Perrier. He sat in one of the armchairs, picked up his pen and yellow legal pad and waited. 'So?' he asked.

'Well,' she began, 'I got a call from John Schmidt yesterday, asking me to meet him again in the Bonaventure Hotel, downtown. He told me that the trial they needed my help in was Abel Pile's trial. I pretended that I didn't know, since he obviously thought he was making a big surprise announcement. I didn't want to spoil his fun. He told me to be in the public section of the federal courthouse tomorrow morning when the trial opens at nine-thirty. He said there'd be lots of press and media people there, so I have to get there an hour early and stand in line to be sure of getting in.'

'What do you have to do?'

'I have to watch jury selection. That's what they begin with. It might take all day. Apparently they call the jurors up by name, but they don't give addresses or phone numbers. This is my first chance to get a look at them all, my only chance to hear them talk. The judge asks them questions, and this is when we try to decide which of them I'm going to hit on.'

Ernest wanted more of a flavour of her conversation with John Schmidt. 'What did he actually say?'

She looked at the ceiling for help. 'He said: "Look inconspicuous. Look different from normal. There's a lot of sitting around in a courtroom, and if you're sitting there looking great the way you look now, everyone'll notice you, the judge, the lawyers, the jury, they'll all recognize you if they see you again and obviously we don't want the juror you hit on to know you have any interest in the case, OK?" I told him I'd be a real little mouse tomorrow. I'm going to wear that brunette wig I wore the day I met you, Norm, remember?'

'But not that mini-skirt that goes all the way up to your crotch?'

'It doesn't go all the way, Norm,' she pouted, 'don't exaggerate.'

'But you're not going to wear it, are you? You've got great legs . . .'

'Why, thank you sir,' she said, playing the Southern belle, fluttering her eyelashes.

'I'm serious, Joanna, please.' Ernest was getting tetchy. 'He's right, you must look plain if you can, nobody should give you a second glance.'

She scowled at him. 'I know that, what do you think I am, some kind of idiot?'

'Sorry,' he said.

'I mean, do you think I want to end up in jail?'

'No.' He felt a little sheepish. 'Go on. What else did he say?'

'I asked him if hitting on just one juror would get his man off. He said that wasn't the whole answer. If only one juror votes not guilty, then it's a hung jury and there'll be a retrial. He said that would be a start, it'd be better than nothing, but obviously he's trying to get an acquittal. So we have to try and hit on a juror who can persuade some of the others if necessary.'

'That's going to be tough, isn't it?'

'That's what I asked. He said "No, not really. We have a case that we could win, we just want to be sure." He said they're allowed to challenge up to twelve jurors. The defence strategy will be to get a jury of ordinary God-fearing simple folk, who will be predisposed to believe Abel Pile's side of the story.'

'So they've got to find twelve jurors who are stupid and gullible.'

'I suppose. Not sophisticated was the way he put it. Anyway, tampering with the jury is just meant to be a sort of insurance policy, to get one definite vote so that at the very least there'll be a hung jury, and to be sure there's someone in the jury room arguing on our side. He says they could win the case anyway.'

'How are you supposed to pick up the guy you select if you don't know where he lives?'

'John said he'd take care of that.'

'Did he say how?'

She shook her head.

Ernest sat and waited. 'What else?'

She sat and thought. 'Nothing really. He told me the kind of people they get on a jury. They're retired, or they work for the government or the aerospace industry or big companies. Mainly they're blue-collar kind of people, unless they're retired.'

'Why's that?'

'John says that economic hardship is an exceptable excuse. They'll let you off. So if you're not being paid a salary or a pension while you're on jury duty it's a hardship, see?'

'He told you nothing else?'

'He told me how to get to the courthouse.'

Ernest hesitated. 'You . . . did nothing else?'

She laughed her delicious husky laugh. 'Ernest, you're such a naughty boy. We really ought to get you a two-way mirror.'

'So you did?'

'Sure. John's got a very big . . . appetite.'

'What happened?'

'That's nothing to do with you.'

'Yes it is. It's all part of my story, your relationship with John Schmidt.'

She giggled again. Ernest had never thought of her as a giggler. For all the world she seemed to be slightly embarrassed. 'Use your imagination, Norm.'

'No. I'd rather know what really happened.' She looked at him, intrigued, smiling, but said nothing. 'Go on,' he insisted, 'it's part of our deal. You said you'd tell me everything.'

'Well . . .' She crossed her legs as if she didn't trust herself, leaned back in the sofa with a little smile and began to talk. 'We were very naughty. We did just about everything.'

'Everything? Like . . . what? What does everything mean?' He felt slightly breathless and panicky.

'I asked him if he wanted to undress me. I always ask that. Some do, some don't, know what I mean? He said he did. So I let him, and he really took his time, he wasn't in any big hurry. He unzipped my skirt first . . .'

'Were you lying down?'

'No, I was standing up. So, he unzipped my skirt and pulled it down over my cheeks.' She was speaking softly now. 'Then he slid my panties down and I stepped out of them. I was still wearing my stockings and garter belt, and my blouse and bra.' She looked over at Ernest, who was listening intently. 'He didn't want to undress me any further. He looked at me for a bit. Then he asked me to take off his clothes for him.'

'So you did?'

'Customer's always right, Norm. This is America. 'Course, by the time I finished undressing him and laying him down on the sofa and everything he was very . . . excited, know what I mean? I was getting wet too. I asked him if I could sit on it. He said not yet.'

'What time of night was this?' asked Ernest without looking up, as busily he wrote down her actual words.

'It wasn't night. It was the middle of the day.'

Ernest was surprised. 'Oh. I thought you usually worked at night.'

'Why?'

'I don't know. It's just what I imagined, somehow. I thought that's when . . . working girls worked.'

'No, I have lots of daytime dates. You know, lunch, followed by a nice time in the afternoon. Married guys have much less problem explaining a long lunch to the wife than some evening appointment.'

'Then what?' asked Ernest.

'He asked me to kneel beside him and he sat up and finished undressing me.'

'Then what?' asked Ernest again.

'He took off my blouse, very slowly, very gently, kissing me all the time. Then my bra – I'm always a bit concerned about that because my tits aren't that big, and that's important to some men, not that it matters, good things come in little packages, so they say, and I come any time.' She laughed.

'Then what?' asked Ernest for the third time, aware that his side of the conversation had become somewhat limited.

'Then, while I was still wearing my stockings and garters, he gently bent me forward over the back of the sofa, and slipped into me from behind. I could hardly wait, I was really wet by then. I was having a great time.'

Ernest stared at her. He pulled himself together, stopped drooling and continued writing. Great, he thought, these'll be the best sex scenes I've ever had in any of my books. Ernest had always felt that sex scenes had been his weakness, even though he was convinced that they had played a major part in the success of his books, at least from the point of view of sales. But he'd always found them difficult. I mean, how many different ways can you describe tits? he'd asked Mark Down. 'Go on,' he said.

'Well ... you'll never guess what happened next,' she whispered playfully.

'You're right,' he whispered back, slightly hoarse. 'So tell me.'

'Three guesses.'

Ernest's mind was racing. Flashing through his head went every fantasy, every perversion, every position he'd ever read about. 'I give up.'

She pulled her knees up in front of her, on the sofa, and clasped her hands in front of them. Her full skirt now covered even her ankles and her feet. She fixed her eyes on his in an unblinking stare. 'Abel Pile came into the room.'

'While you were ...?'

'Exactly. While we were ... you got it, pal!'

Ernest's eyes revolved. 'And?'

'And he had a woman with him.'

'Who?'

'I don't know, Norm, I was being fucked, it wasn't exactly the moment for formal introductions.'

'What did he say?'

'Nothing.'

Ernest got exasperated. 'Well, didn't anybody say anything?'

'No. We just carried on. Then we did everything.'

Ernest stopped writing and looked at her for a moment. 'Everything? What does that mean, everything?' He swallowed nervously. He was aware that his conversation was becoming even more repetitive.

'Well, while John and I finished up, he had her. Then

John had her and Abel had me. Then they wanted to watch me and her together, which she seemed a bit reluctant about but I think she enjoyed it in the end – I told you I've got the best tongue in the business. Then Abel had John.'

Ernest gaped. 'You're kidding.'

'No. Why?'

'It's just that . . . I've never been in an orgy like that.'

'No?' She wasn't very curious, or surprised.

'I'm shocked,' he said. 'I can't exactly explain why, but . . .'

Joanna smiled at him casually. 'Whatever turns you on, Norm. It's not good, being judgemental. 'Course, I know I don't have any right to be judgemental, but have you?'

He didn't have a reply for her. She wrapped up the story. 'So, I'm trying to get to the interesting part. Afterwards we all showered, and got dressed, and then a very strange thing happened.'

'What was that?' whispered Ernest.

'We prayed. Well, they did, all three of them, and I pretended to join in of course. Like I said, the customer's always right. I mean, like, they were paying me, right? They want me to fuck, I fuck. They want me to pray, I pray.'

Ernest was silent for a moment. His mind was racing. Was Abel Pile genuinely religious, in spite of his aberrant behaviour? Was the prayer to impress Joanna, who knew who he was, or certainly would when she saw him the next day in court? But surely not. You wouldn't have a charade like that to impress some hooker. Maybe the prayer was for the benefit of the other woman. He had an idea. 'Was this some kind of perverted sexual quasi-religious rite you were involved in?'

She shrugged. 'I wouldn't know. As far as I was concerned, we were just having a nice time. Anything else you want to know?' She stood up.

'Yes. Can you remember anything about the prayer?'

She had to think for a moment before she replied. 'I think so. He thanked God for giving us this party, he said they believed that sex was good, that it was a gift from God to be enjoyed by men and women, and it was nothing to be ashamed of. After he finished praying he told us that we should never think negatively about our sexuality, but we should be proud of it. You know what? I'm thinking of joining his church if we can keep him out of prison, I felt just great when I left.' She walked to the door and opened it. 'See you in court tomorrow?' she asked.

'Yes. One more thing. What did the girl look like?'

'Jesus, Norm, I thought you were a fucking novelist. Can't you make anything up?' And she walked out of the room, shutting the door behind her.

EIGHTEEN

*We are not onely passive, but active, in our owne
ruine; we do not onely stand under a falling house,
but pull it downe upon us; and, wee are not onely
executed, but wee are executioners and executioners
of our selves.*

John Donne

The United States courthouse stands on the corner of
Temple and Main, downtown. It is right opposite City
Hall, a vast white 1920s version of a neo-classical office
building, ten storeys high with another eighteen storeys of
1930s skyscraper towering out of its centre. Across the
street, just around the corner from Spring Street, which
was built in 1920 and was known as the Wall Street of the
West and came complete with a number of monumental
American 'classical' buildings decorated with Greek,
Roman and Egyptian columns and statuary, stands the
federal courthouse. It's a plainer place, fatter, lower, also
white, like a cigarette pack lying on its side.

Joanna parked in the public parking-lot on nearby
Arcadia Street. Even at eight-thirty in the morning the
day was warming up. She walked across the freeway
overpass, where the rush hour was in full swing fifty feet
below, past some brown, shaggy, neglected-looking palm
trees and some browner, shaggier, even more neglected-
looking panhandlers. She strolled along the sidewalk to
the wide shallow steps of the courthouse, where a couple
of Stars and Stripes hung limply from twin flagpoles and
a bald eagle in the centre of the US Seal, carved in stone,

stared blindly out over the traffic jams and the homeless people being moved along by the cops.

Joanna had indeed dressed discreetly, and no heads turned to watch her as she mounted the steps and entered the gloomy marbled lobby. Dressing discreetly had been her own idea, not John Schmidt's. As she walked she smiled, and thought how easily Ernest had swallowed her story about the meeting with John Schmidt in the hotel yesterday, and the subsequent orgy with Abel Pile. I should be a writer, she thought as she passed through the metal detectors, and paused to look at a ten-foot-tall stone neo-ancient-Egyptian statue of a woman in an apparently tight gown through which her marble nipples were clearly visible, the side of one hand placed over her pubic region and the other hand leaning heavily on a stone tablet on which were carved the words NO LAW IS STRONGER THAN IS THE PUBLIC SENTIMENT WHERE IT IS TO BE ENFORCED - ABRAHAM LINCOLN. Turning to look around through the gloom of the underlit dark green, beige and grey marble lobby, she saw what appeared to be a statue of the young Mr Lincoln at the far end. It was a puzzling monument, showing Abe naked to the waist and with his trousers half open at the top. He had no words beside him, not even about strangely clad women in diaphanous gowns with Ptolemaic hairstyles leaning on his words. Joanna rode the long escalator to the second floor, which turned out to be a magnificently huge hall of Cecil B. de Mille proportions, this time principally veneered with sea-green and mud-brown marble. Old illuminated signs outside the bank of elevators indicated THIS CAR UP/DOWN and, like the New York subway, LOCAL TO THE 13TH. She felt she was in a period movie. It was all very reminiscent of *The Front Page*.

Inside the courtroom, the dark, rich, shining teak panelling which lined the walls reflected the fluorescent yellow panels in the ceiling and the subdued activity as the team of defence lawyers and the attorneys for the people of the State of California, led by a confident-looking Gil Hoolahan, took their seats at their respective tables. Abel Pile was already there, his charisma strangely faded in the gloom of the courtroom. Joanna looked at him with interest. He didn't acknowledge her. She knew why. She saw John Schmidt at the defence table, and their eyes met briefly as he scanned the public seats. He looked at her again with slight surprise, as he recognized her under the modest disguise.

She was not alone on those benches. At the far side of the public section sat Ernest Mayday and Randi Toner, also early arrivals. Joanna's eyes met Ernest's but, as planned, they betrayed no recognition of each other. Sitting between them were thirty or forty members of the public, from whom the jury of twelve would be selected.

The Judge took his seat. He was a tall, lumpy, ungainly fellow, a tired ex-prosecutor with an untidy face, a lazy right eyelid, a couple of warts on his cheek and his chin, bags upon bags under his eyes like a St Bernard and a bulbous bloodhound's nose for a bad legal smell. This was a man who had heard everything. He struck the gavel hard, once, to obtain silence. The clerk of the court selected twelve names at random and Joanna watched and listened carefully as they took their seats in the jury box. Not only were their names given, they were spelled out to avoid confusion, and though their addresses and phone numbers were withheld their neighbourhood was given.

'What is your marital status?' the Judge asked the first juror, a scrawny skinny middle-aged woman with thin hair and thinner lips.

'I'm married.'

'Occupation?'

'I'm an educator.'

'What kind of educator?'

'I teach grade school.'

'Where do you reside?'

'Thousand Oaks.'

'Can you think of any reason why you cannot be a fair and impartial juror in this case?'

'No, sir.'

'Have you ever heard of the defendant, Dr Abel Pile?'

'Yes, sir.'

'Have you read anything about this case in the newspapers, or seen any comment about it on television?'

'Yes, sir. Both.'

'Do you have any view at this point in time about whether Dr Pile is innocent or guilty?'

'Well,' said the woman, 'obviously, if he wasn't guilty he wouldn't be here.'

The Judge suppressed a smile, and raised an untidy shaggy eyebrow in the direction of the defence.

Other jurors too were dismissed in the course of the morning. The Judge was diligent in his questioning. He asked for their children's occupations, and one homemaker was dismissed because she had a son-in-law who was a cop. Some jurors were excused by the defence because on previous jury service they had found the defendants guilty, and others by the prosecution because on previous jury service they had found the defendants not guilty. The Judge continued his methodical questioning. 'Marital status?'

'Divorced.' This one was an overweight, asthmatic bulldog of a woman.

'Juror number three,' continued the Judge, 'have you had previous jury service?'

'Nope, but I bin a witness.'

'Can you put the events of that court case out of your mind?'

'No, Judge, I can't, he got off scot-free, and in my opinion they shoulda fried him.'

'Was it a capital offence?'

'Huh?'

'What was the alleged offence?'

'Huh?'

The Judge tried again. 'What crime did he commit?'

'Weren't no crime, exactly. We was gettin' divorced.'

By three-thirty it was over. Twenty-nine potential jurors had been in the box and twelve of them remained. 'By my count', said the Judge, 'we now have a jury, as the defence has exhausted all its pre-emptive challenges.' Ernest surveyed the jurors. He had imagined, foolishly, that Joanna would have a choice of twelve men to seduce. But seven of the jurors were women. He watched her across the now virtually empty public seats, for the jury panel was gone and only a couple of bored-looking reporters remained. He couldn't tell what she was thinking, but he thought she had to be worried by the lack of choice. The Judge was instructing the jury, rapidly, mechanically, with words he had used a thousand times before, reading them into the record as a matter of form. 'This is a criminal case, brought by the US Government. The indictment is simply a description of the charges and is not evidence. The defendant has pleaded not guilty and is presumed innocent until he is proved guilty beyond a reasonable doubt. You are the sole judges of the facts. The defendant starts out with a clean slate. The defendant has the right to remain silent and he never has to prove his own innocence. The following things are not evidence: statements and arguments by the attorneys, objections by the attorneys, anything I instruct you to disregard, anything you may see or hear when the court is not in session. You should not and must not discuss this case with any other person.' At the back of the courtroom, Joanna permitted herself a little private smile.

As he drove home, Ernest felt that Joanna had various possibilities open to her. Four of the five men on the jury were married. Three of them had been married a long time, had grown up children and respectable jobs. A couple of them said they were churchgoers. He wondered how she would make contact with them. Would she follow them home, would she try to pick them up on the street near the courthouse? How would she dress? Would they be attracted to an obvious hooker, or would she pretend to be a civilian? He knew that he wouldn't see her in court again, for she no longer needed to be there and it was too risky for her to show up on a regular basis.

At home on the answering machine he found a mass of offers and invitations. Virginia Spearmen's assistant had called to arrange dinner so that he and Virginia could discuss the creative aspects of *Lies*, Craig Rosenbaum had called on behalf of the English faculty to follow up on the idea of Ernest's teaching a creative-writing course, Casey Boddichek – the persistent young Creative Executive from International Pictures – had called to 'do' lunch so that they could discuss Cinderella, and Oliver Sudden had simply called.

Meanwhile Gil Hoolahan, on his way home to Woodland Hills in the deepest darkest Valley, called hopefully upon Sandy from Tarzana, the lady who had called in to the TV talk show to confront Abel Pile with her accusation that he had demanded a blowjob in exchange for continued church membership. He had already arranged for her to be interviewed by an FBI investigator, to whom she had confirmed the story and with whom she had gone into further detail. He was now in possession of a written statement from her.

By a stroke of good fortune, otherwise known as a leak from Gil's office, representatives of the tabloid press were doorstepping her house, and they photographed his arrival. At first she mistook him for a journalist and refused to talk to him, but upon realizing her error she let him in. He was not upset to be pictured entering Sandy's house, for he was not sure that he could get her story admitted into the evidence, and at least the jurors would see reports of him investigating the allegation in the papers or on the evening news. And in order for the reports to make sense to the great American public, the press would have no alternative but to repeat the allegation, however discreetly: ABEL PILE DEMANDS ORAL SEX FOR RELIGIOUS RITES. Luck was on Gil Hoolahan's side – Sandy turned out to be an attractive, photogenic, clean-cut all-American young lady in her mid thirties, happily married, God-fearing and righteous, not at all the tarty type he had feared. She was delighted to receive him, though she seemed upset and embarrassed when he asked her to retell her story. She was slightly tearful, and Hoolahan hoped that she would be able to reproduce those emotions in the witness box. After a forty-minute talk over a glass of iced tea she agreed that she would, if necessary, fulfil her public duty and serve as a witness if required.

Hoolahan left, pondering how to get this delightful tidbit admitted into the record. He let none of his doubts show to the ladies and gentlemen of the press who were courteously peering in through the downstairs windows through their Nikon lenses, for he did not really expect a problem: if the defence introduced evidence of Abel Pile's good character the door would be open for him to produce Sandy and the blowjob request. When one of the journalists asked him if he would be calling Sandy as a witness, Hoolahan had a ready reply. 'She has something to add to the deliberations of the court that could constitute both relevant and admissible evidence, that goes to prove both the fiscal and sexual corruption of this scoundrel Abel Pile.' The reporters clamoured for details, at which point he adopted his most high-minded stance. 'No, it would not be fair for me to say anything further at this stage. You must remember that as the prosecutor I am a servant of the court, and my reponsibility is to justice herself. If I were the attorney for the defence I'd be prepared to say anything, to stoop at nothing to get my client off.

Ernest, watching the late-night news, thoroughly enjoyed the mixed metaphor and thought: little does he know how right he is. On TV, Hoolahan was winding up his smug and self-serving remarks: 'That's why it's so much harder to prosecute than to defend – unlike the defence, *I* have a duty to be fair.'

Ernest was back in court the next day, looking for good material. Joanna could not keep showing up there but there was no necessity for Ernest to be discreet. Randi was planning to attend every single day of the trial, and she was thrilled that Ernest was making his support for Abel visible in this way. Gil Hoolahan, conscious that the eyes of Los Angeles were upon him, made a powerful opening statement. His determination to root out the truth was unmistakable.

'You are the sole judges of the facts,' he told the jury, as if totally unaware that the Judge had told them the self-same thing the evening before. He gripped the railing along the front of the jury box and spoke softly, firmly and authoritatively, fixing each juror in turn with his most implacable, gimlet-eyed gaze. 'Members of the jury, you may rest assured, each and every one of you, that we, the Government of the United States of America, will leave every stone unturned in the search for the truth, the whole truth and nothing but the truth about the Reverend Doctor Abel Pile.'

'Every stone?' queried the Judge. Hoolahan looked blank.

The opening statement by the defence was equally impressive.

'Dr Abel Pile is a servant of God,' explained Harris K. Fitch, the shabby, crumpled, down-home Midwestern attorney who had been retained to lead the Pile team. He wore an old sports coat, pockets bulging with a pipe, a tobacco pouch and a few pipe cleaners, into which he stuffed scrappy bits of paper on which he made a note whenever the other side said something that seemed to strike him as new, significant or important. 'Now I'm just a simple country lawyer from Nashville, Tennessee, and I'm gonna do my level best to figure out what the Reverend Pile is bein' accused of here . . . and why! Because, for the life of me, I can't see what he's supposed to have done wrong.' He stopped, and added as an afterthought: 'Though if he has, I'd expect y'all to vote him guilty. That's your job and that's your duty.' Ernest wondered, when it came time to write the book, if he should spell duty the charming way Harris K. Fitch pronounced it, doody. 'But I think you gonna find, ladies and gentlemen, that the charges against the Reverend Pile don't amount to a hill o' beans. Nobody gave money to the Church of the Community of Personal Truth who didn't *want* to give it. Nobody twisted their arms. None of the members of the Church are complainin'. And we will show y'all, in the course of this trial, that the money did not go into Dr Pile's pocket. It's the Church's money, it went to the Church and it's bein' used by the Church to do' – and here Fitch's voice dropped to a deeply respectful murmur – 'the will of God.' He paused, looked at them all, then spoke again with renewed vigour and energy, a sense of innocent outrage and legitimate grievance colouring his mellifluous and expressive voice. 'So why, I can hear you askin', *why* is the government prosecutin' a God-fearin' law-abidin' citizen like this good man here? And it is the government, not the people of the state of California, no, make no mistake, this is a federal case and this is a federal courtroom, it is the *government* in Washington DC that's prosecutin' this case here today. Why? I know y'all are askin' that question because I can see that y'all are a group of highly intelligent men and women. Y'all saw how careful we were in selectin' y'all. That's because we wanted a real intelligent bunch of people, on this jury, because Dr Pile has the right to be judged by a jury of his peers, and I think y'all *are* his peers. Well, I'll tell you what I think is behind it. I think it's the government. They are committed to keepin' prayer out of our schools. Did you know that? Sure you did. They're none too happy about those good people who are trying to build a holy kingdom here on earth. This, my friends, is a political prosecution, and that's not the American way. The first amendment of our constitution guarantees freedom of speech, freedom of expression, freedom of religion. There's nobody, not even in Washington, who has the right to tell us how we can worship God.' Slowly, with dignity, he walked back to his chair, shaking his head in sorrow at Gil Hoolahan. He turned to face the jury. 'We are Americans,' he reminded them and sat down, leaving the jury to contemplate their awesome responsibilities.

That night Harris K. Fitch left his suite at the Beverly Wilshire Hotel to meet his clients for dinner. The jury might not have recognized him in his bespoke-tailored three-piece conservative suit and silk tie. No bulging pockets but a knife-edge crease in his trousers, no tobacco pouch and pipe but a fat Cuban cigar, and almost no Tennessee accent. The shambling country bumpkin was transmuted into a slick city lawyer. It's not that he had lied to the jury, he was indeed from Nashville – he simply had omitted to mention that he had been practising in Washington DC since he left Yale law school thirty years ago.

And that night Ernest Mayday left a message on Joanna's answering machine, ostensibly to inquire if she had made any progress but in reality because he was now obsessed with her. She didn't call him back. He wasn't surprised, he had not expected that she would. The trial was predicted to last for several weeks, and it was bound to take her a little time to make contact with one of the jurors. Randi was out giving massages, trying to make up some of the losses that would inevitably be incurred by spending all day in court. Ernest went out for his much talked-of dinner with Virginia Spearmen.

'It's a comedy, isn't it?' she said as she ordered the Cabernet Sauvignon. In the distance, a group of waiters had gathered around a table to sing 'Happy Birthday' to a customer over a crème brûlée with one lighted candle in the middle.

Ernest felt inhibited by his instructions from Oliver Sudden: 'Don't get drunk, don't fuck her and don't talk about the movie.' How could he avoid discussing the movie? He felt that they had already got off on the wrong foot and he could see no way to duck her question. *Lies* was actually more an adventure, more a romance, more a thriller – in fact, you would have classified it as almost any genre other than comedy, but he certainly didn't want to disagree with her opening gambit So he pretended he hadn't heard. But she persisted. 'You *would* say it's a comedy, wouldn't you?'

The correct answer was unmistakable. 'Yes,' he said. Why risk fucking up the deal? he thought. Let Oliver Sudden explain to her that it's not.

The waiter arrived, pursed his lips, tossed his head and readied himself for his performance of the daily specials. 'We specialize in fusion food. Our soup of the day is watercress with pineapple and cilantro, our pasta special is a chocolate pasta, fusilli with bay shrimp, sweet corn, lox and a light cream sauce, we have a *delicious* grape and goat cheese quesidilla, and our fish of the day is line-caught ahi tuna.'

'Don't you have any *net* caught?' complained Ernest, deadpan.

'What?'

'Nothing.' He decided to heckle no further.

'Shall I leave you to think about it?'

'Please do,' replied Ernest. After the waiter had gone Ernest studied the menu, looking for something he could eat. Virginia stared thoughtfully into the middle distance. 'I think you should put dogshit in, that always works.'

Ernest nodded. 'Why not? Dogshit, great idea, it could hardly taste worse than chocolate pasta.'

She stared at him. 'I was talking about the screenplay.'

Now he was confused. 'Dogshit?'

'Don't you like this restaurant?' She was concerned. 'I think fusion food is very hip.'

Ernest retreated. 'Sure, I've nothing against hip food, *per se*, it's just that ... what do you mean, exactly, dogshit?'

'Dogshit always gets a laugh. You know, stepping in it? We've found it always works, at American Pictures.'

He stared at her, unable to frame a suitably tactful reply. 'I'm not sure that I ... er ...' He petered out.

'Look, don't worry, I'm not trying to make a whole *megillah* out of it,' she explained, 'it's just an idea, you know, if we need an extra laugh somewhere, that's all.'

Ernest decided that Oliver had been right and that it might be better to avoid talking about the movie.

NINETEEN

*'When I use a word,' Humpty Dumpty said, in a
rather scornful tone, 'it means just what I choose it to
mean – neither more nor less.'*

*'The question is,' said Alice, 'whether you can make
words mean so many different things.'*

*'The question is,' said Humpty Dumpty, 'which is to
be master – that's all.'*

Lewis Carroll

Ernest Mayday's life was fuller and more productive than
at any time since his arrival in Los Angeles. Every day he
went to court, where the prosecution confidently and
methodically laid out its case against Abel Pile. He was
accused of both defrauding the members of his Church
and the IRS. Ernest made copious notes, which he
transcribed every evening. Meanwhile, word had gone
around that he and Virginia thought each other were
great at dinner and that *Lies* was on the fast track at
American, although as he had not yet received a cent
from his widely reported million-dollar deal he felt
increased pressure to come up with a new angle on
Cinderella for the ever-enthusiastic Casey Boddichek at
International Studios, whose own 'new directionality' for
the fairy-tale had turned out to be a fairy-tale too. It
seemed that they were prepared to offer him untold sums
of money for the right idea. Unfortunately, he didn't have
any ideas at all.

What he did have was copious invitations to dinner.
Having spent the second day of the trial watching and

listening to Harris K. Fitch, who certainly had a way with words, that night he again met some of the younger members of the university's English faculty, who had a way with semiotic signifiers. Professor Craig Rosenbaum appeared to be offering some sort of stipend if Ernest would give a regular class and occasional lectures at the university, and after the discussion of dogshit with Virginia Spearmen the words that the English faculty used around the dinner table seemed to Ernest to be pleasantly opaque, especially since he had taken the precaution of fortifying himself with several large Scotches before he got there.

'Mineral water?' offered Craig, as he dispensed it to all the other dinner guests.

'Large Scotch,' replied Ernest firmly.

They all sat down to dinner in the next room. It was quail again. 'I've been thinking over your offer, and I'm willing to teach literature,' he began, taking the fight right to the enemy. Leonard Lesser smiled gently, intelligent eyes twinkling behind major major lenses, as he lowered himself carefully into one of the delicate dining-room chairs. Ernest noted that Julian had not been invited back, and that the chair he'd broken was propped up in the bay window. '*Modern* lit.,' Ernest continued firmly. 'Not creative writing, which I don't think can be taught.'

'But literature,' said Alfred Hare, 'with all the old capitalistic, sexist, crypto-fascist baggage, is not what modern, forward-looking state-of-the-art English departments teach today.'

'Speaking as a Euro-centred, capitalistic, sexist, crypto-fascist myself,' replied Ernest amiably, 'I can't see what the problem is.'

'Surely you can understand,' interjected Leonard's tiny, pinched wife Frankie, who had been helping Craig's wife Judy in the kitchen until now, 'that the old liberal-arts education is based on a white, male Euro-culture, which has to go.'

'All I can see is that I'm going to need another very large Scotch,' grinned Ernest. He was beginning to enjoy himself. He turned to face Frankie. 'Are you talking about Shakespeare? And Mozart? And Rembrandt? That sort of white, male Euro-culture? That's the sort of thing that has to go, is it?'

'Of course. Shakespeare, Dante, Goethe, all those old English writers. English literature is not about specific authors any more,' she sneered. 'God, I thought we'd got past that.'

'So what is it about, d'you think?'

'The semiotic method,' said Craig, 'as we explained last time we met.'

'Sequential encounters with signifiers,' added Hare.

'Emancipated subjectivity,' chimed in Craig's wife Judy, who had fetched Ernest's Scotch and was now dutifully serving the vegetables.

'I still don't get it,' admitted Ernest.

Alfred Hare took the lead. 'We have understood that the process of reading is – in reality – a sequential encounter with signifiers, in which the linguistic semiotics are decoded. That's why individual authors are of no importance any more.'

Cora Malloy was nodding in full agreement, pushing her lank yellow hair out of her face so that she could eat.

Ernest was wishing now that he'd had either two Scotches less, or six more. He looked over to Leonard for help. Leonard was hugely enjoying both his dinner and Ernest's confusion. 'Semiotics is the study of signs,' he explained. 'When Cora says "signifiers", she means words. So what she's saying is that the words on the page are still there, but they don't mean anything except what the reader – the person who employs the reading strategies – wants to make of them.'

Ernest turned to Cora. 'So that's why you call it emancipated subjectivity? Because these signifiers mean anything you want them to mean?'

'Not at all,' was her nasal response. 'God! It is that which is *signified* by the signifier that is open to interpretation. I should have thought it was all so *obvious*!'

Ernest stared at her. Then he belched.

'Look, Ernest is just a writer,' interjected Leonard Lesser. Ernest had a sudden feeling of *déjà vu*. 'If you're just a writer, God forbid,' Ernest remembered Max. Kirsch saying to him in the commissary all those months ago, 'you will be ignored, rewritten, sent to get the coffee and bagels, and if you make a suggestion you'll be told to shut the fuck up.' Just a writer? Could Hollywood and the English faculty have more in common than meets the eye – a shared contempt for scribblers, *schmucks* with typewriters as Harry Cohn of Columbia Pictures is said to have said?

Leonard Lesser was still explaining to the others. 'I think Ernest is under the impression that there are people out there called readers, who read his books, and other people's, to enjoy the characters and the story and the human relationships they describe. Is that right?' Ernest nodded. He wasn't paying full attention, his eyes were scanning the room for signs of a decent bottle of wine. 'Well, I guess ordinary people still do that,' continued Lesser, 'but not our friends here in the English faculty – they have moved on to something much more important. Right, fellas?'

'Right,' agreed Hare, failing to detect the irony.

'They're interested in juxtapositions, dissociations, components, psychoanalysis, linguistics, feminist theory, post-Marxism ... you see, to the English department, a literary work is a text waiting to be deconstructed to determine its linguistic significance. But the interesting thing,' added Lesser with a sly smile, 'is that when the deconstructionists have finished analysing a book it always turns out to mean the opposite of what the author intended.'

Everyone chuckled.

'Then they must all be deconstructionists at the major studios,' said Ernest, 'because that's also what happens when Hollywood has finished filming a book.'

The academics were still chuckling at good old Lennie Lesser, who always amused them. 'Lennie's such a cynic,' said Hare.

'But am I right?' Lesser demanded.

'Only', said Alfred Hare, still smiling, 'if you accept the false notion of authors' intentions.'

Ernest put down his knife and fork and stared at Alfred. 'You don't think authors have intentions?'

'They're not *relevant* intentions. Because they're not knowable.'

'They are if you read their books.'

'If we did that,' intervened Cora Malloy contemptuously, 'we'd be back to problematizing the semiotic language along the male axis imaginally.'

'Well, we certainly wouldn't want that, would we?' said Ernest.

'No. Because all texts are equally valid.'

'So you're saying, for instance, that there's no real difference between Jane Austen and Jackie Collins?'

Cora was absolutely firm on this one. 'Not from our viewpoint.'

'I've heard about people like you,' said Ernest, 'but I thought it was just a vicious rumour.' He pushed his untouched quail away, reached across Cora for the extremely average bottle of Californian Cabernet, and poured himself another comfortably full glass. 'So Jane Austen didn't have a clue what she was writing, but you do. And through your insight we can understand it?' Ernest sniggered.

The young Professor Hare smiled patiently. 'Yes

because we know so much more than Jane Austen.'

'In that case,' remarked Ernest, 'shouldn't you be knocking out the odd masterpiece or two on your word processors, then?'

'Ernest, you've missed the point. We know more because of our historical perspective. All eighteenth- and nineteenth-century authors were falsifying words for reasons that they didn't understand, they reproduced the clichés of their respective cultures. But we have understood both the origins of language and the anthropological setting which their cultures inhabited – only by deconstructing them can you understand the culture and the meaning of the language.'

'Give me an example,' Ernest challenged him.

Leonard Lesser raised his hand. 'Let me. I'd be delighted. Ernest, you mentioned Jane Austen. I imagine you'd agree with me if I summarized her attitudes, as revealed in her novels, as a belief in the importance of the social order, property rights, and honest and generous feelings between people . . . perhaps all summed up in the phrase "good marriage"?'

'Yes,' said Ernest. 'Roughly.'

'Well, it so happens that Alfred here has published an important essay on Jane Austen. Can you summarize it for us, in layman's language?'

'I'd be delighted,' smiled Alfred. 'When I refer to "Jane Austen", of course you understand that I'm referring to the text, not the person. The text of any Austen novel reveals a belief in anarchy, support for the notion that property is theft, and a conviction that the most satisfying relationships are to be found in polymorphous and multi-partner sex.'

Ernest's upper lip curled and his nose wrinkled up, as though a plate of rotting fish had just been placed under it. 'Anything else?' he inquired. 'I've read her books and I never noticed all that.'

He meant to sound sarcastic but it obviously didn't work, for Alfred continued: 'Well, yes, I forgot to mention respect for nature, gay and animal rights and environmental protectionism is also clearly discernible, in that since the bad things happen inside houses, ergo the good happens outside them, amongst nature.'

'That's your evidence?'

'Oh my God, no, do you want me to go into detail?' Glazed, Ernest nodded. 'Briefly, then, look at the titles. Let's take *Emma*. Its not quite a palindrome. It's not *Emme* nor is it *Amma*. A word that's so nearly a palindrome is a broken mirror, i.e. not an exact reflection. This indicates that the text is not trustworthy: it is about false reflections. So, let's break the mirror up into *Em* and *Ma* – now we see immediately that *Ma* is motherhood, and by extension everything that motherhood represents about patriarchal authoritarian society. *Em* is printers' terminology for a space, a fixed length of twelve points or one-sixth of an inch ... or, to put it another way, a broken rule. Furthermore, because *em* is a printing image and also part of the title, we can safely assert that the book is drawing attention to itself as a book and not as an account of the real world. It is, after all, the very first syllable of the book.' He held his audience spellbound.

'One more thing: *em* is not only a broken mirror, therefore a distorted reflection, a fraction, and an image of the book *qua* book – it is also a space, which on the printed page performs the dual function of holding things apart and together simultaneously. So let's look at other Jane Austen titles – *Sense and Sensibility*, *Pride and Prejudice*. The *and* is crucial to each of these titles: like the *em*, the *and* is about holding people apart while together. What does that describe? A patriarchal, authoritarian marriage. And what exemplifies being apart yet together? Being alone with as many sexual partners as possible.'

Ernest, sweating, tried to digest all this. 'What about

the title *Northanger Abbey*? It's got no *ems* or *ands*.'

'That's obvious,' answered Hare with delight. 'An abbey is a clerical institution, it owns property, it supports chastity, and formal patriarchal religion. The word *north* has a vertical emphasis, as does *hang*, which not only has vertical tension but also penal implications of death – hanging is what happened to those eighteenth-century unfortunates who broke the property laws. So we have this fascinating juxtaposition between the vertical, deadly, murderous, upright, erect (in both senses) patriarchal design for society – and the *em*, the rule, the ordered space, which shows that we can oppose the rule by creating space for ourselves as individuals.'

There was a reverent pause.

'What are you thinking, Ernest?' Leonard Lesser wanted to know.

'Actually, I was thinking about Bertrand Russell,' Ernest confessed.

'What about him?' asked Craig.

'He once said,' said Ernest, 'the worse your logic, the more interesting its results.'

Hare was unused to bad reviews. He bridled. 'You're suggesting there's something wrong with my logic?'

Ernest carefully considered the question, then decided it was his turn to answer a question with a question. 'Tell me,' he asked, 'have you ever taken a text, deconstructed it, and discovered – for instance – that capitalism and homophobia are the true subtext?'

'Can't say I have.'

Ernest contemplated this reply. 'Well, I can certainly see the practical advantages of this approach. Saves a lot of time reading the text. It's money for old rope, you're on to a bloody good thing, I see that now.'

'I must say, I take exception to that,' snapped Cora. 'We don't just sit around the campus all day with our thumbs up our butts. It took Alfred a long time to deconstruct Jane

Austen, he's written three hundred pages on the subject.'

'I got tenure for it,' interjected Hare with pride.

'Good God!' muttered Ernest, pouring himself more of the plonk.

'I myself,' continued Cora in considerable indignation, 'read a great deal of complex theoretical literature, by Paul de Man, Jacques Derrida, Foucault, Lacan . . .'

'Wait a minute,' Ernest interrupted, 'I've heard of Paul de Man. Wasn't he that Belgian anti-Semite who wrote articles for a Nazi newspaper all through World War II?'

'He was also a leading literary critic and an austere and rigorous philosopher,' piped up Craig Rosenbaum.

'And an ex-Nazi, that must be admitted,' acknowledged Leonard Lesser.

'That doesn't make him any less important, as a scholar,' said his wife, admonishing him for once.

'It does make you wonder about his common sense, though, doesn't it?' asked Leonard.

'And who's Lacan?' Ernest wanted to know.

'Lacan rediscovered Freud,' said Cora. 'Haven't you heard?'

Ernest guffawed. 'I didn't know we'd ever lost him.'

We are not amused, signified most of the faces around the table. And Cora was not to be deflected. 'Lacan rediscovered Freud's real meaning: that all experience is about language, all transactions are linguistic transactions. Of course, he's not a deconstructionist, really, but like us he believes in looking with great intensity at the meaning of every word, in the manner of the poet, opening up clichés and assumptions, forgetting style and subject matter, so that we just look at the words and the language. Looking out for the Freudian slip, in fact.'

'So let me sum this all up,' said Ernest. 'As far as you lot are concerned, the author's intentions are at best a bunch of Freudian slips and, at worst, irrelevant. The words – I'm so sorry, the *signifiers* – simply mean what the reader thinks they mean?' They all nodded, delighted with his progress. This man would, after all, be a worthy addition to the English faculty. 'And if the signifiers don't mean anything except what the reader wants them to mean, then the entire book has no objective meaning either?'

'That's right. That's why we don't care if our students read them or not,' said Cora.

'We don't call them books, remember,' Craig pointed out. 'We call them texts.'

'That's because a text needn't be a book at all,' added Alfred Hare. 'To put it in film terminology, literature is just the McGuffin.'

'For instance, I'm studying Madonna,' interjected Cora. 'Madonna is a really valuable text.'

'You mean,' said Ernest, 'her book and her records are texts?'

'Yes, but she herself is also a text.'

Ernest gaped. 'She is?'

'Oh yes.' Cora waxed enthusiastic. 'There's a lot of critical literature about her now. Interesting papers on her reception and interpretation within the gay community, foundationalist or anti-foundationalist theory and praxis, the ideological force of commodity culture, feminist politics and post-modern seduction, Madonna and the struggle for political articulation.'

'How come?' asked Ernest.

'Because Madonna is a queen of gender disorder and racial deconstruction.'

'And what aspect of her are you studying?' Ernest was now eyeing Cora as if she was a rabid dog.

'I'm studying the contrasts between early and late Madonna.'

Ernest glanced around the table, searching for signs that she was putting him on. But no, they were all listening with attention and respect. 'I'm interested in the change from her Toy Boy phase to her Chameleon phase.'

'You know, what *particularly* interests me', commented Alfred, 'is the fact that Madonna happens to be a real person, one who will always impinge on the field of textual representation, operating within an undeniably intricate matrix of corporeal and corporate relations.'

'Not only that,' added Cora. 'But talking of Lacan, one can't help noticing that in Madonna's "Open Your Heart" video there are some suspiciously academic references to Lacan's essays about "the Gaze", Deleuze and Guattari's "Anti-Oedipus", the feminist critique of woman's film image, and other citations too scholarly to be believed but too precise to be dismissed.'

In the ensuing respectful pause, Craig took the floor. 'And that's why, as I said to you before dinner, we would be so pleased to welcome you aboard, in spite of your hostility and your deeply reactionary views. Your involvement with film and TV writing is a great plus for us, a major plus. Film is particularly fertile territory for semiotic analysis because it contains so many different types of sign: the graphic image, the voice, the music, the text . . . '

'You see,' added Hare enthusiastically, 'what we like about the cinema is that it is a social institution with significant ideological effects.'

'Significant ideological effects?' repeated Ernest. 'I see. I've got it now. You people think that art is about improving society.'

They looked at him in silence. 'Well, isn't it?' inquired Craig.

Ernest made a last ditch effort to explain. 'Art isn't about improving us,' Ernest said. 'Is *King Lear* a better play if it improves us? Do Laurel and Hardy improve us? Does Van Gogh's *Sunflowers* improve us? This is preposterous nonsense. That's how Stalinists judge art – social realism. But that's not even relevant, *improving* us. You judge art by how it moves you, whether it expresses recognizable – and in the case of great art – eternal truths.

Whether it expresses them truthfully, funnily, beautifully. Is the audience, the viewer, the reader, moved to laughter or to tears? That's the only thing that matters. I mean, I'm not against improving society. Like, we're all against sin, right? But you're applying sociological criteria to literature.'

'Literature is *irrelevant*!' snarled Alfred Hare, losing all patience. 'Don't you get it yet? Can't you get that straight? The history of literature is merely part of the history of criticism. The modern English department doesn't confine itself to archaic, paternalistic, privileged texts. For centuries élitist literature has been imposed from above. Political, social and economic barriers are coming down, in literature as elsewhere, and it's high time they did. Traditional authors are white, mostly male and too old.'

'How about too hard?' suggested Lesser.

Ernest grinned. 'By hard do you mean difficult, or erect? And therefore potent.'

Cora looked at him with undisguised contempt. 'That's *exactly* the kind of chauvinistic, phallocentric shit we're trying to get away from.'

'Just let me check one thing,' said Ernest. 'You're saying now that Shakespeare has been read for four hundred years as a function of élitism?'

'Obviously. For centuries literature has been written by entirely the wrong people for entirely the wrong reasons. Malcolm Bradbury said so in the *New York Times Book Review*.'

'Wasn't he joking?' asked Leonard.

'I don't think so.' Cora was fairly confident on that score. 'Not in *The New York Times Book Review*, surely.

'Perhaps you mean *The New York Times Text Review*?' asked Ernest.

He had gone too far. The disappointment in him was palpable. Ernest looked around the table for support.

None was forthcoming. Lesser merely smiled and stayed *shtum*.

Hare spoke, but his manner was cold and it was clear that he was no longer amused by the Englishman. 'We acknowledge, Ernest, that there are such things as books. But texts need not be books. There is no advantage in texts being books. Since a text has no existential author the text itself is what we study, and the text can be anything, anything at all. Graffiti, for instance, can contain a whole treasure trove of human experience, excitement, pain. But not just words – architecture, urban design, junk shops, the campus right here ... when you look at it, the whole of LA is a compaction of ideological signs.'

The curtain fell from before Ernest's eyes. 'I *see*. At last I've got it. So – let me see if I've got this right – not only do you not study literature in the English department, you don't even study language.'

'Attaboy!' said Leonard.

'There are many languages,' replied Alfred Hare. 'We don't limit ourselves to words when there are so many other signifiers all around us. We are beyond language.'

'I see,' said Ernest. 'And beyond intelligent too, I suppose?' he added, as Tiffani's words in the parking-lot of American Pictures suddenly came back to him.

'What does that mean?' asked Judy.

'Nothing. Or anything, I presume, like everything else, since it's a text.'

'Did you say "beyond intelligent"?' asked Alfred.

Craig Rosenbaum nodded slowly. 'You know, that's a very interesting way of putting it.'

'So. Humour me,' persisted Ernest. 'There's just one little thing I still don't get. Since books don't mean anything objectively, why does the English faculty have a course in creative writing, and why would you want me – or anybody, for that matter – to teach it?'

'Your books,' said Hare, 'your texts, the way you use your signifiers, are sequentially formless and uninteresting. The students will not approach them with reverence or respect, and therefore will be open to a healthy, emancipated subjectivity. We hope you can impart your own haphazard approach to the creation of the text to our students, so that they learn that the literary quality of the text is irrelevant and unimportant and may perhaps be able to create their own post-modernist trash.'

Ernest Mayday stared bibulously at him. There was no air-conditioning in the Rosenbaum dining room and Ernest had gone pink and blotchy. Rivulets of sweat were running down his temples and he was beginning to look like a boiled pig. 'If I heard that correctly, I think you're telling me that my books are formless trash.'

'Yes, but you mustn't take that the wrong way.'

'What's the right way to take it, exactly?'

'Trash is too strong a word, anyway,' intervened Judy, trying to keep the peace.

'Oh, I wouldn't say so,' muttered Frankie. 'I've read them. Have you?'

'No, not all the way through,' admitted Judy, 'but that's hardly the point. I think mediocre would be a more accurate way to describe the one I read.'

Ernest was speechless for a few moments. Signifiers failed him. But not for long. 'Look,' said Ernest. 'Let me just get this straight. You're sitting here telling me that you want me to teach a bunch of airheads and surfers in your fucking English faculty because I'm a *bad writer*?'

Alfred Hare smiled. 'Bad writer, good writer, meaningless concepts. If you haven't understood that, you haven't understood a word we've said tonight.'

'You're dead fucking right I haven't.' Ernest stood up from the dinner table abruptly. 'Though I thought there weren't any words any more, only fucking signifiers. And since texts have no objective univocal meaning, I feel sure that when I call you a bunch of moronic cunts you will be able to decode that sequence of sequential signifiers with the appropriate emancipated subjectivity.'

TWENTY

Within a few days Joanna called Ernest. He wasn't home.
'It's Joanna, call me,' was all she said, and she left her
home number with the 818 area code. Randi was out
somewhere, and carefully he erased her message. Not that
it would have mattered if she'd heard it, for she would
have accepted his explanation that Joanna was Oliver's
secretary, or Virginia's, or Fanny's – he couldn't remember
what he'd said last time, but it hardly mattered since
Joanna was such a common name.

He called her back. 'Yes?' was all she said, answering
the phone in her usual incommunicative style.

'Is that Joanna. It's me, Er . . .' He stopped himself in
the nick of time. He'd almost said Ernest. He turned it
into a sort of hesitant speech mannerism. 'Er . . . Er . . .
Norm. De Plume, that is,' he added.

'Thanks for calling back,' she said, very businesslike.

'So, what's going on?'

'I've made a little progress. I have the addresses and
telephone numbers of all five of the men.'

'How? Did you follow them all home?' For a moment
he thought she must be quite an amazing detective.

'No, silly, the trial hasn't even been on five days.'

'So . . . how?'

271

'Our friend John knows someone in the jury commission at City Hall, who gave him the names and all the information.'

'He bribed him?'

'We don't use words like that, Norm, especially not over the telephone, I'm on a cordless.'

'Sorry. But how much was it?'

'How much was what?'

'What did it cost to get the information?'

'Not very much I should think, he's some kind of a low-level clerk, apparently. Also, I think maybe he's a member of SCREAMS or Abel Pile's Church or something, because they knew him before and there didn't seem to be any problem in getting his cooperation.'

'Great,' said Ernest, making notes. 'Wheels within wheels, perfect, I love this.'

'What?'

'Nothing. Just talking to myself. Anything else?'

'No.'

'Have you made a move on any of them yet?'

'No, John's having them followed. He's finding out about them. He's getting credit checks on them. Finding out who's vulnerable to what. I mean, like, for instance, there'd be no point in throwing myself at a gay, you know?'

'Four of them are married, aren't they?'

'That proves nothing. Three of them are married, actually one's divorced, one's single.'

'So the married ones are a better bet, right, they have more to lose?'

'Not necessarily, not if the others are in respectable jobs. Lawyers, doctors, politicians. 'Course, they wouldn't be on a jury unless they're retired, but, like, they don't have to be married so long as they're the kind of man who wouldn't want it known he went with a hooker. If the guy's married, with kids, it's even better, because it could be enough that he's been photographed in bed with another woman. But if he's not married, we can tell him I'm a hooker and threaten him with the vice squad – it's illegal to be a john in this town, remember?'

'Great,' enthused Ernest, writing everything down. He hadn't thought of all these angles, and it would be a big advantage to have the maximum possible information about all the male jurors. Joanna might be able to blackmail one of the men if she could compromise him sexually, but in order to secure an acquittal it would obviously help if they knew all the vulnerabilities of the whole jury. He was impressed that John Schmidt had it all worked out so well. 'Who's doing all his detective work?'

'I asked him. He wouldn't tell me. He didn't tell me who his friend was in the jury commission, either.'

Very smart, thought Ernest. Schmidt only tells Joanna what she needs to know. He made a note of it. 'Anything else?'

'No. I'll get back to you when John's decided which one of them I should go for.'

'Wait a minute,' said Ernest. 'Is he the best judge? Isn't there some element of personal chemistry in this?'

'Not much,' said Joanna. 'Not if I pitch it right. Quite frankly, Norm, very few men refuse a free fuck with a girl like me if given the opportunity. Most men just follow their dicks. They can't help it, they're men, that's what men do, nature just takes its course. I can be very seductive, you know.'

'I don't doubt that,' said Ernest. 'But are you sure? Are there no exceptions?'

'I never get turned down if I offer them a free one. If a guy knows I'm a working girl, he might be one of those macho types who says he doesn't pay for it – though you all pay for it, sooner or later, one way or another. But, like, look at you: when we met, you had something else very specific in mind, a business deal. Obviously a girl can't *always* get inside a guy's pants, not if there's a business relationship there, or if he's afraid his wife or his chick'll find out, or he's scared he'll be all over the *National Enquirer* or something.' She softened her voice, to an intimate whisper. 'But you're scared of all those things and you'd still take the chance. And I didn't even make a play for you – though I might, when all this is over.'

'Might you?'

'I might.'

'Well, yes, you know I would take the chance,' he agreed. He suddenly had a frog in his throat. He cleared it, nervously.

'I know you would. You tried already. And I've seen that bulge in your pants. I can make you hard just by talking to you.' And she hung up.

Oliver Sudden phoned the next morning to say that he needed an urgent meeting, so Ernest's daily trek downtown to the federal courthouse had to be postponed. They met this time at his offices at American Pictures, a long, low, California ranch-style bungalow done up inside with aged pine mock-eighteenth-century fluted columns, country-pine panelling and a huge cut-glass chandelier. Ernest stared at it open-mouthed.

'You like this place? I had it done by a French decorator.' Ernest looked around and wondered how to reply. 'I'm a Francophile. An Anglophile too,' Oliver added hastily. 'I thought of having it all done mock Tudor, you know, like a ye olde pubbe. Or a castle. But then I thought French country style might be classier than Tudor.'

'It certainly is,' agreed Ernest, thankful that he had found something to say that was both positive and honest.

'I spoke to Virginia,' Oliver began, 'she loves you, she thinks you're cool. Which is an incredible kick in the ass.'

Ernest took the news calmly. 'Good, good.'

'She thought you were really laid back.'

'I certainly was. I was virtually horizontal.'

Oliver looked concerned. 'I thought I told you not to get drunk?'

'I didn't.'

'So why were you horizontal? Jesus, you didn't fuck her, I hope? I *told* you not to fuck her.'

'No, I didn't fuck her, though I should think that would be a remarkable experience. Don't panic, Oliver it was a figure of speech: I just meant I was so laid back that I was virtually horizontal.'

Oliver relaxed. 'Got it. OK, let me tell you what this meeting's about, I've decided I'm not going to direct *Lies*, I'm not gonna direct it, OK, so we have to discuss who's going to direct it and how we strategize this whole deal.'

Ernest was instantly worried. Losing the director could throw the future of a whole movie into doubt. 'What'll Virginia say? Won't she be very disappointed?'

'Not if I pitch it right,' said Oliver with absolute confidence. Again Ernest was assailed with a sense of *déjà vu*. Where did I just hear that phrase, Ernest wondered. Then he remembered. From Joanna, of course.

He cleared his throat. 'I'm disappointed about this, can I get you to change your mind?'

'Why are you disappointed? There's a lot of directors out there.'

'But we've got to find the right one. One who's available, and who wants to devote a year of his life to *Lies*. And one who's acceptable to Virginia. One that stars want to work with. That's a lot of hurdles that we have to overcome.'

'These are all opportunities.' Oliver was admonishing him again for being negative. 'We don't talk about hurdles, we talk in terms of opportunities.'

'OK,' said Ernest. 'There's a lot of opportunities that we have to overcome.'

'I thought about Marty Rubb. You think he'd be good?'

'He was great, once,' said Ernest, 'but isn't he a bit of a bear? And weren't you going to try Spielberg next?'

'Who are you kidding? Spielberg? You crazy, why would he wanna do this?'

'Spielberg was your idea. That's what you told Virginia when we pitched it.'

'That was the *pitch*. This is reality we're talkin' about now, OK? Two different things, OK? OK?'

'OK!'

'We'll meet Marty, he's good, you'll like him.'

'Is that a prediction, or a command?'

Oliver glanced at Ernest, and grinned disarmingly. 'We'll meet Marty, that's a plan, he's good, that's my opinion, you'll like him, my prediction – no, my fervent hope and belief, OK?'

'And if I don't like him?'

'You will.'

'Is *that* a command?' Ernest persisted.

'No,' replied Oliver with a still bigger grin, 'it's a threat.'

Ernest still didn't know if Oliver was kidding or not, but the meeting had lasted eight and a half minutes and was clearly over. By the time he reached the door Oliver was in the middle of his next phone call. As he opened the door Oliver waved cheerfully, told the voice at the other end of the line to hang on a minute, cupped his hand over the mouthpiece and said: 'Ernest, don't tell anyone about this, OK, nobody, got that? and that includes Virginia, it's our secret, OK, so you're not gonna tell Virginia, you're not gonna tell *nobody* it case in gets back to Virginia, it is not in our *interest* that the studio knows there's gonna be a change of director, OK? That would be a real kick in the ass, we gotta wait till we got somebody lined up that they love, OK? someone they'll wanna sign off on, then they'll be happy, believe me, I know Virginia, I've done business with her for years, I got her her first job, so you're not telling Virginia, got that?'

'I think I've got the general idea,' Ernest said, and he shut the door behind him.

He couldn't be bothered to go all the way downtown to the courtroom. He knew that if anything significant happened it would be widely reported in the papers and on TV. So instead he dropped in on Max. and Sidney, still working on *Ask Your Father!*, the hit TV comedy half-hour show. They were sitting in the same shoebox office in the seedy two-storey stucco building appropriately known as the Writers' Block, with a whirring, grinding air-conditioner of limited efficiency filling up half of one of the two windows and further darkening the already dingy room. They greeted him with what passes for enthusiasm among elderly comedy-writers on a hot day, morose grunts and jaundiced looks, followed by creeping sceptical smiles as he told them of Oliver Sudden's new plans for the movie.

'You look tired, Max.,' Ernest remarked.

'He always looks tired,' complained Sidney. 'So do I. I look tired. Who wouldn't look tired if they had to write this shit every day of their lives? You know why we look tired? We *are* tired, that's why.'

'I'm tired because of my neighbours,' said Max. 'The wife, she's been *shtupping* some rock-and-roll musician with long hair. She thought her husband was away for a couple more weeks. Well, he came home last night, to surprise her, and boy! was the surprise on the other foot?'

'What happened?'

'There was some shooting, screaming, then the cops came. And the ambulance. I think the husband's pleading justifiable ballicide. And the musician'll be singing soprano from now on.'

The others listened to this tale with awe, empathy and

horror. 'Too many guns in this *fahrshtunkener* town,' said Sidney quietly.

They sipped their decaf thoughtfully, and Max. ate a few pistachio nuts, chucking the shells across the room in a desultory way, pulling a wry face whenever they missed the grey plastic trash bin. 'Why did you come to LA, anyway?' he asked, out of the sombre silence.

'I don't know,' replied Ernest, in all honesty. 'I suppose I was drawn to the glamour of it all.' This induced a few cynical chuckles. 'Well, I'm serious, it is glamorous, in a funny sort of way. I wanted to experience Hollywood myself, I wanted to write about it in my book, I wanted to be involved in the films of my books – which may still happen.'

'They're British books, why not make them into British movies?'

'It's not so much an industry over there as a hobby. There isn't a British film industry, not any more.'

'There isn't an industry here, either,' said Sidney bitterly. 'The auto industry, that's an industry. Or the shoe industry. You design a product, you test it, you try it out, you see if it works and if people like it ... then you go ahead and manufacture it, in thousands or hundreds of thousands. That's what I call an industry. My father was in shoes, I know. But the movie industry, not only is it not an industry, it's not even a business! Half a dozen major studios make a dozen prototypes each, every year. They have no idea if the public's gonna buy them or not – how can they know, each one's unique?'

'Uniquely bad, mostly,' commented Max.

'Bad, good or mediocre – unique. New script, new casting, new chemistry, new everything, and each one costs about twenty million on average, plus another ten to fifteen mill for marketing. So what does it all come down to? Each studio makes a dozen thirty-five million dollar bets. Twelve spins of the roulette wheel. That's not an industry, that's Vegas.'

'It's great if you win the jackpot,' said Max.

'But the odds are too great,' Sidney whined. 'I prefer to eke out a living in television.'

Ernest turned and stared at him. 'Am I mistaken, or is that your BMW 800 series coupé outside? And wasn't that your two-million-dollar house in the Palisades, with a pool and an ocean view, where we played poker last week?'

'So?' Sidney stared back.

'So – *eke* out a living?' repeated Ernest.

'Yes. Eke, eke.'

'Shut the fuck up, OK, Sidney?' requested Max. 'You sound like you're doing farmyard impressions. We've got to write another coupla scenes of this piece of shit, OK?'

'My mother, she's ninety-three, she comes out to California to stay with me every so often, God help me,' said Sidney, totally ignoring Max. 'She lives in the lap of luxury, in my house, and she's disappointed in me. She said to me, "Sidney, I love you whatever you are, a doctor, a lawyer, a disappointment ..." Those were her three categories. The only three she knows. Thanks a lot, Mom.' He wiped a rheumy eye with the back of his hand.

Driving home, Ernest did feel sorry for Sidney and Max., in a way. They must have started out in this business with higher ambitions, he thought, with hopes, with ideals, with stars in their eyes. They must have intended to be real writers, adding a little insight to the human condition. They couldn't have set out as young men to become sitcom sausage machines writing script after script, week after week, year after year, each one marginally different yet each one exactly the same. In their case, Ernest thought as he drove home along Sunset with an ironic smile on his face, the text really *was* out there, it *did* only need to be written down, it was merely waiting to be deconstructed. What had happened to Sidney and Max.? What had gone wrong? With everything they had, how could they enjoy their lives so little? Was it the mortgage and the kids that had trapped them, or the alimony owed to three ex-wives, or were they junkies hooked on the riches they had been unfortunate enough to earn since they were in their twenties? Ernest wondered if money was the worst habit of all to be hooked on. He wouldn't have been sorry for them if they were happy with their lot, in fact he might have despised them. But they were so cynical, so willing to settle for the cheap joke, for cliché-ridden, third-hand, pre-digested characters and relationships, so full of contempt for their audience and themselves, so filled with self-hatred, that they left no space for anyone else to despise them.

He saw no connection between their problems, their fate and his. Bestselling novelists too, as Mark Down of Cockerel Books had explained to him long ago, must write a succession of books that, though superficially different, are fundamentally the same. That is, if they wish to remain bestselling authors. But fortunately Ernest was not in an introspective frame of mind and he spent the rest of the day at home, working on *Flagrante Delicto*. It was coming along nicely. He now had several encounters with Joanna to draw on and her character was shaping up well, even though he felt that he hadn't yet got to the bottom of what she was really about. No hurry. Either he'd get to understand her better or, if absolutely necessary, he'd make something up. Abel Pile and John Schmidt were taking shape too, in a fictional form and under assumed names. The trial was filling up lots of pages, and he was able to write plenty of comment on the American legal system and the curious power that the First Amendment apparently confers on the prosecutor, allowing him to have the case pre-tried in the press, ensuring that all the evidence that is inadmissible in a court of law is trumpeted in the court of public opinion.

Down on Spring Street, as the trial progressed, the

evidence against Dr Abel Pile was mounting. Inside the courtroom (where possible) and outside it (where necessary) Gil Hoolahan was producing evidence of millions of dollars that had been earned and – allegedly – charged as fees for services by the Church of the Community of Personal Truth, expensive tickets cum donations for the Sincerity Awards, massive donations to the Heartwarming Institute and to the Caring and Sharing Foundation, huge fees paid by participants in SCREAMS (the Self-Creating Energization and Activization Mode Seminars), not to mention SPITS (the Spiritual Inner Training Seminars) and major fundraising contributions accepted for the annual Peace and Harmony Day event. Accountants and other expert witnesses eagerly stepped forward day after day to demonstrate the difference between fees (taxable) and donations (non-taxable) – fees were defined as set prices, or set minima, in exchange for specific services rendered. Other witnesses, reluctant and subpoenaed, acknowledged amid much wailing and lamentation that their donations had indeed been in the form of such aforesaid fixed fees. Witnesses and investigators from the Internal Revenue Service explained that in their expert opinion such income was not tax exempt, should have been declared, and that the Church was guilty of tax fraud and owed millions of dollars to the federal government.

But there was a double-pronged attack, not just on the network of Church organizations but also on the good Dr Pile personally. It was suggested that much of the money had been diverted to his personal use – his five cars, his luxury Malibu beach house, his gated mansion and estate up on Mulholland Drive with spectacular three hundred and sixty degree views over both the city and the Valley (near the Marlon Brando gated mansion), his helicopter, his Gulf Stream jet, his yacht, his Seminary in Aspen, his Spiritual Center in New York City and his monastic retreat in Monte Carlo. It was alleged by the prosecution that Abel Pile benefited personally and in the form of undeclared income from these assets. Abel Pile, not yet called to speak in his own defence, sat at the table next to Harris K. Fitch and personified injured innocence.

Finally, it was suggested that this Very Reverend and learned cleric was guilty of knowingly and wilfully defrauding the members and congregation of his Church, in that his Church was alleged to be not a spiritual organization at all but merely a device by which Dr Pile and his associates could criminally accumulate vast wealth for their personal use – an enormous confidence trick, in fact.

Abel Pile sat still and listened carefully. His look of bewilderment combined with an air of compassion for his accusers was an inspiration to all those spectators who believed in his essential goodness. Occasionally he made notes. Harris K. Fitch, his ambling, amiable, country bumpkin of a lawyer, asked occasional questions in cross-examination but made no attempt to dispute the colossal income – indeed, he gloried in it, asking witnesses to agree that it indicated massive public belief in and support for Dr Pile's Christian mission. He got government witnesses to admit that no apparent effort had been made to hide any of the income. Meanwhile, Ernest copied all the evidence down and faithfully wrote it into his rapidly growing novel, just as it happened, changing only the names to protect the guilty. As he did so he smiled to himself, wondering if he had been too hard on those deconstructionist loonies from the English faculty. Perhaps literature *is* already there, just waiting to be called upon.

TWENTY-ONE

America is *deconstruction.*
Jacques Derrida

It had been easy as pie, Joanna told Ernest, for her to nail one of the jurors.

His name was Adrian, she said. He was the blond shaggy-haired one in his forties. She had picked him up in the parking-lot outside the courthouse early in the second week of the trial. At her usual rendezvous with Ernest, a bedroom in the Bel Monde Hotel, she described the scene. 'He was instantly attracted to me. We embraced. Mouth to mouth and belly to belly. Adrian must have the wettest kiss in history. His tongue is everywhere, like the ocean. We are sailing away. His penis (bulging under his corduroy pants) is the tall red smokestack of an ocean liner. And I am moaning around it like the ocean wind.' She giggled. 'And I am saying all the silly things you say while necking in parking-lots, trying somehow to express a longing which is inexpressible – except maybe in poetry. And it all comes out so lame.' She giggled some more. 'I'm saying: I love your mouth. I love your hair. I love your ears. I want you. I want you. I want you. Anything to avoid saying: I love you. Meanwhile, he's got my ass and is cupping it with both hands. He's put my book on the fender of a Volkswagen and he's grabbed my ass instead. "I've never met an ass to rival yours," he says.'

'Is he married?' asked Ernest, eager to sort out first things first.

'Yup. Three kids. It's perfect.'

'Did you make a date to see him again?'

'Lunch, tomorrow.'

'He's not suspicious?'

'Why should he be?'

'What does he know about you?'

'Nothing. Obviously. He thinks I'm a social worker and that I work in City Hall, across the street from the courthouse. I told him I couldn't give him my full name because my husband works out of the same office and I didn't dare.'

'He swallowed that?'

'You want to know what I said to him? I was great! I said I was not against marriage. I believed in it in fact. It was necessary to have one best friend in a hostile world, one person you'd be loyal to no matter what, one person who'd also be loyal to you. But what about all those other longings which after a while marriage did nothing much to appease? The restlessness, the hunger, the thump in the gut, the thump in the cunt, the longing to be filled up, to be fucked through every hole, the yearning for dry champagne and wet kisses . . .'

'This is great,' said Ernest. 'This is *great!*' He was writing as fast as he could, loving her language, thrilled with the whole seduction. 'And what did he say?'

'He agreed. What would you expect? I'm probably the best thing that's happened to him in years. He's married and wants to stay married. He loves his wife and kids. And he meets a girl who's longing to be thoroughly fucked, but who wants to do it in secret and stay married to her husband. He'll never get a better offer and he knows it.'

Excited by everything that Joanna was saying, both mentally and physically, ecstatic also with the material that she was providing for the book, he urged her to carry on talking about it. He felt he was getting a real insight into female sexuality. He had been brought up to believe

284

that nice girls didn't have real lust, which he knew wasn't true but was somehow still hung up on the notion – this perhaps contributed to his growing obsession with Joanna, for he had always been excited by women who didn't pretend to be 'nice'.

She interrupted his thoughts. 'Give me the next instalment of the ten grand.'

'Have they paid you any yet?' asked Ernest.

'No, they say they won't give me any till they have photos of me in bed with Adrian.'

'Do they give it all to you then?'

'No. They say we might have to set up a honey trap for another of the guys on the jury, just in case, just to be safe. So I don't get paid in full until he's acquitted, or there's a hung jury or something. Some result.'

'Well,' Ernest replied cautiously, 'I don't want to be a hardnose but my deal with you was that I'd match what they gave you, dollar for dollar. I've already given you an advance. If you show me the cheque from them, or the cash, or your bank statement, something, some proof, then I'll give you the same. OK?'

She stood up, angry. 'You shit. You pig. I've already given you half the plot for your fucking book, the trial, the conspiracy, Adrian, and you *still* won't give me any money? Well, fuck you! That's it. Forget it. It's over.'

She walked to the door and threw it open. He ran after her and stopped her, grabbing her arm. She shook herself free. 'Let me go, you bastard.'

'I'm sorry,' he said. 'I'm sorry. How much shall I give you?'

She turned to face him, her face set, her lips thin, her eyes cold. 'Five.' She looked ugly, for the first time.

'Five . . . thousand?' Ernest was taken aback.

'Why not? All you need now is the details of how Adrian fucks me, and then how we all fuck him . . .'

'What?' Ernest's eyes widened.

'Not literally – I mean, how they blackmail him and threaten to destroy his life and marriage, OK, and how my relationship with John Schmidt and Abel Pile works out, right? I mean, you'll know the result of the court case from the papers, right? You don't need me for that.'

Ernest said: 'I'll have to get you the cash, I don't have that kind of money on me.'

'That's OK. You can get it to me.'

Again she turned to leave. 'Wait.' Ernest stopped her. 'Did you say they won't give you any cash till they have pictures of you and Adrian in bed together?'

'That's right.'

'Why?'

'Why? Why d'you think? Without the pictures, how can they threaten him?'

'How explicit will they be?'

She stared at him. 'Huh?'

'How . . . explicit will they be?' He swallowed.

'How can a photograph not be explicit?'

'You know what I mean. Sexually explicit.'

'Well, I guess a picture of us having breakfast in bed wouldn't hurt, but we'll be after something a little more hard core, I should imagine.'

'How will you take the pictures?'

'*I* won't take the pictures, Norm, I'll be otherwise occupied.' She rolled her eyes. 'Jeez.'

'I mean, how will they be taken without his knowing?'

'I don't know. Not my problem. A two-way mirror, a peephole in the wall, somebody hiding in the closet – who knows?'

'Can I be there?'

She stared at him for a moment. 'Why?'

'I need to see what happens?'

'Why?'

'You know why. For complete authenticity. For my book.'

She smiled contemptuously. 'Who're you kidding?' And she was gone.

Back home from the Bel Monde, the phone was ringing. It was Professor Craig Rosenbaum, trying to persuade Ernest that he should not abandon the creative-writing course at the university, which apparently had been heavily advertised. A considerable number of students had signed up for it. Perhaps the professor thought that he was pouring oil on troubled waters but as far as Ernest was now concerned Rosenbaum was a leaking tanker, adding to the slick, further polluting the environment. 'No hard feelings, Craig,' Ernest explained without unpleasantness, 'but I've no time for any of those French bullshit critics. I'm really not interested in what Derrida or Lacan or any of those poofters have to say.'

Rosenbaum didn't know the word poofter. It was clear to him that it had some derogatory connotations. 'Is that another word for critic?' he asked.

'In a way,' replied Ernest judiciously. 'Though, on second thoughts, for that kind of critic, wanker would be better.'

'Have you tried Foucault?' persisted the professor.

'Who's that? Another Frog? These guys don't live in the real world.'

'Foucault's rather different. He writes about voyeurism, and how it's a political act.'

Ernest's attention was caught. 'Political? Voyeurism is political?' He chuckled.

'No, seriously, it is,' said Craig Rosenbaum, 'because there is an oppressive relationship between authoritarianism and looking.'

'There is?' He knew that there was, the moment Craig suggested it.

'If you can look and not be seen,' Craig went on, 'you have the ultimate power over other people. Foucault's more of a historian, he wrote a book about the Panopticon, which was an octagonal prison with a guard in the centre and there was a window in each cell which the prisoners couldn't control.'

'Isn't that like any prison?'

'Not in America. In our prisons the cells are like cages at the zoo. The front wall is open bars, floor to ceiling, without any privacy for the inmate. But there's none for the watcher either. There are two essentials for voyeurism: first, that you can see and second, that you *can't be seen*. The voyeur cannot also be an exhibitionist because the excitement of voyeurism lies in its anonymity and secrecy. That's why voyeurs are seldom if ever violent criminals.'

Ernest was feeling distinctly uneasy. 'Why are you telling me all this?' he demanded.

The professor replied without rancour. 'Because you were critical the other night of the notion that texts – literature, if you will – can have unintentional political and historical meaning. People have always seen voyeurism as an erotic concept, whereas in fact it's a political concept . . . the pleasure, the power, the delightful manipulative possibilities of seeing without being seen.'

Ernest suddenly felt that he was swimming in deep water. 'I see what you mean,' he said briefly. 'Well, I'll think about it.' And he hung up.

He was late for his meeting with the celebrated elderly Hollywood director Marty Rubb. The meeting was to be at Oliver Sudden's Bel Air mansion but at the last minute Oliver sent his apologies. 'I have to be more target-orientational with my problematizing, my prioritizing's in a mess,' he explained as they spoke car-phone to car-phone. So Ernest Mayday changed direction and journeyed instead to a sunless corner at the bottom of Mandeville Canyon where deep in the shadows of the oak and eucalyptus trees he found a dark brown redwood house with hardly any windows. Knowing as he did that cinematography, like other photography, was all about light he was mildly surprised to discover that this legendary figure lived like a mushroom. Then again, when he met Marty face to face, overweight, pudgy, pallid, bushy salt-and-pepper hair, he was also surprised by the living legend's air of profound melancholy.

'Where's Oliver?' he demanded, looking up and down the street.

'Not coming,' said Ernest.

'He wants us to discuss my script changes without him?'

'Perhaps he wants to leave it to us?' Ernest suggested.

'Producers!' Marty said, by way of not answering the question, as he ushered Ernest inside and slammed the door. The Goldberg Variations were playing on an old-fashioned record-player with lots of hiss and scratches. 'Pain in the ass. When he's here he holds everything up, when he's missing he delays us, is that a paradox or what?'

Ernest made no comment.

'Producers!' Marty grumbled again. He waved vaguely in the direction of an uneven bulgy old sofa and coughed for a while, a deep, hacking, lung-churning cough that made Ernest's chest ache just from listening to it. He sat on the sofa and waited politely while Marty ambled into the adjoining open-plan kitchen. 'People think movie directors are *auteurs*,' gloomed the legend, spitting a gob of phlegm into the sink and running the tap, 'whatever the fuck that means. We have those fucking French critics to thank for that. I mean, I suppose a few of us are *auteurs*, maybe, once or twice in our lives, if we get lucky. But let's face it, usually we're nothing more than hired hands, trying to get those fucking producers off our backs.'

'But isn't it nice to be thought of as an *auteur*?' Ernest thought he'd like it if it were him.

'No, usually it's shit,' wheezed Marty, pouring two mugs of coffee, 'because they blame you for the movie, instead of blaming the studio that developed the script, and cast it, and hired you. Even the studio blames you – that way they don't have to blame themselves. Like, if this piece of shit . . . what's it called?'

'Which piece of shit?' Ernest was confused.

'This piece of shit,' growled Marty with impatience. 'The piece of shit you're here to discuss. The piece of shit you wrote.'

'Oh, *my* piece of shit,' said Ernest obligingly.

'Yeah, your piece of shit, what's it called?'

'*Lies*,' Ernest reminded him.

'Right, *Lies*, if *Lies* bombs they'll blame me, the studio'll say it was my vision, the critics'll make it look as though it's some kind of important personal statement of mine instead of a piece of shit that Oliver sent me through the mail and that I'm willing to do for the money. Which, by the way, and I don't mean to be offensive, but I feel I should be candid, is the truth.' He took a deep drag from the cigarette he held between his banana yellow forefinger and thumb. Then he coughed wetly for a few minutes. Ernest waited till the spasm subsided.

'But what if it's a success?'

'How many films are successes?' replied Marty, giving Ernest a weary stare from under the famous hooded eyelids. He was very glum.

'So what are directors, if they're not *auteurs*?' asked Ernest, trying a different tack. He wanted to get along with this man, he'd enjoyed many of his movies, but so far he wasn't finding it that easy.

'Directors are control freaks,' said Marty without a second's hesitation, and he smiled his wicked but charming smile. His teeth were even yellower than his fingertips.

'We control people. We manipulate. Just like writers do on the page, we do it on the stage. If we're any good, that is. But we manipulate real people.' I should be a director, thought Ernest smugly, remembering Joanna and her seduction of Adrian. Writers, he was discovering, can manipulate real people too.

'People think', continued Marty, 'that being a director is about making aesthetic choices – the script, the shots, the sets, the costumes, the way the actors play their parts ... well, that's a part of it, but the real skill is in how you handle the people, how you get them to do what you want.'

'Don't you just tell them?'

'Ha,' said Marty, throwing back his head and laughing an entirely unhumorous laugh. 'Ha-ha-ha-ha-ha.' His long teeth were bared, but his eyes weren't laughing. Then his laugh turned into a cough, necessitating another prolonged delay in the conversation. 'No, bud, you don't just tell them,' he croaked finally. 'First of all, actors want to give their own performance, and rightly. You don't buy a dog and bark yourself. And the best actors don't obey orders. They might be cooperative but they're never obedient. You wouldn't want 'em to be. Stars are exciting because they have an air of danger about them. Directors are lion-tamers. You need the bentwood chair and the whip to protect yourself; you may need the actors to perform the tricks but you still want 'em to threaten and snarl. If they were docile there'd be no fun, no excitement, no danger ... and the audience would know. It's the danger that's sexy. Without danger, the audience ain't interested.'

'What else do you look for in a star?'

'Other than danger?' He considered the question for a moment. 'There's only one important quality.'

'What is it?'

'Fuckability.'

'That's it?'

'Yup.'

'You serious?'

'Sure.'

'Men and women?'

'Sure. If the opposite sex in the audience doesn't want to fuck them, forget it, you got a character actor on your hands, not a star.'

'What about good acting?'

'What about it?'

'Isn't that a quality you look for?'

'That helps,' conceded Marty. 'But if you're fuckable enough everyone starts saying you can act. Look at Monroe.'

'So . . . are the audience voyeurs?'

'What else?'

Ernest watched him in silence for a few moments. 'Do you like actors?' he asked suddenly.

Marty smiled at him. 'I love 'em,' he said. 'I hate 'em but I love 'em. They're so brave.'

Ernest was surprised by that word. 'Brave?'

'Sure. Brave. Every time they play a part they risk making fools of themselves in public. When they fail the humiliation is total, it's for all the world to see. There's no other job that takes that risk, not even politicians. They dress up and pretend to be somebody else, they reveal their feelings and their vulnerabilities, they show us their bodies with all their imperfections, magnified on a screen seventy-feet wide and forty-feet high, when most of us won't even risk an honest look in the mirror.'

'Isn't that just narcissism?'

Marty nodded in agreement. 'Narcissism, yes, and ego. But it's also courage. If the public and the critics reject our work, if they don't like your book or my film, they're not quite rejecting us. Actors suffer constant personal rejection – poor babies, how can you not love 'em?'

'Most people round here seem to hate them.'

'That's because they don't understand. Acting's a tough job. It's what you people in England call a working-class job. They're told when to show up for work. They're told when they can go home. Nobody reports to them. I know, I know, they may have an assistant, a manager, some kind of an entourage if they're big movie stars – a personal make-up artist, a hairdresser, a driver, a secretary, people to laugh at their jokes and make their appointments and read their scripts and agree with their opinions – but the fact remains, when they're doing their real job, acting, nobody reports to them. They can't delegate it. When they get to work they're like factory workers: they're told where to go, where to stand, where to walk, when to talk – 'course, if the director's any good he invites their co-operation and collaboration and listens to what they want and how they feel, but finally the director makes the choices. And they hate that. Well, wouldn't you?'

Ernest nodded.

'Now, most actors don't have very stable personalities to start with. If they did, they wouldn't be actors. They all have some kind of identity crisis, they're insecure, that's why they need to dress up and pretend to be somebody else in order to express themselves. Frequently they're very shy people unless they're acting. You, for instance, Ernest, you don't need the love of a thousand strangers every night, eight performances a week, the way a stage actor does. And TV and movie actors need the love of millions of strangers – eight thousand folks a week just doesn't cut it. But actors need this because they're kids – they need the love and attention, "watch me, Daddy, watch me jump in the swimming-pool, watch me jump off the sidewalk, watch me, watch me, catch me . . ."

'And then, when the show opens, they get all this adulation. They get all the attention from the media, they're interviewed as if they thought of the whole thing, as if they *understand* the whole thing, instead of simply being hired to act in it. They take a big bow and receive all the applause on Saturday night. That's fine. They deserve all the applause they can get. Because underneath, *underneath*, they know that they're dispensable, they know that they can be laid off just the same way they lay off the guys on the production line at General Motors. They're scared. And rightly so. Above all, actors are frightened.'

Ernest was intrigued. 'So how do you deal with this?'

'Well, you don't get good work from frightened people. Acting is ninety per cent nerve. Actors are like trapeze artists. A great actor is a high wire act, taking chances, risking everything, every time. If they lose their nerve, they're finished. So my job is to make it safe for them, give them confidence, give them the courage to take big chances – you can't leap a chasm in two steps.'

Ernest was interested. 'So how, exactly, do you give these frightened, dangerous, fuckable people confidence?'

'Well, it's a kind of therapeutic relationship,' said Marty. 'In group therapy eight or nine people meet once a week for two or three years. The therapist gives them boundaries, he protects them from each other, he says what's fair and what's unfair – within those boundaries, they're safe. Well, that's what I do. Except that my group meets for twelve hours a day for twelve weeks, and we're trying to make a movie, we're not trying to solve our personal problems. Well, not ostensibly. But the therapist is Daddy, and so am I. I make it safe for the actors to play. Because that's what they do, that's what they're supposed to do, they play. Like kids – they believe it completely while they're doing it, but they know it's a game. That's why they're called players, and they act in plays. Or screenplays.'

'Where does fuckability fit into kids' games?' asked Ernest.

'Sexuality has a place even in kids' games, didn't you know that? And listen, these are adult kids. What games would you expect them to play?'

Three hours later, Ernest drove home. It had been easy, working with Marty on the script. He hadn't wanted many changes and those that he requested seemed perfectly sensible and weren't hard to do. So a couple of days later he was back in court, watching a real-life drama being played. Was fuckability the secret of Abel Pile's success too? Ernest found himself wondering as he watched the jury watching Abel. Ernest regarded himself as a poor judge of male sex appeal, but if Randi's reaction to him was anything to go by then Abel Pile fitted Marty's definition of a star. He watched Randi watching Abel too, with evident adoration in her shining eyes.

Then he began to wonder again about the identity of that other woman in that orgy Abel Pile and John Schmidt had had in the Bonaventure Hotel with Joanna the night before the trial. Where had Randi been that night? She had seemed evasive when he asked her. He had no particular reason to suspect her ... except that it was becoming plainer day by day that Randi was infatuated with Pile. The question was, was it purely a spiritual infatuation or might there be a physical component? As he considered this question, watching the dust particles dancing in the limelight beams of sunshine streaming in from the high narrow windows above the well of the courtroom while the lawyers droned on, he realized that he was interested but not at all jealous. He was merely curious, and his curiosity was purely on account of his book. If Randi were involved sexually with Abel, he realized, it might even be rather helpful. He'd learn more about him, and this could give him a different perspective on Joanna. He wouldn't learn any more about Randi, of course, she was an open book, but that was OK; he already knew pretty much all there was to know about her. He decided he would have to ask her about that orgy one day, but not yet. She might tell Abel. Then none of them would be safe.

Ernest had gone back to court because of all the trailers on the TV news the night before: the forthcoming attractions on *Eyewitness News* featured Sandy from Tarzana, who was slated to give evidence today about her famous accusation of the blowjob conversation with the Reverend Pile. Harris K. Fitch had blundered the previous day and had questioned one of the witnesses about Abel Pile's previous good character. This was all that Hoolahan needed to bring Sandy into the case. All the TV news programmes interviewed their legal correspondents, who all agreed that Fitch had blown it.

Hoolahan had made sure that all the media knew that Sandy would be on the stand, but by lunchtime, owing to the law's delays, she had not yet made her appearance. All morning the courtroom had been packed with cheerful hacks and the *paparazzi* had shown up in full force outside, lounging about the wide panelled fluorescent corridor. Ernest had been hoping to see Joanna, but she wasn't in the public seats. He studied the jury carefully. There were two men who looked something like her description of Adrian. At lunchtime he hurried out into the heat and around the huge white building in an effort to find where the jury came in and out so he could try to follow the likeliest-looking juryman to his tryst with Joanna. But no luck. He couldn't even find the right door.

At two p.m. he was back in his seat, and the eagerly awaited Sandy took the stand. She looked as hygienic as Doris Day, with her freckled snub nose and big blue eyes. Gil Hoolahan took her slowly and carefully through her story. Yes, she confirmed, she had joined the Church of the Community of Personal Truth twelve years ago. She had been a constant supporter ever since. She had been baptized by the Reverend Pile. She had attended SCREAMS and SPITS and every other available seminar. She had donated more than thirty per cent of her income to the Church. After twelve years she had been let go from work and she was broke; her husband was out of work too and so she had asked the Reverend Pile if she could continue to attend at nominal fees.

'And he replied?' cooed Gil Hoolahan, looking at the jury.

'He said that he could do nothing more for me unless I gave him a blowjob.'

There was a buzz in the courtroom. The Judge called for order and banged his gavel. The hacks smirked, scribbled, then waited, pencils poised. Gil Hoolahan smiled at Harris K. Fitch. 'No more questions,' he said, and sat down.

Fitch rubbed his chin in a puzzled sort of way. Frowning in apparent confusion, he rose and strolled over to Sandy. 'Sandy – may I call you Sandy? – Sandy, this is a very worryin' story that you just told the court.'

She nodded. 'I know that, sir,' she said, and smiled that big, transparently honest wide-eyed smile of hers.

'Now, Sandy, I must remind you that you are under oath,' said Harris.

'I know that, sir,' she said.

'I'm sure you do.'

'I've sworn to tell the truth, the whole truth and nothing but the truth, so help me God,' she said.

'So you have. And that's just what you bin doin', right?' asked Harris, in a worried fashion.

'Yes, sir, I have.'

'Now, you know that Abel Pile says that he's never met you?'

'I saw him say that on TV.'

'So who's tellin' the truth here?'

'I am, sir.'

'I see. Now, do you remember that I came out to your home in Tarzana, to talk to you about all this, a coupla weeks ago?'

'Yes I do, Mr Fitch.'

'And it was a lovely sunny day, wasn't it, and you were swimmin' in your pool in your l'il ole backyard?'

'That's right.' She smiled cheerfully.

'And do you remember you had a little metal antenna on your head?'

'I do.'

'What was that for?'

'So that I could pick up my messages.'

'So where were your messages coming from?'

'Outer space, mainly.'

Jurors glanced at each other, puzzled. Gil Hoolahan stood up, consternation written all over his face. 'Your Honour,' he interrupted, 'I object.'

'I bet you do,' said the Judge, grinning. 'But I want to hear this.'

'Thank you, Judge,' said Harris K. Fitch. He turned back to the witness box, deeply serious. 'Do all your messages come from outer space?'

'Oh no,' said Sandy. 'Some are on my telephone answering machine.'

'Well, that's pretty common. Anywhere else?'

'Some come from my leg.'

'I'm sorry, I didn't quite get that, your what?' Even Harris K. Fitch seemed surprised.

'My leg.'

'Your leg gives you messages?'

'Yes.'

'You mean, it speaks to you?'

'Yes.'

Gil Hoolahan put his head in his hands.

'Anywhere else?'

'Well, some come from the Devil, of course.'

'You believe in the Devil, I take it, bein' a lady of profound religious convictions?'

'Oh yes. I have no doubts on that score.'

'So where is he? The Devil.'

'He's everywhere.'

'Anywhere . . . specific?'

'Over there,' she said, pointing cheerfully to the windowsill above the jury box. They all turned to look.

'There's nothin' much visible to the naked eye except a couple of dead flies,' observed Harris Fitch, after some lengthy and careful scrutiny.

'But I can see him,' she insisted sweetly. 'He's right over there.'

'I'm sure you can.' He glanced at the jury. 'Now, Sandy, do you remember sayin' to me: "Isn't it strange how when I move to the deep end of my pool all the water moves to the shallow end?"'

'I do.'

'Now, Sandy, that didn't make any sense to me. It seemed to me that it kinda defied the laws of physics. I mean, there wouldn't be room in the shallow end for all the water from the deep end, would there?'

'Well, there is. I'm happy to assure you of that.'

'Thank you, thank you, I appreciate that.' He leaned thoughtfully on the witness box front ledge. 'So it doesn't overflow?'

'No.'

'Why does the water move around like that?'

'It's like the waters of the Red Sea, parting for Moses.'

Fitch rubbed his hand over his chin. 'You see, I asked a friend of mine who's a psychiatrist what he made of the remark, and he said it was psychotic. Delusions of grandeur, he called it.'

'Objection,' said Hoolahan wearily, hardly bothering to stand up.

'Sustained,' said the Judge. 'Sorry, Mr Fitch, but you know better than that.'

'Was Moses psychotic?' asked Sandy, ignoring the Judge. 'Are you saying I imagine it? Because I don't. Was Moses psychotic? Does God have delusions of grandeur?'

'Good question,' said Fitch. 'What do you think?'

'Objection!' cried Hoolahan.

'Sustained. Mr Fitch, just ask questions, OK?'

'OK, Judge. Sandy, have you ever had psychiatric treatment?'

'Objection?' tried a not very hopeful Hoolahan once more.

'I don't mind answering,' said Sandy cheerfully.

'Then go right ahead,' suggested the Judge. 'Let's get this over with.'

'I have had treatment, but I'm still telling you the truth.'

Fitch soothed her immediately. 'I'm sure you are. Tell me, how was your condition diagnosed?'

'Schizophrenia. But I'm fine now.'

'I'm mighty glad to hear that,' said Fitch. 'Now tell me, just one last thing: has anybody *else* ever refused to help you unless you gave them a blowjob?'

She nodded with sadness. 'Quite a few people, yes.'

'Anybody we might have heard of?'

'Well, only the President.'

'I'm sorry? The president of what?'

'The President of the United States.'

Harris K. Fitch turned away from Sandy, unable to suppress a smile. Fortunately he turned towards the jury. As he strolled lazily back to his table he grinned at Gil Hoolahan. 'Your witness, pal,' he said.

Gil Hoolahan stood up slowly. 'Let me ask you this again: did Abel Pile demand oral sex from you as your fees for continued participation in the activities of his Church?'

'He did.'

'Did this message come from outer space or your . . . your leg?'

'No. From Abel Pile, definitely.'

'Thank you,' said Gil Hoolahan. He sat down. He sighed heavily. He knew that he would be the laughing stock of Los Angeles for days, if not weeks. Ernest knew that, after the débâcle the court had just witnessed, it would only take one really stubborn juror to turn this jury around. Joanna was riding a winner. Well, he thought, it's just the kind of evidence one might expect from an inhabitant of a rich Californian suburb named after Edgar Rice Burroughs's memorable but incoherent hero.

TWENTY-TWO

Thanks to the Trinity, God is the only person who is
able to have group therapy with himself.

Dr Murray Cox

'Ernest, we have to talk.'

Ernest looked up from his word processor, where he was tapping out the latest instalment of the book. Reluctantly he was leaving out most of Sandy's testimony because it was too easily identified. Besides, he wasn't sure that anyone outside LA would believe it.

'What about?' he asked.

Randi had made one of her very rare forays into his study. Something was definitely up. She seemed upset. She was searching for the right words. 'We . . . we don't seem to have anything much left to say to each other,' she said.

'Then how can we talk?' he asked.

'You know what I mean.'

'Look, can we discuss this later, I'm in the middle of . . .'

'No. Now. I want to discuss it now.'

He had been surprised when she'd driven home with him after the trial that day. Usually she went to the Church, to do some work on herself, as she put it. She hadn't spoken a word, all the way home. 'What do you want to talk about?'

'Us.'

Ernest forced the rest of his features into a sympathetic expression and, having rearranged his face appropriately, waited. She didn't seem to know how to begin. He wasn't sure he wanted her to. 'Ernest, this is difficult to say. I mean, it's really rather personal . . .'

'Would you rather I weren't here?' he offered.

'Shut up,' she said. 'You remember Ellen?'

'You mean Ellen my wife?' She nodded. 'Yes, strangely enough I remember her quite clearly.'

'You remember what you told me she used to say?'

'You mean, that she couldn't get off? Not your problem, surely?'

'No, not that. She used to say that you're not capable of a real relationship with anybody?'

'I remember that, yes.' He was rapidly losing interest in this conversation but he knew from experience that it had hardly started.

'Well, I want to help you with that problem.'

'Wait a minute,' said Ernest. 'Who says I want help? Who says there is a problem? The fact that she used to say that doesn't mean it was true.'

'But it was. And it is.'

'So how do you propose to help?'

'You once told me that as soon as a couple who are having a relationship get married, the sex stops working. I think that's why you won't marry me – you're afraid that'll happen again. Right?'

'Partly.' He didn't want to go into the several hundred other reasons why he didn't want to marry her.

'Well, what else?'

'You know what I told Ellen – the whole deal makes no sense for men today.'

'I suppose', began Randi tentatively, 'that my problem is, I don't think of getting married as a deal, I think of it as a sacrament.'

'The word sacrament signifies nothing to me,' said Ernest. 'The point is, we don't really have a shared life, shared interests. I go to dinner parties that don't interest you – '

'They don't interest you either,' she retorted.

'That's true, they don't interest me either.'

'So why don't you stop going to them?'

He smiled. 'Why? So that I can come to the Church with you?'

'Not necessarily.'

He took her hand in his. 'Randi, you spend your every waking moment at that Church, which interests me even less. Well, that's not true, it does interest me, but only as a sociological phenomenon. Once a week numerous people throughout the world troop into a local big empty building, kneel down, look up and say to nobody "Please can I have . . . ?" or "Thank you . . . " or "Sorry about such and such, it was wrong and I'll try not to do it again, or if I do, which I probably will, I'll say sorry again next Sunday." And they're just talking to the ceiling.'

'I know you don't believe. I'm not asking you to. But you wanted children with Ellen, and I want them now.'

Ernest was taken by surprise. 'You do?' She nodded. She was really very beautiful. She gazed at him with doe-eyed simplicity and hope. 'And are you prepared to stay home and look after them?'

'I don't need to, you're home anyway.'

He was exasperated. 'That's what I mean.'

'I'll stay home with them, yes, up to a point.'

'That's what Ellen said. Look,' he explained as reasonably as he could, 'I can offer a woman – you, in fact – economic security. In return, I wanted kids, housekeeping, sex, the standard deal, OK, I didn't get that from Ellen and I wouldn't get that from you. I offered Ellen economic security and what did she offer me? Economic security. Ergo, no deal. OK, I can offer *you* economic security. What can you offer me? Religion. I don't want religion. Sorry.'

A big tear leaked out of the corner of her left eye and ran slowly down her face. 'But I'll offer you what you wanted from Ellen,' she said very quietly.

He felt like a shit. He tried to be more gentle. 'There's nothing in it for you either. You're not a home-maker. You can't even cook.' He took her hands in his. 'So it boils down to sex ... which you're very creative about, especially recently – but that's just not sufficient incentive.' *I refuse to tie myself up for ever and hand you half of everything I own* were the words he left unspoken.

Then she uttered some dread words of her own. 'I think we ought to see someone.'

'As long as it's not Abel Pile,' he had replied, and thus it was that some days later they found themselves sitting in the office of Dr Julian Genau on the UCLA campus.

'How can I help?' asked Julian, and waited. Randi and Ernest shifted uncomfortably in their chairs. There was a long silence. Julian waited for a few minutes. 'Well?'

'Well,' said Ernest with considerable hesitance, 'see, it's not me, it's Randi.'

'It's not me,' denied Randi immediately. 'I admit I wanted to come and talk to someone, but it's Ernest who has the problem.'

'Not in my opinion,' growled Ernest.

'Ah,' said Julian, and waited some more. He looked first at one of them, then at the other. Neither wanted to speak or even meet his eye. He didn't mind. He found the silence quite relaxing, though – given a choice – he preferred explaining to waiting. So after a while he said: 'I think I should let you know, we're about halfway through the hour that I've allotted to you.'

'It's about Ernest's spiritual crisis,' said Randi.

'Bollocks,' said Ernest. 'She wants to get married and I don't.' He explained his position. Julian nodded, and listened, and nodded again.

When Ernest stopped speaking Julian said: 'So let me see if I understand this correctly. You're really asking this question: why should a man commit himself to taking care of a woman who might at any time run out on him,

305

either to another man, or – what's worse – to a career that could consume all her time and energy?'

'That's it,' said Ernest.

'And you're saying', continued Julian, who hadn't finished his explanatory paraphrase yet and was determined to do so, 'that even if we men owe women a better break, *this* deal – the marriage deal – has no advantages for men. Is that it?'

Ernest was delighted. 'That's it exactly,' he agreed. He turned to Randi. 'Do you see now?'

'Hang on, wait a minute,' said Julian. '*I* don't see.' Ernest looked back at Julian, confused. 'Ernest, marriage is not actually about a deal, is it?'

''Course it is,' said Ernest.

'No it isn't,' said Randi.

'Yes it is,' said Ernest.

'No it isn't,' said Randi.

'Excuse me,' interrupted Julian. 'Randi, what do you think marriage is?'

'It's a sacrament,' said Randi.

'Ah, that's interesting,' said Julian. He shrugged. 'Depends what you mean by sacrament, of course. Let me tell you what I think. I think marriage is about intimacy with another human being, which is why men are frightened of it.'

'Why', asked Ernest, 'should men be more frightened of it than women?'

'Let me explain,' said Dr Genau, happily seizing the opportunity with both hands and embarking at last upon his favourite pastime. 'Both sexes start out as babies, as you know, with an intense primary relationship with the mother. All babies and young kids have a tendency to identify with the mother and her values. It's easy for a girl. She stays with that. But a little boy has to undergo a transition and become a man. To do this, he has to join the men, so his relationship with his father becomes crucial.

All the older men in that boy's world have a responsibility to help the boy leave his mother and join them. Every society has some sort of rites of passage – Jews have barmitzvahs, primitive tribes take them out hunting; we Brits are even more primitive, we send our boys away to boarding-schools if we're middle class or we take them to the soccer match if we're not. It's all tribal behaviour.

'Now, many boys have no relationship with their father, maybe he's away on business all the time, only sees the kids at the weekend and can't be bothered then because he's tired. Boys like that achieve only a shaky male identity ... and this usually manifests itself in some reaction against women – hostility, fear, antagonism, aggression, all the qualities which you display most of the time, Ernest. I hope you don't mind my saying this, it's nothing personal, please don't take this personally, but it could mean that you never really crossed the bridge into adult manhood. Anyway, that's why some men fear making a commitment to a woman. The man experiences a fear that he's got no balls, or that he'll lose them, or that she'll take them.'

Ernest was steaming. He had turned that unpleasant blotchy lobster pink colour. 'What the fuck do you mean, "Don't take this personally"? You're telling me that I have a shaky male identity? That I've got no balls? That I hate women? And then you tell me not to take it personally? How the fuck else can I take it?'

'Look ... I'm just saying it's one of the possibilities. Any man who views marriage as the kind of a deal you described fears intimacy.'

'I've heard all this crap before.' Ernest turned to Randi. 'He's just regurgitating the latest fad in American psychobabble bullshit.'

'No, actually, Ernest, all I'm doing is explaining why some men fear intimacy, that's all.'

'Well, I don't get it. Last time we talked you had the

impertinence to tell me that I was angry with other people all the time because I'm *really* angry with myself.'

'Projection. Yes.' Julian nodded vigorously in agreement with himself. 'I remember.'

'Well, why should I be angry with myself?'

'We were discussing your case of writers' block, remember?'

Randi intervened. 'I think that's caused by his spiritual crisis.'

'Now that's very interesting,' said Julian with his customary enthusiasm for a new thought, however slight. 'That could be another way of looking at the same thing.'

'What the hell are you both talking about?' snapped Ernest.

'Oh, I'm sorry,' said Julian. 'Look, perhaps I didn't make myself clear, let me try to explain again. Both sexes start out, as babies, with a very intense . . .'

Ernest stood up. 'Stop explaining, Julian. You're always fucking explaining. Just shut the fuck up, OK?'

'OK. But this *does* all tie in with our last conversation, you know, d'you remember, at Oliver's party, when you asked if I'd see you professionally?'

'Did you?' Randi turned and stared at Ernest, astonished. 'You never told me.'

'Yes I did,' Ernest snarled. 'Clearly I was wrong.' He stalked out, slamming the door behind him. Randi looked at Julian. He shrugged.

'I want to marry him,' she said simply.

Julian was baffled. 'Why?'

'It's my religion,' she explained. 'It's been explained to me that I should.'

'Ah yes,' nodded Julian. 'Well, in the end most things seem to come down to God or sex. In my opinion everything in life boils down to these two big questions: Is there life after death, and is there sex after marriage?'

*

Still quivering with rage, heart pounding, complexion puce, Ernest slammed his Mercedes out of the campus parking-lot and roared over to the studio for a meeting with Oliver Sudden. There he sat fuming in the waiting area of the French château bungalow for half an hour or more, till Oliver sent for him. This turned out to be a much shorter meeting than Ernest had anticipated. 'I met Marty Rubb', he began, 'and his changes were pretty reasonable, but I just wanted to discuss them with you before I . . .'

Oliver interrupted him. 'Things have changed,' he said.

'Changed? How?'

'I decided to tell Virginia we wanted Marty to direct the film. It was a mistake. She doesn't think he's right, she says he's not young and hip.'

'Well, he's not, but . . .'

'She wants young and hip, we sold her young and hip, boom boom boom, young and hip, remember?'

'I remember,' said Ernest. 'Boom boom boom. How could I forget?'

'She thought I was going to direct it,' said Oliver.

'Only because that's what you told her,' said Ernest.

'I didn't promise, not in so many words, I agree she might have had that impression, anyway that's water under the bridge that ship has sailed know what I mean, that ship has sailed?'

'I know what you mean,' said Ernest. 'You mean that ship has sailed.'

'That's it,' agreed Oliver. 'That ship has sailed. Exactly.'

'So have you promised it to Marty?'

'Yes, but that doesn't mean anything, he knows that, there's no deal yet, he's not pay or play, Marty's a big boy, there's a lot of directors out there.'

'So what's the problem?'

'No problem. There's no problem. Don't ever say what's the problem, that's the negative way of looking at things, you know like is the bottle half empty or half full, know what I mean, every problem is also an *opportunity*, the question here is what *opportunity* does this present us with?'

'It seems to me', said Ernest stubbornly, 'that this opportunity presents us with a problem. Is there a director that Virginia would like?'

'Unfortunately, when I proposed Marty she began to see the whole project as less young and hip than she thought it was, then she started to question the budget, so now she's saying she's worried about the whole thing and she won't greenlight it without casting.'

Ernest was shocked. His million-dollar deal seemed to be disappearing before his very eyes. 'Oliver, this is serious. My neck is on the block here.'

'What about my neck?' said Oliver.

'You've got lots of deals.'

Oliver was insulted. 'You saying my neck isn't on the block?'

'OK,' said Ernest, 'your neck can be too. I'm not worried about exclusivity here, I was just using an idiom: "My neck is on the block."'

'But my neck is too,' insisted Oliver.

Ernest was exasperated. 'Oliver, I don't want to argue with you about a pronoun. *Our* necks are on the block, OK?'

'OK!'

'Who does she want to cast first?' Ernest wanted to know.

'The girl. She thinks it's a great opportunity to get Chelsea Krieger. So here's our opportunity – if we can get Chelsea Krieger we get to make a picture with one of the top three female box-office stars in the world, isn't that great?'

'But', Ernest asked, slightly perplexed, 'isn't everyone trying to cast her in their movies?'

'Of course, didn't you hear what I just said, she's one of the top three female box-office stars in the world.'

'So, what happens if we don't get her?'

'Who knows, maybe Virginia won't greenlight the movie, what we have to do is get Chelsea so I've messengered the script over to her house, she lives in Brentwood, I've asked her to read it today because she leaves for Chicago tomorrow to start on another picture and once she starts work on the other picture she'll never read our picture so I want her to read it before she leaves because if she doesn't read it while she's on the other picture that's twelve weeks or maybe sixteen and then she'll be exhausted and wrung out and she'll need a vacation and she'll go to Hawaii so it'll be four or five months before we get an answer and meantime she'll have been offered twenty other pictures all pay or play and Virginia will have gone cold on *Lies* by then so here's the skinny, I've sent her a big bouquet of flowers and a basket of fruit to show how much we love her and she's gotten the script it's been delivered already and I've spoken to her manager and told him it's the role of a lifetime, a certain nomination, we told her "You play this role you'll be there on Oscar night" and Ginnie's talked to the agent and she's gotten a pay or play offer from Ginnie for six million dollars plus a percentage of first box-office dollar and now, *now*, she wants to talk to you about the role so you gotta drive over to Brentwood right now and answer her questions, any questions, all her questions about the material and about the role, OK?'

Ernest was stunned. 'Me?'

'Yeah, you. You're the writer.'

'You're the producer, for God's sake.'

'I know, but I've got two uncancellable meetings, anyway she wants to talk to you, what can I do? You wrote the book, you created the character, she knows that, she's not dumb, there's no director on board so she wants to talk to you, OK? I can't help it.'

Ernest's day was going from bad to worse. He drove

out to Brentwood, where the meeting with Chelsea Krieger was shorter and even less satisfactory than the meeting with Oliver. The basket of fruit seemed to have had little effect. Ernest waited for nearly an hour in the living room of her Brentwood home, a long low building with white walls, beige sofas, beige armchairs and beige rugs on blond hardwood floors. There was the statutory amount of yellow marble and some small crystal chandeliers that would have looked at home in Golders Green. The room had obviously been done up with great care by a top-class professional decorator and it had all the character of the lobby of a good hotel. A baby was crying somewhere in some distant part of the house. In the wide two-storey hall stood evidence of Ms Krieger's forthcoming trip to Chicago, a mound of that Louis Vuiton luggage so beloved by prostitutes in Paris and movie people in Beverly Hills. He wandered over to the french windows and looked out, down the gentle incline of the green velvet lawn. At the bottom of the garden, behind a chain-link fence, two Dobermanns growled intermittently and hurled themselves snarling and barking against the jangling fence in a desperate but fruitless attempt to savage every passing Mercedes. Elsewhere in the garden a Rottweiler wandered loose.

After an eternity Chelsea hurried in. She did not look like the ravishing sensual beauty who lit up the silver screen. She was a skinny little thing in a tracksuit, almost anorexic, pasty and colourless, no make-up. She looked tired, her hair was greasy and was pulled severely back from her widow's peak and tied on top with an elastic band. 'Nice meeting you,' she said without looking at him. 'Sorry you've been waiting so long, I'm packing, I'm going away tomorrow, my manager's on his way here, then we can talk, OK?' She smiled a brief shy smile, managed a moment of eye contact, and invited him to sit down.

'Nice dog,' said Ernest.

'Don't go out there,' she warned. 'He's a killer.'

'That's nice,' he said. For a while they exchanged the usual pleasantries about the weather, the smog and the traffic and after several minutes of halting conversation the manager arrived, clutching the script of *Lies*.

'Oh good, here's Sergio,' she said. Sergio was followed into the room by the selfsame killer Rottweiler, and it fixed a baleful eye on him. Ernest could see why. Sergio was very short, bearded, and massively overweight. He wore thick spectacles with Giorgio Armani frames and a blue and green tracksuit. He spoke in a creaky, hoarse, high-pitched voice that sounded as though it needed oiling. 'Hi, Sugar, finished your packing?' She shook her head. 'Don't worry, doll, this meeting won't take long.'

'Sergio,' she introduced them, 'this is . . .'

Ernest took a step towards Sergio to shake hands, and the Rottweiler growled. Ernest retreated immediately towards the far corner of the room, under an indoor palm.

'How did this fuckin' dog get in here?' demanded Sergio in his squeaky tones. He certainly gave the impression that he was shouting, he *looked* like he was shouting, but there were no more decibels than before. 'Get him out.' Obediently Chelsea led him out. 'He's a Nazi,' explained Sergio to Ernest. 'Thank God he knows I'm not Jewish. Sit down.'

Chelsea returned and belatedly introduced them. 'Sergio, this is Mr Maypole.' Ernest could hear the dog scratching furiously on the other side of a nearby door, uttering a combination bark, snarl and yelp.

'Mayday, actually,' muttered an embarrassed Ernest. 'Can that dog get back in?'

'No,' she whispered. 'He's locked up.'

Ernest advanced from his corner. Sergio gave Ernest's hand a damp but firm manly shake, though he was looking at Chelsea as he did so. 'You guys discussed this piece of shit yet?' Ernest somehow felt that this question did not bode well for their future working relationship.

'No,' he said in a curt voice.

'Sorry I'm late,' Sergio croaked. 'Traffic from hell.' Ernest surveyed him. Trickles of sweat were running down both sides of Sergio's forehead from under his hairline. His beard was heavy and dark, the kind you have to shave twice a day or you look unkempt. He hadn't had his second shave yet. His face seemed to register permanent distaste, as if there were a bad smell under his nose. 'I said, sit down,' croaked Sergio.

Ernest sat down, and came straight to the point. 'Do you think it's a piece of shit too?' he asked Chelsea. 'And if so, what am I doing here?'

Chelsea Krieger lit a cigarette and smiled a wan smile at both Sergio and Ernest. 'He didn't mean piece of shit literally. Don't take it personally. That's just how people talk about scripts round here.'

'OK. I'll try not to take it personally. I gather you have some questions about it.'

'Well, yes,' said Chelsea. 'You see . . . I didn't quite get it.'

Ernest waited for the question, but she said nothing more and after a while it became clear to him that this *was* the question. He sought elucidation. 'What, exactly, didn't you get?'

'Well,' she began, 'you know I'm going away tomorrow and I only got the script today. So I only had time to read the first eighty pages. But I wanted to be fair to it so I messengered the script over to Sergio in his office.'

Ernest looked at Sergio. Sergio took up the story: 'As she'd already read the first eighty pages, I started on page eighty-one and read all the way through to the end. To be quite candid, Ernest, I didn't get it either.'

Ernest's mouth had dropped open. He closed it. 'Um . . . I don't know how to . . . where to . . . I mean, how could you get it, if you haven't read it all?'

'We have read it all,' Chelsea corrected him.

'Between us,' added Sergio.

'But . . . but . . .' said Ernest, 'but . . .'

'Look, I have ta be honest wid ya, it didn't make no sense to me,' Sergio croaked. 'Sorry, pal, but there it is.'

'Well, how *could* it, you m. . .' Ernest looked at him sharply. He'd been about to say moron, but he caught himself just in time. 'You . . . moranager!' he said. Chelsea and Sergio exchanged puzzled glances. Clearly an English word. Ernest knew that the future of the film was hanging in the balance, so he tried again. 'Chelsea, thank you for reading even part of it when you're so busy, and I quite understand that you haven't had time to read it all. Frankly, I don't see why you can't finish it later, on the plane or something. Still I'm very grateful that you found time to read the first two-thirds of it.' He looked at Sergio. 'But how you can expect to get it if you only read the last third is completely beyond my comprehension. It is, I grant you, sometimes difficult to understand scripts that one has read right through. But I can assure you that, as a general rule, it is exceedingly difficult to understand a script that one hasn't read, even for someone as insightful as a manager.'

Sergio's blood pressure was up. 'OK, pal, OK. I mean, I'm not saying it's no good or that you're not talented. I'm just saying . . . well, the humour, you know, I didn't get . . . the mystery, it just made no sense to me . . .' He sighed and looked helplessly around the room for inspiration. 'But it's nuttin' to get hostile about, it's just words, that's all, they can be changed, so what? See what I mean?'

'Sure,' replied Ernest in a tone of sweet reason. 'What you're saying is, they're just semiotic signifiers waiting to be decoded when sequentially encountered.'

'Huh?' inquired Sergio.

'Sergio, writers don't just choose words arbitrarily. We

don't just write down any old words. If you change the words, you change the meaning.'

'So? I mean, well, Jesus, you writers are always so upset if anyone wants to change your words. I mean, I'm sure they're great words, but if you wrote these great words you can write some other great words, right? Some more great words, see what I mean? Different great words. I mean, why are you so sensitive, pal, what's the big deal?'

'Look – pal – the fact that you don't "get" my script if you haven't read it does not strike me as deeply puzzling.'

'Wait a minute,' intervened Chelsea, showing signs of incipient life. 'Don't be like that. Sergio's opinion is very important to me.'

'I'm sure it is,' said Ernest. 'And I'll be absolutely delighted to help Sergio "get" it just as soon as he's read the first two-thirds of it.' He stood up.

'Are you leaving?' Chelsea was startled.

'Yes please. If you can prevent Cerberus from attacking me.'

'His name's Sergio,' said Chelsea. 'He's not attacking you, he just didn't get your script, that's all.'

'I was referring to the dog. The three-headed devil dog that guards the gates of hell.'

'Oh. Sure.' She rang a bell and the boatman appeared in the form of a Filipino maid, to row Ernest back across the Styx to safety.

TWENTY-THREE

It is the nature of men to feel as much bound by the favours they do as by those they receive.

Machiavelli

Ernest Mayday drove to the bank's instant teller at the junction of Doheny and Sunset on the border of Beverly Hills. It was the place he usually went if he needed cash because it was a safe neighbourhood. As he was getting out of his car he saw a couple of people being held up at gunpoint and deprived of their cash withdrawals, their wallets and credit cards, their car keys and their BMWs, so he got back into the car and drove to the bank itself. There were armed security guards there.

His week had steadily worsened. He had been so pre-occupied with his encounters with Randi, Julian Genau, Oliver Sudden, Chelsea Krieger and Sergio that he forgot he'd promised to pay five thousand dollars to Joanna. As he stood in line at the bank he realized that he didn't know what to do about it. 'You can get it to me,' was all she'd said, giving no instructions. Probably she had intended that he give it to her at one of their usual meeting places, like the Bel Monde Hotel. But Ernest decided that the time had come to find out some more about her by observing her in her native habitat. Clutching five thousand dollars in a padded manila envelope, he hurried to his car and dialled her home number. He was in luck. She was home. 'I've got your money,' he told her.

'Great, Norm, thanks. Where shall we meet?'

'I'm in the Valley,' he lied, trying to sound as casual as

possible. 'I'll be passing Toluca Lake in quarter of an hour, give me your address.'

There was a moment's hesitation. Then she told it to him. As he drove down the Valley side of Laurel Canyon it was a clear fall day. The mountains, invisible for weeks, suddenly looked close enough to reach out and touch. The Santa Anas were gusting hot winds from the north and all the gunge had been blown clean out of the Valley. He motored along Ventura, past the Universal Studios Tour signs, the shining tourist hotels whose mirrored windows reflected the shadowy skyline of the brown hills, past a couple of ramshackle 'adult' motels with their peeling paintwork and flickering neon advertising waterbeds and X-rated videos, left on to Barham and down the long hill past the expensive and heavenly gates of Forest Lawn cemetery.

She lived in a narrow, shabby residential side street somewhere between Warners, NBC and Disney. This proximity to Studio City might sound glamorous to those who don't know Los Angeles, just as the name Broadway still conjures up images of New York's Great White Way to those few remaining out-of-towners who haven't heard about the degradation of Forty-second Street. But Studio City was not the Forty-second Street of LA – that tawdry privilege was reserved for Hollywood Boulevard – no, Joanna's street was just one of thousands of identical shabby suburban roads, with a couple of tired old coconut palms wilting on each corner, lined with long, drab, two- and three-storey apartment buildings with dark concrete subterranean garages protected by automatic steel grille gates, with dim lobbies and endless identical corridors washed out by flickering fluorescents.

He rang her doorbell and it chimed. Joanna opened the door. She was wearing a big green sweater, off the shoulder (the way movie actresses wear evening gowns), black tights and black cowboy boots highly decorated in a silver and gold motif. She was chewing. 'Gum?' She offered a stick by way of a greeting.

He walked in and looked around. The living room was dark because the windows faced out on to a light well at the back. The walls were painted peach, the white plastic venetians hung at an odd angle, apparently unused, for the windows had some unlined floral drapes. There was the original fifties white cottage-cheese ceiling, a slightly stained oatmeal three-piece suite grouped around the obligatory glass-topped coffee table and an off-white shag-pile carpet. It was apparent that the room was rented furnished. He sniffed. A stick of incense was burning in a jam jar.

'You like my apartment?'

'Charming,' he said and handed her the fat little jiffy bag containing the money. 'Can I look around?'

'OK.' She took him to her bedroom. It was very feminine – a king-sized, spindly, new brass four-poster with white gauze drapes, lacey linen sheets and a couple of balding stuffed bears, noses in the air, lounging arrogantly on the pink and white pillows. On the dressing-table was a selection of framed snapshots, some faded, some new. One portrait, carefully and professionally posed, was of a little girl with her hair in pigtails, sitting on the lap of a young man. The child's smile was unmistakable. 'How old were you when this was taken?' asked Ernest.

'Six or seven,' she said. 'Wasn't I adorable?'

'You certainly were,' he agreed. 'You still are,' he ventured, after a pause.

'Norm, darling, you're such a sweetie, what a nice thing to say.' She seemed genuinely pleased. Ernest looked at another photo, of Joanna at her high school graduation. The same man was with her, smiling, squinting because of the sun, his arms around her shoulder. As in the posed portrait, the family resemblance was obvious.

'Who's the man?' he asked.

'My father.'

'Where's your mother?'

'She took the picture.'

Next to the photos was an opened letter. He picked it up and glanced at the envelope. It was addressed to Jane Montgomery. Joanna stepped forward and took it out of his hand. 'Stop prying,' she admonished him, playfully slapping the back of his hand.

'I'm just doing what you taught me to do,' he grinned. 'Who's Jane Montgomery?'

'My room-mate,' she said, leading him out of the bedroom and sitting down next to him on the sofa, 'and stop trying to read her mail.'

'I thought your room-mate was called Pamela.'

'Pamela?'

'You showed me a picture of her.'

'Oh, she moved out ages ago. Listen, I have great news for you. I've got Adrian just where we want him.'

Ernest's jaw dropped. 'You mean . . .?'

She grinned. 'Yup.'

'What happened? You've done it already? Why didn't you tell me?'

'I'm telling you now.'

Ernest was angry. 'I told you I wanted to know in advance.'

'What's the difference?' she asked mischievously. She knew why he was upset, only too well, but she wanted him to say it.

'I . . . wanted to see what happened . . .'

'You're so *kinky* . . . I *love* it, you seem so straight . . .'

'I'm not kinky, I'm a writer . . . if I saw what happened I could write it up my own way.'

'You can write it up any way you like. I'm not stopping you.'

He sat down, and got out his ballpoint pen. 'Fire away.'

'Actually, I've written it out for you,' she said, and shyly handed him several sheets of handwriting on a yellow legal pad. Surprised, he took it and looked at it. Her handwriting was big and round and childish. What she had written was not.

We were tasting each other. We were upside down and his tongue was playing music in my cunt.

'You've a lovely cunt,' he said, 'and the greatest ass I've ever seen. Too bad you've got no tits.'

'Thanks.'

I kept sucking away but as soon as he got hard, he'd get soft again.

'I don't really want to fuck you anyway.'

'Why?'

'Dunno why – I just don't feel like it.'

Adrian wanted to be loved for himself alone, and not his yellow hair. (Or his pink prick.) It was rather touching, actually. He didn't want to be a fucking machine.

'I can fuck with the best of them when I feel like it,' he said defiantly.

Irritated, Ernest put down the yellow pad. 'What is all this, exactly?' he demanded.

'It's what we said to each other. What I was thinking. What we were doing. All the details.'

'I don't want you to write my fucking dialogue.' He was quite angry.

'Oh really?' she said, hands on her hips. 'I thought that's exactly what you did want.'

'What I want is . . . I want to know what happened, that's all. How did you get him up to the hotel, who reserved the room, who took the pictures, how were they taken without his knowledge, was this before, during or after jury duty . . .?'

'Norm, you're so pedestrian.' She sighed. 'OK. It was after jury duty. I told him I wanted him. He could hardly wait. It didn't occur to him that this might have any connection with the trial. John had rented an apartment in a rooming-house near the courthouse. I told him that's where I live. He was so horny he didn't question anything. John had installed a two-way mirror and took pictures from the room next door. Why didn't I let you come and watch? – well, *obviously*, Norm, I don't want John Schmidt and Abel Pile to know that I'm telling you everything, for you to put it all in a fucking book. These are dangerous guys. I'm not suicidal even if you are. And if this got out, any of it, and even if Abel didn't have us killed, if the cops got hold of it it'd land us all in prison for years for jury tampering, you and me as well as Abel and John. So I'm working on the assumption that nobody should ever know about our little arrangement, OK? Which means you can't get involved, right?'

Ernest nodded. She was correct of course. He didn't know what he'd been thinking of. 'So, how can I get to see the pictures?' he asked quietly.

'I don't know. I don't see how you can. John took them. He's got them. I can ask for copies, but I doubt if he'll give them to me. So now I want the rest of the money, OK?'

'The rest of the money?'

'The balance. The full ten grand.'

He was astounded. 'No way. When John Schmidt pays you in full, I do too. That's the deal.'

'How do you know he hasn't paid me already?'

Ernest realized he didn't know. 'Has he?'

'No.'

Ernest smiled. 'There you are then.'

'You just don't get it, do you, you smug bastard? I could have said he had, couldn't I? And you would never have known. Why can't you trust me, after all this time? It's because I'm a hooker, right? I must be untrustworthy, unreliable, sub-human, is that it? Well, fuck you.' She was crying.

Ernest didn't know what to do. Gingerly, he put one

arm around her heaving shoulders. She shook him off, and jumped up. Tears were streaming down her cheeks. They seemed to be tears of rage or frustration rather than self-pity. 'Well, what's the difference? You've got your story, I've written it for you. But I can't control the result of the case, I can't guarantee they'll be able to use these pictures to get Abel Pile acquitted, and I think you should pay me what you owe me. My mother's *dying*, for God's sake.'

Ernest tried to take some of the heat out of her conversation. 'No, you can't control the result of the case – but maybe it's not over yet. Maybe more will happen.'

'Like what?' She had found herself a tissue and was wiping the damp mascara from around her panda eyes. She blew her red, runny nose.

Ernest stayed calm. 'Like – we have to see if Adrian gives in to the blackmail. What if he doesn't? What if he confesses to his wife? Or tells the judge? . . . There'd be a mis-trial declared, and the cops would come after you, so you may not be able to go back to the courthouse in case Adrian recognizes you. You certainly can't go back there till you know which way he's going to jump. I mean, are you going to be there when they show him the pictures? Or are *you* the one who'll show him the pictures?'

She shrugged. 'I hope not. He might get pretty angry with me.' And she went into the bathroom to wash her face.

'Exactly.' Ernest followed her enthusiastically to the bathroom door. 'But don't you see, it's a great scene for my book if he does. And I want to know exactly what happens. Or he may just cave in. But if he does, he's still got to win the fight in the jury room. And what if he can't? You'd have to seduce another juror, right? That's what they told you. I mean, who knows what could happen? *Anything* could happen. So I'm not giving you the rest of the money because if I do you'll have no incentive to phone me and I might never hear from you again. That's perfectly reasonable, isn't it?'

She stared at him in the bathroom mirror, then began repairing her eye make-up. 'Has your publisher seen any of our book yet?' she asked.

'My book?' he said, correcting her. 'Yes. The first few chapters. I've been sending them off in instalments.'

'He likes it?'

'He's very excited about it. Why?'

She thought for a moment, and then spoke calmly, quietly, unemotionally. 'You have no reason to distrust me. I've told you everything that's happened, just like I said I would. But you treat me like shit. I've saved your ass. You needed my story, but prying money out of you is too difficult and I've had it with you, you cheap son of a bitch.' She finished the make-up job and brushed past him, heading for the little kitchen where she started making some coffee.

'I'm flabbergasted,' said Ernest. 'Dammit, I just gave you five thousand dollars, didn't I?'

'I'm renegotiating,' she replied. 'I would have settled for ten grand, but not any more. It seems to me that I've given you the story of your book, and I want a percentage.'

Ernest's eyes spun. 'A what?'

'A percentage. A share. I want a big piece of the profits, it's my story.'

She had regained her self-control. Now Ernest lost his. 'Bullshit.'

She smiled at him, a superior smile. 'Why bullshit?'

'We made a deal,' he shouted. 'You're not a writer. You're just part of my research, that's all.'

'Oh, is that all I am? Well I don't agree. Your book is about me. It *is* me. You've been writing down my story. It's my life you're using, I'm the one taking the risks here, aren't I entitled to a share, don't I get anything?'

'You get ten grand, that's what we agreed.'

'As a matter of fact *I* think', she said, enjoying torturing him, 'that it ought to say that I wrote it. You know, as told to Norm de Plume, like those sports stars do.'

Ernest's heart was thumping. His mouth was dry. If she went public on this he'd be ruined. Then, suddenly, he realized that she was just yanking his chain. She couldn't go public, it couldn't be an 'as told to' book, it would mean a jail sentence for her, maybe even a death sentence if Pile or Schmidt took out a contract on her. He relaxed. He smiled. His pulse rate dropped. 'Who are you kidding? You can't take that chance.' He sat down at the kitchen table. 'And by the way, I don't just write down everything you tell me.' He held up his hand to pre-empt her argumentative reply. 'Sure, I admit that everything you've been doing is the basis of my book. I told you it would be. But I'm a novelist, not a reporter. I'm like a painter, not a photographer. As I write I reshape real life, I change the composition, I adapt what actually happened, I interpret it, I edit it, so that what emerges is art.'

She stared at him sceptically. 'So art equals lies?' she asked. 'Is that it?'

'Not lies, no. Well, not exactly. Because art doesn't pretend to be true. Except to itself.'

She chewed her gum. 'Sounds like a lot of shit to me. This story *is* true. So if you say that it's not mine, that's a lie. And it's my story, and if you say that it's not mine that's another lie.'

'You're missing the point.' He tried to explain once more, aware that he was in danger of angering her again if his tone was too patronizing. 'Look, no one cares whether a novel is true or not true, or based on truth, or completely made up. That's not the point! The Booker Prize, a prize they give for fiction in England, has even been won by a novel that wasn't fiction at all. It was all true. Fact, fiction, faction, it doesn't matter, it just matters how it's written, that's all. And that's what I do, I do the writing. You're not actually writing any of this book. It's not yours, it's mine.'

'I don't think I'm missing the point at all. It may not seem like the point to you, but it's the point to me. I've been completely straight with you. You're telling *my* story, about *me*, without me there wouldn't be a story. You make a lot of money. I want more than ten thousand. Or else.'

'Or else what?'

'Try me,' she said grimly, poured herself a black coffee and sipped it, eyeing him over the rim of her Mickey Mouse mug.

'Are you threatening me?' he asked.

She was indignant. 'No. But I'm the one person who can finger John and Abel. As soon as anyone hears about this book I expect to be in considerable danger. If Abel Pile or John Schmidt ever associate me with this book, I'm dead meat. They're lethal. You know that. Even if I don't claim any credit – even if I *deny* any connection with it – they may spot it. It could easily be drawn to their attention that this book is really about them.'

'By whom?'

'The newspapers.' She stared at him. 'Or by me.'

'You?'

'To cover my ass.'

'You're crazy.'

'No, I'm not. If I tell them about it, you're the one in danger, not me.'

'Me *and* you. We'd both be screwed.'

'Not if I help them suppress the book.'

Ernest swallowed. 'You think you'd survive?'

'I might. But you wouldn't.'

He stared at her, shocked by this new and hitherto unimagined threat of betrayal. 'So what, exactly, are you asking for?'

'Substantially more.'

Ernest drummed his fingers on the oatmeal arm of the chair. Suddenly he was excited. He saw at once that he had no choice but to acquiesce, but in a funny way he didn't mind . . . for he had suddenly seen an exciting way to end the book. Until now he'd thought of no way to put any thrills into the final section. Whatever the outcome of the trial, the novel had seemed headed for an anti-climactic finish. But now, unwittingly, she had presented him with the bones of a potentially heart-stopping ending, in which Joanna – tracked down, threatened, tortured perhaps – reveals the name of the writer whom she's been tipping off. Of course, his sense of self-preservation dictated that he couldn't take any such risks in real life. 'OK,' he agreed. 'I'll give you a bit more. But I'm not giving you a percentage,' he added hastily.

There was an old typewriter on the sideboard. Joanna went over to it, put down the steaming mug, rolled a sheet of copy paper into the carriage and typed with two fingers. As she concentrated on her typing her tongue moved down behind her lower teeth, then stuck out of the corner of her mouth, like a little girl learning to write or draw. Ernest waited with curiosity. She pulled the paper out and handed it to him. It said: 'I, Ernest Mayday, promise to pay Joanna Aimes the sum of twenty thousand dollars in full and final settlement for the rights to her story about the trial of Abel Pile.'

Ernest read it through. 'Twenty thousand?' He was appalled. 'No way.'

'I thought you'd agreed to give me more.'

'More, not double.'

'That's the price. Or you can kiss your ass goodbye.'

He fumed for a few seconds. Actually, she had pitched her demand with considerable shrewdness – twenty thousand dollars was a drop in the ocean to Ernest, who expected to sell the American rights to the book for nearly a million. 'OK,' he grunted. He took out his pen and was about to sign his name when he realized suddenly that the paper said 'I, Ernest Mayday . . .' He looked up at her.

She wasn't smiling. How long had she known his real name? 'Sign it Ernest Mayday, by the way, not Norm de Plume,' she said.

He felt hot and sweaty. He cleared his throat. 'How long have you known?' he whispered, mortified. He was croaking. There was still a frog in his throat. Suddenly he sounded like Sergio.

'Norm de Plume? You think I'm an idiot?'

'No.' Ernest denied it emphatically. 'I don't. When I wrote to you originally I thought you'd realize it was a joke name. But when we met you seemed to take it seriously. So I didn't say anything. How long have you known who I am?'

'All along. Your name is on your answering machine, you dickhead. And on your cheque book – you tried to hide it from me that day at the Hamburger Hamlet, but I'm not blind.'

'Why did you pretend you didn't know?'

'I had no reason not to. Till now.'

Ernest felt ridiculous, and profoundly embarrassed. Reddening, he looked down at her little contract and reread it. 'We shouldn't have anything in writing,' he said. 'I don't want to sign this.'

'It's only temporary,' said Joanna. 'When you pay me in full you get this piece of paper back. Then it's up to you what you do with it. Till then, I want something in writing, OK?'

'When do you want the money?' he asked.

'Now would be acceptable,' she suggested.

'Nobody carries that kind of cash on them.'

'I'll take a cheque,' she offered. 'You've no reason not to give me one now. Now that I know who you are.'

He thought fast. 'That's not the only reason. What I said to you all along's still true – I don't want to write you a cheque, because I just don't think there should be anything in writing.'

'OK. So get me cash. But meantime, sign on the dotted line.'

Ernest signed.

Ernest sat alone in his library that night. It was a chilly evening. The Santa Anas had stopped blowing as suddenly as they had started. There was no message on the answering machine from Randi. Presumably she was at the Church. He hadn't seen her or heard from her since his petulant tantrum at Julian Genau's when he had stalked out of their couples' therapy session. In view of her claim that she wanted to marry him, this silence was both surprising and significant. Perhaps she'd changed her mind. He couldn't blame her if she had. But he began to think (for the first time) that maybe marrying her was not such a bad idea after all. Perhaps he did need some intimacy, some relationship, perhaps there was more to marriage than the mutually beneficial deal . . . he certainly felt a void, something lacking in his life, some unidentified, unfulfilled longing. Now he sat by himself, wallowing in self-pity on his opulent leather sofa opposite his vast picture window until it got dark, watching the blazing sunset. As night fell he didn't even get up to switch on the lights. Inertia overwhelmed him. He felt depressed, exhausted, gutted.

And curiously, above all, the emotion he felt most strongly was guilt. He wanted to feel anger, which was one of the feelings he most enjoyed. But since leaving Julian's office that most pleasurable of feelings had proved elusive. Instead, a sense of guilt persistently intruded and ruined that self-righteous sense of outrage that he was struggling so unsuccessfully to indulge. He felt guilty that he'd lied to Joanna. He felt ashamed that he, the respectable, upright citizen, the pillar of society, the celebrity, the author, the man of letters, had been shown once again to be lacking in trust and honesty in their relationship, and he was humiliated that a whore had demonstrated her moral superiority over him. And he couldn't deny it. She had never done anything to deserve his distrust. She had never lied to him. She had always kept her side of the bargain. But he had lied persistently, continually distrusted her and, worst of all, he had been caught.

But the lying was nothing in comparison to the rest. He could easily have justified that. There were much bigger issues that concerned him. Had he swindled her? What about her claim to share the authorship of *Flagrante Delicto*? Was it just? Did she have a moral right to the story? The more he thought about it, the more he was unable to decide. And the more he considered her demands, the more some of the other questions surged uncomfortably to the surface. There was the matter of his voyeurism, which he could no longer avoid facing. And then there was the question of his moral responsibility in encouraging her to get involved in something illegal and possibly dangerous, just for his profit.

He had managed to justify it to himself until now. After all, she had placed the advertisement originally. He would never have found her if the initial impetus hadn't come from her. Why should any of this be my responsibility, he asked himself? If I hadn't answered the ad, he thought, if I wasn't giving her the money, maybe somebody else would be. But he knew that this argument didn't wash. All the other replies she had ever received were to hire her as a call girl. Well, that's illegal and possibly dangerous too, he reasoned, maybe I'm saving her from that. But that argument didn't hold up either. After all, not only was she – at his behest – now involved in a criminal conspiracy to defeat the course of justice, she was *still* prostituting herself, this time with Adrian the juror. And for Ernest's profit as well as hers. Did this make him a pimp as well as a voyeur, he wondered? Until now Ernest had never considered the moral implications of helping to finance her prostitution. After all, he was in the film business. And was this kind of subterfuge essentially different from cheque-book journalism, kiss-and-tell autobiographies, Kitty Kelly's books, the Oprah Winfrey Show, the *National Enquirer* here or the *Sun* back home? The answer was an emphatic no, it was not essentially different, but these were all cultural phenomena of which he thoroughly disapproved.

He drank some more Scotch and tried looking at it another way. He had paid Joanna a lot of money, and was shortly to pay her in full. Didn't his paying her relieve him of all responsibility?

Furthermore, wasn't the money to be put to good use? Her mother was sick, dying even, without health insurance in a country where the medical care is poor if you are poor, where thirty-seven million people struggle along without insurance because they can't afford it or no insurance company will grant them the privilege. Joanna was desperate for the money. That's why she'd placed the advertisement. Surely he had merely been a good Samaritan? The fact that he benefited as well ·was coincidental. And he hadn't made her a whore, she was one already.

But the guilt simply wouldn't go away. For if Joanna was truly desperate, what was his moral position in exploiting her? Novelists play God with their stories and their characters, and Ernest saw that he had been playing God's game not with a character based on Joanna, but with Joanna herself. On a high – and as if he were on high – he had been manipulating her, albeit with her full cooperation, into an increasingly dangerous situation. And why? To create his own world, selfishly, on paper, in his book. When God's little games go wrong, as so often they seem to do, does He merely wash His hands of us and cite Free Will? Apparently so. Can He, without guilt, brush off all accusations of irresponsibility? 'I created the

Universe,' saith the Almighty. 'After that, *que sera sera.*' What kind of an ego does God have, and what kind of a macabre sense of humour? And if it is OK for God to play Pontius Pilate, thought Ernest, why shouldn't it be OK for me?

Ernest sat, self-indulgent and alone in his unlit mansion, emotionally numb, delving deeply into his soul. But his hands were coming up empty. He looked inside himself and saw only a void, a profound sense of his own sin. That plus a weird sense of disconnection, and a stomach-churning fear of the growing encroachment of the one feeling that was unacceptable in California: negativity. Was this a clinical depression? Was it the spiritual crisis that Randi had for so long predicted? Or was it the DTs, long overdue?

He went to bed around midnight. Just before dawn, after hours of sleeplessness, he finally fell into a fitful doze. One thing he did know. Whatever he'd got himself into, there was no backing out now. He knew he would regret his involvement with Joanna and the trial of Abel Pile for the rest of his life, if he lived that long.

TWENTY-FOUR

If you can dream and not make dreams your master,
If you can think and not make thoughts your aim,
If you can meet with Triumph and Disaster
And treat those two imposters just the same . . .
                                                    Rudyard Kipling

As he slept Ernest dreamed that he was a roast chestnut.
But not only was he a roast chestnut, he was a General
roast chestnut in command of an army of roast chestnuts.
(Well, in the dream it seemed to be called an army but it
wasn't all that big, there weren't that many chestnuts, it
looked more like a regiment than a whole army, or even a
battalion.) It was dawn. Ernest was on horseback. His
army of several hundred chestnuts stretched out before
him. They all had little stick legs and arms, each held a
sabre flashing silver and orange in the dawn sun, and each
chestnut wore a sash of red, white and blue. Ernest stared
down at his army from his white charger. Even after he
woke up he could see it all quite clearly, right down to his
horse's flowing white mane.

Ernest and his army occupied a commanding hilltop
position. In the distance he heard a trumpet call reveille.
The enemy were expected to pass through the deep valley
below. You didn't have to be Napoleon to be confident,
as Ernest was, that he and his roast chestnut troops had
the advantage not only of the commanding position but
also of surprise. They waited, and watched, and slowly the
enemy cavalry trotted into view out of the morning mist
at the distant end of the valley. They thundered briskly

below, apparently unaware of the catastrophe that was about to befall them. Ernest studied the enemy through his binoculars and saw that they were men, not chestnuts. But even though they were men, and all on horseback (his chestnuts were infantry), he wasn't worried. He was about to give his non-commissioned nuts the order to charge, to race down the steep grassy slope and surprise the enemy, when the enemy standard-bearer looked up and saw them. Without any ado the enemy cavalry simply turned and galloped straight up the hill towards Ernest's army. Ernest and his troops stood there, paralysed, overwhelmed by the superior speed and will of the enemy. He sat motionless in his saddle and watched as the enemy soldiers galloped through his army, spearing his chestnut soldiers with their swords, peeling them and eating them. Then, when Ernest's entire army was eaten, they galloped away into the cool blue morning leaving Ernest, still on his horse, sabre in hand, alone on the deserted field of battle amongst a pile of red, white and blue sashes and burnt chestnut peelings.

He woke at dawn. The light in the bedroom was the same as the light in his dream. He remembered the dream vividly and in colour, like a 70mm showprint. He lay in bed, pondering it, still depressed from the night before. He wondered if he was suffering from a nostalgia for England, for the cottage in Haslemere and his first marriage, for those cosy and romantic Christmases when he and Ellen used to roast chestnuts on the log fire. It was natural, he decided, for his thoughts to turn to log fires and damp spaniels as the year drew to a close. He had tried a log fire once in LA, the year that he bought the house, but great gusts of smoke had blown back down the chimney into his living room during a dinner party and choked a roomful of A-list guests, hospitalizing seven of them temporarily at Cedar Sinai for smoke inhalation tests. (Unfortunately one of his guests that evening had

334

been a doctor, so simple remedies like coughing and wiping the eyes were deemed to be insufficient – tests all round were mandatory.) The next day Ernest had called a chimney sweep that he found in the yellow pages. The man arrived on the doorstep wearing a candy-striped waistcoat and a top hat, switched on his portable boom-box as soon as Ernest opened the front door and insisted that he sang 'Chim-Chiminee, Chim-Chiminee, Chim-chim cheree' the whole way through before he would come in and clean the chimney. He didn't get that far. Roundabout the middle of the third chorus Ernest had had enough and he shut the front door in his face, refusing to re-open it for the rest of the day. Central heating was much less trouble anyway, Ernest decided, and so far the men who serviced the furnace had not revealed any show business ambitions.

When he staggered downstairs after his dream to make some urgently needed coffee he glanced at the *Los Angeles Times* and saw that Abel Pile had given evidence in his own defence yesterday. Pile had been asked if people who had subscribed to his Church had been swindled. 'No,' he replied. 'They wanted faith. That's what they paid for. That's what they got.' Ernest felt that the court would have no option but to agree to that proposition and numerous witnesses could presumably be called for substantiation, if not for trans-substantiation.

He had intended to return to the courthouse to watch Abel Pile on the witness stand, for he knew that it would be helpful to the book. Also, he wanted to take a close look at the men in the jury box, for he still wasn't sure which one Adrian was. But paralysing inertia set in once more. Lethargy and apathy overwhelmed him. He hardly moved a muscle when Consuela arrived and cleaned the kitchen around him, joyfully throwing virtually everything from the fridge into the garbage. Dark bags under his eyes, emotionally wrung out, the morose and exhausted

Ernest watched her for a while, grateful that they had no language in common.

By late morning he found the energy to call Julian Genau. 'I need help,' he said, without energy. 'Can I see you alone?'

'When?'

'Now?'

'What's the big hurry?' asked Julian.

His eyes were welling up. 'I'm feeling really down. I'm completely without energy. I feel very guilty about something. I need to talk.'

'What on earth's happened?' inquired Julian.

'Last night,' he said tearfully, 'I dreamed I was a roast chestnut.'

There was a brief silence at the other end of the line. 'That's nothing,' Julian contended cheerfully. 'Kafka dreamed he was a cockroach.'

'A beetle, actually,' Ernest corrected him. He didn't care for Julian's dismissive attitude towards his dream. 'And only in a book.'

'OK, a beetle. And when he woke up, he was one.'

'Well I'm awake, Julian, and I'm not a chestnut.'

'Glad to hear it,' boomed Julian with his customary enthusiasm. 'Look, Ernest, I'm just here in LA to teach. I don't mind chatting to you and Randi about your problems if I can be of any help but if you want regular sessions I think I should refer you to some properly qualified American analyst. Besides, I'm busy writing my next lecture. I'll refer you to someone I've heard is pretty good.'

So Ernest found himself sitting in Glen Tornoff's office. Glen was plump, with a scarlet lipstick gash mouth that smiled but eyes that didn't, unwashed long brown hair and fingernails that were not entirely clean. As they shook hands Ernest caught a whiff of bourbon and mouth freshener. It was only ten a.m. She smoked too. 'You seem ill at ease,' she commented, taking a deep drag on her cigarette.

He didn't want to tell her that he hated inhaling her smoke, so he lied. 'Well, it's only that ... I didn't really want to talk about my private life with a woman.' Especially a grubby alcoholic woman, he wanted to add.

'Do you often have sexist feelings?' she inquired.

Ernest felt that old rage boiling up inside him. This was a leading question, a how-often-do-you-beat-your-wife? type of question. 'I'm not a sexist,' he replied, icy calm. 'Some of my best friends are women.' He could see that she didn't believe him.

'Sure,' she said with heavy irony, 'some of my best friends are Jews.' Now he hated her, and they'd only met five minutes ago. Furthermore, he certainly didn't want to discuss his personal problems with her. She seemed to have quite enough of her own. So, reluctant to open up to her about Joanna, he told her about his dream which for some reason he was finding increasingly disturbing. He told her the whole thing, from start to finish. She said nothing. 'Well?' he asked finally, impatiently, after she lit up another cigarette and he had joined her once more in a little secondary smoke.

'Well what?'

'Is this dream significant?'

'This is not for me to say. This is for the analysand to say.'

'The what?'

'You. What did you feel about it?' she asked, stubbing out her Camel.

'Well ... it made me think nostalgically of roasting chestnuts in England, with my ex-wife.'

She stared at him. 'That's it?'

'Yes. Why?'

'Sounds like there's some denial going on here,' she remarked. Denial, he thought, that's rich. You seem to know plenty about denial, he thought, but he remained silent.

'What are you thinking?' she asked, after some minutes of silence.

Ernest hesitated. 'I'm really supposed to say what I'm thinking?'

She nodded. 'Otherwise I can't help you.'

'I'm thinking: *Physician, heal thyself.*'

'Meaning . . .?'

'OK,' he said. 'I'm thinking: how can this grubby, overweight, chainsmoking alcoholic help me when presumably she can't help herself?'

Glen stared at him. 'I'm not smoking at the moment.'

'Fine,' said Ernest. '*Now* I'm thinking: if I have a problem with denial I've certainly come to the right emporium.'

After a long and expensive silence she spoke again. 'You didn't consider whether you have a problem with maternal aggressivity?' She seemed irritated. But not as irritated as Ernest was.

'Do you mean aggression?' he asked, feigning puzzlement.

'I guess so,' she acknowledged. 'What's the difference?'

'Elegance?' he suggested. 'Literacy, perhaps?'

'I think you're being somewhat anal.'

'As a matter of fact, I'm being somewhat aural.'

'What I'm getting at', she tried again, 'is the possibility of some familiar causality, some maternal aggressivity, some precocious experience in your neuro-psychological maturation, some . . . some imperfect complementarity in the triangulation of the mother, infant and male figure of symbolic phallic power.'

'Goodbye,' said Ernest.

He rose and left the room. When he got home he phoned Julian again. Julian seemed apologetic and sympathetic so he told him about his dream in more detail. Julian was delighted. 'That's an absolutely splendid dream, old chap.' He was crowing with delight. 'An absolute corker. 'Course, I don't know exactly how it relates to you, but obviously it's a dream about being helpless. About being exposed. It's about having your skin removed too, or maybe that's purely a symbolic skin in the dream in which case it's about your fear of having your exterior peeled so that others will see what you really are. It says that your attempts at leadership are futile, there's always a larger authoritarian figure with more equipment – perhaps mental, or perhaps with a bigger penis – who will expose you and eat you up.'

Ernest wasn't sure that he wanted to know any more. 'Is this supposed to help me?' he asked.

'No, wait, that's just a superficial interpretation.' Julian was just beginning to warm up. 'On a *deeper* level, it's an annihilation dream. A dream which shows that you fear being consumed. A fear of engulfment. A fear of being swallowed up.'

Ernest was astonished. 'By whom?' he demanded.

'I don't know,' said Julian. 'Could it be Randi?'

'Maybe it doesn't mean anything at all,' said Ernest, sorry that he'd started this particular hare. 'It's nothing. It's just a dream.'

'Oh, it definitely means *something*,' said Julian. 'Dreams are messages from our unconscious minds, when our consciousness is in the missionary position, as it were, over our unconscious. Allegorically speaking, the unconscious is female and it controls our imagination. Creativity, for most people, exists largely or only in their dreams.'

Ernest lay on his sofa and contemplated Julian's instant interpretation of his dream. Certainly it was true that intimacy bothered him. Perhaps he did fear it. Whether or not he feared being swallowed up, whether indeed he had a male fear of women's mystical power and of being engulfed by a woman, he didn't know. But he certainly had an uneasy feeling that sex was the bait and marriage the ultimate trap. Did this mean he was paranoid, he wondered? Or was it reality that he feared?

Ernest thought that he would be able to pull himself together and get through the rest of the day without falling into any more emotional pits, but at that moment Oliver Sudden called.

'We've had a real kick in the ass,' he announced.

'We have?' Ernest's spirits lifted in hope.

'A *real* kick in the ass.'

'Great.'

'What's great about it? Virginia pulled the plug on the movie.'

Ernest sat down and took a deep breath. He felt close to tears again. 'Why?'

'Chelsea Krieger passed on it.'

'So what?' Ernest took off his glasses and rubbed his aching eyes. 'Is that what greenlighting a movie depends on – an *actress's* opinion?'

'Yup.'

'But she's so dumb.'

'But she's a great actress,' said Oliver. 'We needed her. Marty's not young and hip.'

'But he's a great director, he's won two Academy Awards.'

'The studio's looking for the young audience. No one gives a shit if the Academy likes him. The average age of the Academy is deceased.'

'What about trying another studio?'

'I'm looking into it.'

Ernest knew at that moment that his much-publicized million-dollar deal on *Lies* had been a mirage. Certainly he had received no money yet. And he'd signed no contract. Suddenly he was completely out of energy. He couldn't be bothered to prolong the conversation. He simply hung up, and sat looking at the phone for an hour or so. Then young Casey Boddichek called, still hoping that Ernest would have an idea for a modern *Cinderella*. Ernest told him that he was working on it. Trying to suppress the rising feeling of desperation, unsure of the outcome of his novel and suddenly a million dollars poorer, he sat down at his desk, switched on his word processor and began typing.

INTERIOR. A PSYCHIATRIST'S OFFICE. DAY

[*Cinderella enters. It is raining outside. She shakes the rainwater off her umbrella, hauls off her galoshes and lies down on Dr Fuchs's couch. He sits behind her and waits patiently, forever ready with his understanding nod. There is a long pause while she considers her options.*]

CINDERELLA: I'm hungry.

[*Dr Fuchs nods carefully, considering deeply the psychological implications of this remark.*]

DR FUCHS: [*In a Viennese accent*] Hungry for love, perhaps?

CINDERELLA: No, I want a hot dog.

DR FUCHS: Aha! As I thought. You vish for phallocentric oral gratification.

CINDERELLA: No, I'm just hungry, I didn't get lunch. Listen, I want to tell you about my dream.

DR FUCHS: Good, good. Already I love it. [*He waits hopefully.*]

CINDERELLA: It's about that prince again.

DR FUCHS: Of course.

CINDERELLA: I want to marry him.

DR FUCHS: Aha!

CINDERELLA: But my stepsisters and my stepmother, whom I hate, cheated me out of all my money and made me sleep in a filthy cellar with a singing ratman.

341

DR FUCHS: Vell, superficially zis is a simple vish fulfilment dream about marrying a prince and living happily ever after. Yet, symbolically, it is also a classical Oedipal dream, a most waluable regression, taking you straight back to your potty training.

CINDERELLA: Are you sure?

DR FUCHS: Of course I'm sure, it's obvious. You see, every child believes secretly that he, or she, deserves to be degraded. Because of secret dirty vishes. [*A sudden thought*] You do have dirty vishes, I hope.

CINDERELLA: I'm afraid I do.

DR FUCHS: Good, good. Abnormal desires are perfectly normal. But they make a child feel unvorthy to be loved. Because you vanted to be your father's sexual partner.

CINDERELLA: [*Shocked*] I did not.

DR FUCHS: You did, I'm telling you, you did. Shut ze fuck up and listen, OK? Good, good. Now, in your dream, the mother figure – who symbolizes the mother figure – prefers your sisters, encourages sibling rivalry and allows them to punish you. It shows how dirty and guilty you still feel.

CINDERELLA: But . . .

DR FUCHS: And yet . . . and yet! . . . in the same dream you marry a prince. This shows that subconsciously you believe that you can triumph over your degradation. [*Dr Fuchs has noticed something of extreme psychoanalytical significance. Excitably*] You see?! Look at those galoshes, Cinderella. They are most rewealing.

CINDERELLA: They are?

DR FUCHS: You know, of course, that there is a children's fairy-tale in vhich a prince finds a glass slipper. Zis glass slipper symbolizes the wagina – small, delicate, fragile, a symbol of wirginity. But what do you vear instead? Galoshes!

342

CINDERELLA: So?

DR FUCHS: So! [*He picks up a galosh.*] This shoe is big and made of rubber. Zis suggests that, subconsciously, you regard your wagina as exceptionally flexible and capacious.

CINDERELLA: Stop making personal remarks.

DR FUCHS: That's my job. Vhat else should I do?

CINDERELLA: Dr Fuchs – just listen. What would you say if I told you it wasn't a dream, that I've been telling you a true story?

DR FUCHS: I'd say . . . same time tomorrow.

CINDERELLA: But I'm telling you it was real. Can't you recognize reality?

DR FUCHS: No, I'm no good at that, I'm a psychiatrist.

Ernest read the scene through. He sat for a while, sighed deeply and pressed DELETE on the word processor. He phoned Casey Boddichek and told him that he had no ideas at all for *Cinderella* and that Casey should look for another writer. He phoned Julian Genau, told him he was coming over to his office whether Julian liked it or not, and hurried out to the car. He was glad that he didn't have Randi with him. He wanted to talk to Julian alone. And he no longer wanted to discuss his dream. By now he wanted to discuss his whole situation in life. He wanted to discuss his relationship with Randi. Above all, he wanted to tell Genau about Joanna. He needed to confess. If marriage, about which he was now deeply confused, was indeed the answer to his problems, would it be absurd to consider marrying Joanna? He asked Julian.

'Well . . . describe your feelings about her,' suggested the doctor.

'I get a panic attack just being in the same room as her,' said Ernest.

'Hmm,' mused Julian. 'You feel that this is a good basis for marriage?'

'You think not?'

'Well, panic's not an *ideal* response to one's spouse.' He thought for a moment. 'Better than hatred, of course.'

'What I mean,' Ernest hastened to explain, 'is that I think I'm in love with her. She's the only woman for years that I ever think about or fantasize about if she's not actually right there in the room.'

'And what do you fantasize?'

'I fantasize about fantastic uninhibited sex. I also fantasize that she loves me.'

'Perhaps you're not in love with her, but in lust with her.'

'Would that be so bad?'

'Well ... do you fantasize that she'd do all the other things that you look for in a wife, things that you mentioned last time? Cook and clean for you? Bear children and care for them? Be a faithful wife? That sort of thing?'

'Why not?'

'And give up prostitution?'

'Why not? She wouldn't need the money.'

'So she's a tart with a heart of gold, is that what you're telling me?' Julian's mouth was quivering at the edges. He was trying hard not to smile.

'She's completely, refreshingly honest and she's got plenty of common sense,' said Ernest with defiance. 'I'm not saying she's a tart with a heart of gold, no.'

'But she is a tart,' reiterated Julian.

'Yes.'

'And you *are* saying she has a heart of gold?' he persisted. Ernest scowled at him. 'I rest my case, m'lud.' Julian leaned back in his chair.

'Look,' said Ernest through clenched teeth, 'I'm aware

that it's a literary cliché. And I'm aware that you are trying to ridicule what I'm saying . . .'

'No, I'm just trying to do some reality testing,' interrupted Julian.

'Clichés are always based on truth,' said Ernest, determined not to listen, steam-rollering him out of the way. 'Why shouldn't there be such a thing as a tart with a heart of gold? Where else does the cliché come from, if not from real life?'

'From male fantasies, obviously,' said Julian.

Ernest said nothing. There was silence for a while during which Julian, ever the psychotherapist and for want of anything better to do, filled the time with a little occasional nodding. Eventually, tired of nodding, he spoke again. 'You've never had sex with her?' Ernest shook his head. 'Well, why don't you. Try it a few times. Wear a condom, though. Then see if you're still fantasizing about her.'

'I don't want to,' Ernest replied untruthfully.

'So you'd rather stick with the fantasy than try the reality?'

'Don't you understand?' cried Ernest. His eyes were brimming and he didn't know why. 'This is not just about sex. I'm talking love, romance, dishonesty, betrayal.'

'Whose dishonesty and betrayal?'

'Mine.' He was weeping now. He still didn't know why. All he knew was that he seemed to be cracking up and he could do nothing about it.

'Ernest, who are you weeping for? Yourself?' Ernest couldn't answer. He was shaking, his nose and eyes were running. He searched hopelessly for a handkerchief. Julian handed him a tissue and continued remorselessly. 'Joanna stimulates your fantasies, as Hollywood and hookers will, until real life catches up. Finally, you have to involve yourself in the lives of other human beings. And the fantasies may be better unfulfilled.'

'But I think I love her,' wailed Ernest.

'You're talking shit,' Julian remarked with psycho-analytic dispassion.

'I'm talking shit?' cried Ernest, jumping up, massively indignant. 'No, that's what you people do. What about that Glen woman you sent me to talk to? She's an alcoholic. And what was all that crap about maternal aggressivity, neuro-psychological maturation and imperfect complementarity in the mother, infant and male figure triangulation. And some other phallocentric power bullshit?'

'It's very unfortunate,' Julian readily agreed, 'that Glen talks in such jargon. But what she was saying was quite sensible, even if she does need to dry out.'

'What was she saying, then?'

'She was questioning your relationship with your father. She was essentially raising the same questions that I raised when you and Randi came to talk to me.'

'You mean, my famous shaky male identity?'

Julian sighed, and tried again. 'You have difficulty with your relationships with women, right?'

'What man doesn't?'

'You're right – but you are concerned about it, that's what you came here to talk about. What we're both saying – Glen was trying to say it too, but in regrettable jargon – is that you need to see your relationships in a fuller, deeper, less fragmented sort of way. Not as a deal. You need intimacy, real intimacy, and that would lead to something more fun, richer . . .'

'But *why*?' Ernest pleaded desperately for an explanation that he could understand. 'I don't see why.'

'Because . . . you would be understood. Then you'd grow. But instead, you are one of those men whom we see all around us, running for cover. You see sex as a form of entrapment, entrapment in a relationship over which men today have limited control. And that's why you're obsessing about Joanna – she doesn't want a relationship either,

346

so she's not a threat, merely a desirable fantasy. But it's not an answer.'

Ernest thought for a moment. 'I see,' he said. 'I think.' For some reason, in his relationship with Julian he felt like a woman: helpless, dependent and vulnerable. Except that women didn't seem to feel like that any more, not the women he knew.

'Now, let's start from the beginning,' said Julian. 'How did you meet Joanna?'

Ernest recounted the story of his writers' block, the attendant depression, and the idea that had struck him when he'd seen Joanna's ad. He told Julian about Randi's rebirth as a fundamentalist Christian. He confessed that Joanna was committing a considerable number of crimes at his instigation, with his connivance and for his benefit. 'She's probably going to get Abel Pile acquitted,' whispered Ernest, 'and I know he's guilty.'

'How do you know?'

'I just know.'

Genau considered this latest symptom of omnipotent feelings, nodding. 'Let's recap, shall we? This whole problem with Joanna started when you were depressed because you were blocked?' Ernest nodded. 'You had readers' block and writers' block. They often go together. Two quite interesting symptoms. Let's look at the others. You're rich, you're successful, a beautiful woman – Randi – wants to marry you, and yet no matter what happens you never feel good. You're very labile. You are also, according to your own account, which I can confirm from my own observation, chronically angry and paranoid. So. My guess is that you have what is called here a bi-polar condition or what we in England call a manic-depressive illness.'

'But that's ... what I thought ... Randi ... had.' Ernest's body was wracked with sobs. He didn't know why. But he could only get the words out piecemeal.

'We're not talking about Randi, we're diagnosing you. Now,' continued Julian calmly, handing Ernest another tissue, 'if I'm right, about the bi-polar condition, that's not wholly bad news, because if you're manic-depressive you have an excellent chance of being creative – it doesn't guarantee it, but it certainly helps.'

'Wait a minute,' said Ernest. 'You're saying I'm creative because I'm manic-depressive?' Julian nodded. 'But just now you were saying that I'm blocked because I'm manic-depressive.'

'That's right,' Julian was still nodding.

'Well . . . which is it?'

'Both, if necessary, I presume,' said Julian. 'Amusingly paradoxical, isn't it?' He crossed his right leg over his left with tremendous energy. 'Now, you also say that you haven't been able to concentrate on reading fiction for some time now? That's only to be expected. Depressed people can't read fiction. And the reason you can't write in the first person – you tried, and abandoned the plan – is because you haven't reached a developmental stage in which you feel safe to use the word "I".'

'No, it's because I didn't want people to think it was me.'

'That's what I said,' nodded Julian.

'I didn't know . . . I was . . . so neurotic,' gasped Ernest, between sobs, his eyes blurred, his nose running like a river, his glasses all fogged up.

'Don't fight it,' said Julian cheerfully. 'It's a help in your job. You're an artist. What are the paintings of Van Gogh if not symptoms? Have you seen his *Mulberry Tree* at the Norton Simon? No sane man could have painted that. All art is just symptomatology.'

'Paintings maybe. Not books,' gasped Ernest between sobs, stubborn as ever.

'No? What's *Crime and Punishment* but a symptom of Dostoyevsky's neurotic guilt?' Julian inquired rhetorically.

'No, the interesting question here is – what brought on this particular attack?'

'I've often had these feelings, ever since I was a teenager,' said Ernest.

'But not when you were a child?'

Ernest shook his head, no. It was the answer Julian expected. 'That's because it's only in childhood that one has a sense of blessedness. As we grow up we start losing it. Perhaps that's why St Augustine created the notion of original sin. Freud shared his view, of course. Psychoanalysis, as you know, though invented by a Jew, was founded on the theory of original sin. But today we know that the primacy of the phallus is a fallacy, today we're more influenced by people like Winnicott, who believed in the theory of original innocence.'

Ernest had never heard of Winnicott and couldn't have cared less. 'What's all this to do with me?' he whimpered. 'I just want to feel better.'

Julian was getting to it. 'You are an extraordinary case. You, in your personal life, represent this whole dichotomy in modern psychiatry: you are torn between a born-again Christian fundamentalist woman who believes in original sin and your own desire – because of your infatuation with a prostitute and your refusal to accept the implications of this problem – to believe in original innocence. Freud v. Winnicott. Fascinating.'

'Are you sure I'm manic-depressive?' was all that Ernest wanted to know. Julian noticed a pleading tone in his voice.

'Why? Would you feel better, knowing that your misery has a name?' Ernest nodded, and blew his nose with a massive trumpeting sound. 'Would it be comforting to know that you suffer from a known clinical condition?'

'Yes, it would,' he acknowledged weakly.

'Well, I can't make you any promises,' said Julian

apologetically. 'It's an awfully difficult condition to diagnose. But I can give you a definite maybe.'

Ernest was confused. 'But I thought . . . I mean, well, what else could it be?'

Julian shrugged. 'Well, there is one other possibility. It might be nothing at all. You might just be an angry, miserable, mean-spirited son of a bitch with a negative personality.'

Ernest broke down again. He wept uncontrollably. 'Oh God,' he said, 'please make me a manic-depressive.'

Then he realized he was praying.

TWENTY-FIVE

To marry a second time represents the triumph of hope over experience.

Samuel Johnson

Was the fact that Ernest started praying a sign that he had found God, or was it just despair? Or was God a symptom too? Ernest was searching, but for what? Religious consolation or psychological revelation? He didn't know.

He was due to return to Julian for another session two days later. On his way out of the front door the phone rang.

'I'm in trouble,' said Joanna.

'Trouble? What do you mean, trouble?'

'I went on a date with John Schmidt last night. I got very bad vibes.'

'Why?'

'He was asking me if I'd told anyone anything. I said of course I hadn't. He was hinting darkly about indiscretions. I told him I was very discreet.'

'Did he buy it?'

'I don't know. But I don't think it makes any difference. I'm frightened. I think that once the trial's over, they'll kill me.'

'Why?'

'Why should they keep me alive? I know too much. Dead, I'm no threat. I'm frightened, Ernest, I need your help.'

Ernest didn't feel up to this crisis. 'What can I do?'

'I need another thirty grand.'

He exploded. 'What do you think I am? Stupid?'

She stayed calm. 'No, Ernest, you're not stupid and that's why you'll give it to me.'

'What do you mean?'

'I've got to be ready to run, and run fast. Running fast costs money. They won't let me survive. I've got to get to another country, with another identity.'

'And if I don't give you another thirty grand?'

'You know the risk. We discussed it last time. If you don't give me the money, they'll catch up with me – and *then* they'll catch up with you. I don't plan to be a hero on your account.'

There it was, on the table, the blackmail threat again. Ernest said cautiously: 'You know, I've been thinking about that. Why should they believe you?'

'Because of your book.'

'That won't be out for a year or two. I'll hide the book. I'll show them some other manuscript. If they're convicted, it'll be safe to publish it – if they're acquitted, I'll make sure that no one can ever recognize them from it. There's no reason at all for them to believe you. There's nothing to connect us, I always paid you in cash, I've been careful where I've met with you, there's absolutely nothing to link you to me. They simply won't believe you.'

There was a pause. Then Joanna said: 'Let me read you something. "I, Ernest Mayday, promise to pay Joanna Aimes the sum of twenty thousand dollars in full and final settlement for the rights to her story about the trial of Abel Pile."'

Ernest saw at once that this was the beginning of a nightmare, one that might not only bankrupt him but could also threaten his life. But he refused to concede immediately. He needed time. 'I'll have to think about it,' said Ernest. 'It's a lot of money.' And he hung up.

*

'You look bushed,' Julian told him as he settled into the chair.

'Well . . . I'm having some trouble with the plot of my new thriller,' explained Ernest.

'Is it a detective story?' asked Julian.

'More of a suspense story, really,' Ernest said. 'But I don't want to go into it now.' Actually he *did* want to go into it, he was desperate to tell somebody about Joanna's demands for money, but there was something so superior about Julian that he still couldn't bring himself to admit that his new book was nothing more than a hooker's experiences as told to Ernest Mayday.

'Psychoanalysis was born as a detective story,' Julian remarked.

'A detective story?' repeated Ernest weakly. 'Was it really?'

'Actually, by a strange coincidence, this is what my lecture's about, the one I'm preparing at the moment.' Apparently, in Julian Genau's mind, the strange coincidence lay in the fact that he was now talking about the subject that he was also writing about, and talking, furthermore, with absolutely tremendous enthusiasm for his chosen subject, his hair and his eyebrows nearly perpendicular with excitement with the sheer pleasure of explaining. 'As you probably know, Freud based the whole *shmeer* on *Oedipus*, the first detective story. What we psychiatrists do, every day, with all our patients, is look for clues. Every patient is a unique mystery story. Psychoanalysis, like the Bible and Agatha Christie, is based upon murder and human sacrifice.' Here he paused dramatically. 'And so is the Church.' Ernest's attention had been wandering, but the word 'church', made him focus, a sort of Pavlovian reaction from living with Randi.

'Freud, you see,' continued Julian Genau, gesticulating and pacing around his office with boundless energy like an intellectual Worzel Gummidge, 'discovered in the play by Sophocles the fundamental human need to sacrifice the father. Don't forget what Freud said about play – the opposite of play isn't what's serious, it is what's *real*. That's the opposite of *a* play too. In the Oedipus complex, though Freud himself never fully understood his own brilliant insight, the child wishes to kill the father in order to have the mother.'

'I know that,' said Ernest. 'Everyone knows that.'

'But did you ever *realize* that, just as in the story of Oedipus, in Christian mythology the father is also sacrificed and accordingly becomes Our Father who art in Heaven.' Ernest was struggling to see what this had to do with him. 'What Freud never saw was that the *essential* meaning of the Oedipus complex is the need for human sacrifice *in general*, especially the sacrifice of the child.'

'Please ... Julian, stop,' Ernest begged with increasing desperation. He felt he was being battered to death by the torrent of Julian's language, a Niagara Falls of words, coming down in sheets. Like an actor, Julian suffered from emphasitis, the dread condition in which you over-emphasize at *least* one key *word* in *every* sentence. 'Please ...' repeated Ernest pitifully, 'how does this affect me?'

'Doesn't, really,' admitted Julian. 'Just thought you'd be interested, seeing as how Randi's so concerned with the sacrifice of the child.'

'Child? Which child?' Ernest's mind was reeling. 'Randi hasn't got a child, what the fuck are you talking about?'

'No, not Randi's child ... I mean Christ! The Christ child,' said Julian. He picked up an upright chair, swung it around and sat astride it, almost nose to nose with Ernest. 'Jesus Christ, the son who was sacrificed to save us all. Randi's a born-again Christian, isn't she?'

'Yes,' said Ernest, baffled.

'Don't you see? Christ was the son as well as the Father, and Christ's sacrifice, the sacrifice of the child,

God's own child, enables him to be our judge. The authority of the super ego – the conscience – comes from the act of sacrifice. He who offers himself as a sacrifice becomes holy, for if he died for us he has the right to judge us and save us. That's the theory, see? I mean, that much is totally obvious, right?'

It hadn't been totally obvious to Ernest, but he nodded. More words tumbled out of Julian Genau's motor-mouth and swirled about his head, later to be hopelessly jumbled up in his reeling brain as he tried to recall what Julian had said while he drove home. Till now, he had always assumed that Christianity inhabited a completely different world from psychoanalysis. Having believed in neither he suddenly found himself tempted by both. He knew that the symbolic sacrifice of the child was as old as religion itself, and as old as literature, for hadn't God said to Abraham:

Take now thy son, thy only son Isaac, whom thou lovest and get thee into the land of Moriah; and offer him there for a burnt offering upon one of the mountains which I will tell thee of . . .

And Abraham stretched forth his hand, and took the knife to slay his son.

And the Angel of the LORD called unto him out of heaven, and said, Abraham, Abraham: and he said, Here *am* I.

And he said, Lay not thine hand upon the lad, neither do thou any thing unto him: for now I know that thou fearest God, seeing thou hast not withheld thy son, thine only *son* from me.

Ernest, who had always regarded guilt as the one essential prop that all religions need (for without the need to be saved or punished God would be redundant), saw for the first time that the Christian myth of the crucifixion told him about God's own guilt for creating the world as it is, for which He offered His son in penitence.

But he was in the depths of misery and melancholy, not knowing which way to turn, whether to psychiatry or idolatry, his brain boiling with panic and confusion, his intelligence blurred by guilt (even though he thought he didn't believe in guilt) and blurred also by Johnny Walker (perhaps the only thing he did believe in). In the play, Oedipus is the only person who doesn't know whodunnit and Ernest now found that he, like Oedipus, was looking for that part of himself which is most secretly feared and most profoundly defended, but without which happiness would not be possible.

Sadly, however, it is not easy to find something when you don't know what you're looking for and wouldn't recognize it even if you saw it. For the first time in his life Ernest was struggling to understand the myths that he knew so well. What did they really mean? What did they mean to *him*? Biblical stories, stories of God's great works and Satan's, stories of the curse on Thebes brought about by the incest of the King, stories that teach us how to survive the threats that are all around us, whether personal or tribal. For that is why we tell stories, go to plays, watch films – to see the mistakes that we might all make ourselves, to experience vicariously the many pitfalls of real life so that we may learn to avoid them. Like the characters in a play, we have the same human frailties. We empathize with them if we are watching drama or tragedy and we laugh at them if we are watching a comedy or a farce – and from this experience we learn what could happen to us if we don't watch out. We tell each other stories in order to heal ourselves. That is what literature is. And our dreams are the stories we tell to ourselves instead of to each other, the stories we get when we let loose our unconscious imaginative power. But in order to create these most potent, most creative, most healing imaginative fantasies, our dreams, no work is required and no talent is required. Each and every one of us can create imaginative images of the most profound and disturbing nature, and we do so, every night.

Are God and the imagination one, Ernest wondered? Where is the imagination situated? In the soul? Or in the neurons? No autopsy has yet identified a soul, but the religious would have us believe that that's because souls have already departed for their final destination. Neurologists tell us that the imagination is in reality situated in the neurons. So is God in the neurons too? If God is everywhere, why not? But can a guilty God who exists only in our neurons offer up for sacrifice His only son in penitence? Perhaps He exists in our neurons but not *only* in our neurons. Ernest feverishly considered all these questions and became convinced of one thing, and one thing only: that he was losing his mind.

He might have found solace without the help of either God or Freud if he had followed Dr Julian Genau's recommendation, obtained a prescription from his doctor and tried taking Prozac for a couple of weeks. But this simple solution seemed unsatisfactory to a man who suddenly found that he wanted to indulge in, enjoy and repent his complex guilty feelings. Months ago he had explained patronizingly to Randi that guilt was a powerful feeling, a strong feeling, that it was preferable to feel guilty than to feel helpless or insignificant – guilt gives us a valuable feeling of importance, for one can't be guilty of anything serious if one is impotent, trivial or of no consequence. Guilt, he had explained with contempt as he tried to demolish her religious feelings, was a narcissistic feeling. Yet now Ernest Mayday, the internationally known novelist and narcissist, had managed what he had always maintained was impossible: to feel simultaneously trivial, helpless, impotent *and* guilty.

It is no coincidence that Prozac has come under attack from some of the more expensive Californian cult churches, for if it removes anxiety, depression and guilt for a mere thirty dollars a month what need would there be for EST and SCREAMS and all those other expensive quasi-therapeutic activities that are so well attended? Left to his own devices, Ernest might have tried the medicine but Randi, familiar with the teachings of the Church of the Community of Personal Truth, advised him most strongly against it. 'It's caused some murders,' she explained darkly. 'It makes people very violent.'

'That's not what Julian said,' Ernest told her.

'Then he simply doesn't know,' she replied with total certainty, 'but he ought to. I mean, it's been in all the papers and everything.' She probably didn't know who placed all the stories in the papers, and he was too upset and confused to argue. So, reluctant to try psychoanalysis in case his already shaky talent was indeed a symptom of his neurosis or psychosis, and still unwilling to ditch his lifelong atheism, he turned to his ever-ready emotional-support system, Randi Toner, and her ever-present solution to his problem: marriage.

It was coming up to the Thanksgiving weekend, a four-day public holiday. Abel's trial would be suspended. Randi knew that she would miss nothing by leaving town, and she bore in mind that months ago Abel Pile had entrusted her with the task of getting God's blessing upon her relationship with Ernest. So when Ernest rang up and invited her to Las Vegas for Thanksgiving, she accepted with alacrity.

They rented a car. It was a five-hour journey across the Mojave Desert, so they planned to drive there and fly home. It took nearly two hours to clear suburban Los Angeles, and they still had two hundred miles to go. The views were majestic as they climbed into the high desert where the tumbleweed aimlessly wheels and the Joshua trees are the only trees that can survive, cactus trees out of Samuel Beckett growing in sculpturally agonized shapes, so named by the early settlers who hadn't read *Waiting For Godot* and thought that the trees resembled Joshua with his arms raised to God. Mountains are ranged behind mountains: brown with black shadows in the foreground, purple with navy blue shadows in the middle distance, behind them lilac mountains, then light blue, then pale grey as they recede into the distance.

Three hours later they crossed the border into Nevada, and motored past the first casinos, *Whiskey Pete's* and *Cactus Kate's*, and they reached Vegas at three p.m. Ernest was shocked to see the same thick blanket of yellow smog hovering above this small desert town as he had left behind him in LA.

They checked in at the hotel, into a vast and crowded lobby filled with slot machines, freshened air and Muzak. They decided to go to a seven-thirty show and then have a late dinner. Randi went to their room for a rest and Ernest found himself with time on his hands and John Schmidt's threats on his mind. He was unable to stop himself worrying about what Schmidt knew or did not know. He found a bank of telephones and rang Joanna, to check that she was still in one piece.

She answered at once. 'Who is this?' she asked in a guarded tone.

'It's Ernest,' he said.

'Oh, hello, Mom,' said Joanna. 'How's things in Savannah?'

'No, it's Ernest,' he said.

'I know,' she replied.

He had a horrible empty feeling in the pit of his stomach. 'Have you got someone with you?'

'Yes,' came the reply. No details.

'Who?' he asked. She didn't say anything. 'Is something wrong?'

'Mom, you know I don't want to talk to you about that.'

'You don't have to say anything, just answer yes or no: is somebody there?'

'Yes.'

'Are you frightened?'

'Yes.'

'Is it John Schmidt?'

'Absolutely.'

'Is he threatening you?'

'Oh yes.'

Ernest's heart beat faster. 'Does he know about you and me?'

'No. I don't think so. Not yet. At least, I don't know.' She cupped her hand over the mouthpiece and called to somebody else in the room: 'My mom wants to come visit me here in LA.' She spoke into the phone again. 'Mom, it's fine with me. I think you should come right away. With that money.'

'I can't,' said Ernest. 'I'm out of town.'

'For how long?'

'A day or two.'

'Don't leave it any longer,' she said. 'I really can't wait to see you, Mom,' and she hung up.

Ernest was in a state of shock. What was happening to him? 'What the fuck am I going to do?' he wanted to scream, but he stayed silent. This was only supposed to be a novel, for Christ's sake! and it was turning into real life. Everything was going disastrously wrong. Ernest, one of life's natural watchers, a manipulator not a participant, a master at keeping life at arm's length, realized that he was no longer detached. He was losing control over the chain of events that he himself had set in motion, he seemed to be becoming the main character in somebody else's novel, the puppeteer was becoming the puppet. He was sweating. He couldn't breathe. Fear and panic rising uncontrollably, he rushed outside for some fresh air and sat down on the edge of the sidewalk, not seeing the tourists, the bellmen, the hawkers, the crowds. After a few minutes he stood up and walked around the outside of the mammoth hotel, then returned to the men's room to splash cold water on his face. He tried to get his thoughts in order. What about going straight back to Haslemere? Maybe one could fly Las Vegas–Heathrow, direct? He found a bar and ordered a drink. With the help of a double Johnny Walker he recovered his nerve a little and he realized that he could run but he couldn't hide, and that both for Joanna and for his own self-respect he had no choice but to return to LA and confront the situation.

But he could think of no excuse to leave immediately. What would he say to Randi? They'd only just checked in. The earliest they could go would be tomorrow morning. He called his travel agent – all the early flights were fully booked, so he made reservations for late morning. It was still a while before he was due to wake Randi to see the show. He wandered over to a five-dollar blackjack table and watched for a few minutes. He had never played blackjack but he quickly recognized it as *vingt-et-un* so he sat down and joined in. Ira, the dealer, shuffled neatly. 'You here for Thanksgiving?'

Ernest acknowledged that he was.

'Where you from?'

Ernest kept it simple, and left out London, Haslemere and the rest. 'LA.'

'I don't know what you give thanks for,' said Ira, 'but I give thanks every day that I don't live in LA.'

'You do? Why?'

'I'm a New Yorker. Even though I live here now.'

'So?'

'So. LA is hardly a cultural centre. I guess it's an OK place if you like surfers and airheads.'

'This, from a resident of a town where the ability to count to twenty-one is the only education you need,' replied Ernest, 'and a plant that isn't plastic constitutes a cultural

361

event?' Ira grinned, and won ten more dollars from Ernest. Ernest, by now under the influence of his third double Scotch, suddenly found that he had acquired patriotic feelings for LA verging on the jingoistic. 'Besides, LA has plenty of culture,' he added. 'We have a fine orchestra, superb art galleries, enough opera, and who gives a fuck about the theatre anyway – New Yorkers don't, look at Broadway today.'

'So,' said Ira again. It was his favourite opening gambit. 'I don't suppose you celebrate Thanksgiving at all, being British.'

'I certainly do,' said Ernest. 'I give thanks that I didn't make the crossing on the *Mayflower* but on Pan Am, may it rest in peace, and first class at that. I give thanks that I didn't experience the first winter, the second winter, the Civil War, Custer's Last Stand, Wounded Knee, the Wall Street Crash, the Great Depression or Arnold Palmer taking twelve strokes on the eighteenth at Rancho Park in 1981.'

'So do you celebrate the Fourth of July as well?'

'Certainly I do. I celebrate that we're no longer responsible for you,' said Ernest.

Ira, still grinning, relieved Ernest of a few more chips. Ernest, feeling he'd lost enough, a couple of hundred dollars by now, abandoned the game and wandered around the hotel looking for a room with natural daylight. There were none. He sat down in one of the restaurants and ordered some potato skins and salad to keep him going. Steaks were being offered for 13.95, including baked potato and soup or salad and coffee. Ernest wondered how they could operate restaurants so impossibly cheaply. The secret must lie in the turnover. There must be one vast kitchen under Las Vegas, he decided, serving everyone, and this would explain why every hotel on the Strip served food that tasted exactly the same.

Randi awoke refreshed and they went to see *Jubilee* at

another hotel. He managed to hide his sombre mood from her. The show was like the *Folies Bergère* only bigger and American. First there was a Hollywood medley, sung by plump strangled tenors, masses of girl dancers – well, girl walkers really – and a few topless showgirls posing. Then came a succession of epic scenes from history, all somehow featuring girls with bare breasts, false eyelashes and bored faces. There was a Samson and Delilah scene. The topless cuties sang

> Hey there, Hey there Samson,
> Are you as strong as you think you are?
> Hey there Samson,

and so on. Boy dancers jumped and pirouetted around and about, wearing bulging leather jock straps with big brass studs. 'She's got the hots for a guy named Sam,' squawked the energetic young ladies with bare breasts and runs in their panty-hose as Delilah danced on in her nylon wig from K-Mart. Samson made his entrance. The wig on his head was appropriately long but he had shaved his arms and legs and armpits. Delilah did a little dance and unerotically revealed her tits, they kissed on a bed in front of a vast backcloth which was then raised to reveal the Temple in all its tatty grandeur. Samson was brought on in chains by the brass and leather jockstrap brigade, his hair was 'cut' and he pulled down the mighty hinged pillars of the collapsible temple with much smoke and dry ice and rumbling and music, while lots of showgirls hurried hither and thither in tempo and breasts bounced freely all over the stage.

Ernest was distracted and not entirely sober, half watching the show, partly ruminating on the Samson and Delilah legend and what it said or didn't say to him about relations between men and women, while a host of unanswerable questions jockeyed for position in his head.

What did Schmidt know by now? Should he have gone straight back? Were they going to kill Joanna? Would they kidnap her? Would they want to exchange her for him? Would they want a ransom? Should he now tell Randi that her friend John seemed to be threatening to kill Joanna? And that his own life could be in danger? What, above all, could he do to get himself out of this alive? He had only one idea: marriage. It had been the thought of marriage to Randi that originally made him propose this trip. If he married Randi, he said to himself, he'd be a part of their team, he'd be one of them, she'd have more money to give them and they'd be grateful to him. He could see no other way that could even possibly get him off the hook.

As they strolled back to their hotel down Las Vegas Boulevard Ernest's spirits lifted a little. He thought about the naked bouncing bosoms he'd been watching all evening and suddenly found himself singing 'I've got a loverly bunch of coconuts'. Randi laughed uproariously. 'Big ones, small ones, some as big as your 'ead.' They sat down to a leisurely late dinner together, dwarfed amid the giant plastic vegetation surrounding the hotel's best but nearly empty restaurant. At the far end of the room a group of waitresses sang 'Happy Birthday' to a middle-aged lady, her husband in a red and green plaid sports jacket smiling appreciatively. Randi watched, then leaned across to him suddenly while he was toying with the red snapper, took his hand and placed it on her thigh. 'Feel this,' she said. 'Isn't it firm? I'm stronger than ever.'

'Very firm,' he agreed, slightly baffled.

She moved his hand along her thigh, under the table-cloth, to her knee. There he felt a strange contraption of two plastic-covered metal loops linked by a spring, forming a sort of figure of eight between her knees. 'What's this?'

'It's firming up my thighs. You can exercise any time,

like now, when we're just sitting in a restaurant. Isn't it great? It's the latest thing, I'm recommending it to all my clients. Like this cord . . .' She produced a long elasticated cord from her handbag. 'You can get fit using just this, why don't you try it? It's for isometric exercises.'

'What are isometric exercises?' Ernest asked.

'Exercises where you work against yourself.'

Ernest smiled, but his eyes were full of sadness. 'My whole life is an isometric exercise,' he said.

She held his hand. Her hand felt cool and strong. 'Why did you ask me to Las Vegas for Thanksgiving?'

He found himself saying it. 'I thought, maybe, we could get married.'

Tears welled up in her big brown eyes. She blinked them back. Then she took his face in her hands and gave him a gentle kiss. 'When?' she asked.

'Why not tomorrow?'

She kissed him again. This time it was a delicious erotic kiss. Her tongue explored his mouth. And as he was being kissed by his wife-to-be, he thought of Joanna. Would she kiss any better than this, he wondered? Randi's erotic skills had come a long way in the past few months, he noticed. He didn't know why, perhaps she'd been learning from somebody else, maybe she *was* the other girl in the orgy at the Bonaventure Hotel with Abel Pile and John Schmidt . . . and so his thoughts wandered on, strangely disconnected with the kiss that was still taking place, thinking only that he might as well face up to the fact that if he got out of this alive he'd have no future with Joanna anyway, that this was his best chance to get out of it alive, and that furthermore the only way for his conscious mind to get the upper hand over his unconscious and show that he was definitely not frightened of being annihilated, engulfed, consumed or otherwise swallowed up by Randi, was to tie the knot.

They abandoned dinner, hurried to their bedroom,

undressed each other and made love, their room brightly lit by the sunbursts of neon right outside their window at eleven-second intervals. In the morning, which was hardly any brighter than the night, they went for a drive down the Strip in their rental car. Ernest felt strangely numb, not personally involved, a spectator. They drove past a couple of schools for dealers, then slowed down at the first wedding chapel they came to. Chapel of the Bells, it was called. Randi didn't like the look of it. Nor did she fancy the Cupid Wedding Chapel, with neon hearts and cupids in the window. Ernest insisted on looking inside, but Randi turned out to be right. It smelled of stale smoke. 'It'd be like getting married in an ashtray,' she said, pulling a face. Weddings on Wheels – *Phone 369-LOVE* – was simply a large motor home which would come to you for your wedding, and which wasn't necessary since Ernest and Randi had already come to it. Finally they came to a little clean white shack with a tiny spire, maybe fifteen feet high, and a huge sign reading 'Little White Chapel' and an enormous lit-up red plastic heart. '24-Hour Drive-up Wedding Window' said the sign immediately below the heart. They parked around the back and went in. The cosy manageress with greying ginger bushy hair and bifocals fished around below the front counter and gave them a glossy brochure with all the details. Joan Collins had married Michael Jordan there, it seemed. 'Who's Michael Jordan?' asked Ernest. 'Joan Collins's husband,' said the manageress unnecessarily. 'We've been featured on *The Today Show*, *Joan Rivers* and *Life Styles Of The Rich And Famous*,' she added with pride. She told them where they could get their marriage licence in forty-five minutes, and they took a brochure out to the car.

Next they stopped at the Chapel L'Amour. They took a brochure there too. 'L'Amour means "Love",' it explained. 'A beautiful stairway leading into the chapel will excite your heart as your bride enters the chapel from the Stairway of Love into your arms for ever.' It seemed that at the Chapel L'Amour their wedding would be performed by one Charlotte, the 'Wedding Queen of the West, the President of L'Amour Chapel and a long-time Nevada resident with over thirty years' experience in uniting loved ones.' Apparently the notches on her belt included Frank Sinatra, Judy Garland, Mickey Rooney, Joan Collins – again – and Bruce Willis. For $149 they could have the French-Lace Package. For a further hundred bucks they'd get a video taping of the ceremony. The Chapel L'Amour Special Package included such delights as photographs, an album, wedding cake for twenty and a Wedding Garter. Ernest didn't know what that was.

While they queued at City Hall for the licence Randi debated the relative merits of the competing chapels. The Little White Chapel seemed to offer dressing rooms in which to change into one's rented bridal gown and tuxedo, but Ernest pointed out that he had no intention of dressing up like a fool. Competing offers of cakes of various tiers seemed equally irrelevant since there were to be no guests, as did the champagne glasses. The Little White Chapel was offering candlelit ceremonies, marriage certificates and holders, a 'beautifully etched marriage scroll', a bride's garter (could this be the same as a wedding garter?) and a Free Love Recipe – Ernest couldn't imagine what the recipe could be either. Was it a free recipe for love, or a recipe for free love?

He was about to suggest that they find out when he noticed, at the bottom of the Little White Chapel's brochure, the item that had caused him to stop outside it to begin with: 'World Famous Drive-up Wedding Window' – $25'. How blissfully and typically American, he thought. A drive-up wedding. A short-order wedding. A fast-food wedding. The McDonald's of weddings. 'Be married in your favorite car', it said. And for only twenty-five dollars. The Joan Collins Special was $499 complete ('Prices subject to change without notice', said a footnote), and the L'Amour Chapel's top of the line job, the Eiffel Tower Special, was $949. As far as Ernest was concerned, there was no contest.

Armed with the marriage licence he strode out of City Hall on Carson Street, and crawled back along the Strip in the Thanksgiving traffic jam. Vegas was full for the holiday. They drove up to the window, and a couple of minutes later they were married. 'Let's be truly American,' said Ernest wickedly. 'Let's do the whole thing in the car. Let's have the honeymoon in the car too.' He reversed away from the drive-in window and accelerated into the deserted parking-lot behind the Little White Chapel. Laughing raucously, Randi lay back in the front passenger seat, pulled down her panties, opened her legs, stuck them out through the sunroof and they fucked, she with triumph and exultation and he with anger and despair. 'Make Today a Happy Memory' exhorted a painted sign above their rocking car. He was doing his level best but he wasn't sure that it was working.

TWENTY-SIX

How do you make God laugh? You tell him your future plans.

Woody Allen

They flew back from Las Vegas airport that morning. Ernest was in such a state of *angst* at the airport that he didn't have time to focus on his usual fear: that the airport bookshop might no longer be stocking *Lies*. Although he immediately spotted a couple of copies, moderately well displayed, this did little to help him relax, so he decided to buy a book. He sensed that the only way to keep the rising tide of panic at bay was to carry on doing things normally.

It wasn't his marriage that morning that increased his tension. He felt curiously fatalistic about that. The wedding had been followed with a kind of eerie calm in Ernest's mind. Randi, he could see, was utterly content and was giving no indication whatsoever that she was suffering from Buyer's Remorse. Ernest, on the other hand, had been wondering why on earth he'd done it. In the sober light of day he realized that marriage to Randi did not necessarily make him safe from John Schmidt and Abel Pile – on the contrary, it might simply put her in danger from them as well. And if he had really done it just to prove to Julian Genau that he had balls, that he wasn't frightened of being engulfed by women, he saw now it proved no such thing.

Reviewing his recent actions, struggling to find a positive way to look at the consequences of his impulsive behaviour, he told himself that Randi seemed willing to do anything to be a good wife, other than make a home for him. 'I'll always be there for you, baby,' she had replied in a low voice and gently chewed his earlobe at the Drive-up Wedding Window when asked if she would love, honour and cherish Ernest. He couldn't see how that would translate into anything practical, exactly, other than sex, but it sounded as good as he was going to get.

After the consummation of their marriage in the rental car they had driven back to their hotel for breakfast and to check out. While breakfast was *en route* from room service Ernest turned on the TV set and there, to his surprise, was the trial of Abel Pile. The judge had not recessed for Thanksgiving after all. Abel was still in the witness box. It was his third day on the stand and he didn't seemed to have cracked. On the contrary, he looked cool and collected as he answered a variety of questions from the harassed Gil Hoolahan, who had never recovered from the damage done by Sandy from Tarzana. 'Isn't it true,' snarled Hoolahan ineffectually, 'that some members of your 'church' (somehow he managed to say the word in quotes) have paid as much as two hundred and fifty thousand dollars in fees?'

'Absolutely not,' replied Pile with quiet courtesy and patience. 'Nobody pays us fees. I've explained this before. Many members of the Church give us donations.'

'Up to a *quarter of a million* dollars?'

'In some cases, perhaps, yes.'

'Isn't that rather a lot?'

'That rather depends on how much you have, doesn't it?'

'*I'm* asking the questions here, Mr Pile.'

Pile allowed himself a small smile. 'I understand that,' he acknowledged.

'So,' went on Hoolahan, without any real sense of where he was heading, 'what did they get for these vast sums of money?'

'Specifically? That depends,' replied Pile. 'But they got what they paid for.'

Hoolahan hesitated. 'And what was that?'

Hoolahan had bowled a full toss. Pile hit it for six, right out of the park. 'Faith, in a word. Also reassurance, support, religious education. Help, in one form or another.'

The hapless Hoolahan had no answer. He changed tack. 'So where did all the money go?'

'The poor.' The answer was given with an absolutely straight face. Ernest was entranced. He was getting to love Abel Pile almost as much as Randi did, though for entirely different reasons. He loved his poise, his assurance, his magnificent hypocrisy.

'And what about your mansion at Malibu, your helicopter, your yacht?'

'As you know, these are all owned by the Church,' replied Pile calmly. 'They are available to members, they are used by others more than by me, they are not my personal property. You might as well accuse the Pope of expropriating the Church of Rome's money because he lives in the Vatican.'

The camera picked up one of the jurors, nodding. Ernest, in the hotel room, shook his head in silent admiration. 'Why are you shaking your head?' Randi was concerned. 'Did he say something wrong? Did he make a mistake?'

'On the contrary,' said Ernest. Room service had just arrived, and he poured hot coffee for them both. 'He's doing just great.'

'Do you think they're going to convict him?' She was anxious.

'Very, very unlikely.' Ernest spread some honey on his hot buttered English muffin. He loved English muffins, an American delicacy disappointingly unobtainable in England.

'Why are you so sure?'

'First of all, the prosecution already shot itself in the foot, trying to pin a sex scandal on him.'

'Have they any evidence of one?'

'If so, they haven't produced it yet.' He thought she looked relieved. Again Ernest wondered if she was relieved for Abel or for herself. He still didn't want to pursue it. 'And they don't seem to be shaking his story under cross-examination.'

'When you say they shot themselves in the foot – how, exactly?'

'Don't you remember that loony woman from Tarzana, with her sex fantasies about him and all that psychotic raving about the Devil? She was barking mad. No jury could miss that.'

Randi took Ernest's hand in hers. Her grasp was cool and firm. She turned his face to her. 'I believe in the Devil, Ernest,' she said, looking him in the eye. 'I want you to know that.'

'You do?' He was surprised but, after a moment's reflection, not very surprised. 'Why?'

'Jesus believed in a personal devil.'

'He did?'

'So does Abel.'

At least, he says he does, thought Ernest. That's what he's selling, insurance policies against the Devil. 'What does he say about it?' The trial droned on in the background.

'He asks the question: Is there such a thing as evil? If so, there must be a Devil.'

'Is that who the Angel of Darkness reports to? The Devil?'

Randi thought for a moment, taking the question seriously. 'No,' she answered. 'I don't see how. I mean, the Angel of Darkness enforces the rules of the Church. So it must be a fundamentally good angel, wouldn't you say?'

'Then why,' inquired Ernest, 'would it be called the Angel of Darkness? And why should people be afraid of it if it's good?' Randi had no answer for these questions. She shrugged. 'I think,' said Ernest, deciding to help her out, 'that human beings *need* devils because we don't want to confront the cruelty within ourselves. Perhaps it's better to blame the Devil.'

'Yes, but that doesn't explain', said Randi slowly, 'why we should fear the Angel of Darkness if he's doing God's work.'

'Sure it does,' said Ernest. 'The Bible's always telling us to fear the Lord. 'Course,' he smiled mischievously, 'there is one other explanation.' She looked at him, expectantly. 'Maybe God's bad.'

She laughed, and hit him with a pillow. 'I know you don't mean that.'

'Ouch. I do. I do.' He tried to ward her off.

'You don't.' She pushed him back on the bed, and kissed him. It was nice. 'Evil', she explained to him, 'is caused by Satan. That's basic. Everyone knows that. How come you don't?'

'Evil', replied Ernest, kissing her nose, 'is not an absolute. Evil is a matter of opinion.'

'How can it be?' she argued. 'Evil's always bad.'

'Of course,' he agreed. 'But it depends what you mean by bad.'

'I know what I mean. Evil is unmistakable. You know it and I know it. And Abel says that if evil is more than the sum total of human misdeeds, then you must believe in Satan.'

'And you do?'

She nodded seriously, and brushed her long brown hair back out of her eyes. 'Ernest, tell me . . . you're not saying that's why the woman from Tarzana was mad, are you? Just because she believed in Satan?'

'No.' He was emphatic. 'It was all that stuff about the

swimming pool parting like the Red Sea. And getting messages from her leg.' Randi giggled. 'She was off her trolley. She really damaged the prosecution.'

'You said that was the first reason.'

'Right. Well, the second thing is, the prosecution don't seem to have proved that he defrauded his congregation. I mean, *I* think he did, you know that, I've never hidden it from you, but they haven't made it stick. I don't know about the tax angle, but generally when the prosecution makes such a pig's breakfast out of a case the jury loses faith and throws the whole thing out lock, stock and barrel. And with *this* jury that's a certainty.'

The words were out of his mouth before he realized what he'd said. 'What do you mean, this jury?' she asked.

He hesitated. 'Nothing,' he said unconvincingly.

'No, come on,' she wheedled, putting her tongue in his ear. 'What did you mean?'

'Nothing,' he insisted. And then he told her about John Schmidt, Joanna and their conspiracy to subvert the jury. He couldn't help it. He'd been desperate to tell somebody. The words just popped out. And anyway, she was his wife now, why shouldn't he tell her? She sat up and listened, goggle-eyed. 'So you see,' he finished, 'even if there's some doubt left in the jury's mind, I think that by the time they've finished blackmailing that unfortunate guy Adrian with photos of him and Joanna in *flagrante delicto* there's not much chance of a guilty verdict. And even if it were a hung jury, the case has looked so flimsy that they'd never put Abel on trial again. So I reckon that, all things being equal, he'll be off the hook in another week or two. Happy?'

'Yes,' she said. 'But ... then, I don't think I ... you mean, you're going to put it all in your book? And publish it? Surely not.'

'Believe me, no one'll make any connection. No one ever does when you fictionalize things. It'll just be a novel.'

But as soon as he had told her all this, he regretted it. So he didn't tell her about Joanna's latest demands for money. And immediately after breakfast Ernest encouraged Randi to go down to the hotel exercise centre for a sauna and a work out. He'd been unable to get the threats from John Schmidt out of his mind, his anxiety level was rising and as soon as Randi was gone he phoned Joanna to check that she was still in one piece.

There was no reply.

When Randi came back from the sauna Ernest was packed and ready. He didn't want to wait for lunch, he told her, he just wanted to get back to LA. They took a taxi to the airport. Randi tried talking to him a few times while they waited in Departures, but eventually gave up. He explained that he was preoccupied with his writing. Then he started worrying not only about Joanna's safety and his safety, but also about his own spiritual condition. 'Let me ask you a question,' he said suddenly, turning to Randi as they settled into their seats and fastened their safety belts. 'Can you make a Faustian pact if you don't believe in the Devil?'

She thought for a moment. 'I should have thought so, yes,' she answered. 'I mean, the Devil's there, whether you believe in him or not.'

'Why should he want you? Or me?'

'The Devil wants us all,' replied Randi with quiet conviction. 'But he doesn't just want you. The Devil likes to make a deal. He very rarely wants just your soul. He's using you to get somebody else's too. Isn't that what happens in a Faustian pact?' Is he using me to get Joanna's soul? Ernest wondered. Or Joanna to get mine? 'Why?' asked Randi. Ernest shrugged. He didn't want to pursue the conversation. He didn't know why he'd started it.

The plane journey from Vegas to LA took only about an hour. Randi settled down for a snooze. Ernest put the earphones on, switched from Easy Listening (whatever that was) to the classical music programme which was playing Mahler's Symphony No. 2, and, hoping to distract himself, opened up the book he'd bought at the airport, *Fear of Flying* by Erica Jong. He'd read it when it first came out, years ago, and loved it. But he couldn't remember it well, and he wanted to play safe and read something that he knew he would enjoy, a hilarious earthy roller-coaster, something that would distract him from the panic of his life. He pulled it out of the airport plastic shopping bag and, as was his way, flipped through the pages, browsing before reading. A sentence caught his eye. He stared at it, uncomprehending. He couldn't quite believe he was reading what he was reading. He looked at it again. It said:

I was not against marriage. I believed in it in fact. It was necessary to have one best friend in a hostile world, one person you'd be loyal to no matter what, one person who'd always be loyal to you. But what about all those other longings which after a while marriage did nothing much to appease? The restlessness, the hunger, the thump in the gut, the thump in the cunt, the longing to be filled up, to be fucked through every hole, the yearning for dry champagne and wet kisses . . .

The strident, dissonant, brassy chords of *Auferstehun-Sinfonie*, allegro maestoso, resounded in his head. Or in his earphones. What were these words? These were the very words, the actual words, that Joanna had told him she'd said to Adrian when she was seducing him in the parking-lot outside the courthouse. These words were now in his novel. But they weren't his. And now it transpired that they weren't even Joanna's. They were Erica Jong's. Ernest was aghast. No wonder Joanna's language was so good, so immediate, so strong, so descriptive . . . she'd got it out of a great book!

He raced through the pages, trying to speed-read, not even attempting to follow the story, just trying to see if anything else Joanna said had come from the book. On page seventy-seven his eye caught the phrase 'Mouth to mouth and belly to belly.' He remembered typing those words. With a dry mouth but a sweaty upper lip he read:

Adrian must have the wettest kiss in history. His tongue is everywhere, like the ocean. We are sailing away. His penis (bulging under his corduroy pants) is the tall red smokestack of an ocean liner. And I am moaning around it like an ocean wind.

He remembered noting, at the time, the sudden poetry of Joanna's language as she described her first encounter with Adrian.

Adrian! But – thought Ernest – that's the name of the character in the *book*. What an amazing coincidence that the juror was called Adrian too. Absurd! Obviously there was no coincidence here, she must have made up the juror's name. But why? Why would she call him Adrian? There was only one possible answer: the juror wasn't called Adrian at all. Perhaps, since she borrowed the name from *Fear of Flying*, she'd never met the juror at all. Which would mean that she'd never seduced him. Which meant that there were no photographs. Which meant there was no blackmail. Which meant . . . his mind was reeling. He picked up the book and read on.

And I am saying all the silly things you say while necking in parking-lots, trying somehow to express a longing which is inexpressible – except maybe in poetry. And it all comes out so lame. I love your mouth. I love your hair. I love your ears. I want you. I want you. I want you. Anything to avoid saying: I love you.

He looked up from the page, staring unseeing out of the porthole at the pale blue sky. She had memorized this. He looked back at the page. She'd skipped the next bit, then he saw, ' "I've never met an ass to rival yours," he says.'

Now he started wondering about the lines she'd written out for him on that yellow lined pad. Ten pages further on, he found them:

We were tasting each other. We were upside down and his tongue was playing music in my cunt.

'You've got a lovely cunt,' he said, 'and the greatest ass I've ever seen. Too bad you've got no tits.'

'Thanks.'

I kept sucking away but as soon as he got hard, he'd get soft again.

'I don't really want to fuck you anyway.'

'Why?'

'Dunno why – I just don't feel like it.'

Adrian wanted to be loved for himself alone, and not his yellow hair. (Or his pink prick.) It was rather touching, actually. He didn't want to be a fucking machine.

'I can fuck with the best of them when I feel like it,' he said defiantly.

Ernest put the book down on his lap. Then, in a desultory way, he flipped through the rest of the pages. He put it down again. Nothing else seemed to have been taken from it. But everything that Joanna had ever told him was suddenly open to question. And to think that he had been reproaching himself for his lack of frankness with her.

He was in a daze as they landed at Los Angeles. Randi had checked in her suitcase and although they were travelling first class they had an unexpectedly long wait by the carousel. Luggage is a great leveller. They didn't talk much. Ernest couldn't have managed a conversation if his life had depended on it, and to his relief Randi seemed tired and preoccupied too and didn't seem to want to talk. They drove to his house in silence.

Downtown, at the federal courthouse, Abel's three-day

ordeal in the witness box was over. After the court adjourned for the day he walked out to the car with John Schmidt, who congratulated him on his performance. 'I loved that moment when you said the money goes to the poor,' Schmidt sniggered. 'And I think the jury bought it.'

'We do have figures to support that, don't we?' Abel wanted to be sure.

'Natch. We give some of the money away, always did. Not too much, though.'

'Of course not,' commented Abel with a smile. 'After all, God loves the poor. It would be wrong to make them any richer. We don't want to deprive them of God's love, do we?'

John Schmidt laughed heartily, stepped off the kerb and straight into the path of an oncoming eighteen-wheeler which he had not seen speeding along Spring Street. To say that he died instantly, or that he didn't feel a thing, would not be true – but perhaps he didn't suffer for long. In any case, the hospital pronounced him dead on arrival.

TWENTY-SEVEN

The woman who cannot be ugly cannot be beautiful.
                                                    Karl Kraus

By lunchtime John Schmidt's untimely demise was on all the local TV stations and the front page of the *Los Angeles Times*. Randi was distraught but Ernest was somewhat relieved. With Schmidt dead, he felt safer. Even if Abel Pile knew that Joanna had been revealing her work for him to Ernest, it might not matter now. Schmidt was the enforcer. Now that he was dead, it wasn't dangerous any more. No one would come after them now. Unless there were other enforcers . . .

Randi hurried off tearfully, brushing aside Ernest's half-hearted noises of sympathy. As soon as Randi left for the Church he phoned the object of his ire. He demanded to see her. She invited him over. He sped over the hill, down to Toluca Lake, hung a left at the wilting coconut palms on the corner of her street, scraped his paintwork against a concrete pillar as he hurled the Mercedes into a tight parking space in her garage, and burst into her apartment as she opened her front door. His rage was barely under control. He slammed the door behind him. His face was blotchy from anger, raised blood pressure and a lot of Grant's twelve-year-old whisky, special reserve. Fearful, she retreated to the living room. 'What's wrong?' she asked.

'I hardly know where to begin,' he began. 'But let me put it this way: I reread *Fear of Flying* on the plane.'

'Oh, is that all?' she replied, smiling broadly. 'Well, I

suppose I knew that you'd catch on sooner or later. I mean, there was bound to be someone at your publisher's who'd recognize it.'

'So you don't deny it?'

'Of course not. I'd be pretty stupid to do that, wouldn't you say?'

'So how much have you lied to me?'

She shrugged. 'Quite a lot, I guess.' She strolled into the kitchen, apparently quite relaxed. 'Want a diet soda?'

'Well, let's start from the beginning,' he said grimly. 'For instance, is your name Joanna?'

She swung around, staring at him dangerously. 'My name isn't Joanna any more than yours is Norm, baby.'

'So what is it? Jane Montgomery?'

'Right.'

'So there's no room-mate either, I take it.'

Coolly she poured her coke into a large tumbler. 'You sure you don't want some?'

'You lying bitch.' He marched into her bedroom and searched through all the photographs there. She followed him to the doorway, and stood watching him, leaning against the frame, holding the cool drink against her cheek. 'As I thought,' he snarled. 'No sign of mother, not in any of these pictures. Your mother's dead, right? She died years ago, right?'

'Right again.' She didn't appear to be the slightest bit upset or embarrassed. But she was watching him with caution.

'So all this shit about needing the money for a dying mother . . .?'

'Shit,' she acknowledged, nodding cheerfully. 'It worked though, didn't it? I mean, like, you must admit you believed it.'

He sat down on the bed. Her refusal to deny anything had taken the wind out of his sails. She was still leaning in the doorway. 'So . . . I mean, I don't . . .' He couldn't find the words. 'I don't get it.'

'What is it you don't get, exactly?'

He stared at her. 'What I don't get is . . . why?'

'Why? Why did I make this up? For the money, obviously.' She sipped the drink. 'Though it wasn't enough.'

'You thought it was easier than hooking?'

'Yup. And it was, I should think.'

'What do you mean, you should think?'

She sat down on the floor, leaning against the wall of the bedroom. 'Norm – sorry, Ernest, I mean – I'm not a hooker.'

He stared at her. 'You're not?'

'I'm not. Sorry.'

He didn't know whether he was disappointed or simply confused. 'So . . . what are you?'

'I'm an actress. Like everyone else in Hollywood. What else would I be?'

Ernest stared at her. He was trying to get his thoughts straight. 'But you said you were a hooker.'

'I lied,' she said simply.

'But a woman from an escort agency rang me, and you were there . . .'

'I was that woman. That was my voice.'

'It didn't sound like you.'

'I'm an actress.'

He tried to straighten everything out in his head. 'So that's why you wouldn't . . .'

'Wouldn't sleep with you? That's right.'

'I see. No I don't.' He stared at the wall. Then he looked at her again, and spoke softly. 'I don't think I understand anything that's been going on. What about all that stuff you said about actresses being the same as hookers?'

'I didn't mean it, obviously. Well, to be truthful, I half meant it. Does that mean I hate myself?' She giggled. 'Anyway, when you're doing improv, you have to believe in it or it doesn't work. It sounded great, didn't you think?'

'How come you know so much about hookers?'

'I've had friends who've tried it.'

'But if you're not a hooker, what was your ad all about?'

'I needed money. That was true. I still do. I advertised, I hoped something good would come out of it. Or something exciting. Who knows? I didn't know what to expect. And I was as naïve as you. I'd often seen ads like that in the papers, I didn't guess they were hookers' ads either, till I got some replies. Then it was all too clear. All the replies I got were for sex – except yours. But you wanted to exploit me too, in a different way. I told you I was a hooker because it was the easy thing to tell you that evening – and because by then I was sure that I wasn't going to get any replies of the sort that you were hoping for, and I was hoping for. After you dropped me off here that night, outside this apartment, I was sure I'd never see you again.'

'But what about the second time we met? At the Beverly Westwood. You were offering to sleep with me then, weren't you?'

'But I knew you wouldn't. For a start, you were on your way to a dinner party. No, I was just hoping you'd want to do a book about a hooker. Then I'd make something up, get some dirt from my girlfriends who've done it, get some money that way. But it didn't work.'

'But then', said Ernest, 'you *did* get a reply. From John Schmidt. Wanting the trial fixed. Wanting you to nobble the jury.'

She smiled and shook her head. 'You still haven't got it, have you?'

'What do you mean? What haven't I got?'

'I never had a call from John Schmidt.'

'Never?'

She shook her head. 'Never.'

'He never replied to your ad?' She shook her head

again. Ernest put his head in his hands. 'Please ...
explain.'

'Well, after I went home I had an idea for your novel. I
thought that, since I'd told you I was a hooker, I'd try
and think of some good thriller plot that a hooker might
be involved in. I mean, that was what you wanted. And
around that time there was some mob boss on trial in
Chicago for jury tampering so I thought ... why not try
out the jury tampering idea on you?'

'You made it all up?'

She nodded proudly. 'Yup. Every bit. And you bought
it.' She grimaced. 'But I never really meant it to go so far.
Actually, I never thought at all, really. I just wanted some
money. And you gave me some.'

Ernest was still having trouble assimilating the basic
facts. 'But Schmidt never wrote you or called you?'

'Nope.'

'You did know him, or you didn't? Which is it?'

'Well ... actually, I knew him a little. I went to a
SCREAMS seminar a couple of years ago, and he was
one of the tutors there. Afterwards we had a little ... like,
a little fling. But I hadn't seen him since. Then I ran into
him on Fairfax and Beverly, outside the Authentic Café.
We had a coffee together. He told me he had a client who
was probably going to be indicted.'

'So he tipped you off that they were putting Abel Pile
on trial?'

'No, Ernest, that's all he said. He mentioned no names.
I saw it on the TV news, just like you. I'd been waiting for
the right trial to come along that I could pretend to you
that I was involved in and when I saw John and Abel Pile
on the news that night I knew this was perfect, this was
the kind of thing you were looking for. I knew something
about his bullshit Church from way back, I knew John, I
knew what scumbags they were, I knew I'd be able to
make up outrageous stories that would still ring true.'

'So you never seduced any juror? You never had photos taken?'

'That's why I couldn't show them to you. That's why you couldn't be there when they were taken.' She laughed. 'It was so funny, you know, because you were *real* disappointed.'

Ernest was not amused. 'And ... wait a minute, does that mean you never met Schmidt and Abel Pile in that hotel downtown? There never was an orgy either?' All this time, he now realized, he had doubted Randi quite unfairly.

She pulled an apologetic little face. 'No. Sorry.'

'And ... you haven't been out on any dates with Schmidt, he never threatened you? ... So who was here when I rang you yesterday and you were too frightened to talk?'

She answered in a little voice. 'No one. Sorry.'

'No one? *No one!*' She shrugged. 'I don't understand, why did you do it, why did you torture me like this?'

'For the money. And because Schmidt coming after me is what was bound to happen next. It was obvious.' She stared at him. 'I was helping. It's the inevitable climax of the book.'

Ernest was aghast. 'I don't know what to say. I can't *believe* you did this to me! I'm appalled.'

'Ernest, if you hadn't read *Fear of Flying* on the plane you'd have written this all up. Then I could have vanished tomorrow. You might have followed me, you probably would. Who knows what else I might have thought up? I was inventing a fucking great finish for you. Thrilling. I think the phrase you're looking for is "thank you". You should be fucking grateful.'

'Grateful? Yesterday I thought you only had a few hours to live. I thought *I* didn't have much longer. I thought I was going to be a victim of my own book. I was really scared.'

She smiled. 'But now you love it – the threat to my life, the threat to yours – what a great ending, huh?'

Ernest looked at her for a moment. Suddenly his book didn't matter to him. 'So we're safe. Both of us.'

She grinned. 'Yup. It's only a novel.'

He sat down. She watched him. 'Just tell me,' he said. 'Was *anything* you told me about yourself true?'

'Well, some of it, yes, obviously. I mean, I am from Atlanta. I was trained as a nurse. And I have been a table dancer since I got here – it pays a whole lot better than waiting on tables, which is what most actresses do in LA. But I never went home with a guy. I swear.'

'So the escort agency . . .?' He paused.

'An answering service, that's all.'

'They said it was an escort agency.'

She grinned. 'Honestly, you're so gullible, Ernest. *I* said that.'

He stood up and walked around her little bedroom. Then he turned to her accusingly. 'I thought we trusted each other.'

She laughed aloud. 'Whatever gave you that idea? You certainly never trusted me.'

'Rightly,' he said, 'as it turns out.'

'I've never done you any harm.'

'I just can't believe you told me so many lies.'

'They weren't lies. They were fiction.'

'No,' said Ernest. 'You led me to believe that you were telling me the truth. That's lies.'

'OK,' she acknowledged. 'Maybe it was lies. But now that I'm not pretending that it's true, that makes it fiction again, right?'

'Don't you see why I'm upset? I feel I was entitled to the truth.'

'No. That wasn't our deal. You were entitled to a story – and you got one – better than the truth.' She smiled. 'And I was very inventive, wasn't I?'

Her smile infuriated him. He felt completely humiliated. 'You bitch,' he said. 'How do you think I feel?'

'Don't call me a bitch,' she said, suddenly indignant. 'Aren't you forgetting something? If I hadn't made up all these lies, you wouldn't have a book. Which you have now. Thanks to me.'

'A book full of Erica Jong's dialogue,' he snarled. 'Oh, thank you. Thank you very much.'

'Hardly full of it,' she retorted. 'Twenty or thirty lines, at most. I just put them in to embarrass you later, you cheap son of a bitch. It was my little joke. I knew someone would spot them. Take 'em out now, you've got no problems, you've gotten a complete original novel, with a story, and a potentially nail-biting ending, which is something that you didn't have and couldn't think of till you met me, OK? You should be grateful, you should be down on your fucking knees, not standing there abusing me.'

'You keep telling me I should be grateful. Grateful for what? For being made to look like an idiot?'

'You don't look like an idiot to anyone else, only to me.'

'Thanks a lot.'

'Hey, I'm sorry, OK? But I don't have that much to apologize for. I mean, you've got your next bestseller now. Which I want my share of, by the way. Fifty-fifty.'

Aghast, he stared at her. 'Fifty-fifty?'

'Sure. We're the joint authors, wouldn't you say that?'

'No, I would not say that.'

'But it's my story.'

'Which I thought was *true*. I mean, I was even prepared to give you thirty thousand more when you asked me to before, which I thought was pretty generous by the way, I mean that came to a total of fifty grand, but I was prepared to do it for your *sick mother*!' he snarled bitterly. 'But not now. Absolutely not.'

'Why not? Before, you were just writing about something that you thought had happened to me – now you know that I made it all up. If that's not being an author, what is?'

'You want to know?' demanded Ernest. 'I'll tell you. Writing is telling the story well, the ability to write good, interesting, funny, real dialogue, the creation of characters who are believable and stay with you when you've forgotten what they actually said. It's the hard mental and physical slog, sitting at your desk hour after hour, day after day, month after month, trying to perfect every phrase, writing down every tiny transient thought before it escapes, perhaps for ever, in case it opens a new door, creates a new plot twist or an insight into character. It all has to be turned into some sort of magical confection that makes the mouth water, that keeps the reader turning the pages, that makes you want to know what happens next. And it has to have resonances beyond the immediate struggles of the characters, so that readers feel that the story, however unlike their own lives, relates to them. That's what I do when I write a book, or try to. The story is just a coat-hanger. Stories are two a penny.'

'You couldn't think of one,' she pointed out.

'I could think of dozens,' he retorted. 'There are stories everywhere you look. I just couldn't get *going*. I couldn't get started. I was blocked. Everyone I've ever met, at least every educated person, thinks they have a novel in them. Well, maybe they have and maybe they haven't. I'm sure they've all got a story to tell. But they don't do it, do they? Because they just can't get themselves up for it. And if you can't do that, you're not a writer. That's what it takes. If you think you're such an author, why didn't you write it yourself?'

'I can talk, I can improvise, I can invent, but ... you're right, I'm an out-of-work actress, not a writer. Anyway, who would publish any book I wrote? And if they did, I wouldn't get the kind of money you get and which you're going to give me half of.'

Ernest laughed. 'Half? You're out of your fucking mind. Half? No way.' He walked up to her, and stuck his face into hers. 'No way.'

'Why are you so angry?' she asked softly. 'I've saved you, and you know it.'

'You've been manipulating me,' he said.

'I get it,' she said. 'You're angry because you thought you were manipulating me and it turns out it's the other way round.'

'That's not the reason,' he said.

'Then what is it?'

'I don't trust you any more.'

'Why not? You know the whole truth about me now.'

'The whole truth? I doubt it, I hardly know you.'

'Well, let me put it this way: all that you know about me now, however little, is the truth.'

'I still don't trust you.'

'Why not?'

'One never trusts anyone whom one has deceived.'

'So, in your case, I guess that means you never trust the women in your life? I guess you've deceived them all.'

'I'm deceiving my wife right now,' said Ernest softly, his face still close to hers. 'In my heart at least. Because I still want you.'

'I didn't know you were married,' she whispered. 'How long have you been married?

'Since this morning,' said Ernest. And he started laughing. She started laughing at him. He clutched his head melodramatically, and lurched around the room. 'Oh my God, what a mistake!' He was howling now, and so was she. Tears were streaming down his face. Together they staggered round the room, holding each other, clutching their sides. Laughing and weeping and laughing, hysterical with hilarity and pain, not knowing if he were laughing or crying, he fell on the bed. She fell beside him. They lay there, fighting for breath, staring at the cottage cheese ceiling, till the laughter finally subsided. Then they looked at each other for a moment, eyes wet, and kissed.

After they'd made love Jane asked Ernest, 'How long have you wanted me?'

'Since the moment I met you.' He turned to look at her. 'How long have you wanted me?'

'Five minutes,' she said.

TWENTY-EIGHT

The birth of the reader must be at the cost of the death of the author.

Roland Barthes

They made love several times that afternoon. Ernest knew that he had found the woman he could be with the rest of his life. She would have been the answer to his prayers, if he'd ever prayed. Instinctively he knew, as he had always known, that she was his salvation, that he could find redemption through Jane and her *doppelgänger* Joanna. She had been clever enough to concoct the plot of his novel, smart enough to take him on, captivating enough that he would let her. She was his ideal fantasy foil. She had put him through the wringer the way he put everyone else through it, she knew him better than anyone else had ever been allowed to know him, she had succeeded in holding up this vast mirror to him – you're not pretty, it said, but maybe there's hope for you. His feelings of release and of gratitude to her had created the possibility of a relationship filled with infinite promise.

Ernest knew that he'd got many things wrong in his life and suddenly he wanted to start putting them right before it was too late. Originally, he had had his share of humanity. In the days before he was rich and successful he'd been ironic, passionate and clear-sighted. But increasingly he had confused his prejudices with his identity, and he saw now that over the years he had retreated to a hollow wasteland of an emotional and intellectual life that consisted simply of tearing everyone else apart. He had become the reverse of a communicator. By expressing strong opinions he told himself that he made a strong impression, whereas all he'd been doing intellectually was cutting other people off at the knees. Even though his personal, professional and emotional life had been miserably bitter and empty, Ernest had always managed to make everything work for him on a superficial level: money, a slim, fabulous-looking centrefold quality girlfriend, two fat bestsellers, an LA mansion ... Life had gone in the direction he wanted it to go, but never with any real pleasure. Now, for the first time, he had hope. He saw that things could change with a woman who was worthy of him – a worthy companion, a worthy adversary, a worthy lover. Even amid the *angst*, the chaos, the disorder, uncertainty and panic of Ernest's life, he recognized these qualities in Jane and the sex between them that day was easy, relaxed, beautiful and delightfully unimportant, simply because they were right for each other.

Outside it was dusk – magic hour, as it is known to movie people because of the mysteriously translucent beauty of the light when twilight falls, electric lights are switched on and it looks like both day and night. They lay on the bed in the semi-darkness, touching each other gently. She played with the hair on his chest. 'About the book,' he said.

'Mmm?' she grunted lazily.

'You do know that, legally speaking, you haven't got a leg to stand on?'

'So?'

He raised himself up on one elbow, and looked into her clear grey eyes. 'So ... if I share the book with you, will you share your life with me?'

'You got a deal,' she whispered and gently pulled his face down on to her breasts. They lay still for a moment. 'But what are you going to tell your wife?' Ernest had been wondering about the very same thing. Now prepared to make a commitment to real life, Ernest was willing at last to involve himself in the life of another human being. Unfortunately, it was not the one whom he had married that morning.

Ernest believed that he had made the journey from fantasy to reality, from Joanna to Jane, but simultaneously he was moving from one fantasy to another. Unwittingly he had become the main character in his novel, the novel that he had instigated but which Jane had fabricated. Yet his ability to turn fact into fiction and fiction into money would no longer help him if the events of Jane's novel became real: Ernest knew how a good story worked, how to control the characters, how to create a thrilling climax, but in his desperation to achieve the fantasy one more time he had allowed the distinction between fiction and truth to become dangerously blurred. These two people were right for each other, yet this fleeting day of love, this excitement, exhilaration, this moment of warmth and sublime contentment could not prevent Ernest from being overwhelmed by the inevitable events that he himself had put into motion. Was Jane his salvation or his nemesis? Ernest would have time to consider this question as his life spun out of control, deconstructing itself into interestingly intellectual pieces.

He hadn't answered Jane's question, 'What are you going to tell your wife?' It was still hanging in the air, that particular Sword of Damocles. He knew she was waiting for some kind of answer. Unsure of what to say, knowing only that his second marriage was over and that his third was about to begin, he kissed her. And he stayed out at Jane's apartment all night.

His second wife, however, came home. She had spent the afternoon supervising the funeral arrangements for her mentor, the late John Schmidt, and fighting off the press, and worrying about the outcome of the trial – the jury were sent out to deliberate that very afternoon. Over the past few months Randi had slept at the Seminary down on Sunset more often than she stayed overnight at Ernest's mansion in the hills, and Ernest didn't think that she would turn up that night. Since she moved into the Seminary she had only slept over at his place when he'd invited her. But he'd forgotten one small detail: that he'd married her only that day; or maybe he forgot that marriage changes things a little and that she, his bride, would now consider Ernest's home her own.

She still had her key. She let herself in. The house was in total darkness. Clearly Ernest was not home. She didn't know where he was, and there were no messages on the answering machine. She ate a little fruit, wandered around aimlessly, glanced at the story about Schmidt's death in the papers, watched some television – and became increasingly anxious. Where could he be? And on the first night of their marriage. There was only one possibility. He must be with that hooker, the one who he was using to help put the fix in on Abel Pile's trial. She wasn't sure how she felt about all that. Of course she wanted Abel to be acquitted, but she wasn't happy about a book that might show that John Schmidt or even Abel were involved in some criminal conspiracy. She switched off the TV and wandered into Ernest's study. There on the desk was a manuscript, nearly four hundred pages long, recently printed out. She sat down at the desk and started to read.

She was still at the desk as dawn broke. Ernest had not returned. She finished the book – as far as it went – walked slowly up the wide sweep of the elegant curved Spanish staircase to Ernest's bedroom (my bedroom now, she thought) and took a shower. She dressed, returned to the study to pick up the manuscript, took it out to the car and drove out to Malibu to see Abel Pile. It took less than forty-five minutes because she was driving against the rush-hour traffic. She phoned Abel Pile from the car, so when she arrived he was waiting for her in the sunny breakfast room.

'What's all this about?' he asked, his curiosity aroused. Randi told him about the plot to tamper with the jury that John Schmidt had been working on with Joanna. He was incredulous. Then she told him that Ernest was using it as the basis for his new book.

At first Abel Pile was quite unable to take her seriously. 'I don't think so,' he chuckled. 'John would never have gotten involved with that kind of thing without my knowing. Far too risky.'

'But he did.' She was insistent.

'No way.'

'Are you sure?'

'Sure I'm sure,' said Pile, with his usual easy confidence. 'The trial's going far too well for that kind of a risk to be necessary. They're going to acquit me today, it's obvious.'

'It looks that way now. But you couldn't have known that from the start.'

His eyes twinkled. 'I put my trust in God.'

'Well, John didn't,' she insisted. 'And it's all in Ernest's book. Look.'

Pile took the manuscript and glanced at the chapter in which Ernest described Joanna's meeting with John Schmidt. Then she showed him the chapter in which the conspiracy was outlined, and Joanna's role in it. The names were altered but the similarities to Abel, John and Randi seemed unmistakable. 'Did Ernest give you this book?'

'No. I found it in the house, on his desk.'

'What were you doing in Vegas?' Pile wanted to know.

'We got married.'

Abel Pile kissed her on the lips. 'Congratulations,' he said. 'You made it, Mrs Mayday.'

'I'm not sure,' she said, troubled, breaking out of his embrace. 'I mean, yes, we are married, but I think he's having second thoughts or something. He didn't come home last night. I didn't even know about this hooker till yesterday, and obviously he's been seeing her for months. Maybe he's having an affair with her.'

'Maybe,' said Abel. 'So what?'

'So . . . he's my husband!'

'Sexual fidelity isn't everything. We've talked about that. You haven't been faithful to him over these past few months, either.'

'But I would be, now that we're married.'

Abel seemed less than delighted with this snippet of information. 'Oh?'

'Well, don't you think I should be?'

'I guess so, if that's what you feel is right.'

'But the point is,' said Randi, 'it's because of this hooker that I know that this whole story is true. Look. Here's a bit where he describes an orgy that she told him about. This character's called Jan Smith, he's the preacher's lawyer. I mean, Jan Smith obviously equals John Schmidt, right? Here's Joanna, that's the hooker Jan's screwing, and that's Ernest's snitch, Joanna, he hasn't even bothered to change her name. And look – over the page, into the room comes the charismatic evangelist and he's got me with him. See, this description fits me perfectly. And then they all have sex together. How does Ernest know all this, unless he was told by Joanna? And if she told him all this accurately, if she then told him that she was tampering with the jury on John Schmidt's instructions I'd be inclined to believe it.'

Abel took the pages and read them carefully. 'I don't understand,' he remarked, puzzled. 'We've never had a hooker at any of our spiritual sexuality orientation seminars. All the ladies have been High Priestesses of the Church, like you. Pilgrim initiates. I thought you understood that to enjoy sexual rites with John and myself was always the highest accolade that the Church of the Community of Personal Truth could bestow.'

'I know that, believe me,' Randi reassured him sincerely,

'and you know how grateful I've always been that you honoured me that way. I was willing to do it, not just willing, I don't mean to sound negative, I mean it was great because it was God's will. Also,' and here her eyes filled with tears, 'you're an inspirational lover. But the point is, one of our initiates must be this hooker Joanna. That's the only explanation I can think of. Because she's infiltrated somehow. Read this for yourself. The only difference is that he's set the scene in some fancy-shmancy downtown hotel when it actually happened here at the house. But how else could he have known, if he didn't get it from her?' She was anguished. 'And he's putting it in a *book*.'

Abel Pile thought for a moment. 'So you think that John did tamper with the jury?' She nodded. 'And yet he didn't tell me? Why not?'

She shrugged.

'I wonder', he said thoughtfully, 'if Joanna, whoever she is, could have made the whole thing up, or heard rumours and fleshed them out?'

'No way of knowing,' said Randi.

He sighed. 'Well, maybe you're right,' he said. 'And if you are, we don't want any of this to get out. Ever.'

'So should I confront Ernest about this?'

Abel sighed. 'Yes,' he agreed. 'I think you'd better.'

'What shall I say?'

'First,' said Abel gravely, 'we must pray together.'

Abel was right in his prediction about his trial. The jury had deliberated for only four or five hours when they announced their verdict of not guilty on all counts. By lunchtime Abel Pile was a free man. Randi, with a few loyal followers, was there to celebrate.

Ernest came home early that afternoon. He went into his study and found her sitting there, at his desk, staring out of the window. She turned slowly and stared at him.

'Hi,' he greeted her casually.

'You've been with her, haven't you?' she asked quietly. 'On our wedding night.'

He had been wondering how to tell Randi that he wanted a divorce. He opted for humour. 'Yup. Who says Hollywood marriages don't last?'

She didn't smile. 'What's that supposed to mean?'

'Randi, I'm sorry, I made a mistake marrying you. I'm really sorry.'

'That's not the only mistake you made.' She picked up the manuscript of the book with both hands. 'Burn this.'

'Don't be silly, Randi.'

'I'm not being silly. This book is dangerous. Dangerous books must be burned. I told you once about the Angel of Darkness. Well, Abel Pile told me to tell you that you're in danger.'

Ernest wrinkled up his nose as he stared at her with rank disbelief. 'Don't be silly, Randi. The Angel of Darkness? There's no such thing.'

'There is!' She crossed the room and took his hand in both of hers. 'Please. I'm pleading with you. You won't be allowed to say these terrible things about Abel. You won't be allowed to say that his trial was fixed.'

'Look, Randi . . .' He sat her down next to him on the big leather sofa. 'I'm not going to burn this. First of all, it's taken me months of hard work to write. Second, I think it's good. Third, there's a little old thing called the First Amendment, which guarantees the right of free speech – and even if there wasn't, I should still claim the right to write what I like. And fourth, it's all fiction – I was wrong. I discovered last night that Joanna made the whole thing up, there was no plot to get Abel acquitted and no orgy with him and John Schmidt. So there's no reason at all for me to burn the book. And I'm not going to.'

'What about the offence it will cause to all of Abel's followers, and all the other religions you ridicule in here?'

'What about the offence all those religions cause to me? And to the rest of us? We have to put up with them – they have to put up with me. That's the deal in a free society.'

Her eyes narrowed. 'Sorry, Ernest, but this is your last chance. Save yourself. Burn this book now. Don't underestimate the Angel of Darkness.'

Ernest lost patience. 'Randi, just fuck off. OK? I think you're off your fucking trolley. I don't believe all that superstitious bullshit, and you can't frighten me. There's no such thing as the Angel of Darkness.'

Randi took a pair of gloves from her purse and put them on. While Ernest was trying to make sense of this latest weirdness she produced a dainty Saturday Night Special from her purse and pointed it at him. 'I'm the Angel of Darkness, Ernest.'

He gaped.

'I don't believe that this hooker made up that story,' she continued. 'I think it was true. And anyway, it makes no difference – people might think it's true, and that makes it dangerous to us.'

'Us?'

'Abel and me. The Church. Us.'

Ernest was now speaking very quietly and calmly. 'Put that gun away, Randi, it might go off.'

'It will go off,' she said. 'That's a promise.'

Ernest wasn't even frightened. He simply could not believe this was happening to him. It seemed more like a dream than reality. Randi wouldn't really shoot him, he knew that. He just wanted to understand. 'I thought you loved me.'

'I do.' Big tears were rolling down her cheeks. 'That's why I have to do this. Abel explained it to me. It's a sin to do this except out of love for your transcendental soul. That's why Abel chose me to be the Angel of Darkness this time.'

'What do you mean, *this time*? How often has this happened?'

'I don't know. I just know now that there's no permanent Angel – it's horses for courses.'

'Horses for courses?' Ernest gaped. Even at this surrealist moment of high panic and advanced terror he couldn't prevent himself from exclaiming at the inappropriate metaphor. '*Horses for courses?*'

'It's a racing expression.'

'I know that!'

'I have to do it now, Ernest. OK?'

'No! It's not OK, Randi. Look, if you're serious about this, I'll burn the book.'

She shook her head. Tears were streaming down her face. 'It's too late. Now that you know about the Angel of Darkness, it's too late. Don't you see?'

Ernest began to see. What he saw was that she was truly whacko. 'Randi,' he began carefully, 'I don't want to die.' Never taking his eyes off her, he backed slowly away, out of the french windows, back towards the tall Cypress trees and the fence.

'We don't refer to death,' she reminded him as she followed him out on to the sunny terrace. 'Death is not real. We do not utter that word.'

'You just did.'

'Shut up. You are not dying. I am not killing you. Do you think I could kill you? How could you even think that of me?'

'Because that's what you . . .'

'Ernest, all that is happening is that you are transitioning to a different plane.'

'I like this plane, Randi.'

'This is God's will,' she explained, 'so tough shit.' And she pulled the trigger. Simultaneously a dying rat bellyflopped out of the tree above her and bounced off her head on to the terrace. She screamed. Ernest screamed too. Her shot went hopelessly wide. For a brief moment Randi and Ernest gaped at each other and at the twitching rodent, lying between them. Ernest reacted first. He took off down the driveway. She pulled herself together and followed. He reached the electric gate, the gate he'd installed at such expense to protect him. But this was something nobody had planned for – his assailant was on the inside, with him. He pressed the button. It was a heavy solid steel gate, and there was always a slight delay before it moved. By which time Randi was upon him. 'Sorry,' she said, and she pressed the trigger five times more.

TWENTY-NINE

There is darkness without, and when I die there will be darkness within.

Bertrand Russell

The rest was easy. She carried his body into the house. She slid the manuscript into a carrier bag. She took the floppy disk that she had seen Ernest using to make a safety copy of his book. Still keeping her gloves on, she took the cash and credit cards from Ernest's wallet, and his Rolex from his wrist. She set the Armed Response alarm, stepped outside the front door and locked it, broke a window and forced it open, calmly walked out to her car and motored down the winding hill to Sunset and thence to Malibu. It was the middle of the day and no neighbours were home. As she drove away she could hear the security system siren still hooting, but as yet there was no sign of any Armed Response.

When she reached the house at Topanga Canyon she drove on into the hills. There, in a deserted spot, she tipped a small can of gasoline over the book and burned it. She took the bag with the gun, the Rolex and the credit cards and, beating the undergrowth hard with a stick to frighten away any rattlesnakes, buried it deep in the brush. She got back into the car and once down in Malibu Village she dropped the floppy disk down a drain in the street. Then she drove home to Ernest Mayday's mansion and was met by the police, who broke the news to her that he had been murdered by an intruder. They were very sympathetic. They knew she'd married him only yesterday. She wept. And she wasn't acting.

The murder was big news, and the tabloids on both sides of the Atlantic revelled in the tragic story of a beautiful woman widowed only twenty-four hours after she was married. The widow in question was too upset to talk to the press, except for one brave and tearful statement in which she said that she was obliged to accept God's will. The resulting debate on law and order led, naturally, to ... more debate. Much was made of the dangers of living in America by the British press, even though nineteen people had been killed or maimed by another Irish bomb outside Victoria Station the previous week. The quality London papers carried brief obituaries of Mayday, all suggesting that his move to the United States was vaguely disloyal if not unpatriotic, and that his decision to live in Los Angeles was proof indeed that he was an intellectual lightweight, if not mentally out to lunch. Furthermore, several of them hinted that his inability to write any more books – and even perhaps his untimely demise – was what you might reasonably expect if you sell out to Hollywood.

His death was reported in the trades too, but as he wasn't that hot any more his funeral was sparsely attended. His agent Fanny Rush was there, and his lawyer Dylan Kanpinchowitz, both of whom were slightly miffed that they hadn't known of Ernest's marriage to Randi until they read about it in the newspapers after he died, but they offered their warmest sympathy and condolences to the new Mrs Mayday. Mark Down couldn't make it but he sent a telegram from London, Oliver Sudden had a major major deal coming down so he couldn't make it either, but he sent Tiffani and Chuck who couldn't find anyone much to network with. Julian Genau came and so did Craig Rosenbaum and Leonard Lesser, but the other professors of his acquaintance found that they had urgent teaching commitments. Consuela the housekeeper, being the only mourner who had been completely unable to understand a word that Ernest had ever said to her, grieved the most.

Randi, escorted by Abel Pile, mourned deeply. Jane Montgomery, escorted by nobody, stood at a distance, watching them, knowing that she could prove nothing even if the book were found. And indeed it was: a book can be burned but the memory lingers on, in this case on the hard disk. In the course of their routine investigation the police printed out everything on Ernest Mayday's computer, but although the novel contained a fictional trial not unlike that of Abel Pile it offered no evidence as to who might have murdered Ernest.

At the end of the funeral, after his casket was lowered into open ground, Sidney Byte (who with Max. Kirsch had taken a couple of hours off from *Ask Your Mother!*, the hot new spin-off from *Ask Your Father!*) turned and put on his hat.

'Too bad, huh?' remarked Max. Kirsch.

'Yes,' said Sidney. 'He really was an asshole, God rest his soul.'

Flagrante Delicto had never been finished and so the new Mrs Mayday understandably refused to let it be published. Mark Down generously let her keep the advance. The money went to the Church of the Community of Personal Truth to defray legal costs and Harris K. Fitch's bill. The Mayday Mansion, as the press began calling it, was put on the market but because of the recession in real estate values and because a much-publicized murder had taken place there it stood empty for many months, during which time City Hall, under pressure from the environmentalist lobby, introduced an Adopt-A-Rat programme. Then the rains came, the house leaked (if you want to go to California and make your fortune, be a roofer not an actor), the moisture encouraged the termites, and Ernest's beloved house in the sun was eventually sold for a knock-down price to be knocked down The proceeds were put towards the next year's Sincerity Awards.

EPILOGUE

Come on and try your luck,
You could be Donald Duck,
Hooray for Hollywood.
                    Johnny Mercer

Five years later Oliver Sudden remembered that Ernest had been writing a book at the time of his death. It took him some time to contact Randi, his widow, who had left LA and now lived alone in a simple ranch house in rural Montana. Oliver asked if he could read it. Fortunately, the police had returned their print-out of *Flagrante Delicto* from Ernest's word processor when it proved no help in their investigations, and Randi had kept it.

She removed the manuscript from her bottom drawer, read it through and, after some thought, sent it to him. Abel's trial was long forgotten and there seemed to be no risk any more. In any case, she insisted upon script approval of any future film. But Randi had been grateful when she heard from Oliver because eventually she had run out of Ernest's money, whereupon she had found herself unwelcome at the Church of the Community of Personal Truth unless she continued to offer sexual favours to Dr Pile. This she was no longer willing to do.

Flagrante Delicto was unfinished, but Oliver saw at once that Ernest had somehow become the principal character in his own book and had then been written out. As the book itself had no ending, Oliver had no problem in reshaping it a little. He was certain of one thing: he didn't want the novelist to die at the end. He wanted the film to be commercial.

Six different teams of writers were hired over the next four years, and they all worked hard on developing the script. Their efforts were rewarded, the film was greenlighted and, nine years after Ernest's death, the movie was completed. In the final version Ernest was saved from death at the hands of an intruder by his loving wife, Randi.

The movie was released over a holiday weekend. Jane, twice married and divorced and now living alone in the Valley, didn't go to see it. But it was a major major hit – Siskel and Ebert each gave it a Thumbs Up on their TV show and it was the only romantic comedy to gross over two hundred million dollars that year.

ACKNOWLEDGEMENTS

I should like to thank Clare Alexander and Mark Lucas for their encouragement, numerous helpful comments and suggestions. I thank Dr James S. Grotstein for his explanations of the Oedipus complex. I also thank Dr Marion Solomon, whose book *Narcissism and Intimacy* gave me considerable insight into couples therapy. My thanks are also due to Professor Al Hutter and Hargurchet Bhabra for their insights into (and examples of) post-structuralism. I acknowledge a debt of gratitude to Charles J. Sykes for the information in his book *Profscam*, and to Michiko Kakutani for the entertaining review of *The Madonna Connection* in *The New York Times*. Thank you also to my friends Jack Kaplan, Antony Jay and Rob Wyke, and to Elaine Pagels for permission to quote from her book *Adam, Eve and the Serpent*. The author especially wishes to thank Erica Jong for allowing him to put her words from *Fear of Flying*™ in the mouths of his characters.